Living la Vida Loca

Living la Vida Loca

BELINDA JONES

First published in Great Britain 2010
by
Hodder & Stoughton

Published in Large Print 2011 by ISIS Publishing Ltd.,
7 Centremead, Osney Mead, Oxford OX2 0ES
by arrangement with
Hodder & Stoughton
An Hachette UK Company

British Library Cataloguing in Publication Data
Jones, Belinda.
Living la vida loca.
1. Flamenco - - Spain - - Fiction.
2. Tango (Dance) - - Argentina - - Fiction.
3. Salsa (Dance) - - Cuba - - Fiction.
4. Reality television programs - - Fiction.
5. Female friendship - - Fiction.
6. Women - - Travel - - Fiction.
7. Love stories.
8. Large type books.
I. Title
823.9'2–dc22

ISBN 978–0–7531–8800–2 (hb)
ISBN 978–0–7531–8801–9 (pb)

Printed and bound in Great Britain by
T. J. International Ltd., Padstow, Cornwall

For Jonathan Aseibiri Gbenekama
(my favourite dance partner)

LIVING LA VIDA LOCA PLAYLIST

ARGENTINA

La Cumparsita — The Tango Project
Hernando's Hideaway — Alfred Hause's Orchestra
Whatever Lola Wants — Sarah Vaughn & Gotan Project
Jealousy — 101 Strings Orchestra
Santa Maria — Gotan Project

SPAIN

La Dona — Gipsy Kings
Espana Cani — Ballroom Latin Dance
A Boy from Nowhere — Tom Jones (live or youtube)
Halo — Beyoncé
Habanera from Carmen — Bizet, Classic Moments

CUBA

Everything I Can't Have — Robin Thicke
Cuba — Gibson Brothers
I Still Haven't Found What I'm Looking For
— Coco Freeman and U2
Un Montan de Estrellas — Polo Montanez
La Vida Es Un Carnaval — Lucy or Celia Cruz

Dancing is just discovery, discovery, discovery.
Dance guru Martha Graham.

PROLOGUE

Meet Carmen and Beth, aged eight. They won't actually meet each other for another twenty years but on this particular Saturday night, way past their official bedtime, they have the same dream: to step away from the humdrumness of their suburban weekend and enter the twirly-sparkly TV wonderland that is *Come Dancing*.

Beth longs for the day when she has a number pinned to her back and a trophy raised above her head. Carmen can't wait until she's pretty enough to wear a bubblegum pink gown with a calf-tickling marabou feather trim, although she suspects that aquamarine is more her colour.

With just minutes to go before the opening credits, each girl has a different pre-show ritual: Beth is limbering up her dolls with arm windmills, toe touches and head rotations. She understands that it's all too easy to crick your neck when ratcheting it into position for the foxtrot, that peculiar pose where the woman looks like she's been partially adjusted by a chiropractor and then frozen . . .

Beth had been having trouble getting the angle right until her mother explained it thus: "Imagine your arms are the curve of a martini glass and your head is the olive, resting on the rim."

She never was one for age-appropriate metaphors, Mrs Harding. But she does have an extensive array of perfumes in old-fashioned bottles with pumps and tassels and so each doll gets its own signature squirt before they step into the spotlight.

Meanwhile, some way across town, Carmen is creeping down the stairs hoping not to wake the sleeping beastie guarding the TV, a.k.a her gin-soaked dad.

Each week she has the same palpitations, convinced even the squeak of the carpet might wake him. Oh-so-tentatively she lowers the volume, hoping to ease the transition from the agitated commentary of *Match of the Day* to the serene strings of the Viennese Waltz. She checks once more on the rhythm of her father's snore and then lays out her art pad and set of coloured felt-tip pens — a rainbow range as long as a piano keyboard. Her fingers hover eagerly over them, not knowing whether she will be called upon to reach left for the pale lemon or far right for African violet . . .

The dancers are so close now she can practically smell the Elnett.

"Oooohhh!" the girls sigh in unwitting unison as the reams of chiffon begin to undulate and flounce in perfect synchronisation.

As Carmen's pen moves around the page so Beth moves around her room, mimicking the dips and skips and giving her own scores to Manchester and the Home Counties.

For the duration of the programme life is perfect. No one yells, no one cries and everyone looks like a princess.

It is very clear to these two young girls that life gets a lot more glamorous when you are a grown-up.

"I can't wait!" they squeak as they snug into their respective pillows. "I can't wait until I'm old enough to have a dream-come-true!"

CHAPTER ONE

"Youch!" shrieks Aurelia. "This is meant to be a costume fitting not an acupuncture session! You do this practically every week, Carmen!"

I want to tell the West End's leading lady that we wouldn't have to make such frequent adjustments to the black taffeta waistline if her weight wasn't always yo-yo-ing to such extremes but she's right, it is my fault. Ever since my split from Lee, I've been overwhelmed with tears at the most inconvenient times and when I well up the line between flesh and fabric blurs.

"Perhaps our eyes need to be washed by our tears once in a while, so that we can see life with a clearer view." My best friend, Beth, recently offered consolation via quotation.

It was certainly a nice idea but the fact is I'm more confused and in the dark than ever. Wasn't splitting up meant to be liberating? Wasn't this supposed to be the right thing, the *only* thing to do? I don't know quite how this is possible but I actually feel worse.

I'm just thankful that the show ends its run next week — putting on a brave face every night is so wearing, though I've now realised that if I keep a set of pins in my mouth, no one expects me to smile.

"OWWWW!"

I've done it again. This time was actually on purpose. I need Aurelia out of my sewing room so I can get on with finishing Beth's new dance outfit. It's not quite the dazzler I would have liked but it's been a while since I worked on a production with any colour or pizazz so I've had to get resourceful with the rather drab palette of this period drama.

"Okay, let's have a look at you!"

I step away from the sewing machine and hold up the lavishly-corseted take on a Victorian chambermaid's outfit.

Although it's a surprise for Beth, I know her measurements so well these flirty frills should sit exactly at her hip and bounce with every step she takes. Equal parts sexy and cute. Perfect!

I'm reaching under the desk for a bag to protect my handiwork from the elements when Toby, one of the dressers, enters the room.

"Oh my God, is there a little person joining the show?"

"It's for Beth," I tut, prising the ruffles away from his grasp.

"Oh, that's a shame, I'd love to have seen Dame Judi in that!" He hops up onto the counter top. "So what's her new job?"

My eyes light up. "Picture velvet booths, a live band and a woman sashaying on stage, slowly peeling off a long satin glove —"

"Burlesque?" he gasps.

"Yes!"

"*Beth?!*"

I must confess I'd had the same initial reaction. I mean it's obvious why they'd pay her over the odds — it's not often you find a real-life platinum blonde Vargas Girl who happens to have the elegance and flexibility of a classically-trained dancer — but she's always been staunchly against anything stripperesque.

"Remember last year — she wouldn't even jump out of that footballer's birthday cake and he was offering £500 for one quick '*Ta-daaaa!*'" Toby reminds me.

"Yes, but they wanted her to wear a bra made out of two halves of a football. This place is pure sophistication," I assure him, just as Beth assured me. "All the women receive a corsage when they enter, every man is in a tux and the bandleader looks like George Clooney!" I recall her words. "It's pink champagne and tinkling laughter all the way — just how we always wished London nightlife would be!"

"Sounds like heaven!" Toby succumbs to the sell. "You have to do her a number in baby blue satin next, she'll look a total doll. So what's the name of the club?" He prepares to tap the details into his iPhone.

"Peep!" I pep. "Isn't that cute?"

Toby's face drops. "Peep on Pimm Street?"

"Yes," I cheer, reaching for my coat. "I'm going there now to surprise her."

"Girl, I think you might be the one getting the surprise." Toby puts his phone back in his pocket and prepares to exit.

"Not so fast!" I pull him back by his faux-schoolboy sweater. "What do you know that I don't?"

He appears conflicted.

"Toby . . .?" I adopt my "tell Mummy the truth now" tone.

"Look, I hate to ruin your illusions — or Beth's for that matter — but that place . . ." He gives me an apologetic grimace. "Less Dita Von Teese, more Venereal Disease!"

"Oh gross!" I push him away. "You must have it confused with somewhere else."

"You do know Pimm Street is only about three buildings long?" he asserts. "And I know I'm not muddling it up with the classy joint next door because, trust me, there *is* no classy joint next door."

"Is it really that bad?"

"Sticky floors, drink scams . . . There's nothing to set it apart from all the other Soho dives, except the DJ is supposed to be slamming."

This doesn't make any sense. "But she turned down an eight-month cruise ship contract for this job!"

He looks unconvinced. "You're sure it wasn't a P&O ferry?"

I narrow my eyes. "It was a luxury liner in the Caribbean. You remember the pictures from her last trip — it was like a floating Versace mansion!"

"Then I don't know what to tell you. Except maybe you shouldn't go there tonight. If for some reason she wants you to think —"

"Are you crazy?" I cut in, pushing past him to get to the door. "If it's anything near as scuzzy as you say, I have to get her out of there."

"Don't forget your hand sanitiser," Toby calls after me. Which really doesn't help.

* * *

As I bear headfirst through the West End crowds and splattering rain, I try to come up with some rational explanation for why Beth would choose a seedy club over St Kitts? Why would she lie about getting a better offer here in town? And how could she think she was going to get away with hiding the truth for any length of time? She said she didn't want me to visit until her routine was perfect but she's such a quick study that would really only buy her a week.

Of course, if someone was guessing why I'd done something disturbingly out-of-character they would suspect a man but that's never the case with Beth. Her mum gave up her dancing career for marriage and motherhood and then spent the next thirty years drinking away her regrets. (Booze of choice: vodka from her native Ukraine.) As a consequence, Beth swore she'd resist all romantic entanglements until she'd "made it".

And as that status eluded Beth, so she eluded her suitors.

Naturally there has been the occasional fling but, nine times out of ten, she dismisses those proffering hearts and flowers without even the promise of a callback. I guess it somehow redresses all the rejections in her career. But as much as I wish she'd give these men more of a chance, it also makes it all the more unlikely that she has accidentally pledged herself to an underworld pimp.

"*Do You Love Me?*" A group of girls howl at the moon as they stumble out of *Dirty Dancing: The Musical*.

I miss that show. Not least because that is where Beth and I first met . . .

"Snap!" I cheered as my last chorus-girl costume fitting of the day skipped into Wardrobe sporting the same white plimsolls as me.

"Don't you just love this look?" Beth struck a coy toes-together pose. "It's so innocent!"

"Wait 'til you see the watermelon print fabric I've found!" I scrabbled for the roll.

"Whatever you put me in will be some kind of wonderful," she trilled. "I'm just happy I can finally ditch the minimiser bra!"

She was right about the brief to let her curves show: there was no need for her to blend in with an identikit chorus here, the choreographer actually wanted the background dancers to look as real and individual as possible.

"You wouldn't believe what a burden these have been until now," Beth confided as my tape measure encircled her upper body, relating how she was on course for the Royal Ballet School until the summer holiday her teenage chest inflated like a lifevest.

"Nowhere to hide in a pastel pink leotard," I tutted.

"Exactly!" she confirmed. "Madame Celeriac took one look at me and then shooshed me out of the studio as if my new-found cleavage might be contagious!"

"Seriously? That was it?"

Beth nodded. "She told me I would be more 'comfortable' in the Jazz and Tap department. When I protested, she said, '*Your body has decreed it!*' "

She may have been laughing as she mimicked the severity of her teacher but I could only imagine how crushing it must have been to be dismissed after all those years of intensive training.

"You know who kept me going?"

I expect her to say her mother but in fact she credits Canadian dance legend Miriam Gilbert.

"You know Miriam Gilbert?" I gawped. "I love her!"

She's got to be nearly sixty now and last time I saw her was a few years back as a highly impassioned judge on a TV dance competition recreating scenes from her most famous movies.

"I thought she was practically a recluse these days?"

"That's what I hear too and it's not like I've ever actually met her, she's just the woman I admire the most in the business." She leaned in closer. "I've actually got this little shrine dedicated to her — all her interview clippings and DVDs."

"Her movies are the best," I confirmed. "You can't beat the *Once More With Feeling* trilogy."

"I know!" Beth cheered. "I always watch that when I'm feeling down. Anyway, I really feel my luck is changing now!" she asserted. "I mean, does it get any better than *Dirty Dancing?*"

I felt the same way. After years of assisting, this was my first big break since completing my BA in Costume for Performance. Come to think of it, I had yet to toast my new success . . .

"Here, switch those plimsolls for these heels," I said, sourcing two pairs of strappy silver dance shoes and slotting my own feet into the second. "I think this calls for a celebration!"

Sipping lychee martinis at the Art Deco cocktail bar next door, we shared backstage gossip from all our previous shows, gleefully calling "Snap!" again as we realised just how many people had overlapped in our lives. By the third martini we'd traced our career paths back to our eight-year-old selves watching *Come Dancing*.

"My dad could never understand why I would spend the last of my pocket money on satin-faced organza," I chuckled. "He said my Sindy doll was better dressed than I was."

"Oh my God!" Beth hooted. "You've just reminded me I actually had a Barbie dress copied for one competition. And if that wasn't enough, I stuck sequins on the paper number on my back!" Her eyes got a little misty. "You know my one big regret? When I got ejected from the ballet studio, I wanted to go back to my first love of ballroom but my mother said there was no living to be earned there."

I clunked my forehead, picturing Beth fitting so perfectly alongside the glittering cast of *Strictly*, in particular, Ola Jordan, or "Exhibit C cup" as Beth had dubbed her.

"To think it could have been you on the cover of *Woman's Own*!" I wailed. "You might have even fallen in love with your celebrity partner!"

"And then we could've adopted orphaned children from around the world to create our very own formation dance team!" Beth chuckled as she reached for her glass. "You know, I have to say, it's very refreshing to talk to someone who's not bent over flexing their toes while you're speaking to them."

"You need never worry about that happening with me," I confirmed with a chink.

It's curious to think that Beth was the serious one back then. Until we met, she had such tunnelvision regarding dancing that every Sunday activity I suggested — be it a Eurostar trip to Brussels or a stroll around the National Portrait Gallery — was a whole new experience for her. Even though we were the same age, I felt like her older sister, showing her the wider world.

Those were fun days. We always seemed to be laughing ourselves silly about something. Either that or sipping after-show hot chocolates on Old Compton Street, huddled over our wish lists. Beth was big on these: "'Without leaps of the imagination, or dreaming, we lose the excitement of possibilities,'" she would quote the wonderfully bold feminist, Gloria Steinem, whenever possible. "'Dreaming, after all, is a form of planning.'"

Number one on her list: a leading role. For me? A leading man.

And then one day it seemed as if these wishes might just come true.

It was an otherwise unremarkable Wednesday night when the director asked Beth to hang back after the show and then told her he was considering her for the role of Penny — more dancing than acting and, let's face it, who better than Beth to "shake her maracas"?

When the official nod came, we set to work on the creation of a show-stopping red dress — experimenting with endless textures and silhouettes, eager to create an outfit that further enhanced the dance, one that somehow accentuated the speed of the spins and would fall sensuously away to reveal Beth's balletic leg extension when she placed her heel on Johnny's shoulder.

"This is it," she beamed when we finally got it right. "This is my star-is-born dress!" Then she looked at me, confident as anything, and said, "Now it's your turn."

And the very next day, along came Lee.

The prop department had been looking to get real vintage cars on stage — the Houseman's '63 Oldsmobile Dynamic and Johnny's '57 Chevrolet Bel Air — and Lee was the man who could make that happen.

"Carmen, meet the Car Man," the prop man quipped.

It seemed like fate. You could practically hear the engine revving every time we looked at each other. A brief chat about the interior colour schemes and he was asking me on a date. And then another and another.

"So it's finally happened!" Beth cheered at the news. "I've got my dream role and you've got your dream lover!"

For three weeks we were on a high. Beth was rehearsing every available hour, eager that her debut as

Penny would be received with ovation rapture, while I was spending every spare moment with Lee — his vintage Buick purring at the stage door each night, ready to glide me home. He was the first man I'd ever actually slept all night entwined with. (Normally I'd wake up on the far side of the bed, or unable to sleep at all.) I'd never had a boyfriend who wanted to see so much of me, or who actually seemed in it for the long haul. I couldn't believe my luck.

And then came what was due to be Beth's last Saturday night as chorus — the night of her accident. Not that it was really *her* accident at all, she was an innocent bystander. Baby went for her iconic "*Time of Your Life*" lift, Johnny's knee gave way and sent her diving over his head into Beth, who broke Baby's fall and two of her own ribs.

The pain didn't even register on her face, all I saw as she was slotted into the back of the ambulance was the awful realisation that her chance at the big time was gone.

Shortly after she went home to recuperate, my life also took a downturn, though in a much more slow-burn way.

I don't say any of this to garner sympathy. If anything, you'll want to stick a few pins in me. I just want you to understand my frame of mind at this time. So how best do I explain?

Imagine having to choose between two men . . .

The first is protectively broad with playful denim blue eyes, an arousingly deep rumble of a voice and the sweetest of kisses. He's a little bit rock'n'roll but a homebody at heart and makes the best Sunday breakfasts, smells delicious without wearing any aftershave and is never shy of saying, "I love you!"

And in his arms all your troubles — past, present and future — simply melt away . . .

The second is surly, undermining, demeaning, quick-tempered, prone to lewd comments, drunk-driving and humiliating you in front of your friends and colleagues.

The choice is obvious, of course. What person in their right mind would want to be with the second option?

But what if these particular characteristics and foibles belong to the *same* person? What if the man who has the ability to make you feel so cherished is also the one who leaves you tear-stained and bewildered. Then what would you do?

You'd leave him. You'd have to. Only a masochist would stay.

Or so I thought.

That was before I was privy to all the subtle slidings that can occur — compliments were replaced by reminders that he didn't want a "fat girlfriend" every time so much as a Malteser would pass my lips. He stopped texting cuteness and started answering the phone to me with a barked "*Go!*". When I'd welcome him with open arms, he'd stride past me with a dismissive "Not now." Somehow I'd gone from being the person he wanted to spend every spare minute with to an irritating waste of time.

Obviously I thought he wanted to break up but no, he said he had marriage in mind.

"Surely you wouldn't even consider it?" Beth was scandalised.

"Well I'm not exactly getting a lot of other offers."

"Carmen, he left you alone on your birthday to play football with his mates."

"Well, I knew he'd just feel he was missing out if he stayed in with me. I didn't want to be around him if he was all grumpy."

"It doesn't worry you that his moods seem to be getting worse?"

"He'd never be violent towards me, if that's what you're implying."

"What about the time he said he wanted to beat you with a baseball bat?"

"Oh, he was really drunk when he said that."

"What a novelty!"

I couldn't deny that his drinking was excessive. One soul-searching night he told me he was afraid he was an alcoholic. His vulnerability touched me. I wanted to help him face his demons.

"You know it's not your job to save him, Carmen." Beth was beyond exasperated. "I really don't know why you stay."

"Because I remember how sweet he was at the beginning," I told her. "I know he has it in him to be wonderful. If I could just figure out what I'm doing that's triggering him —"

"Don't you go taking the blame for his bad behaviour!"

I didn't reply. Part of me wanted the fault to be mine — if my ineptitude was the root cause then maybe there was still hope, maybe I could fix it. Then one day I was online searching for relationship advice and I came across a quiz on Verbal Abuse. I took it and found I could tick eighteen out of twenty boxes.

"What are you waiting for, a full house?" Beth wanted to know.

That night I sat him down and told him I couldn't go on if he couldn't be nicer to me. I couldn't take the surliness, the foul language, the daily criticisms.

"So it's all me is it?" He was instantly defensive. "You're perfect and I'm the ogre? Well, for your information, this morning you left your dishes in the wrong side of the sink!"

"What?" I was stunned. Did he really consider the two things on a par?

Maybe Beth was right. Maybe he was an incurable bully but I couldn't possibly be the pathetic doormat in this scenario. I mean, let's be frank — those kind of emotionally degrading relationships are the domain of the weak, meek and needy. I just didn't fit the profile: I loved my job, had great friends and a wide streak of independence. I felt good about myself. Except in terms of love, of course. If you added up all my man encounters you would see that they would only account for a total of two years out of my thirteen of dating. Naturally, four thousand nights alone can take their toll but was I really so desperate to be wanted that I was willing to put up with the worst kind of behaviour from this man, simply because he said — over and again — that he loved me and would never leave me?

The answer — in equal parts surprising and depressing — would appear to be "yes".

CHAPTER TWO

I stand before Peep, its pink neon signage reflecting in the rain-glossed pavement.

The entrance is little more than a beaded curtain and a downward flight of stairs. Now I come to think of it, it was an offer from a place just like this that prompted Beth to take that first contract as a cruise ship dancer a year ago.

"People used to tell me what a great little Von Trapp kid I'd make, now I get solicited by strip clubs!" She had rolled her eyes. "I think it's time for me to get back to work."

At first, Beth was dreading hoofing in velcro and lamé on a stage that tilted like a funfair ride with every ocean swell but, as it turned out, she had a blast — getting to do what she loved most in the world, twice nightly at 8p.m. and 10p.m.

Besides, she didn't exactly have a lot of other options — her big *après*-rib-crack comeback had not gone according to plan. While she was repairing and retraining her body, a new breed had taken over. Beth called them the "So You Think You Can Dancers" — stronger, faster, sexier.

And *younger*.

The director who championed her at *Dirty Dancing* had moved on and when she went to new auditions the recurring feedback was that they were looking for something "fresher" and "edgier". Apparently she needed to lose the "old-school/stage school cheese". And the truth is, that's tough to reverse, the Layla Kay Academy may as well brand you as you graduate. But we refused to be daunted. We knew Beth had both technical brilliance and experience on her side so we worked on a new look — roughed her up a little, sourced some street clothes — and she adopted a sassier attitude to match.

Then came the comments about her "lack of connection with the audience".

"I think I liked it better when they just blamed it on my boobs ruining the symmetry of the chorus line."

It didn't seem fair — as a dancer you have to have the hide of a rhino to withstand all the rejections and hardships of show business but the second you set a toe on stage, your skin needs to be transparent.

"I really don't know what more I have to do to 'move' people," Beth had despaired. "Short of lap-dancing every person in the stalls."

And so it comes to this.

Pushing through my apprehension and repulsion, I step forward and explain to the mush-faced doorman that I just need a quick word with my friend.

"It won't take a minute," I tell him. (Get in, get her out. That's my plan.)

He's having none of it.

"Girls pay too," he grunts. "You could be Lindsay Lohan for all I know."

"Well, I'm not entirely sure I've even got the right place," I say, still clinging to the hope that I'm wrong about the street or club name. "Do you know if a Beth Harding works here? Or maybe Bette Noir?" I recall the stage name we were joking about just last night.

He shakes his head. "Names don't mean a thing."

"She's blonde," I begin.

"They're all blonde," he cuts me off.

I go to describe her facial features — her cute nose and rosebud pout — but figure this is probably not a "face" man. It's then I notice the glass panel of photos advertising the girls within and I get to play my trump card. "Her boobs are real!"

"She start this week?" he enquires.

"Yes!" I cheer, only to realise that this is actually bad news — she's really here. "I'm just here to drop off a costume for her . . ." I remember my prop, giving him a flash of the lace.

He gives me one more look up and down then steps aside. "When you get to the bottom of the stairs, tell them Ron said to show you backstage."

"Thank you," I say, hurrying into the damp, sickly-sweet blackness.

There appear to be car air fresheners at every turn. Cherry, if I'm not mistaken. But instead of putting me in mind of candied fruit, all I can think of is the odours they are trying to mask. I try not to touch the banister on the way down and push backwards through the door that opens onto the dressing room.

"Oh! Sorry!" I stumble as I'm instantly confronted with an array of bulbous body parts and stringy hair extensions, most of which look like they've been raided from the local stables. "Um, I'm just looking for Beth, the new girl . . .?"

I was going to mention that I have a costume for her but I don't think vintage corsetry would sit well with outfits that appear to be made from fluorescent chewing gum, so I keep it stashed in my bag.

"She's just gone on." A woman with a strong Scottish accent calls over to me. "Shame she didn't have a pal here five minutes ago — poor wee thing was chucking up buckets — it's always so nerve-racking the first time you —" She makes an unleashing motion level with her breasts.

"What?" I gasp. "No!"

"She had exactly the same reaction but that's how Dirk gets you — says it's just podium dancing in lingerie. Then a couple of days in, when you're loving the money, he says, 'It's topless or jobless. You decide!' "

This is worse than I thought.

"I have to speak to her." I panic, looking for the passageway to the stage.

"Good luck with that." She nods to a door at the far end.

The music slams into me as I emerge, appropriately enough, *In Da Club*. I reach to steady myself on the wall and feel the whole room vibrating to the bass. I guess they're going for a younger crowd, not that I can discern anyone's age in this darkness. I can just about make out the prowling waitresses but the only lit area is the stage.

And there she is.

For a second I stand transfixed — her moves are pure Fosse, though whether anyone recognises the steals from *All That Jazz* and *Big Spender* is doubtful, particularly when performed to 50 Cent.

"Beth!" I yell as she moves towards the front of the stage, waving my arms wildly, but the spotlight is blocking her vision. At least she's still sporting her satin bustier, I try to look on the bright side as I thrust between two particularly vocal men and make a grab for her ankle. Uh oh. Not a good move — now I've alerted the bouncer. And she's starting to unhook the clasps. The bouncer is gaining; I don't know how to stop this!

"Hey, mind my beer!" one of the salivating males cautions me.

And then it happens: in one swift move, I've grabbed his pint and sloshed it upwards, hitting Beth directly in the face.

"PAH!" she spits, reeling backwards, disorientated at first and then angrily looking around for the culprit.

"It's me!" I pogo on the spot. "Carmen!"

"Is this part of the act?" The salivater looks between me and his empty beer glass.

And then I feel a pair of meaty hands clamp onto my arms and my feet are no longer touching the floor. I'm already envisioning my shoulder hitting wet pavement when I hear Beth cry, "*Wait — she's my friend!*"

The bouncer gives her a dubious look. "She just threw a pint of beer in your face."

"Well, it wouldn't have been my first choice," I reason. "I didn't see anyone drinking Amarula."

He looks confused.

"It's kind of like Baileys but with a strawberry cream flavour . . ."

Beth subdues a smile as she jumps down beside us, only for her face to change as she sees a small, bristly man approaching. There's something about his hyena-like demeanour that tells me this is Dirk. I wonder if I can persuade him that my recent action was a homage to wet t-shirt contests, only this time with beer and a bustier. Hmmm — B&B — that has a certain ring to it. Maybe I could trade him the copyright for Beth?

He gives me a withering look as I make my garbled pitch and then turns to Beth:

"You want me to fire you, don't you?" he snarls at her.

"Yes please."

He shakes his head. "Get outta here."

We're down the street and round the corner before we dare expel a breath.

"Don't say anything!" she whimpers, shaking her head, as if she can't quite believe what just happened. And, worse still, what nearly happened.

"It's not drugs, is it?" I feel compelled to ask, facing my worst fear first, still clueless as to why she would have chosen to put herself in such a situation.

"No, no!" she insists, still averting her smeared eyes.

"I just don't understand." I speak softly. "I mean, I know Dirk promised it was only going to be podium work but even so, the place is a dive." I pull her into a doorway so we can talk face to face. "Why would you turn down the cruise ship for this?"

"It doesn't matter, it's done now."

"It does matter, Beth. Something is wrong. You have to tell me what it is."

"Honestly, it's not a big deal. I'll get something better. It was temporary anyway. I just needed money for the rent —"

"You know I would have lent it to you!"

"I haven't paid you back for last month's yet."

"Well, that's still no reason," I sigh. "Besides, you wouldn't be paying rent at all if you were on the cruise ship. All meals provided, endless sunshine. You said you were desperate to go back to the Caribbean —"

"Well, eight months is a long time."

"It didn't bother you last time."

"But look what happened while I was gone!" she blurts. I'm trying to think which missed audition would still be eating her up when she murmurs, "You went back to him."

"What?" It takes me a moment to process what she is saying. "You mean Lee?"

She nods.

"You turned down the cruise ship job because you were afraid that I might go back to Lee?"

"Well, it's not so far-fetched, is it?"

"No," I have to concede.

Three times we've split up. This last time was about as final and no-turning-back as it could be and yet a sense of unfinished business remains. It's as if part of me still belongs to him. And vice versa. Sounds creepy, doesn't it? It is.

"But, Beth, it's not your responsibility to watch over me like that. It's not your job to protect me. You're my friend not my guardian angel."

"Says the woman who just swooped in and saved me from a strip club."

"Well, that didn't cost me my job or my passion," I reason. "Seriously, I can't bear the thought of you barely scraping a living here in the rain because then that's two of us miserable and what's the point in that?"

"I'd be miserable in the sunshine if I thought you were even thinking of going back to him." She takes a quavery breath. "It just feels like there's not that much of the old you left. I'm afraid that, if you did it again, you would disappear altogether."

"Oh, that's not going to happen."

"*Carmen, you could've died!*"

I thought I'd had all the horrible wake-up calls I was due. But here's another. I had no idea my situation was haunting Beth this way. She's always so bolstering of me, so dismissive of Lee's hold. We haven't spoken of The Incident in so long it was beginning to seem like a nasty dream. I sigh to myself. Though I'm definitely comforted to know how much she cares, there is also an equal measure of guilt at what I am putting her through.

"And I don't want you feeling guilty about this." She reads my mind, and no doubt my teary eyes. "This is my decision and I stand by it."

And then she leans back on the shopfront and peels off her pink-tipped eyelashes. “God, how did this happen? How did our lives become this?” She looks up at me. “It wasn’t supposed to be this way, was it?”

I shake my head, still somewhat in shock.

“Seriously Carmen, I don’t understand — why does everyone else get the breaks? I see girls that aren’t a patch on you with these great, devoted guys, you deserve one more than anyone and look what you got!”

I smile sadly back at her. “I feel the same way about you and your dancing — you looked amazing up there tonight. For a second I thought I was watching a solo in *Chicago*!”

She gives a disbelieving snuffle. “Ten years I’ve been doing this. Ten years of hope. Now it feels like all I have is my imagination — I go to bed at night and I dream all these wonderful scenes and every morning when I wake up the gap between what I want and what the day will bring seems to be growing bigger.”

And then she shivers.

“Jeez what are we doing out in the rain?” I come to my senses. “We need to get you home.”

We try in vain to get a taxi but not one illuminated yellow light passes our way.

“Come on.” I link my arm in hers. “Let’s go back to the theatre and call one from there.”

I’m fiddling with the multitude of locks at the stage door and when I turn back to check on Beth, I find she is an absolute mess of chugging tears.

"Oh honey!" I gasp, quickly pulling her into my arms. I've never seen her like this before. I can't bear to think that her warrior-like optimism has been defeated.

"I'm sorry," she apologises through the snot.

"Talk to me," I urge, sensing there is something more.

As I hold her by her shoulders, she looks up at me with a kind of pleading in her eyes. I hardly recognise her voice, it's so small. "What do you do when you realise that you're not good enough to have your dreams come true?" Her face is trembling as she speaks. "All these things I depend on to keep me going, they're never going to happen. I look ahead and all I see is emptiness . . ."

My heart actually aches for her. I look out into the appropriately blurry world surrounding us and drag up a sigh from the pit of my stomach. "There's only one thing you can do." I tell her. "You have to come up with new dreams."

CHAPTER THREE

"Turns out beer really is good for your hair." Beth tries to look on the bright side as she emerges from the shower. "I've never been so shiny!"

I give her a sympathetic squeeze and then frown at the costume rack. "Sorry there's nothing snuggly to wrap you in — they didn't have a lot of fleecy robes in the Victorian era."

"Don't worry about it," she smiles bravely. "Grey sackcloth is apt — I've been rescued from sin and now I am entering purgatory."

Oh Lord.

"Well, on the upside, this particular house of redemption has a very liberal drinks policy," I wink. "Back in a mo!"

Of course the official booze for shock is a warming whisky but the best I can manage is chilled champagne, purloined from the leading man's dressing room. I'm aware that the celebratory associations of this drink are a tad inappropriate but convince myself that, if I bring along three bottles of the stuff, the message becomes more: "Let's drink until all this misery goes away!"

"Oh!" I startle as I return to Wardrobe. Instead of finding Beth in some high-collared, floor-sweeping dress of penance, she is sporting a wing-collared shirt and tailored trousers.

"You know, if I were a guy, I'd book a job tomorrow."

I stall in the doorway.

"Girl dancers, they're a dime a dozen," she expounds. "There must have been a hundred of us up for that last spot on *Oliver*. And then the guys come in, and there's only a handful that are any good." She smoothes her hair away from her freshly-washed face. "Do you think I could do it?"

"Do what?"

"Pass as a man."

Her question seems in earnest so I give it due consideration. "Well, for starters we'd have to give you an enormous belly to balance out the boobs."

"You couldn't just flatten them down? You know, like Gwyneth Paltrow in *Shakespeare in Love*."

"You have rather different proportions . . ." I put it as delicately as I can.

"What about Barbra Streisand in *Yentl*?"

"Absolutely we could do that look," I agree. "But a Hasidic Jew trying to blend in with the cast of *Grease*?" I pull a face, trying to make her smile before pointing out that of all the careers in which you could attempt to pass as a man, this has to be the hardest. "I mean, you don't get more body-specific than a dancer . . ."

As I get on with popping the champagne and fill us two unceremonial mugs, Beth heaves a wretched sigh and grabs angrily at her chest. "These are such a curse! I wish I could wake up tomorrow and find them gone."

And then her face changes.

"Oh my God." She turns to me. "Carmen! Why didn't I think of it before? I can have them reduced!"

"What?!" I splutter. "Surely you don't mean —"

"Surgery, yes!" She ignores my offer of champagne and settles in front of my laptop, more interested in googling Breast Reduction. "Amazing. All these years I've been burdened with this excess and if I just did this one thing —"

"Beth. Hold on." I lower the screen so I can get her attention. "You can't possibly be talking about hacking off bits of your body for work?"

"Why not? Women do the reverse for men all the time. At least this is for me."

"But it's so extreme!"

"Not when you think of what I'd get in return," she reasons. "Finally I'd be the right shape — I could blend unnoticed into the chorus line."

My face falls, horrified that it's come to this. This beautiful girl who dreamed of being a principal dancer is now willing to go under the knife, just so she can get lost in the crowd? Or is it partly to make sure that she'll never get tempted back to stripping? Either way, I'm too depressed to protest as she lifts up the screen and starts eagerly scanning the pages.

"Look at this — you can get a breast reduction *and* a ten-day holiday in Tunisia all for £2,500!" I blink in disbelief as she adds, "Mind you, all those camels with their humps . . ." Her nose wrinkles. "It would be hard to take your mind off what had just occurred. Czech Republic sounds a better option and it's only £1,600."

"Bargain," I mutter. "But where exactly would you find that kind of money? You haven't even got this month's rent."

"I'll get a loan," she pouts. "You know, a career investment one."

"Oh yes, I can just see you discussing your 'assets' down the bank."

It worries me that she's having these thoughts before she's even had a drink. Mind you, I don't know how many it took to get her on stage earlier tonight.

"Listen to this." She tugs me to her side, undeterred. "The surgery takes just two hours, I'd be asleep the whole time and I could be back dancing in four to six weeks!"

"Let's take a little look at the risks involved, shall we?" I elbow her out of the way and read out loud about the severing of nerve endings that can lead to permanent sensation loss, the dangers of hyperpigmentation and permanent bruising, of scarring irregularities and wound separation. I'm just getting to fat and tissue necrosis when she halts me and reaches for her mug of champagne. "Okay, that's enough for now."

"You know, I really feel for the women who need this kind of operation but you don't. Maybe there's a reason you are the shape you are, we just haven't discovered what it is yet."

"Well, I need to find out soon or I'm going to do it, I mean it!" She takes another swig.

"Of course. Why wouldn't you? The threat of haematoma alone sounds so enticing."

I've gone too far. Beth suddenly looks on the verge of tears.

"Come on," I soothe, placing her hands back on the keyboard. "Let's see if *The Stage* has finally come through for you: blonde dancer required, real-deal 34DD, to play the lead role in *Marilyn, The Musical*."

We spend the next hour trawling assorted websites looking for podium-free dance work.

One ad offers two weeks in Cheshire earning £50 a night. Details of the show's theme include a worrying misspelling of Moulin Rouge . . .

"Moulin Rough?!" Beth hoots. "Well, that really inspires confidence."

As we scroll through the other options, the requests for special skills get more absurd — tumbling, mat-wrestling, nipple-tassel twirling . . .

"What exactly is a fire dancer?" I want to know. "And why would a house DJ be looking for *en pointe* ballet dancers?"

I'm peeling the thick foil off the second bottle of champagne and suggesting we start looking at some career aptitude tests to see what else Beth might be suited to, when suddenly her hand has my wrist in a vice.

"Oh. My. God." Her grip tightens. "It's like someone has turned my dreams into a job ad!"

"Really?" I gulp, already fearing this will only lead to more disappointment.

Beth is actually trembling as she reads:

"EXPERIENCE TV are searching for a woman aged 25–45 to learn three of the world's most popular and passionate dances in their countries of origin:
Tango in Buenos Aires, Argentina
Paso Doble in Seville, Spain
Salsa in Havana, Cuba"

She looks up at me, eyes wide with wonder.

I am a little stunned myself. It sounds too good to be true. "Go on," I encourage.

"The selected candidate will spend three weeks travelling to these exotic destinations where she will learn the most authentic form of each dance." Beth is on her feet now, pacing the room, unable to read further for sheer excitement. "This is it, Carmen. This is my chance. And it's even better than theatre 'cos I'll reach a bigger audience and think of how everything could open up for me! They say you have to hit rock bottom before you bounce back up and this, my friend, is my trampoline!"

While her mind races ahead I read the smaller print. The production company's credits are impressive — all the big-name reality shows are of their creation. All expenses are covered: flights, hotels, food. Obviously Beth won't have a problem with the fact that the candidate needs to be able to leave the country next week — she'd go tonight if she could. The application deadline is tomorrow morning and they require passport details upfront but this is fine too because Beth always carries hers with her, just in case. So far so good.

But then I get onto the qualifications.

Oh no.

Beth has altered her CV to fit a myriad different scenarios but this would be the biggest stretch of all . . .

"There's a problem." I reach for her hand, reluctantly tugging her back down to earth. I wait until her eyes meet mine so I can be sure she is going to hear me and then I say, "It specifically says non-dancers."

"What?" She looks confused. "You mean like no dance experience required?"

"No." I point to the offending line. "'Zero dance experience *essential*.' They don't want to see any applications from trained dancers."

"What are you saying?" She is utterly incredulous, even after she reads the line for herself. "What *is* this? Now even dancers can't get the dancing jobs?"

I heave a resigned sigh. "I guess they don't want it to come too easy, they want to show the struggle, the evolution . . ."

Beth only paces more. There is no way she's letting this one go.

"Right. Well, technically, you know I've only done ballroom Tango, never *Argentine* style and, if you remember correctly, even a pro like Brendan Cole struggled when he had to teach Lisa Snowdon because he'd never done it before." She looks back at the list. "Paso Doble, I'd be a total newbie at that and as for Salsa, every woman and her granny has had at least one Salsa lesson, they just tend not to pursue it because the class is invariably populated with the kind of men who would never get to touch a woman in real life." She looks up at me. "Didn't you try it once?"

I nod, flinching slightly at the memory. It actually wasn't the men in the workshop that put me off, but the instructor. He arrived brandishing a can of deodorant jeering, "I'm not afraid to use it!" The irony being that he, in his nylon/Lycra cycling shirt, smelt so bad you lost your footing when he demonstrated an underarm turn on you. Worse still was the way he tried to drum the "*1–2–3 pause 5–6–7 pause*" Salsa beat into our heads. He had us stomping like a marching band while chanting, "Pie and mash pause pie and mash!"

Not exactly the way to conjure steamy, Mojito-fuelled nights with the Buena Vista Social Club.

When my focus returns to Beth, I find she is halfway through completing the online application.

"What are you doing?" I gawp at her.

"They don't need to know I'm a dancer, do they?" she shrugs as she types.

"Um," I wince. "Do you really think you can disguise that fact?"

"For the chance to do all this . . ." She motions to the silhouette of a couple in a fervent embrace, dancing against a tropical backdrop. "Yes," she confirms. "I think I could fake it."

I fully understand her motivation but it's still not right. I have to be harsh. "You mean fake it as in completely lie?" I venture. "Fake it as in take this chance away from someone who genuinely fits the criteria?"

She looks at me, eyes glistening with a mixture of desperation and desire. "It could never mean as much to them as it would to me."

I hesitate. It's hard to argue with that.

"Besides, I'd be doing the TV company a favour." Her mania returns. "I'd start off being a complete Kate Garraway and suddenly my natural aptitude would be discovered and then I would become a phenomenon, we'd come back to Britain and I'd get my own show — and you could do all the costumes! See? It's perfect! I'll be doing you a favour too!"

I can see simple reasoning isn't going to stop this runaway train. My best tactic seems to be to try and get her to pass out before she sends the application.

"More champagne?"

"Maybe just a little. And can you grab one of the headshots from my bag? They need to see a photo."

She really isn't thinking straight. "You don't think that would ever-so-slightly give the game away — a *professional* headshot?"

"Oh." Her shoulders sag.

"Anyway, you're too blonde bombshell in this," I say as I contemplate the image. "You need to look more . . . *ordinary*. They'll be looking for someone the viewers can root for, someone more like them."

"Mmmm . . ." She gives this notion due consideration. "You mean someone more like you?"

"Well, not necessarily —" I falter.

"No, I think you'd be perfect — how do you think I'd look as a brunette?"

As she jumps up and starts rifling through the wig collection I wonder at my reaction to being the template for ordinary. I suppose I could be seen that way. But it's not exactly a look anyone aspires to . . .

"Jeez, do you have a single wig that's not knotted into a bun?"

I nudge her foraging hands away and find her a longish bob. Not dissimilar to my own . . . Oh dear.

"That'll do." She fixes the hairline and gives herself an approving nod before tilting her face expectantly towards me. "Now, can you do my make-up in sepia tone, like you do?"

"Sepia?" I frown, confused.

"You know all those brown hues — neutral, natural, whatever you call it."

I glance at my reflection. It's true. I am a living, breathing, olde tyme photograph. The most exciting thing that has happened to my beauty regime of late is that I somehow managed to get chocolate on my ghd's and now every time I use them the room fills with the aroma of home-baked cookies.

I oblige her with the make-up but then it falls to me to make a devastating physical criticism: "You're a bit toned."

"What?"

"I think you might look too fit for the job."

Beth throws up her arms in despair. "Well they want someone who's *capable* of doing these dances not someone who's going to struggle to reach around their own *vast* circumference to get to the instructor!"

"I know," I soothe. "But you know what these programmes are like — they love a transformation. They'll want to see that there's room for improvement. What you need is a bit of this." I tap my stomach. "Years of intermission ice-creams in the making!"

She gives my midriff a covetous look and then expels a long, frustrated breath.

I think for a moment we've come to a halt but then her face lights up. "Where do you keep your costume padding?"

Before I can even direct her to the trunk, Beth has located a pre-formed belly and an assortment of arm and leg tubes. "What are you waiting for?" She hustles me to my feet. "*Super-size me!*"

We begin by loosening her bra straps so she doesn't look quite so "sweater girl" thrusting. Then we bulk out her mid-section and thighs and recycle a bustle for her bottom. A pair of fishnets helps blend the sections without flattening them.

"What about my calves?"

"I think we should leave those in case you need to wear a skirt. Besides, plenty of women taper down in that area, look at Letitia Dean."

"Now there's a fighter!" Beth's jaw juts proudly. "But she also let us see her break down. I might have to do that at the audition — you know, shed a few tears . . ."

"We've got glycerine here." I nod over to the cabinet. "Aurelia uses a dab of that for her big cry in Act Three."

"I won't need it — I'll just think how I'll feel if I don't get this job." Beth braces herself against the nearest wall as I yank a line of tape around her middle, deciding she could do with some semblance of a waist.

"Not too tight, is it?" I ask as she catches her breath.

"No, it's fine. You know, you really are good at this, Carmen," she asserts, running her hands over the pouffe of her stomach like a proud mum-to-be. "I think this is going to look pretty convincing."

I agree. Maybe a little too convincing.

I stop my finessing and sit back on my heels. "You're not worried that what we're doing here could be construed as illegal?"

"What?" she scoffs. "Impersonating a plumper version of myself?"

"No, you know, the non-dancing bit . . ."

Beth shakes her head. "I told you, I've hardly done two of those dances. Besides, what are they going to do? Confiscate my tutu?"

"Seriously, Beth." I give her an earnest look. "What if someone recognised you and you got blacklisted by the dance community? What if no one was allowed to employ you again?"

"Well, maybe that's what I need," she says, ever defiant. "Maybe that's what it would take to get me to let go and try something else."

I look at my best friend — this patchwork quilt of mismatched body parts, swigging champagne from the bottle — and I think, *Maybe she's right. Maybe the strip club wasn't rock bottom. Maybe this is.*

And then I make a decision: tomorrow Beth can add this foolish exercise to the list of Things Never To Be Mentioned Again. But for tonight, while she is still energised with hope, I shall cease raining on her parade.

"You're all done," I announce, slinging the roll of tape back in the drawer.

"Great! All I need now is a more appropriate outfit . . ." She eyes my jersey wrap dress.

My brows raise in disbelief. "You've got my hair, my make-up, my body and now you want my dress?" I hoot. "Anything else?"

"Actually yes . . ." She gets a devious look in her eye. "Your love life."

Now that is a step too far.

"Why on earth would you want that?" I splutter. "I wouldn't wish it on my worst enemy!"

"*Exactly!* We need something that arouses sympathy, like that girl on *Diet on the Dancefloor* whose fiancé dumped her just months before the wedding." Beth resumes her seat at the computer and starts typing.

I can't believe it. I have officially created a monster.

"What are you writing?" I enquire, feeling suddenly vulnerable.

"Just that I need this trip to escape the magnetic lure of my repugnant and terrifying ex."

Reading her summary of my relationship with Lee has me flushing with shame. It's no picnic seeing the shortcomings of your life spelled out in black and white.

"Do you really think they need to know all this?" I squirm.

"Don't worry, I'm not going to put the worst bit. No need to relive that."

Sensing that I am about to do that very thing, Beth clicks her fingers in front of my face. "I need your help — remember the last time we were watching *Strictly* and you were telling me how you envied the partnerships the celebs had with the pros? Tell me that again."

I take a seat and close my eyes, picturing the faces sweating so diligently in the dance studios, the secret words of encouragement as they make their way on stage and the euphoria as they conclude their routine.

"I think, more than anything, it's the idea of the bond they have. The fact that they're working so hard towards a common goal. You really get the sense they are in this together. I've always wanted that feeling — that me and my guy are on the same team, lost in our own world." I heave a wistful sigh.

"And do you remember what you said then?"

I'm almost in a trance now. "*I don't need a boyfriend, I need a dance partner!*"

I take a moment to think how different my life might have been if I'd taken that statement literally. If, instead of going back to Lee, I had devoted myself to the Cha Cha Cha.

I'm on the verge of being engulfed by utter hopelessness when Beth gives me another nudge. "What do you think of this for a concluding sentence:

‘You may not be able to outrun heartache but maybe, just maybe, you can out-dance it.’”

“That’s pretty good,” I concede.

“Thank you.”

Now if only such a thing could work . . .

CHAPTER FOUR

You know you've had a heavy night when you can only move your eyeballs. And even that hurts.

From my squinty perspective, I deduce that Beth and I chose to create an impromptu rag mattress by piling every available costume on the floor. I've got a wool frockcoat over me. Beth's top layer appears to be a starched apron. Cosy.

I take a moment to process my memories of the night before — the fantasy job ad and the subsequent hysteria of wigs, padding and sepia make-up . . . Well that would explain why I dreamt that Beth dressed as me for Hallowe'en.

My dress was actually perfect on her, the flexibility of the fabric gave her a soft outline while the distracting swirly pattern disguised any unevenness. It was just the posing for the picture that was tricky — trying to get her to switch off her beauty pageant face and bow that perfect posture. For a while, I was concerned about the blurriness in her eyes —

"You look drunk!"

"*I am drunk!*"

But we managed to find a headshot and full-length that worked and sent off the application. I sigh to myself. I meant to stop her, honestly I did. I meant to suggest I read through for *Moulin Rough*-style typos and then somehow divert her application to drafts. But she was too quick for me. That's the trouble with emails, they're so much worse than drunk dialling because the next day there is documented proof of your misdemeanour.

Water. I need water. I'm just wondering if I had the presence of mind to set a glass within reach when I spy something damp and straggly. Ah yes. Sometime in the wee small hours, Beth decided to adopt one of the toupees as a pet. She named it Gerald and the last thing I remember was her giving it its own saucer of champagne.

I close my eyes, somewhat daunted by the clean-up that lies ahead. Not just of the Wardrobe, but of our lives . . .

"Beth?" I wheeze while attempting her name.

I go to give her a wake-up prod but all I feel is fabric. Still lying flat on my back, I start flipping back layer after layer — a.k.a. hour after hour of ironing — wondering if Beth did some kind of a reverse "princess and the pea" scenario, sleeping *beneath* rather than *atop* this material mountain. Resilient tweeds follow scrumpled silks until, ultimately, I find the pea — in this case, a gentleman's fob watch — but no princess.

Maybe she went home already but didn't want to wake me? I look over to the computer, half expecting to find a note but instead see the plastic surgery page on the screen. *Please say that's just a leftover from last night* . . . I scramble too fast to my feet — forced to wait a moment for my head to cease the sensation of hanging backwards off a playground roundabout — then stumble through to the kitchenette.

Empty. I feel the side of the kettle. Cold plastic. I tap the loo door. No reply. My concern grows as I feel my way along the corridor to the stage.

Perhaps she has decided to take a symbolic last bow?

But no, the boards are bare.

I sigh, my heart heavy. There is nothing sadder than an empty auditorium.

I wonder if this is how Beth feels about her life? Here she stands, the willing performer, but no one has come to see her. There's not even a panel of judges sitting seven rows back, waiting to critique her. No music, no one to cue her. No man to lift her and spin her, no chorus line to link arms with.

Tentatively, I leave my default position amid the drapery of the wings and tiptoe to the very centre of the stage. Even with no one watching, I feel exposed. I've never once felt comfortable out here, even during humble school productions. All those eyes upon me . . . I suppose you hope the audience is assessing you favourably but there's no guarantee. They could just as easily be preparing to denounce you. So what is it that drives these people to put themselves up for such scrutiny? What is this need in them that cannot be sated in any other way? I used to think it was simple exhibitionism — even the great Lord Olivier defined the compulsion as "*Look at me, look at me, look at me!*" But as I stand here now I can't help but admire the performers' bravery for stepping into the spotlight. The way they are willing to make themselves vulnerable, all for our viewing pleasure . . .

"Let me entertain you!" I murmur and then remember Beth telling me about the endless dance performances she prepared as a child, how she would tie long ribbons to her wrists and borrow the cats' collars so her ankles would have little bells that tinkled as she sprang around the carpet. All this for the benefit of a row of teddy bears and dolls — because her mum seemed incapable of staying conscious long enough to see the whole show. Suddenly it all seems so obvious . . .

"Ta-daaaa!"

A clunking of glass announces a presence stage left. I turn to find Beth brandishing three new bottles of Moët & Chandon.

"Oh God, I couldn't drink another drop!" I crumple.

Beth rolls her eyes. "It's to re-stock Vaughn's dressing room, you ninny! Your personal beverage awaits at your desk . . ."

She beckons me with perplexing jauntiness. Can all the angst of last night really be so easily dismissed? Then again, maybe she's still drunk.

"Chai latte," Beth hands me a steaming cardboard-jacketed cup.

"Thank you." I gurgle appreciatively as I inhale the spicy-sweet aroma.

"Blueberry muffin —"

"Oooh, yummy!" I coo, sinking my fingers into its yielding, purple-stained sponginess.

"Havana Brown."

The third package set on the table gives me pause. It's a box of Feria permanent hair dye.

No need to overreact, I tell myself. Lots of women decide to radically change their hairdo in a crisis and compared to surgery —

"Do you see the name?" Beth cuts into my rationale, tapping the lettering. "*Havana* Brown. Of all the names on all the boxes — the Garniers, Clairols, L'Oreals — not one other city was mentioned! No Stockholm Blonde, no Marrakech Mahogany —"

"No Burgundy Burgundy?" I get strangely sucked into her game.

"Nope." She gives me a triumphant look. "So how's that for a sign!"

Oh God, that's why she's so perky. She still thinks she's in with a chance with the TV show.

"And how cute is this — they give you a little aroma ampoule to make everything smell nice!" Beth sings as she sets out assorted bottles, nozzles and protective gloves.

"Don't you think it's worth waiting until you get the call?"

"I already did," she says as she opens the outsize instruction sheet. "While I was out getting the champagne."

"*What?!*"

She looks up at me and gives a whinnying shriek, unable to conceal her euphoria a second longer. "They want to see me!" she squeaks, casting aside the sheet and clutching at my crumb-coated hands. "Lucy from Experience TV rang and said I sound exactly like the kind of woman they are looking for."

My jaw gapes further as she adds, "We've got approximately one hundred and eighty minutes to make me a curvy brunette with two left feet!"

First comes the dye — pasting purplish goo onto her angelic tresses feels borderline sacrilegious. "You're absolutely sure about this?" I hesitate before applying the concluding dollop.

Beth gives an affirmative nod but, as we watch the colour deepen to a murky aubergine, she gives an involuntary shiver and murmurs, "I have officially entered the dark side . . ."

While my slept-in dress churns suds in the washing machine, I set to work streamlining and securing the padding. I don't want to crumple any more of the show costumes so I'm now sporting the handyman's work dungarees, causing Beth much mirth.

"You're so Dexy's Midnight Runners!" she hoots as I re-enter the bathroom to check on her hair.

It's a look I've been deliberately avoiding my whole life — my middle name being Eileen, after my grandmother on my father's side. No big deal? Try saying my first name and my middle name in quick succession . . .

"*Carmen Eileen!*" Beth can't resist a quick sing-song.

"Time to rinse!" I growl.

In the minutes it takes for the water to run clear, I realise I am now as much invested in this process as Beth. Her optimism is contagious. This may be the most ludicrous project we've embarked on but I find myself blow-drying her hair with that bit of extra care, as if she really has finally won the leading role.

"Tawny eyeshadow and a soft peach lipgloss complete the transformation," I simper, pretending I'm hosting a make-under show.

"Wow!" Beth marvels at her new reflection. "I look like a nice person, don't I?"

"You looked like a nice person before!" I tut.

"Yes, but now women won't be gripping their boyfriends a little tighter in my presence."

"Right, let's amp you up a few dress-sizes . . ." I lead her through to the fitting area.

I'm much more nervous about the makeshift body suit today, knowing she'll have to be walking around in it and, worse yet, dancing . . .

"What are you doing?" Beth looks bemused as I take her on an experimental waltz around the room.

"I just worry that all this wadding might feel weird to your dance partner — they're bound to give you a test spin —"

"Oh, don't worry about that." She swats away my concern. "What woman feels real any more? It's all Wonderbras, Spanx and support tights!"

She has a point.

"Besides, I've got jiggle in the area that matters most."

I can't help but smile. At least all notions of a breast reduction have passed.

"So," Beth reaches for my hands and inhales deeply, "Wish me luck!"

My brow rucks into a frown. "You don't want me to come with you?"

"Of course but I know you don't approve."

"Well . . ." I falter. "It's not just about that, is it? I mean, you didn't approve of Lee but you were still there for me when I was fool enough to carry on seeing him."

"Yes but that wasn't borderline illegal."

"No, it was a lot worse." I let go of her hands and reach for my coat. "I want to come."

Still she hesitates. "You're not worried about how this could affect you professionally?"

I survey the avalanche of formerly pristine clothes, the empty champagne bottles and Gerald the drunken toupee, and give a hapless shrug. "In for a penny, in for a pound."

"Or about thirty pounds in this case," Beth mutters as she manoeuvres her newly ample physique out the door.

We take a quick cab via my flat so I can change out of the handyman's dungarees and then twenty minutes later we're at the studio, by which time Beth is starting to sweat.

"Jeez, what's this padding made of — insulation fibre?" she bristles as we take our squeakily-synthetic seats in reception.

"You're just nervous," I tell her, trying to gloss over the fact that she is essentially wearing Puffa underwear. "Here, let me get you some water."

I glug out two plastic cups from the spherical dispenser featuring optical illusion goldfish, noticing a slight tremble to my hand as I do so. The sheer glare of this place is unsettling me — after the olde worlde creakings of the theatre, all these shiny white surfaces and acid bright furnishings are like a flick to the eye with an elastic band.

Even more agitating is the vast wall of TV screens simultaneously broadcasting the production company's full repertoire of shows. I don't know how the receptionists cope with this excess of stimuli — their call desk alone resembles the control deck of the Starship Enterprise. And whatever happened to writing your name in the visitor's book using a biro attached to a piece of string? Here an angle-poised camera takes your photograph (face-on and profile), then scans it onto a laminated card, which in turn triggers the security gate. At the time, Beth joked that these passes could later double up as our mugshots. But she's not laughing now.

"I wish you hadn't made my bum so big!" She struggles to detach herself from the orange rubber cocoon seemingly suctioned to her rear.

I give her a concerned look. "Do you want me to ask if that chair comes in a larger size?"

She narrows her eyes at me. "I just feel so bulky."

"Welcome to my world," I mutter as a walkie-talkie touting redhead approaches, only to stall in front of us, seemingly unsure who to greet first.

"Beth Harding?"

"Hi! That's me!" Beth springs to her feet, mercifully without the sound of a cork popping loose of its bottle. "This is my friend, Carmen, along for moral support."

"Oh for a minute there, I thought you two were sisters!" she chuckles. "You probably get that a lot —"

"Actually, it's a first," I note, diverting my gaze to the floor, taking in her orange leggings and run-everywhere pumps.

"Well!" She takes a rousing breath. "My name is Lucy, I'm the researcher for the show, why don't you come through and we'll have a little chat?"

For all the peppiness in her voice, Lucy's twenty-something eyes show signs of seventy-something fatigue. I wonder if Experience TV employees are ever allowed home to sleep? They probably just slot them into a pod for a twenty-minute power nap and then blast them with fake daylight.

"So, just to fill you in, you're auditioning for a reality show looking at the origins of dance in three Spanish-speaking countries as part of Channel 4's *Living La Vida Loca* special."

"I think I've seen posters for that!" I chirrup.

"Yes," she grimaces. "Always nerve-racking when they start promoting something you haven't made yet!"

"Have you worked on many of these programmes?" I nod to the digital gallery lining the walls.

"Nearly a dozen, but this will be my first time getting a researcher credit," she reveals, before inhaling the words: "Fingers crossed!"

I want to clarify this element of uncertainty but Beth is clawing urgently at my elbow.

I turn and see a dark-haired man in a Fedora fast approaching us.

"Just nipping out for a quick ciggy, Lucy." The man gives a courtesy tug to his hat brim as he passes.

"It amazes me how many dancers smoke," Lucy tuts as she holds open the door for us to pass through. "That's Benicio." She addresses Beth. "He's your test partner."

Beth jerks back from the door. "I'll be dancing with that guy?"

"Yes but it's not like we've got Len Goodman standing by to critique you!" Lucy tinkles. "It's just to assess your natural aptitude. Or ineptitude!" she quips. "Either way, I'm sure you'll be fine, please don't worry."

"Um," Beth gulps, continuing to look stricken.

I give her a quizzical look. I need to know if she's planning on bolting because I'm not sure I'm up to hurdling the reception gate.

"Beth?" I try to bring her round.

"Do you mind if I just quickly nip to the loo?" she blurts, clamping onto my hand.

"Of course not." Lucy directs us down another corridor. "Don't be put off by the fact that it looks like you have to walk through a waterfall to get in there, it's not real, it's just a hologram."

"I can't believe it!" Beth wails.

"Did something come loose already?" I fret as she hurriedly closes the door behind us.

"I know that guy," she hisses at me as she begins pacing the floor. "We worked together on the *Footballers' Wives* musical."

"Oh. Well. That was a really short run," I remind her. "Do you think he'd remember?"

"I slept with him."

"Ah." For a moment I wonder if the bathroom air vent leads to one of those crawl-along escape tunnels oft found in the movies but then it dawns on me: "You've got absolutely nothing to worry about — Blonde Slim Beth slept with him! He'll never recognise you as you are!" I thrust her in front of the full-length mirror, just to emphasise the point.

"Oh my God!" Her face falls as she takes in her reflection anew. "I can't do this! I can't be this *hologram*!" She jabs at the glass. "I don't know what I was thinking."

"I do," I speak softly. "You were thinking that this could be your last chance to show the world what you've got. You were thinking of balmy nights in Buenos Aires and Seville and Havana." I remind her. "You were thinking of how it might feel to have a man who wasn't partnering you because he was cast in that role, but simply because he wanted to move with you to the music.

For a second she pauses, her chest inflates and all the former dreaminess returns to her eyes but just as quickly the light dims and she exhales. "No." She shakes her head. "Look how nice that girl Lucy is — I'd feel awful misleading her on her first big job. We have to make an excuse and leave."

"Everything alright?" It's Lucy, popping her eager head around the door.

"I'm so sorry." Beth rushes to her side. "I'm probably messing up your whole schedule, please go onto the next candidate."

"Well, as a matter of fact, you're it." She tries to maintain her former pep but her voice quavers as she adds, "My last hope."

"There's no one else?" My brows knit together.

"Not today. There have been many, many others. *Many*." She looks pained.

"What happened to them all?" Beth and I chorus.

Lucy checks the corridor and then scoots inside to join us. Leaning on the trough-style sink, she explains how their first ad was less detailed and consequently a number of applicants had second thoughts when they found out exactly what was involved — all of a sudden husbands didn't like the idea of their wives being pressed groin to groin with some "sweaty Latin lover type" six thousand miles from home or their employers couldn't hold their jobs for three weeks or they'd only applied in the hope of getting to dance with a celebrity or they worried about getting caught up in another revolution in Havana . . .

"Plus, several of them had heard the rumour that they serve cold Brussels sprouts at breakfast in Cuba."

"How ridiculous!" I tsk.

"Actually, that is true," Lucy admits.

"But to let that put them off?" Beth splutters. "This is a once-in-a-lifetime opportunity!"

"You're right and plenty of them were ready to embrace it all but when I narrowed the list down to what I thought were the twenty-five best options, the producer vetoed them all."

"But why?"

Lucy sighs wearily. "Most of them weren't 'camera-friendly' in his eyes."

"Not pretty enough?" I translate.

She concedes a nod. "Half a dozen were too skinny, others too well-off, three of them lied about their age, four were too good-looking and thus not relatable for the audience, a couple swore too much when they made mistakes which would just make for one long bleeeeep and the rest didn't have the right accent —"

"What *is* the right accent?"

"Whatever doesn't grate on him that day." Lucy flicks the antennae of her walkie-talkie. "You know, one woman ended up shagging Benicio!"

"Imagine that!" I hoot, stealing a look at Beth.

"Actually, that was in her favour, they love a bit of scandal here but when she came back for her second interview, Rick — that's the producer — decided she was too gummy when she smiled."

As our eyes widen in disbelief, Lucy gets blabber's remorse. "I'm sorry, I'm being incredibly unprofessional. It's just that when your application came through, I thought, '*That's her! That's our dancing queen!*' "

"Really?" Beth blinks back at her.

She nods and then hangs her head. "But what do I know?"

"Oh, Lucy, just because this guy Rick doesn't share your vision doesn't mean you should doubt your abilities." Beth reaches out with a comforting hand. "I'm sure you're very good at your job."

"I thought I was going to be," she sighs. "I thought I just needed the chance to prove myself but now I've finally got that chance . . ." She swallows down the lump in her throat. "It's not exactly going according to plan . . ."

I can practically hear Beth's heart twang in sympathy. "You mustn't give up. Not yet."

"I don't really have a choice any more. Today is it — my final deadline." She tries to buck herself up. "But it's okay, they said they'd always have me back as a runner on *Stars Behind Bars*."

"Oh no! No, no no." A suddenly brusque Beth takes her by the arm. "Come on, we're going to make this last chance count."

"Then you'll do it?" Her eyes brighten with hope.

"We'll do it," she asserts.

I follow behind the two of them, smiling. Maybe in some warped way this is all meant to be.

But then we enter the studio and there stands producer Rick — the one man standing between Beth and her dream.

CHAPTER FIVE

No handshake, no eye contact, positively no pleasantries. As Lucy forewarned, Rick does not suffer fools gladly.

And by his definition, anyone volunteering to appear on a reality show is a fool.

And he's certainly not going to waste his breath introducing himself to a candidate who may not even make the grade, less so her friend. Which is a shame because I am extremely curious to hear *his* accent.

On the upside, the fact that I'm all but invisible means I can loiter close enough to see what he is writing on Beth's assessment sheet.

Interesting . . . That disdainful arch to his brow doesn't necessarily reflect his inner opinion — she's already got a tick for Face, Physique and Outfit. I feel quite chuffed, having had a hand in all three. While they fit Beth's microphone, I decide to turn the tables on him — would I be so liberal with *my* ticks?

The answer is yes, if I were looking to cast a gaunt but stylish villain. His nose looks as if I had threaded one of my needles through its tip and tugged it to a point. His thin lips seem to be hemmed shut. His dark, fashionably-tufted hair could do with a little darning at the crown but I can't fault his dress sense — the slim-cut trousers and structured polo-neck have a kind of futuristic severity to them. I bet he was quite a hipster in his twenties, assessing the crowd from the corner of the club, just as he's scrutinising Beth now.

Holy annunciation! She just got a tick for her accent. And he's made a note that he likes the pluck of her eyebrows. I'm just wondering whether he's gay or straight when Beth bends to adjust the strap of her shoe and the extra weight of the microphone clip causes the crossover aspect of her dress to gape provocatively.

"Oops, I think we need to make that a little more secure!" The soundman rushes back, more than a little pink-faced.

As he continues to bungle the re-alignment of the V, I catch a glimpse of stomach padding — *noooo!* But when my eyes dart anxiously back at Rick's page, instead of finding him stabbing out the word "Imposter!", I see him doodling a little smiley face.

I smile too — I knew those boobs would come in useful some day! I'm so glad she decided to keep them.

Finally the sound guy gives Lucy the thumbs up and Rick etches a definitive loop around the words: *dance ability*.

"Benicio!" He summons Beth's dance partner as if calling forth his favourite gladiator.

The next twenty minutes are excruciating.

Beth's former fluster returns with a vengeance — her hands are noticeably clammy, her body tense, her neck blotched.

"Look me in the eye," Benicio urges as he pulls her closer. "It will help us to connect."

I can practically hear the prayer she mutters before she jerks her face towards his. I know she's wishing she'd worn coloured contacts — her eyes are a very particular amber and for a second it looks like Benicio is having some form of lusty recognition. "Have we —"

Beth tries to pull away before he completes his sentence but he tugs her back, forcing her into a spin but also giving her the opportunity to clomp down hard on his left foot.

As Benicio lets out a yelp, Rick shakes his head and sneers his first full sentence: "Not too used to the company of men, is she?"

You should've seen her last night at the strip club, I think to myself.

Beth steps on Benicio's toes several more times during the course of the try-out but I suspect this is no longer deliberate. Her newly cumbersome form has altered her centre of gravity and affected her natural balance — even if she wanted to exhibit grace and poise she would probably still lurch and stumble. On the plus side, every misstep seems to please Lucy more — this being the one assessment where you get extra points for errors.

"Let me lead you," Benicio urges at one point. "I can feel you trying to anticipate every move. Don't think so much."

Her face is indeed a picture of concentration and frustration.

"Relaaaax!" he says.

But how can she let go? She can't risk letting the trained dancer in her take over. She has to remain vigilant.

So far, I have recognised some basic Salsa steps, the stompier form of the Paso Doble and now Benicio seems to be slinking into position for the Tango. I hold my breath, praying that she'll be able to make this look bad. Busty blondes aren't exactly synonymous with this most sinewy of dances but it is the form she has studied most keenly.

"Close your eyes," he commands.

She obeys, making me more nervous. *Don't forget where you are!* I want to cry. *Don't forget to falter!*

She gets off to an awkward start but all too soon she's looking suspiciously smooth and instinctive. And then it happens . . .

"Wow!" Benicio reels as she unthinkingly unleashes a perfect ocho on him. "Where did that come from?"

"What did I do?" Her eyes startle open.

He repeats the swivel-turn move back to her.

She gives her feet a scowl of reproach and then brazens, "Oh that? It's just something I saw Flavia do on *Strictly Come Dancing*."

"Nice, I like it," he approves. "For a clumsy girl, you've got potential."

He then looks to Lucy who nods and announces a water break, a.k.a. a chance to mutter intently with your cohorts.

"How was I?" Beth quizzes me, still quaking as she downs a whole bottle of Evian.

"Awful," I shudder.

"Really?" She looks hopeful. "You're not just saying that?"

"Honestly, it was jittery and off-kilter and you looked like you might throw up at any point."

"But what about the ocho?" she cringes.

"You totally got away with it," I insist. "I'm sure everyone's tried to mimic a move or two off the telly."

She doesn't look convinced.

"Okay, Beth . . ." Lucy gets our attention. "Ready for a little chat?"

She actually looks ready to pass out but nods regardless.

"You were very thorough with your answers on the application but we need to see how you come across on camera," Lucy explains, inviting Beth to take a seat opposite her.

Only now do I notice the cameraman who must have been lurking in the shadows the whole time. He's very tall; I wonder if this helps him get a greater variety of angles?

When I turn back to check on Rick, I find he is now focused solely on his desk monitor so he can see Beth just as the viewer would.

I shuffle closer, feeling a pang as I see my friend looking so utterly terrified. After all the audition processes she's been through in great cavernous theatres, who would have guessed a boxy little TV studio would be so stressful? Then again, she doesn't normally have to *speak* . . .

"Why don't you begin by telling us your earliest memory of wanting to dance?" Lucy adopts a psychiatrist-patient tone.

Beth sets off at a great pace, chirpily describing her childhood fascination with *Come Dancing* and indulging in a little wishful-thinking as she claims her mother refused to enroll her in stage school, insisting she instead concentrate on her real strengths in art and history. I almost expect a buzzer to go off as she tells her first whopper but then I remember I'm the only one who knows the truth.

"The only formal dance training I've ever had was a few ballroom lessons aged ten," she lies, once again drawing from my personal history. "Due to a shortage of boys and the fact that the other girl enrolling was so pretty and dainty, I was assigned the man's role in the partnership."

"The whole time you were there?" Lucy gawps.

Beth nods. "I remember we entered a novice dance competition and the girl, Charlotte, arrived in some wispy-wafty number while I strode onto the dance floor in a plaid skirt and denim waistcoat pinned with a sheriff's badge!"

This is all too true. It was the most manly accessory in my jewellery box but, I can see now, a curious match for the Lilac Waltz.

"Everyone else on the dance floor had these fixed, slightly manic grins but I kept a stern poker face because, in my mind, real men didn't smile."

She gets a laugh with this comment but in terms of accuracy, she's spot on — that's exactly what I used to think!

"We actually came third," Beth concludes the story. "But then my dad pulled me out of the class, convinced it was giving me a complex about my lack of femininity."

"I'd imagine it would," Lucy sympathises. "Reminds me of that great quote by the American writer Christopher Morley: 'Dancing is wonderful training for girls, it's the first way you learn to guess what a man is going to do before he does it!' "

Beth laughs out loud and then shoots me a sideways glance. "Well, that certainly explains a few things!"

"So when was the first time you actually danced the girls' steps?"

"Gosh, not until the Under 18s disco."

"Why the shudder?" Lucy enquires.

"I never liked dancing with boys then. The way they pressed so close, so hard into you during the slow dances." Beth looks genuinely disturbed. "It used to scare me — I could feel their bodies shaking. They smelt . . . musty. I didn't like it."

"I could see traces of that discomfort when you were dancing with Benicio . . ." Lucy misdiagnoses.

"Mmmm." Beth is non-committal. "I guess I've always wanted to dance with a man who is more interested in the dance itself than how it feels to have me pressed against him."

She's speaking as herself here — hence her affinity with musical theatre where nine out of ten partners are gay.

"While we're on the subject of men," Lucy tiptoes forward, "you mentioned in your application that you have recently split from your boyfriend . . ."

"Yes."

"And you say that is part of your motivation for wanting to do this show."

"Absolutely," Beth confirms. "I'm afraid that if I don't do something radical, really change myself in some way, that I'll go back to him. Again."

"So you have left him before?"

Beth nods. "Three times."

"And what is it that draws you back?"

Beth's eyes flick to me and she takes a deep breath, as if inhaling my point of view.

"It's like there's a part of me that only he can reach. A pain only he can soothe." She pauses. "Because he created it."

Lucy shivers. "It sounds like a kind of addiction?"

Beth nods. "That's how my friends see it. They say he's twisted my mind and left me so confused I don't know which way is up. They can't understand the hold he has over me."

"It's never easy to see a close friend with the wrong man."

"No, it's not," Beth asserts.

"So have you always been attracted to men like this?"

"Never this extreme but in a way, now I come to think about it, it's almost as if all the men I've dated have led me to this point." She pauses for a moment and then muses, "Every guy that cheats on you and puts you down and makes false promises gradually chips away at your faith in love. After a while, you start to doubt that there is someone truly wonderful out there, just for you. If there was, wouldn't he have shown up by now?" Beth expels a heartfelt sigh. "So you tell yourself you have other things in your life — your friends, your family, your career. You try not to dwell on the lack. But still you long to have a love of your own and so when someone comes along and says he is willing to take you on and that he won't leave you *no matter what*, you're just so grateful. You see the red flags but you ignore them because you don't want to go back to where you were before — alone."

The whole room is now in a slump.

"Anyway," she snaps out of the fug, "the point is, I don't want to spend the rest of my life at the mercy of this man and these feelings. I want to shake things up and I believe this could really work for me — the distance, doing something physical, something challenging!"

I'm really rooting for her now. I want to see her cast off those shackles and dance! If she can do it, I can do it! Suddenly I don't know where Beth begins and I end.

But then Rick sits back in his chair and gives her a scornful look. "Sounds to me like you just see this trip as a means of escape."

"Isn't that what all dance is?" Beth is swift with her retort. "I know when I'm —" she catches herself, "dancing at home, letting the music decide my movements, nothing can touch me. In that moment, I am free."

He opens his mouth to speak again but she's not done. "Besides, Tango is not dancing to forget. Quite the contrary." She leans forward, intent on getting her point across. "These days there's such a massive pressure to be seen to be 'moving on'. It's the modern way. But Tango allows you to wear your darkest emotions on the outside. You have permission to let the pain show, to express vulnerability and regret." She tilts her head. "Am I not the perfect candidate for that?"

As Rick's eyes narrow, my heart chills. She's blown it. I told Beth to try and keep a lid on her expertise but her desire to dazzle has got the better of her.

I wait for Rick to accuse her of being suspiciously well-informed but he has a different concern: "I'm just not sure the viewers are going to want to immerse themselves in your woes. No offence but your situation is a little pathetic: '*Oh, he was so mean to me but I still love him!*' "

"Actually Rick," Lucy steps in, "I think there are a lot of women who'll be able to relate to that. Even Jennifer Lopez has spoken about experiencing emotional abuse in former relationships and she's no wallflower." He doesn't cut her off so she continues: "I think it would be great to take a closer look at what happens next — so you got away from him, now what?"

"You seem to be forgetting that this is a programme about dance," he huffs. "Not abusive relationships."

"You're right. But I don't think it would hurt to have a second thread running through the series about the healing power of dance. I mean, isn't that what you've always taught me — it's all about amping up the 'journey'?"

Rick taps the table with his nails. Knowing how easily he can cross hopefuls off the list, he must feel some attachment to Beth to even hear Lucy out.

"What do you think?" He turns on me suddenly.

I'm absolutely stunned, not just that he's asked my opinion but that he's acknowledging my existence.

"Well, I . . ." I'm not quite sure how to answer, seeing as they are essentially arguing about me without even knowing it.

He raises his eyebrows expectantly.

"I think we all have regrets in life." I decide to keep it simple. "Love — or something we mistake for love — causes us to do strange things."

"So you can relate to Beth's situation?"

"More than I can say," I gulp.

"And that is precisely why the Tango is so popular." Beth saves me from further scrutiny. "We all wish that, when we felt that desperation, there had been someone to cling on to, someone who held us tight and led us through the feelings. When we see these dancers clasped together, it moves us because they are expressing things we wouldn't even know how to."

There is a different kind of hush in the room now.

Rick blinks back at her, speechless for once. Lucy is dabbing away a tear, the cameraman has zoomed in closer and the sound guy, well, he looks like he's just fallen in love.

As for me, my heart is brimming with pride.

But Rick isn't done yet. Ding, ding, get ready for Round Two.

"Okay, I get it — your tortured soul is the ideal match for the Tango but what happens when you're asked to do the Paso Doble?"

Beth cocks her head and quips, "Well, the only problem I might have with that is being some man's cape."

Lucy chuckles at her bravado but Rick just gets spikier.

"Really?" He raises a brow. "Isn't that exactly what you have been?"

Beth's eyes darken. I know she's offended on my behalf. Her jaw juts as she responds, "All the more reason for me to want to fight back, wouldn't you say?"

Rick looks unconvinced but his cynicism is no match for Beth's dance knowledge: "You know there is an alternative influence for the woman in Paso Doble — the Flamenco dancer. And you don't get more feisty and in touch with your female power than that."

"Wouldn't that be something of a stretch?" Rick taunts.

"Isn't that the point?" Beth bites back at him. "To learn something new?"

I wonder if she should dial down this fighting spirit, as it may not be entirely "in character". I certainly question whether I could summon the oomph to stomp out my feminine power right now.

"All right." Rick holds up his hands. "Let's say I'm buying what you're selling — the Tango is your period of mourning, the Paso is somehow cathartic. What happens when we get to the real party dance — the Salsa?"

"You don't think I'd be ready to loosen up and have some fun by then?" Beth dares to tease him. "From what I've seen, the joy of Salsa is contagious. I won't have any choice but to let my hair down and go with it."

"You really believe that?"

"I have to," she tells him, earnestly. "It's my happy ending."

Rick suddenly sits upright and barks at Lucy, "Are we filming in that order?"

She checks her notes. "Actually we are doing Argentina-Cuba-Spain."

"Switch it."

"But logistically —"

"I don't care." He disregards her protest. "Re-schedule."

He then gathers up his notes and strides towards the door with new verve.

"Wait!" Lucy lunges after him, blocking his path. "What's your decision?"

"About what?" he frowns impatiently.

"Is Beth our girl or not?"

"Of course!" he roars. "She's perfect!"

"Hold on!" It's Beth's turn to call out to Rick now.

As he slowly turns back to face her, Lucy and I exchange a nervous look. Is she really going to risk having him change his mind by speaking out now?

"There's just one condition."

Rick snorts in disbelief. "*You* have a condition for *me*?"

"I need Carmen along with me." She reaches for my hand and clasps it tight. "She'll be invaluable to the show. You know she's a professional costume designer and wardrobe mistress —"

"This is a reality show, love," Rick cuts her off. "You do your own styling."

"What about ironing?" she blurts. "Everyone hates that and she's really good."

Rick shakes his head. "You want us to fly your friend around the world with us in return for ironing duties?"

"Yes," Beth asserts, staring him directly in the eye.

"Well it's a good thing we've budgeted for a companion then, isn't it?"

"What?" She stumbles forward.

"We won't always be around to babysit you so that's part of the deal — you get to bring a friend."

Now it's my turn for my jaw to hit the floor. "I'm going too?"

Beth squeals and grabs me into the kind of rib-crushing hug that makes me wish I was the one with the padding.

"Th-thank you!" I stammer, twisting around in Rick's direction.

"I'm holding you to the ironing." He gives me a stern look. "Don't make me regret this."

"We won't," Beth and I chorus, even though Rick has just potentially made the worst decision of his career.

CHAPTER SIX

Beth and I barely see each other in the lead up to the flight. For me, the next few days are spent perfecting her padding and tailoring the new clothes she has been busily shopping for.

"It's so unbelievably frustrating!" she humphs after a particularly hardcore session at Debenhams. "Why is everything sleeveless and cut to the knee? Dress after dress after dress! I think, 'Oh, that's pretty!' until I hold it up against me and see it's five inches too short. And the cardigans they have to 'match'!" she scoffs. "You've got all these cool and wispy cotton dresses and they team them with polyester and acrylic! Can you imagine having that on your skin on a humid day? I should know — I have to dance in that stuff all the time, it's vile!"

I go to speak but her rant isn't over yet.

"If manufacturers just added a few inches more fabric to the arms and hems, we could all waft around feeling comfortable and free instead of desperately trying to hide all the dodgy bits they have cruelly left out on display!"

"Tell me about it," I say as I begin letting down yet another hem.

"You should start a clothing line for women your shape," Beth continues. "I saw so many of them today looking crestfallen at their reflection. Two of them asked where I got my dress with — shocker! — *sleeves* and when I said that you'd added them in for me, they looked all sad again, like I was a member of some elite, unreachable club."

"Really?"

"Yes! I don't know what I'd be doing now if I didn't have my own personal seamstress."

"My own personal seamstress . . ." I repeat. "Isn't that a Depeche Mode song?"

Beth's too busy opening up today's giant cake box to get my joke — one éclair for me, five for her, all in a bid to plump up her face to match her new body.

"I'm just saying, maybe you could think about making your own capsule range available to these women? It could be a sideline to your theatre work. You know, for the inbetween-times."

It's not a bad idea. I've already had to make a couple of things from scratch for this trip, including a dress for some big night in Buenos Aires that Beth needs to be particularly "glitzed up" for. I'm quite pleased with how that's turned out — I've used drapes and folds to cover any giveaway seams and the old ballroom trick of working in flesh-colour fabric to give the illusion of skin. Tonight I'm getting Beth to apply the crystals around the cleavage; it's so fiddly and time-consuming but she's always liked shiny, sparkly things so I think she'll be in her element.

"By the way," I tell her as I point out the dab of fresh cream on her chin, "I've got a new body suit prototype for you to try — this one comes in two halves. I thought it might make your hip movements more distinct when you are dancing, so it's not the whole midriff twisting . . ."

As it happens, she likes it so much she decides to wear it to travel in. I'm just hoping she doesn't get a pat-down search at airport security. Or a bag check for that matter — they might wonder why she has packed so many bottles of Febreze.

We meet at Paddington station to board the Heathrow Express together but it's only when the train starts moving that the magnitude of what we're facing hits.

I thought we'd be babbling excitably about the adventure ahead but instead we're sitting in stunned silence.

"You okay?" I ask Beth, who is staring fixedly at a laminated postcard of Miriam Gilbert — her version of a lucky charm.

She nods, looking anything but. "I know technically I've done wrong by deceiving them." She is speaking slowly and deliberately as if presenting her case for the defence. "But I've done everything right my whole life and got nowhere. All I ask is that I get away with this one bad thing." She's looking out of the window now, as if pleading to the gods of station graffiti. "Just let me have this dance!"

I wish I had the power to guarantee her success. But all I can really do is make sure she looks suitably attired along the way.

I still can't quite believe that we're about to jet off around the world — not quite the hibernation I had in mind. Last night I voiced my concern to Beth that I might be a bit of a downer in my current state but she was having none of it.

"It's going to be amazing — *life-changing!* — trust me. Besides, I remember you saying that you've always wanted to go to Havana."

Actually it was Lee who had the hankering, not for the dancing but for the classic cars. He once told me that there are over fifty thousand vintage American automobiles in Cuba, hence the saying: "This country does not have a great car museum. It *is* a great car museum!" I know he would have forgone the city tour for a chance to hang out with a native mechanic, known to be the most ingenious in the world. (Frankly having no alternative but to fix the beauties from the Forties and the Fifties.)

"*Resist!*" I tell myself as I experience a sentimental pang. God! Why does this longing for him linger on and on? I just want it gone! I want to be the ordinary person I was before we met.

Well, I say that. A few weeks ago, in despair of my own slow processing, I rang a hypnotist specialising in break-up cures and when he pipped, "So, are you ready to have this man completely gone from your heart?" I found myself hesitating. It sounded like goodbye all over again and I couldn't do it — couldn't bear the idea of being even more alone.

Lee is still, in the weirdest way, company for me.

"You've got a text!" Beth informs me, always more attuned to that particular bleep than me.

Oh my God. I flush at the initial on the display: L. It's almost like he knows when I'm thinking of him.

"Who is it?" Beth asks absently.

"Toby," I lie. "Just saying '*Bon Voyage*'."

I click off the phone but the words remain: *I love you so much. I wish you could feel it and you'd come home* . . .

I close my eyes and take a breath. *Home*. The concept makes my stomach dip. What a lure.

For a second I allow myself to imagine how good his hug would feel. All the promises to treat me right this time. The special care he'd take in preparing my favourite meal.

But then I imagine all the belittlings and recriminations that would follow and suddenly a sixteen-hour flight doesn't seem nearly long enough . . .

Though Lucy and the crew have already gone on ahead, there is one more sequence for us to film at Heathrow — just a few basic "What are your expectations?" sound-bites, with Beth carefully positioned with the Aerolineas Argentinas plane in the background, for one of those not so subtle product-placement shots.

"So," the substitute Lucy studies her notes, "what image do you have in your mind of Buenos Aires?"

Beth thinks for a moment and then smoulders, "Smoky halls filled with mysterious, serious figures. Dark-eyed men in spats leaning on lamp posts. People not so much walking as stalking the streets. I don't see any daylight or greenery, just a lot of tall, ornate buildings — they say it's the Paris of South America, don't they?"

"And if we were going to play word association with Argentina?"

"Ohhh, *Evita* of course!" Beth gets peppier. "Che Guevara, polo horses, giant steaks, Malbec wine, Diego Maradona and —" She hesitates. "I'm not sure if I should go on?"

The interviewer nods encouragement.

"Well, aren't Argentinians known for their mullets?"

This produces a snigger. I'd say Beth is off to a good start.

Waved on our way, we proceed through the airport without a glitch, though the chap at passport control does do an initial double-take.

"I'm trying a new look!" Beth grins winningly and then decides that she needs a new perfume to go with her new style — always an *Angel* wearer before, we now conclude that *Obsession* is better suited to her Tango alter ego.

We also get a bottle of Absolut vodka for the room (well, it came with its own special edition red sequinned disco jacket — how could we resist?) and stock up on sweets for the flight. No magazines though — Lucy has given us DVDs of assorted Tango movies to get us in the mood.

"Here we are, 27A and B." Beth cues the man in the aisle seat to jump up and let us in.

No sooner is he back in position than she wants to get out again.

"Are they kidding with these seats? I can't believe how small they are!"

"Actually I think they're pretty standard."

"But I'm all wedged in!" she complains, still not used to the excess bummage. "Excuse me, do you mind . . .?"

She's up again, struggling to squeeze back out, catching herself on the armrests as she does so.

I wonder if she's going to try and finagle a last-minute upgrade using her new-found TV credentials but, five minutes later, she's back, busily adding to the overhead locker and then chirruping, "No need to get up," as she slides easily past Aisle Man and back into her middle seat.

"Now that's better!" she says as she reaches for her bottle of water.

Aisle Man looks utterly perplexed. I can see he's desperate to know her secret — the five-minute weight-loss solution that makes your seat all roomy and delightful — but it's not exactly something she can share.

"You took off your bottom half, didn't you?" I hiss, utterly envious.

"Well, there's no filming on board. I'll get back in character just before we land."

The plane's engines start revving, the pressure builds and we hold on as we are forced back into our seats. And then there's the lift.

Wow.

Now there's a sensation I haven't experienced in a long time — hope.

Once the plane has levelled itself, I get out Lucy's printout about the history of the Tango. Apparently Beth needs to be familiar with this information before she arrives and I feel duty-bound to play schoolteacher. However, when I clear my throat and read the headline — "*The Origins of Tango*" — Beth morphs into the slumpy child at the back of the class.

"Do I have to do my homework right now?"

"Wouldn't you rather get it out of the way so we can enjoy the movies?"

"Spose," she pouts.

"I don't get it," I tut. "I thought you'd want to know every last detail about the dance?"

"How to do it, yes, but I've never been a big fan of history."

"Why don't I tell it to you like a 'Once Upon A Time' story?"

"Okay!" Beth brightens before snuggling up and resting her head on my shoulder.

I adopt my most soothing and alluring voice and begin: "Once upon a time, towards the end of the 19th century, Argentina found itself to be full of promise in terms of exporting its agricultural goodies — all thanks to the newly installed railroads. The only snag was the shortage of workers. You still awake?"

"Yes," she giggles. "Go on."

"In a bid to recruit able bodies from around the world, the government offered certain incentives — free accommodation and food for the first week, assistance finding work and sometimes even subsidised passage. Men poured in from Spain, Italy etc., but all too soon the numbers far exceeded the demand and poverty and depression were the inevitable outcome."

"Oh dear."

"Lonely and homesick, these immigrants lived in crowded *conventillos* — basically tenement blocks built around central patios. As the majority of workers were single men, the competition for women was intense. So do you know what set a man apart, what made him an appealing prospect? Not money in this case, because no one had any —"

"His ability to dance!" Beth guesses correctly. "Is this where the brothels come in?"

"Yes but not in the way that is commonly told. The myth is that these lonesome men went to dance Tango with the prostitutes but frankly those women were engaged in more lucrative pursuits!"

"Oh my!" Beth feigns fanning herself.

"What actually happened was this — the brothel owners hired Tango musicians to keep the waiting men amused. This is where the image of men dancing with men comes from — here was an opportunity for these macho labourers to practise the very thing that could some day help them get a woman of their own."

"One they didn't have to pay for!"

"Exactly!" I then quote the next line out loud to Beth. " 'And so the Tango became something more than just a dance — it became an expression of a fundamental human need: *The hunger of the soul for contact with another soul.*' "

Beth and I sigh wistfully and then she tilts her head and gives me a quizzical look. "I wonder what the word 'Tango' means?"

"Well, they actually list a few possible origins here but I like the one that claims it's from the Portuguese *tanguere*, to touch."

The man in the seat next to us shifts in his seat. I can tell he's bursting to join in.

"Yes?"

"There is something else you should know about the brothels . . ."

Beth looks a little unsure of where he might be going with this but I nod to him to proceed.

"They were one of the only places where different classes would socialise side by side: so you'd have the literate elite slumming it for kicks and then going home and writing up what they saw."

"Like a ye olde Tweet?"

He looks bewildered by Beth's suggestion.

"I'm just saying that it must have made quite an impression on them."

"It was the risque nature of the dance," he explains. "They certainly didn't get to clasp their partner that intimately in polite society!"

"He's right," I confirm. "It actually says here that Tango was only the third dance in history that featured a man and a woman facing each other in the now classic hold."

"What was the first?" Beth's interest is genuine now.

"The Viennese Waltz. The second was the Polka. Anyway, back to Tango," I read on: "Considered too vulgar in its homeland, the monied jetsetters took the dance to Paris and used their Latin charm to persuade women it was all the rage. And soon enough it was!" I grin. "London, Berlin, New York . . . and then finally — re-branded as fashionable and refined — it returned to Buenos Aires where it was embraced by high society!"

"I can't believe we're actually flying there right now!" Beth grins.

"You know something else appropriate?" our neighbour chips in. "Tango is the international flight code for the letter T."

"Oh yes!" I laugh.

"Alpha, Bravo, Charlie," he begins reeling them off. "Delta, Echo —"

"Foxtrot!" I blurt and then jiggle Beth. "Isn't that funny, I never realised before there were two dance styles in that code!"

She gives me a withering look and taps my laptop. "Can we watch a movie now?"

The celluloid Tangos are great — everything from Al Pacino manipulating Gabrielle Anwar's tiny shoulder blades in *Scent of A Woman* to Jack Lemmon in Twenties drag in *Some Like It Hot*. Even more hilarious, though not intentionally so, is a cowboy-booted Rudolph Valentino in *The Four Horsemen of the Apocalypse*, dragging his partner around like a rubber-legged ragdoll.

"*Dum-dum-dum-dum de-de-de-dur-dur-dum-dum-dum-dum* . . ." Beth and I hum along to that most familiar of Tango tunes — *La Cumparsita*.

"You know when I was a little girl I thought that song was called 'The Camper Seater'!"

"What?" Beth giggles.

"That's what my dad told me! My Granny Eileen had it playing at her funeral. I was only ten but I remember thinking it was a really odd choice — all squeaky and weird, not nearly solemn enough for the occasion. Turns out she loved that song so much she bought the record before she even had a record player!"

"Bless her!"

"But get this — she hired one so she could listen to her record at home but her husband, my grandfather, went berserk, saying it was a terrible waste of money and made her return it."

"Oh, that's so mean!"

"I know." I look out of the window at the clouds, on the verge of wondering if I inherited more than my grandmother's love of sherry trifle when Beth nudges me.

"We're about level with heaven, wouldn't you say?" She points back out of the window. "Why don't you invite her along with us?"

I give her a tentative smile. "Really?"

She nods.

"Okay, I think I will."

Looking out at the swirly sky, I can almost picture the surprise and delight upon her face. I see her packing her best dress and her favourite shoes with the little buckle straps and me tucking a flower behind her ear to set the mood.

"Just six more hours to go," I tell both her and Beth.

"I suppose we should try and get some sleep?" Beth proposes. "You know those cameras are going to be rolling the second we step off the plane."

"You're right," I stifle a yawn. "Night then!"

"Night!"

Beth settles back in her seat — her eyes close but her smile remains. As I huddle up and rest my head upon her shoulder, I find myself smiling too — it feels good to be so close to a dream come true.

A couple of cricked necks and kinked hairdos later, we bump down on South American tarmac.

Rounding the corner at the terminal, we see the TV crew waiting for us as promised, including the tall cameraman and the pink-cheeked soundman but, unsurprisingly, no Rick, not exactly the type to be holding up a welcome banner and bouquet.

I wave cheerily at Lucy whereas Beth has a sudden spasm.

"Oh my God!" she panics. "I left my bum in the overhead locker!"

Before I can even respond, she's fighting her way back through the disembarkers, leaving me to greet and appease Lucy.

"She'll just be a second," I say, praying they weren't filming our approach, or some eagle-eyed continuity person is going to have issue. "She left her passport in the seatback pocket."

"Forgot my iPod!" Beth puffs when she returns.

"As well as your passport?" I tut.

"Oh, I know!" She quickly cottons on. "I'd forget my own body parts if they weren't attached!"

Brazen, she is.

"Okay, well, I understand you're probably exhausted from your flight but we just want to grab a few initial reaction shots from you on the way to the hotel." Lucy places her hand on my arm. "I know this is going to be frustrating for you, Carmen, but we need you to hang with us so you're not in shot."

"No problem," I assure her. "I'm an 'out of shot' kinda gal!"

Beth, on the other hand, is ready for her close up.

Argentina

CHAPTER SEVEN

"I had no idea that Buenos Aires was so vast!" Beth marvels as we contemplate the *Avenida 9 de Julio* and its twelve — *yes twelve!!!!* — lanes of traffic. This isn't even a motorway, rather the main artery of the city and home to the imposing Obelisk monument — a pointy white needle soaring two hundred and twenty feet high.

"Wow, that's over forty Flavias put head to toe." Beth gives the measurement her own particular context.

There are indeed plenty of architectural delights making sense of the "Paris of South America" moniker and a definite sense of former grandeur, verging on snootiness. But then we divert to the oldest neighbourhood of the city, La Boca.

"Look at all the pretty colours!" Beth admires the aquamarine, tangerine and calamine paintwork of the corrugated iron and salvaged wood that make up the buildings.

I can't deny that the patchwork effect lends a certain beach-hut jollity but the reality is that the original residents — mostly those Tangoing immigrant port workers — couldn't afford new paint so they had to make do with leftovers from the pots in the shipyard.

It's still a poor area today and thus all the more of a jolting contrast when we cross the river to Puerto Madera and enter one of Buenos Aires' most expensive hotels . . .

"Faena Hotel + Universe," Beth quizzically assesses the hotel insignia. "What's with the name?"

As I look for clues along the catwalk-like parade of celebrity portraits lining this dramatic warehouse conversion, we learn that Faena (pronounced Fee-na, rhyming with Argentina) is the surname of the fashion magnate owner but also, coincidentally, a term used in bullfighting — the "faena" being the series of passes the matador makes at the bull immediately before the kill.

"Aha — a foreshadowing of the forthcoming Paso Doble!" Beth notes, grabbing at one of the velvet drapes and flourishing it at the camera.

I don't have to alter anything in my being to do the perfect impression of the bull — wounded, disorientated and unsteady on its feet.

"Aren't you going to charge?" Beth enquires, when we're told that we're free to do as we please for the next hour.

I shrug disinterestedly. The long journey is now taking its toll and suddenly I can't imagine making a flamboyant gesture ever again. Even the frantic leg-flicking of the Tango seems like too much effort to me.

"Come on." Beth offers me a supportive arm. "Let's check out our bargain-basement room, only $500 a night!"

Easier said than done.

The hotel has clearly taken the concept of mood lighting too far — we pass people literally feeling their way along the blackened corridor to their rooms — but fortunately all my childhood years sneaking around the house after dark pays off and minutes later we're collapsing onto the puffy white cloud that is the bed. Now that feels good. Just wake me up when it's time to fly to Seville . . .

"So this is how the other half live!" Beth is already back on her feet, flittering around the room like a kid on Christmas morning. "Even the blinds are remote controlled," she whoops, setting the shiny slats in motion. "And this mirrored cabinet rotates . . ." She makes a magician-like flourish: "Ta daaa! — here's the TV!"

"Miraculous," I mumble.

"I'm sensing Philippe Starck," Beth correctly deduces as she wipes away her fingerprints with her cuff.

Everything in the room is glass and mirrors — advisable to walk with your arms outstretched or risk thudding into plate glass and bloodying your nose.

"I like the chair." I muster enthusiasm for the silver swan carving but Beth is already onto the bathroom.

"Come and look at this!"

"You'll have to bring it here to show me," I muffle from the pillow.

"I can't," she replies. "It's the sink." But then she adds, somewhat intriguingly, "Or maybe I can . . ."

Continuing with her Houdini motif, Beth then returns to the room and draws back the red velvet curtain I thought was a room divider, only to reveal the cube of glass encasing the bathroom.

Now this does make me prise open an eyelid — I can see right through to the chrome tissue-box holder and vase of Cala lilies on the marble sink top. The most curious factor is that the curtain is on the exterior of the glass so the person left in the bedroom can whisk it back at any moment. Seems the wrong way round to me — rather like putting the lock on the outside of the loo. Of course I suppose they presume that if you are sharing a room with someone then you must trust them but I know if Lee were here I'd be feeling very uneasy.

All too often when I was in the shower he would creep up on me and ram back the sliding door and stare at me. Not in a loving "Can I soap your back?" way but because he knew it made me uncomfortable beyond measure. I'd shrink against the tiles trying to cover my sudsy form, begging him to close the door. But still he'd stand there.

It was the same thing with the sudden ripping back of the bedsheets. Never in a playful way. I'd try to grab them back but I was no match for his brawn and inevitably I'd be left scrunched in a foetal position. I wish I'd had the nerve to splay out unfazed but even if I had the perfect body, or at least felt good about it, I still don't think I'd like the sheet to be ripped off like a wax-strip. I mean, where's the seduction in that?

I take a deep breath. I have to find a way to lay these ghosts to rest. You would think a gorgeous hotel room would be an excellent first step — the pristine new environment creating a "fresh start" vibe — but look at me: still prone and wallowing.

If I could grab my own shoulders and shake myself out of this fug, I would. But all I want to do now is play hide and sleep.

"Would you mind if I didn't go to the show tonight?" I test the water with Beth.

"What?" she squawks. "You know it's literally downstairs?"

"I know but I'm just such a lifeless wretch," I mumble, melding deeper with the mattress.

Beth folds her arms as she studies me. "I thought misery loved company!"

"The company of more misery," I clarify.

"Well, I've got you there!" she cheers. "This is Tango, remember? You'll fit right in."

Afraid I'll conk out if she doesn't keep me moving, our typically leisurely getting-ready ritual closer resembles the last seconds prior to a military inspection — lots of scrabbling around yanking on clothes, grooming hair and polishing boots, only in our case our shoes, being patent leather stilettos, already have a lovely shine.

"Look, we've even got time for a pre-show drink!" Beth enthuses leading me forcibly into the luxe Library Lounge.

The room is reassuringly dark with ceiling-high shelves of old books and the softest leather sofas either of us have ever encountered.

"I think this cow had spa treatments," Beth coos as she runs her hands across its copper-brown sheen.

I'm feeling decidedly woozy now even without a drink, which is just as well as no cocktails are forthcoming.

We placed our order directly at the bar when we walked in but even though we're the only guests in the room they don't seem to be in any hurry to quench our thirst.

"It's just possible that the staff have been employed for their visual appeal as opposed to any actual ability to do their job," I propose a theory.

We certainly can't take our eyes off the lost soul in a sumptuously slippery evening gown, gliding about the room like a cross between a supermodel and Lady Macbeth.

After twenty minutes' study, Beth's fascination becomes exasperation. "What exactly is her purpose?" Her brow furrows. "She's not a greeter or a server, she doesn't check on the well-being of the customers, she doesn't play the piano there or dance the Tango. She doesn't even smile!"

We watch as she pauses to contemplate her reflection in a lacquered panel. Up until now her facial expression would best be captioned "unclouded by thought" but now the subtitles are clearly reading, "I wonder . . . does my hair look better behind my ear or swept forward? Behind or forward?"

"I think she's a professional wafter," I conclude.

"Like moving décor," Beth agrees.

The funny thing is, as beautiful as she is, I don't envy her. I've wished a million times lately to be numb, to feel *nothing* . . . but now that I am in the presence of the human embodiment of lifeless blankness, I change my mind. *That's not living* . . .

"That's twenty-five minutes." Beth taps her watch. "Still no drink."

"Next time we'll call down ahead," I suggest. "You know, like pre-ordering interval drinks at the theatre? Ah, here they come now."

First one and then a second waiter set down a bowl of nuts on the table. And then stand back to admire their handiwork.

"And our drinks?" Beth asks, hopefully.

They look at each other in bemusement. We're tempted to clunk their heads together, ready to question whether this joint even has a liquor licence when in walks Rick.

Immediately we feel like we're doing something that we shouldn't and freeze.

He stalls too, midway between the entrance and our sofa, and then puts out his left hand as if he's indicating. Within milliseconds, a Scotch on the rocks meets his palm, presented by — would you believe it? — the wafter.

"Do you think she's in his personal employ?" Beth gasps as he downs his drink in one.

I don't get a chance to reply because Rick is now looking directly at us, channelling Jack Nicholson as he raises one brow and rasps, "*Showtime!*"

★ ★ ★

The Rojo Tango room is darker still with yet more red drapery, black tablecloths and the kind of cane-back cabaret chairs that make you want to straddle them Sally Bowles style. In utter contrast to the library bar, there is no issue with getting a drink here — our wine glasses are topped up after every sip by an aging and studiedly sullen waiter.

I like the *Hernando's Hideaway* vibe but Rick is not happy with the position of Beth's table and I have to concede it isn't ideal — there's a group of twenty or so loosened-tied businessmen between her and the stage, taking full advantage of the free-flowing booze. It doesn't help that the main chanteuse is sporting boobs from the Victoria Beckham collection. One fellow is particularly indiscreet — snuffling and phwoar-ing and nudging his friend. He's got to be fifty but has the peep show giggles of a teen. I wonder if he ever stops to think what this says about him — i.e. *Boobs are a total novelty in my world*.

"We're going to have to find someone to switch tables with her," Lucy frets. "These guys are going to totally ruin the vibe."

"How about the old ladies by the band?" I suggest, noticing one of them has her fingers wedged firmly into her ears. "That spot by the accordion player has a great view."

"Good call!" Lucy sets the transfer in motion. "Just don't let any locals hear you call that instrument an accordion, it's a *bandoneón*."

"What's the difference?" I ask, wondering if it's a size thing.

"Read this." She answers by handing me her guidebook open to a highlighted quote from Tango composer Astor Piazzola: "*The accordion has an acid sound, a sharp sound. It's a very happy instrument. The* bandoneón *has a velvet sound, a religious sound. It was made to play sad music*."

I sigh as I hand the book back to her, suspecting that this show isn't going to be a laugh a minute. "Speaking of using the correct terminology," I perk up, "I don't actually know the names of your crew guys?"

"Easy to remember." Lucy tells me her trick. "Dan Dan the Cameraman and then the sound guy is Simon — so I think Simon Says, only actually he *listens* more than anything."

"Got it!" I smile back at her.

"I would have introduced you at the airport but Rick prefers to keep them in the background, not least because Experience TV has very strict rules about talent mixing with crew."

"And when you say mixing —"

"I mean having sex," she confirms. "It's a fireable offence."

"Really?" I gasp.

As Lucy nods emphatically, I can't help but steal a look at these two forbidden men: Simon, the more sweet-looking of the two, is wearing a dark green T-shirt and multi-pocketed combats. I can't tell whether he has beautiful ears — all the better to hear us with — because he's wearing squooshy headphones. But he certainly has appealing eyes — big, honest, cuddle-me brown. I've yet to get a proper look at Dan's eyes as they're typically gazing down his lens, as indeed they are right now. I wonder if he's ever tempted to rest that camera on Simon's head? He's got to be at least five inches taller, over six feet, I'm guessing, with a lean but strong physique. He's one of those men with really good hair, but in a cool, accidental way as opposed to overtly styled. I like the way his shirt-sleeves are pushed up to his elbows rather than folded. I also like how thin and worn-soft the cotton looks. He's actually rather attractive. I wonder if Lucy agrees but decide not to ask for fear of looking like I'm sizing him up.

"What about crew-on-crew action?" I ask her instead.

"That's a no-no too," she asserts. But then a smile creeps across her face. "Which isn't to say it never happens . . ."

I raise an eyebrow.

"It was just this one time, last summer, when I was a runner on this celebrity farmyard show. There was this gorgeous producer — Kieran — and he took to sending me on late-night errands so I would end up back at his barn after dark . . ."

"And?" I'm agog.

"Best roll in the hay ever!"

I chink her wine glass and then hoot, "Gives new meaning to the phrase 'doing a runner!' " And then I frown. "Sorry, that was inappropriate!"

"It's fine," she shrugs. "Besides, in many ways it's inevitable — when you're on location, so far removed from reality, this group of people becomes your world . . ." She casts a glance at Rick & co. "Whether you like it or not, three weeks from now we're all going to know each other pretty well."

I can't imagine my opinion of Rick changing too much — the man just finger-clicked Lucy to get her to heel.

Apparently the dancing is about to begin.

As the curtain rises, the honeymooning couple to my right snuggle closer and I experience not so much of a tug at my heart as a two-handed yank. What I wouldn't do to feel that blissful togetherness. With Lee, it would only really occur on the day of our reconciliations — we'd cling to each other with such relief and urgency and the kisses would feel so pure and charged with emotion. It was the best feeling in the world, as if we were meant to be together and everything was going to be all right. By the next day that feeling would be gone. Normal life would resume.

Watching the performers give themselves over to their more primal instincts on stage, it hits me: that this is precisely why Tango is so popular — here she can run and throw herself into her man's arms, push him away, pull him back. Everything with intensity! You wouldn't picture any of these body-locked couples texting someone else while out at dinner together.

Not that any of them look like they've eaten any time in the last decade. Their bodies are just as taut and razor sharp as their moves.

"Look at him!" Lucy giggles as she returns to her seat beside me, pointing at a petite but wily chap with a face identical to Al Pacino's prosthetically-enhanced character in *Dick Tracy*. His hair is so brilliantined he looks like he has varnished strips of liquorice on his head.

I wonder for a moment if he's the comedy element but when he begins his predatory tormenting of not one but two women, he commands the floor.

"It's such a masterful dance, isn't it?" Lucy coos. "So different to the aimless shuffling the average British male does at discos and wedding receptions."

"Makes you wonder how different our culture would be if a dance like this was the norm." I ponder, and then frown to myself. "Now I come to think of it, I don't actually know what our national dance is . . ."

Lucy knits her brows and then offers, "Morris Dancing?"

I roll my eyes. "Says it all really."

"Don't mind if I do . . ." I'm just accepting yet another top-up on the wine when the music accelerates to a frenzied staccato. The already devilishly slick dancers now exhibit such attack that, if you'd never seen Tango before, you might mistake it for an Argentine martial art.

"Is this like extreme Tango?" I shrink back, a little unnerved.

"There does seem to be rather a lot of gymnastics involved." Lucy winces at a sequence of lethal scissor-legged tricks. "I hope Beth isn't too daunted."

Little does she know that Beth's probably wishing that she were up there performing alongside them.

"Ah, now that I like!" I nod at the move where the man lifts the woman onto his hip so she can perch, legs crossed and toes neatly pointed, as if she's a 1940s secretary about to take dictation. At a push I reckon I could probably trace my extended leg in a full circle like a geometry compass if the man kept me steady. But I doubt whether I could ever be pointy or precise enough for the vertical footsie — all that sliding one's foot up and down the shin and then hooking it and switching between each other's legs just looks like a lot of bruises waiting to happen.

It's a relief when the tempo changes and the costumes soften from black to ivory lace lingerie. So pretty! Until an older woman strides on in big Bridget Jones pants and — what?! — no top!

I look around, startled — is this some kind of wardrobe malfunction? There was just no lead up to this nudity! Does she realise she's forgotten her camisole?

"Beth's not going to have to do that, is she?" I gulp, getting a disturbing vision of my dear friend skimping around in her padding like something from a *French & Saunders* sketch.

But when I look to my side, I find Lucy gone again. Rick certainly keeps her on her toes.

Speaking of which, I hope the camera can't see Beth's feet as I can, expertly tracing the steps of the dancers on the floor beneath the table. She's always had an affinity with the Tango. But if I'm absolutely honest, I'm not enjoying this as much as I thought I would. I prefer watching the more sensual, slo-mo version of the dance — these aggressive stylings make me uncomfortable: all the tussling and resistance and then the succumbing to partnerships that are clearly bringing no joy. I know it is not the role of the spectator to judge the relationship portrayed but I find myself doing just that, almost getting impatient with one pair of dancers — just like people did with me: *If he causes you so much misery, why do you keep going back?*

I don't want to believe that love is pain but this seems to be confirming my worst fears.

And then he slaps her.

I flinch, the only person in the room who now has her hand up beside her cheek.

Suddenly I feel sick and vulnerable and on edge. Maybe this was a mistake. Maybe this dance is not a good match for my state of mind. I remember one of the films noting that Tango takes you deeper — "*Whatever your current emotion, when you Tango you feel it more . . .*" Well, I don't want my emotions magnified, they're already like a form of madness to me.

My claustrophobia increases as the music takes a menacing turn and starts to strain and tangle with my brain. The thought of spending a week immersed in this is just too much! I have to get away. I try to will Beth to turn my way so I can mouth a message to her but her eyes are locked on stage and, besides, the camera is locked on her.

No doubt they will want to film her after the show, maybe there will even be some interactions with the performers. She doesn't need me for that. No one will miss me if I just slip away . . .

Discreetly I inch back my chair and then, when I am certain that no one is looking my way, I slip out of the door and up to the room. Tanguistas may wear their emotions on their sleeves but when I unleash all the agonies of my heart I prefer to do it in private.

Closing the bathroom door behind me, I fall sobbing to the floor, realising too late that I am entirely surrounded by glass.

CHAPTER EIGHT

"Carmen, you have to get up."

Suddenly I am aware that Beth is crouched beside me.

"I just want to lie here for a while," I tell her, without opening my eyes.

She places her hand upon my arm. "I need you."

"What for?" I squint up at her through puffy lids.

"I need you to dance for me."

Is she joking? "I'm not really in the mood —"

"Not for entertainment," she tuts. "For research."

It's then I notice the man standing behind her in the doorway. Or at least the pair of pinstripe trousers. As she helps me to my feet, I draw level with his face and see that it's the liquorice-haired man from the show.

"Rafael is going to help us," Beth explains. "I can't risk messing up like I did at the audition. I need to watch you with him, to see how a real novice would Tango."

I go to protest, to explain that I'm too leaden, too crumpled to even move but Beth is already leading me through to the bedroom and smoothing my hair in preparation.

"Beth —"

"I know you don't feel like it but the class is first thing tomorrow."

"The show must go on?" I mumble.

"You know it."

Beth isn't being inconsiderate, she's just in "whatever it takes" mode. She's always that way when it comes to performance — there are no cop-outs, no waving of white flags. I'm not made that way myself. I do give up. Fortunately Beth is motivated enough for both of us.

She beckons Rafael who, until this point, has remained at a respectful distance. Even now he does not approach directly but sidles up to me on a curve. I would normally feel self-conscious looking such a wreck in front of a stranger but his dark eyes are filled with limpid empathy and, as he reaches for my hand, his fingers surround my wrist in such a gentle way he could be a nurse taking my pulse.

"Is there going to be enough room to dance in here?" I motion to the limited area between the bed and the glass of the bathroom.

"This is all the space we would have in a crowded dance hall," he tells me. "And when our bodies are together, this is all the space we need."

Wow.

Beth is busily trying to clean up my mascara streaks but Rafael halts her hand and then reaches for the silk scarf I have draped around my neck. Oh so carefully, he slides it over my shoulder and then places the soft fabric over my sore eyes, tying it securely at the back of my head.

Instantly I feel a sense of relief. He understands that I want to hide.

"Are you okay?" Beth checks on me.

I nod, strangely calm in the darkness.

"Well, before we begin, I want to offer you a few words of advice about partner dancing."

"Courtesy of Miriam Gilbert?" I predict.

"Yes," Beth confirms, and then lowers her voice as if she is saying grace. "There is a moment as you step into the man's strong frame, that you get to drop being a professional woman. Here, in this safe place, you can rest your head on that broad shoulder and *exhale*." She pauses to allow me to do just that. "And we're not talking about forever, and it's not to scare him or to be needy, but just for a moment allow yourself to be cradled and sigh."

It's such a beautiful sentiment, I feel a fresh tear spill from my eye, but this time it is absorbed into the scarf.

"Ready?" Beth asks me.

"Yes," I breathe.

I feel in good hands with Rafael — the first man to hold me since Lee.

The major difference is that I know he won't let go. Lee would always pull away from me before I was ready, rationing his hugs in five-second increments. I like knowing that Rafael is going to hold me for a whole song. Even if I don't have any idea of the steps to come . . .

"Is just walking," Rafael assures me, as the music starts up.

"Really?" After what I saw him do in the showroom, I'm dubious.

"*Si*," he assures me. "If you can walk, you can Tango."

And so we begin to move. At first it is little more than rocking. Then we step back and forth and to the side.

I sense Beth moving around us as she studies my form, scribbling on the page and at one point running the end of her pencil down my spine as if assessing its curvature.

Still, Rafael holds me close.

"Tell me what you are thinking, what you are feeling . . ." Beth requests.

"Is this a therapy session too?" I frown.

"I need to know, for the interview afterwards. Does it feel different to how you expected?"

I re-position my fingers on Rafael's back as I consider her question and then reply, "I thought I'd find the Tango hold restricting, claustrophobic even, being so closely governed."

"But in reality?"

"It's actually very comforting."

"So you don't find it overly sexual?"

"Beth!" I squeak, embarrassed.

"The dance may be suggestive but what we are actually embracing is the *music*."

Rafael's voice is so deep and seductive I have to reach out and give Beth a stealth pinch as if to say, "Okay, *now* it feels sexual!"

"What else?" Beth prompts.

I take a moment to compose myself and then reflect. "I was a bit resistant to the idea of the man leading, that notion of surrender . . ."

"So you had trust issues?"

"You could say that."

"You know, a man can lead but you have a choice whether or not you follow," Rafael offers.

I blink beneath my blindfold. Suddenly it seems so simple.

"I do not instruct you," he continues. "I offer you an invitation to join me."

He's so gracious, how can I resist?

As we move, I continue with my commentary. "This is nowhere near as aggressive or jerky as I was expecting. I prefer it this way — smoother and more sympathetic."

"I have you," Rafael assures me.

But then I take the "lean on me" motif too far and cause a stumble.

"Careful there!" Beth steps in to correct me. "I know you've seen those dramatic full body leans in performance Tango but really, for the most part, both the man and the woman should remain on their own axis."

"If you remove the man, the woman should still be able to stand," Rafael confirms.

"That's where I've been going wrong all these years!"

For the remaining minutes, Beth turns up the music on the stereo and lets me revel in the sense of connection and absolution. Somehow, through a combination of this man's sheer proximity and quiet tenderness, I feel my pain ease.

"*Gracias*, Rafael!" Beth thanks him as the *bandoneón* wheezes the concluding note.

I go to remove my blindfold but Rafael's hands are already there. He places the scarf in my open palm and then lifts my fingers to his lips.

I didn't think I had a smile in me tonight but there it is.

Once the door has closed behind him, I fall back on the bed, presuming that we're done, but Beth has one more item on the agenda.

"Remember the ochos from the audition? I made it look too easy before. I need to see you perform it."

"You really are a stickler for detail, aren't you?"

"And you're not?" Beth reminds me of the care I put into my costumes.

"All right, let's do it."

She demonstrates the move once and then asks me to copy.

"Gosh," I grimace as I swivel, turning on alternate feet. "That's actually harder than it looks."

"Again!" She stands facing me, hands gripping mine so I can transfer my inelegance to her.

We keep practising until she gets worse and I get better. This is really quite bizarre, watching her unlearn a dance. Using her talent in reverse.

When she is finally satisfied, she rewards me with the last of the minibar chocolates.

"That was a good session," she decides. "Last question?"

"Go on . . ."

"What would you say is the one thing you feel now above all else?"

I take a deep berry-fondant breath as I ponder. And then I feel another smile coming. "That I want to do it again!"

"*Yes!*" she cheers, pulling me into a gleeful hug. "Welcome to my world!"

CHAPTER NINE

The next morning we awake feeling confident and prepared, enjoying a leisurely room service breakfast, until Lucy calls up to say they want to begin the day filming at the pool.

"What?" I shriek when Beth relays the bad news. Even if we'd packed one of those voluminous Victorian bathing suits, a minute in the water would turn Beth into a big, sopping sponge. "We can't," I protest. "You'd sink for sure."

"I told her I need to dance off a few pounds before I'm ready for swimwear."

"Good thinking, what did she say?"

" 'It's just a scene-setter not *Girls Gone Wild*. Wear whatever makes you comfortable.' "

We both opt for a sundress and shrug combo and then carefully apply sunscreen to all our exposed areas — i.e. face and hands.

Beth holds up the Factor 60 like she's in an ad. "Go tan!" she cheers, tapping the bottle. "Tango! See, it all ties in."

Her good humour wanes a little in the heat. Even the lowest tog-rating of padding makes her feel like she's wearing one of those synthetic weight-loss shell suits. It doesn't help that the pool girls with their perfect *dulce de leche* skin are walking around with Beth's real figure, snazzily attired in red bikini tops and white shorts, a perfect match for the two-tone sunloungers and towels.

"Are you sure you don't want to get in the water?" Lucy offers, a little concerned at Beth's perspiration levels. "We can film you at the edge of the pool from the neck up."

Beth looks almost tempted.

"Heat rash," I blurt. "She's prone to coming out in big red blotches, I don't think it's wise."

"Well, if you're sure. We'll just prop you under this shade and film you ordering a cocktail."

"I don't see the crew . . ." Beth scans the area.

"We had to stash them to the side of the pool bar so we don't freak out the other guests," she explains and then points to a chair where I can sit safely out of shot. "The waitress will be along in a minute."

"Okay!" Beth grimaces, and then discreetly stuffs a couple of ice-cubes down her padding. "Oooh, that's better."

I'm tempted to do the same myself but a familiar skein of hair catches my eye.

"Will you look at that? — it's the wafter!" I giggle as the decorative woman we saw in the library bar last night teeters up and presents Beth with the drinks list.

"Something tells me this poolside scenario is more for her benefit than mine," Beth mutters to me from behind the red alligator skin of the menu while her server poses camera-ward and gives her hair a self-conscious swish.

"Okay, Maritza." Lucy hurries over to address her. "Can we try that again? This time Rick wants you to lean down to Beth's level to take her order so we can get you both in shot."

I can't believe Beth is being out eye-candied! If only they knew what lay beneath her floral frock. Not that she seems to care.

"I think you should get a Love Juice," Beth advises me, while Maritza prepares for her second take.

"What's in it?"

"Carrot, beetroot, Vitamin E and honey."

"Oh." I can't hide my disappointment — I wanted there to be some mysterious Argentine ingredient I'd never heard of — as if a cure for all heartache could be as simple as a Drink Me potion.

"I'm going to plan ahead and have the Morning After," Beth decides. "Just in case we have *una larga noche* . . ."

"Here she comes again!" I turn away so Beth can concentrate on her interaction.

As I tune into the slosh of water, my mind inevitably goes back to the last time I was poolside — in Cyprus with Lee. It was night and he was drunk. He looked so eerie in that blue-ish light. I was afraid of what might happen if I left him unattended but he wouldn't come out of the water so I slipped in beside him, hoping to switch the mood to something playful, romantic even.

As he pulled me into a hug, I smoothed his wet hair and kissed him and told him he was getting cold —

wouldn't he like to come inside? And that's when he started to force me downwards.

"What are you doing?" I panicked, scrabbling to stay above the water and reaching for the side to bear myself up.

"Let me hold you under," he pleaded.

My heart was thumping but I tried to make light of it, spluttering, "Why would you want to do that?"

"To prove that you trust me."

All I could think was, *But I don't!* Not that I thought he would intentionally drown me but he wasn't fully in control of his faculties and, besides, how could he know the breath capacity of my lungs? I don't even know that! Was this really how I wanted to go?

As he reached for me again, I went to tell him that he was scaring me but I worried that would make things worse, so instead I feigned narkiness to hide the fear, telling him I didn't want to get my hair all wet. And then I kicked away in a huff, grateful that he couldn't distinguish my tears from the pool water, or my shaking from shivering.

"You surely can't be cold?" Beth brings me back to the present moment.

"No, I was just thinking of something unpleasant," I explain my shudder.

"Speaking of which — I've made my body suit all soggy with the ice-cubes . . ." Beth delivers a "help me!" look.

"How long have we got before we leave for the next location?"

"Ten minutes."

"Well, it's a good thing we both brought hairdryers then, isn't it?"

The dance studio is just three kilometres away in historic San Telmo and within the walls of a very different hotel, the Mansion Dandi Royal.

"It's actually a Residential Tango Academy," Lucy explains as we enter. "Most of the people staying here are taking daily classes. They even pipe live Tango music into the rooms."

"This is more what I was expecting," Beth confesses as we take in the tall arched doorways, beaded lamps and Louis XIV-style furnishings. "Something old-fashioned and a little tarnished."

"I actually had us booked here initially," Lucy confides. "But then Rick went for a drink at the Faena + Universe —"

"And there was Maritza, waiting to be discovered." Beth guesses the next step.

"I think it's something of a signature with him. You know how Alfred Hitchcock would make a discreet cameo in all his movies? With Rick's TV work, there is always a 'featured waitress'."

"Ick!" Beth cringes. Then switches swiftly from distaste to delight as she is introduced to her dance tutors, real-life couple, Adriana and Adriano.

Talk about "your other half", they really do mirror each other in looks — long, lean bodies, high cheekbones and matching black ponytails, they must look amazing when they are moving together as one.

"How funny that they essentially have the same name," Beth comments to Simon as he attaches her microphone.

"Apparently it means 'the dark one'," he informs her.

I give a little shudder and walk towards the light — in this case, the picture window overlooking the street.

Outside, I see a dog-walker wrestling with a dozen dogs. Literally, one slender man being tugged forward by twelve highly-animated leashes.

"Makes you wonder why he doesn't go the whole hog and get himself a sled!" Dan jests, giving me the benefit of his distinctive, slate grey eyes for the first time.

I intend to make a smart little remark back but instead stand with my mouth slightly agape — I don't think I've ever seen eyes quite that colour before.

He raises a brow.

"Would you look at the face on that pug!" I quickly turn back to the pack; and then wonder out loud: "You much of a dog-lover?"

"I've certainly been called at least half that term in my time!"

Before I can clarify which half, Rick demands we get started.

"Dan!" I call after him.

"Yes!" he turns back and it happens again — I become Lady Slack Jaw.

I pinch myself back to coherence. "I was going to ask you — where should I stand so I don't get in the shot?"

He gives me a reassuring wink. "Stay right by my side, you'll be just fine."

And so for the rest of the afternoon, wherever he moves around the room, I go too. He doesn't know it but we're doing our own little partner dance.

Beth, meanwhile, is proving to be a good student — as in convincingly mimicking my inexpert moves from last night. All the corrections she was giving me, she is now receiving herself.

I find it quite charming how Adriana reduces the complexities of Tango to "a combination of walking, turning, stopping and *adornas*."

"Adornments," Adriano translates. "Or decorations. Like the *gancho* which means 'hook'."

Her foot locks around his calf in demonstration.

"Above all, Argentine Tango is improvisation. We show you steps to instruct you but at the *milonga* —"

"*Milonga*?" Beth frowns.

"*Milonga* is where we go to dance Tango socially," his wife explains to Beth. "You will see tonight."

Adriano nods. "There, everything relies on communication and contact — to be a success you must remain in the sensuality of the present moment."

I have to stop myself ooo-ing out loud. Why is it that everything related to dance sounds so darn romantic?

Beth, however, is immune to such whimsy and remains in calculating mode.

"Do you think I should have a tantrum?" she asks me on her break.

"Whatever for?"

"Well, you know whenever they show training footage of these kinds of things someone is always storming out, wailing, 'I can't do it!' "

"You might want to pace yourself," I suggest. "No one wants to see a cry baby on the first class."

"Right, right," she agrees. "Maybe day three I'll have a crisis, you know, to spice things up around the mid-point."

"The only note I would offer is that you should apologise more. That's what us amateurs do — instead of accepting that it's a learning process and thus we will inevitably get things wrong, we get all tense and say sorry every five seconds."

"That's a good one," Beth enthuses. "I wonder how you say sorry in Spanish?"

"*Lo siento*," Simon chips in.

It flusters us a little that he was listening in, though hopefully he just heard Beth's last line. I wait until he is over on the far side of the room before continuing.

"He seems to be hanging on your every word, that one," I observe. "Then again, I suppose that is his job."

"I may also have encouraged him a little," Beth cringes.

"What? That's not like you!"

"It wasn't intentional — he was asking me about my life back in London and I was so afraid of giving myself away that I started bombarding *him* with questions about where he lived and did he have any pets and how did he become a sound guy and what does he listen to when he's not working," she snatches a breath, "and now I have a horrible feeling that he thinks I'm into him."

"Well, at least you can console yourself that he'll get fired if he makes a move. Is he a terrible bore?"

"Actually, he's pretty interesting. Especially when you get him talking about music."

"Really?"

"We have very similar taste. Don't look at me like that!"

"Like what?" I splutter.

"With those ever-hopeful matchmaking eyes of yours! It's not going to happen."

"I wasn't thinking that at all," I lie. "What about the cameraman?"

"Carmen!"

"For me!" I quickly explain.

She doesn't even look up. "Honey, I wouldn't care if you had a crush on the ghost of President Perón, whatever it takes to keep you away from Lee."

CHAPTER TEN

A lovers' tussle. A face clawed with scarlet nails. Maybe a stabbing . . .

This is what Beth expects to see at tonight's *milonga*.

My vision is far more unnerving — packs of smoky-eyed women with slicked back hair and glossy red lips à la Robert Palmer's *Addicted to Love* video.

I'm dreading feeling even frumpier than normal. Especially since Dan's grey eyes will surely leave me for them. I enjoyed his attention earlier today, even if it was sparing on account of Rick's constant monitoring. I liked the secret looks he gave me. Admittedly they were primarily, "Can you believe this tool I have to call boss?" but there was a gleam that made me perk up and reminded me of something long forgotten — the pleasure of a secret crush . . .

"I suppose in a way a *milonga* is like a confessional," Beth muses as we approach our destination. "Sharing your sins in the shadows . . ."

"That's very poetic," I commend her.

"Thank you," she grins. "I'm getting into this talking lark."

And then the minibus halts and Simon gallantly offers us a steadying hand as we step down.

"Try not to be the one getting stabbed tonight," he urges Beth, quite earnestly, I suspect.

"Don't worry about her," I chirp. "She's practically armour-plated."

And then I look around me.

There is nothing picturesque or remarkable about this street, not even a cluster of bodies at the club entrance to create the requisite buzz. For a minute I wonder if Lucy has the right address but then the door opens and we're lured forth by the hearthside glow.

It couldn't be more of a contrast to our visions: the room is large and open, like a community hall, with a vibe more akin to a family gathering than paid nightlife — I've never seen such a range of ages on the dancefloor. Instead of the golden oldies tapping their toes on the periphery, they're the ones dominating the floor with flair and expertise.

Apparently the stick-thin caricatures we saw at the Faena last night are the preserve of *show* Tango. These are real people with real bodies dancing with relatable emotion. No silent movie exaggerations here, the steps are more understated yet somehow all the more poignant for it.

But what surprises me most is the overall vibe of happiness. I honestly thought people Tangoed to make themselves miserable but apparently there is plenty of pleasure to be had too.

"Look at that girl." Beth points to a twenty-something blonde dancing with a trim gentleman with a dashing whisk of silver hair. "She looks in absolute ecstasy!"

"She's probably drunk," Dan opines.

I give him a playful swat and then retract my hand like I did something unlawful.

"I have to get out there!" Beth is chomping at the bit. "Is it okay if I go and ask someone to dance?" she checks with Lucy.

"Actually no, the man has to ask the woman."

"You're joking, right?"

Lucy shakes her head. "Adriana and Adriano will be here shortly to explain the *milonga* etiquette to you but I definitely remember that cardinal rule from my research."

Beth can't hide her dismay.

"On the upside, they've reserved us a table right on the edge of the dance floor so you'll be in the frontline in terms of exposure and opportunity," Lucy tries to console her. "Let me just find out where that is."

Beth waits until Lucy is out of earshot and then pouts, "No one's going to ask me until they've seen how I dance — I know how these things work, they want someone else to take that initial risk."

"Well, maybe in your case it's a good thing they don't know," I remind her of her amateur status. "Besides, I don't think you're going to attract anyone with that scowl of injustice. Relax!" I give her a loosening jiggle. "Did Beth Harding ever go shy of male attention back home?"

"No but Beth Harding was never a brunette before."

"Personally I think dark hair is more in keeping with the Tango, don't you?"

"Spose."

"Anyway, forget hair colour — what did you always tell me?"

"It's all in the eyes," she mumbles.

"So use them."

Rising to the challenge, Beth visually stalks each man we pass en route to our table, making sure he knows she is open to invitation, should he be so gracious as to proposition her . . .

"Here we are!" Lucy replaces the reserved sign with her bag and suggests Beth takes the seat set off to the side so she will be easily accessible when her moment comes.

I, meanwhile, tuck myself decidedly out of reach.

It's a cosy arrangement — each chair seems to be touching the next and thus, when Dan sits down beside me, I feel his thigh aligning with my own. All the way from hip to knee. Though he appears oblivious as he chats with Simon, I'm wildly aware of the increasing warmth being generated.

But then I catch Rick looking in my direction and quickly try to turn myself inwards, crossing my legs and entwining my arms to create some space between myself and Dan. After a day spent in such close proximity, I can't believe how self-conscious I suddenly feel around him. When Simon moves away I catch my hand halfway to flouncing my hair but then quickly return it to my lap — I don't want to look like I'm preening. Just act natural. Let's think, what would I normally be saying now? Would I be asking him about the shots he is hoping to get? Or respect that he needs to concentrate on adjusting his camera and thus keep quiet? Before I get the chance to debate further, he is gone, off on his B-roll mission.

I glance around to see if anyone else has noticed my mild fluster but they are all involved in their own business: Lucy studying her schedule, Rick moving through the crowd like a secret service operative, Beth still working on her dance partner recruitment drive and Simon watching Beth, clearly bemused at the way she is playing come hither with the nimble-limbed septuagenarians.

No one knows a certain change has occurred in me, that the mere touch of Dan has triggered an internal homing device that means I am now ultra aware of where his body is in relation to my own. Like right now, I am all too conscious of the fact that he is making his way back to the seat beside me . . .

"Anyone want a drink?" I jump to my feet.

"It's waiter service," Lucy tells me.

"Oh."

He's upon us now. No time to escape.

I sit back down and quickly link arms with Beth, as if this will somehow anchor me and help me resist this sudden pull I feel towards him.

"Wow, there are some crazy partnerships going on out there," he chuckles to no one in particular.

No need to respond to that.

But then he elbows me. "See that little guy with the woman in the green dress?"

There is no missing her voluptuous form.

"I think he keeps bumping into the other dancers so he can use her boobs as airbags."

Darnit! I'm blushing, I can feel it. "Do you dance?" I ask, trying to neutralise the conversation.

"You mean other than horizontally?"

I can't believe it! He's just made it worse!

"Not so much," he continues, seemingly unaware of the effect he's having on me. "I bet *you'd* be good though. I saw you getting into the tunes earlier today." He smiles my way, then adds: "It must be pretty frustrating for you to be relegated to the sidelines like this."

"Oh no, I'm happy to be one of life's observers," I assure him and then give his camera a light tap. "I'm sure you can relate."

He pulls a face. "I may be a 'watcher' by profession but on my downtime I make sure there is plenty of doing."

Why does everything he's saying tonight seem to have a saucy edge? I'm almost nervous as I ask, "And what is it that you like to do?"

He holds my gaze until my toes scrunch up and then says, "*Everything*."

"Everything?" I repeat, mostly out of an inability to come up with a whole sentence of my own.

Thankfully he chooses to elaborate, describing adrenaline-fuelled passions from sand-boarding to shark-diving. I sigh as he reveals his plans to explore the rest of Cuba after we conclude in Havana. I love the idea of all that untamed energy. I tell him that my last boyfriend was such a sapper in that direction, poo-pooing every activity I ever proposed.

"I remember the Sunday I suggested taking a rowboat out on the Thames — good grief, you'd have thought I was proposing an expedition down the Amazon!"

"And now here you are in South America!"

I smile back at him, something about his comment making me feel as if I've made a personal achievement just by being here.

As Simon steps in to consult about filming the live band, I find myself wondering what Dan would really like to be doing in this city tonight? If I dared him to ditch the *milonga*, where might we go? I've always been curious about the myth of the spontaneous man. Does anyone really know that guy who packs a suitcase for his girlfriend and whisks her off to Paris on a whim? I could be wrong but I think Dan would be that type. Only he'd probably pick somewhere edgier like Berlin or Zanzibar.

I turn back to Beth, who is looking ever more mesmerised by the scene before her.

"Did you hear any of that?" I whisper, cocking my head towards Dan.

"What?" She gives me a dreamy look.

"Never mind, I'll tell you later," I decide. "What's going on with you?"

"Oh, I'm just thinking how wonderful it is that all these people are here for the love of the dance."

"As opposed to killing themselves trying to earn a living?"

She nods. "Have you noticed how many of the women have their eyes closed out there?" She points out examples of heads resting upon the man's chest or chin or cheek, depending on the height difference.

"All wearing imaginary blindfolds," I smile.

"Exactly."

Then again, when I tried that, I was in the privacy and safety of a hotel room with my best friend watching over me, I'm not so convinced about doing it in a crowded *milonga*.

"I mean, how could you be sure this stranger has your back?"

"Well, there does seem to be a certain order to proceedings," Beth observes. "For a start, everyone is dancing in anticlockwise rotation."

"Yes but there's still a good chance you could clip a chair or get slashed by another woman's stiletto if he didn't guide you right."

"I guess they think it's worth the risk," Beth shrugs.

And maybe it is — when the song ends and the couplings disengage, several women look almost surprised to find themselves back in the real world. As if they have been sleepwalking through a dream.

Not that the *milonga* environment is exactly the real world — the more I study the scene before me, the more it seems like some parallel universe where the usual pecking order of attractiveness does not apply: here the prettiest girl in the room remains a wallflower if she hasn't got the moves, while her deft-footed friend — the one who would be overlooked in a regular club — becomes the belle of the ball.

And then we have Beth — pretty *and* skilled. The only hitch is that she can't let on. So even when she gets her wish and a man invites her to dance, she has to keep in mind that this is just day one of her Tango education. Yes, if he is masterful, he can make her look good but she must react to him as a total novice.

Now, if only she had waited one more moment, she could see how this is really done . . .

"Oh no, I couldn't!" I protest when a white-suited thirty-something approaches me.

I must confess I had been looking in his direction but only because the glare of his suit had made him stand out so much.

"*Ensámbleme por favor*!" Please join me. He makes a gracious bow and for a moment I am distracted by the ostentatious bling on his fingers. But then I come back to my senses.

"No, no! *Inglese*! Can't dance! Sorry."

"Go on," Lucy eggs me on. "How often are you going to get a chance like this?"

I can feel myself wavering. "He is very sparkly, I'll give him that."

As he implores me one more time, I re-connect to my "gimme more!" feeling from last night. A quick twirl couldn't hurt. Besides, I'd be doing Beth a favour by being a live demo. And, better yet, Dan's camera will be trained on *her* so at least he won't see any of my stumbles.

Nonetheless as I take this man's experienced hand I feel hideously out of my depth, like I'm being forced on stage for the debut of a West End show — naturally the rest of the cast are perfectly rehearsed whereas I have barely skimmed the lines.

More than anything, I seem to be feeling embarrassed. And that annoys me. Why is there such shame associated with being new to something? Or is it just me? He knows what he's letting himself in for and he's willing to try anyway. My God, it's hot in here.

And breathe.

Maybe I should close my eyes after all? It certainly would help me forget the couple of hundred people in the room. I try the blindfold approach but lose my footing the minute we set off. Rafael seemed to come with a built-in safety net but I need to keep my wits about me with this fellow — his hold is a little too tight, possibly in an attempt to gain some control over me. Either way, I'm stressing out.

On the plus side I know the Spanish for "Sorry!" now and use it liberally.

Not that it seems to be appeasing his impatience. "No!" he scolds repeatedly, getting rougher in his corrections. As he presses me ever closer, his hold feels increasingly inappropriate. I try to wriggle away but he yanks me back. If I hadn't had such a transcendent experience last night, I would feel that I was to blame for this terrible off-kilter tension. How can two dance partners be so different?

And then I have a chilling thought — I am dancing with the equivalent of Lee: manhandling me, blaming me for everything . . . The one consolation is that I don't actually understand his insults, though the tone is enough to turn my stomach.

I scan the dancefloor for Beth, desperate for some sympathetic eye contact or to see if she can rescue me, though it won't be quite as easy as the disco shuffle where you shimmy up between your friend and the offending dancer and *Love Train* her on her way.

Unfortunately there's no sign of her. But then the music changes and he releases me. He seems to want to lead me back to the table as if everything is hunky-dory but I squirm away and make a break for the bar.

That felt awful — out of sync, clumsy, disturbing. I down my drink, glad it's over. Never again. Not with him at least.

And then I have another thought. I felt exactly like that eighty per cent of the time with Lee and yet I was willing to hand over my entire dance card to him! Where's the logic in that?

With old Twinkletoes here, I knew a minute in that it felt wrong and so now, even if I was desperate for one more spin around the dancefloor and no other man was asking, I wouldn't go back to him. I wonder how I managed to convince myself that Lee was my last chance? Why couldn't I see all the other possibilities around me? Other than the wives who came here with their husbands, none of these other women know where their next dance is coming from but they all have faith that it will come, or they wouldn't be here.

I could learn a thing or two from them . . .

"How was your first real *milonga* Tango?" Lucy looks up expectantly when I return to the table.

I go to say "horrendous" and then change my mind. "Illuminating!" I tell her and then ask, "Any idea where Beth is?" I still can't see her.

"Loo," she replies. "Actually, maybe you could check on her? She's been a while."

Oh no. I feel a twang of concern — something must have gone wrong with her padding.

"Are we going to be here much longer tonight?" I ask, trying to sound casual.

"Flagging?"

"A little," I confess, summoning a yawn. "It's been a long day."

"Well, I'm sure once we've done the etiquette chat, we can call it a night."

"Great!" I smile, praying my emergency repair kit will suffice.

I give Adriana and Adriano a friendly wave as I pass them and then forge through the crowd, locate the Ladies and then start checking the cubicles for familiar shoes.

"Beth?"

On my first call, a door flies open and I'm yanked in.

"What is it?" I gasp. "Did something come adrift?"

She shakes her head, unable to speak, looking utterly distraught.

"Oooh!" I cotton on. "You decided to have your tantrum early. Looks pretty convincing."

"I'm not pretending," she blurts.

"What's wrong then?"

I watch her take a few steadying breaths and then she bleats, "I just want to be able to let go on the dancefloor!"

I nod in sympathy. "It must be really frustrating."

"It's beyond frustrating," she wails. "I mean, this is my dream, Carmen! I've spent most of my life dancing in strip-lit studios and now I'm here, in Argentina, in the arms of a man who first heard the *bandoneón* in his crib and I can feel him interpreting the music so *soulfully* and he's directing me so *artfully* and all I'm doing is resisting and contradicting him and it feels so wrong, so disrespectful!" She tries to gulp back her exasperation. "You know, between the songs I could see this questioning look in his eyes — 'Why are you doing this?' — as if he knew I was faking. Like my body was telling on me." She slumps down on the toilet seat. "I can't believe I'm complaining about being here. It just feels so *suffocating* all of a sudden!"

"Well, it is kind of cramped in here!" I try to make a joke. "Barely bigger than a confession box."

And then she looks up at me, eyes searching mine. "Do you think this is my punishment for the deception? I get all the way here and I never really get to dance . . ."

I crouch beside her and smooth down her hair, because it's the only bit of her I can be sure she'll be able to feel. And then I have an idea.

"You know, Lucy says we'll be done after this chat with Adriano and Adriana. And this place doesn't close until 4a.m. . . ."

Beth blinks back at me. "You mean we could sneak back out later?"

I nod. "You could even wear your real body and we'll style your hair differently so no one recognises you . . ."

"Oh, Carmen!" She pulls me into a fierce embrace. "You're the best!"

"Ready to face the music?" I ask, reaching behind me to open the door.

She nods but I want more. "Say it!"

A big grin spreads over her face as she hollers her favourite catchphrase: "*The showgirl must go on!*"

CHAPTER ELEVEN

Everyone is in position by the time we return, all that remains is for Beth to step into the frame.

"And action!"

Rick cues Adriano, who manages to address both Beth and the camera simultaneously. "Now I would like to explain to you the *codigas* of the *milonga*."

So interested am I in hearing this, I huddle up without even realising.

"Er, Carmen," Lucy winces. "You're in the shot."

"Oop, sorry!" I turn and collide with Dan, catching the edge of the camera lens on my forehead.

"Oh God, did I clunk you?" His hand reaches for my brow.

"No, no, it's fine," I say, stumbling to get past him. But there's no space for me to move into so I tuck directly behind him, now in danger of getting clunked by the rear end of the camera, so I sit down just to get out of the way and now I'm level with his groin. Great.

"It is not my intention to chastise you with my first breath," Adriano begins. "But we hear that you broke away from your last dance partner before you had completed the full *tanda*."

Beth looks confused. "I don't know what a *tanda* is but I waited until the song had finished —"

"The song, yes, but when a man asks you to dance it is for a sequence of four — a *tanda*. It is very bad form to part in the middle of that. You must wait for the *cortina* — what we call the musical curtain."

Naturally Beth understands the concept of leaving a scene mid-performance but still she wants to know — as do I — "What if he's *really* awful?"

Adriana shrugs. "We are talking of a matter of minutes, for the sake of manners, you can spare the time."

"Oh! I didn't mean to come across as rude . . ."

She places a cool hand upon Beth's. "Is okay. A simple mistake. But if that happens again, at least allow him to escort you back to your chair. You do not walk in separate directions from the dancefloor."

Uh oh. Turns out I broke a rule too.

"No abandoning your partners," Beth logs the information.

In spite of my recent ordeal, that sounds rather civilised — even when you "break up" with someone, you are both still courteous. I like that.

"But what if you do like your partner and you want to carry on dancing after the *cortina*?" Beth asks. "How do you signal that?"

"Oh no, no." Adriano shakes his head. "There is no signal, you must change partners."

"But say you have perfect chemistry? Say you are happy dancing with them?"

"It is not the etiquette. Unless you walk in with a partner, you do not spend the evening with one man. The more partners the better."

"The old brothel influence, huh?" Beth retorts.

He looks mildly offended.

"Sorry, I'm just trying to understand the reasoning —"

"We don't say you must never dance with the same partner again, but not in succession. You must leave an appropriate gap."

This puts me in mind of the American tradition of dating several men at once so you can really weigh up what you are looking for in a partner, as opposed to settling on a guy you accidentally kissed at closing time.

Lucy asks Beth what she thinks of the rules so far.

"Well, I really like the fact that you don't have to come up with an elaborate excuse to end the dance session — the getaway plan is in-built. No worries about offending people."

Adriana confirms that this is also the case with the initial invitation to dance.

"It's all in the eyes," she says, causing Beth to smile. "We call this the *cabeceo*. First, the man will attempt to engage you with eye contact. This protects a woman's vulnerability — if you don't like the look of this suitor, you let your glance glide onwards and do not return it to him. He will get the message but no one else will know, thus his ego is protected. If you do want to accept his offer, a slight nod will confirm it."

"Like at a silent auction?"

"Exactly!"

We survey the room — there is indeed a distinct lack of "Coo-eee!" finger-waving and thumbs-up signals. It's almost impossible to predict who is about to approach whom. As a woman, you clearly need to be alert and ready to go. If, for example, you were utterly preoccupied with the last man you danced with, jealously watching him on the floor with another woman, you probably wouldn't notice the man across the room trying to make eye contact with you right now.

"The other thing you should know is that even when you have acquiesced with your gaze, you do not go to the man, you let him come to you."

Adriano nods confirmation. "He is the one who must traverse the dancefloor." Only when he is standing before you, do you rise to meet him."

I can't help but groan, thinking of all the times I've metaphorically leapt up, over-eager, trying too hard to please.

No wonder people are so keen to adhere to these rules — you really can't get into too much trouble on the dancefloor this way, though of course a few of the men are giving it their best shot . . .

Here comes Twinkletoes again — somehow he has lured one of the best female dancers onto the floor. That should shut him up, I think, but then I am stunned to see that he is criticising and manhandling her in exactly the same way he did with me.

I kneel up on my seat so I can track their progression around the dancefloor and, as I watch him muttering and tutting and jolting her, my mouth falls opens in disbelief. Since we arrived, I've seen this woman moving nothing but gracefully, I know she's way out of his league talent-wise and yet he'd have her believe that she's doing it all wrong. Now it really hits home that his earlier behaviour was nothing to do with my novice status. He's just a bully. Putting women down to make himself feel more powerful.

I shake my head, remembering when I told my dad about some of the more serious problems I was having with Lee and he said, "Well, different people bring out different things in each other. You put him with a stronger woman and he'd know he couldn't speak to her that way."

He may as well have said it was my fault. My weakness. I certainly believed that someone else, someone less "irritating", would be able to bring out a better side to him. But, looking at this reflection before me, I realise that certain men are never going to change. Their behaviour is their character, not merely a consequence of who they are with.

Wow.

"Deep thought?"

Dan is back.

"Oh yes, very deep," I confirm. "But unlike Beth, I'm not contractually obliged to share my thoughts with you."

Dan chuckles delightedly. "A woman of mystery, huh?"

"Would you do it?" I'm suddenly curious. "Bare your soul for a reality show?"

"Hmm. Maybe one of those action-adventure types like *Survivor* or *The Amazing Race* but to do what Beth is doing — attempting to learn something I have no natural talent for —" he halts himself. "Or maybe she does . . ."

We watch her moving on the dancefloor with the silver fox we saw when we first arrived, looking almost relaxed in his elegant arms. Possibly because she knows the camera isn't on her right now.

Which prompts the question: "How come you're not filming them?"

"Rick was happy with the first half of the *tanda*."

"Oh, get you with the lingo!" I giggle.

He rolls his eyes. "This always happens. I swear I'm not going to get drawn in and then all of sudden I have an opinion on everything. I'm such a sucker."

I smile. "I know what you mean. Last night I was so turned off by all that frantic kicking at the show. But now —"

"You're turned on?" he proposes.

For a moment I am still. Too dumbfounded to speak.

Then he gets to his feet and says, "Come on!" as if he's decided it's time for us to cut to the chase and get a room. When in fact he is merely letting me know that it's time for us all to leave the *milonga*.

On the dark drive back to the hotel, we pass dozens of people out on the streets going through the rubbish.

"These are the *Cartoneros*," Lucy tells us, explaining that during the economic collapse of 2001 so many people lost their jobs and homes they were forced to make a living from collecting discarded cardboard boxes — dismantling, flattening and packing them before selling them on to a recycling depository.

It's strange to see families working so methodically and competitively under cover of darkness.

"Look, they've got a child out with them!" Beth points to one metal trolley with a toddler tucked in the front.

"What else are they going to do? Pay for a babysitter?"

It's a humbling sight.

"And to think I was freaking out because I didn't get to dance the way I wanted tonight," Beth whispers shamefacedly to me.

"What about me? Losing my mind because I didn't get loved the right way?"

Our mood remains reflective and by the time we're back in our starkly deluxe room, we no longer have the oomph to return to the *milonga*, choosing instead to sleep away our uneasiness.

"Tomorrow we're going to wake up with a new, improved gratitude attitude," Beth decides.

I whole heartedly agree. "A change is coming, I can feel it!"

CHAPTER TWELVE

The new day does indeed bring new possibilities — during class, Dan lets slip that we're going to be left to our own devices for the latter part of that night's *milonga* as the team need to work on the first edit to send back to the UK. Strange to think the show begins broadcasting in just two days. Stranger still to think that we'll be praying that no one we know will be watching. Originally it wasn't going to air until we were safely home but apparently another show dropped out so they've pulled our slot forward and they'll be showing half hour segments of our adventures every day. Lucy says it's putting them under a lot more pressure but, on the upside, they can now tailor our show according to viewer feedback.

This new development means that Rick is often out of the room making important business calls. Every time his exit coincides with a dance break, Simon and Beth huddle up for an iPod song exchange, urging the other to "Listen to this!"

As for Dan and myself . . . Now that I've got to grips with his penchant for innuendo, I am less flummoxed by his quips and conversation progresses onto more conventional topics, like favourite movies . . .

"Have you seen *Inglourious Basterds*?" he asks me.

"Nearly skipped it because the trailers looked so violent but I'm so glad I did go — those Nazi interrogation scenes were just genius."

"What about that ultra tense one in the basement bar?"

I nod excitably. "You know the funny thing about that — the British Lieutenant who got caught out for having a phoney German accent . . ."

"Yes?"

"German is actually that actor's first language — he was born in Heidelberg!"

"I did not know that." He looks strangely pleased with me and then adds, "You know, I couldn't conceive of being friends with anyone who doesn't get Quentin Tarantino."

"I feel the same way about pizza," I note.

"What?" he laughs.

"You know — whether a person favours thick or thin crust? What are you?"

"Thick," he replies. "Every time."

I shake my head and sigh, "That's it, we're done — I can only commune with thin-crusters."

"Well then, I'd like to rescind my preference," he says, sounding serious for once.

My heart does a little flip. Perhaps it's indicative of just how dreadful my last relationship was, but this actually sounds romantic to me!

The day's session concludes with Adriana and Adriano putting on a dynamic display for us outside the *Casa*

Rosada, a.k.a. the Presidential Palace, a.k.a. the "pink house". (For the record, it's actually more of a pinky-beige plasticine colour than anything Paris Hilton would want to lay claim to.)

Their performance causes quite a stir with the tourists gathering in *Plaza de Mayo* and I know Beth wishes it was her generating the ooohs and aahhhs.

She does, however, get a kick waving from the same balcony as Eva Perón. So much so that she forgets herself for a minute and reveals that when she was in a Forties fashion phase people would often compare her to Evita.

I can see the crew wondering how this plump brunette would prompt such comparisons so I quickly add, "Of course, Evita had dark hair when she was growing up in the Pampas — remember Madonna in the movie?"

"Oh, she was great!" Beth enthuses. "But most of all I remember my mum playing the West End show soundtrack over and over, especially *You Must Love Me* —"

"Before we get into a lengthy Elaine Paige retrospective," Rick interrupts, "may I remind you to tie your hair back for the *milonga* tonight? I was looking at last night's footage and you look like Cousin It in the majority of the shots."

My eyes widen at his rudeness.

"I take it you didn't play back any of the etiquette lesson?" Beth snipes back.

I place a hand on her arm to let her know that she doesn't want to go any further.

"Why don't we go and try some of those *alfajores* at Café Tortoni?" I suggest, seeing as we have a couple of hours before the *milonga* and Adriana has insisted we must experience a) this historic venue and b) the national cookie.

"Actually I was thinking we should probably have a siesta so we'll be able to get through the night." Beth gives me a particular look, reminding me that we are planning to stay out a little later than the rest.

"Oh, yes." I nod, a little disappointed but conceding it is the more sensible thing to do.

I'm just about to board the minibus bound for the hotel when Dan asks if I'd help him with a piece of his equipment. I wonder why he doesn't ask Simon until he says, "I'll take you there."

"Where?"

"Café Tortoni. I've seen the schedule for tomorrow. We'll be done by 11p.m."

"B-ut," I falter checking no one can hear us. "We can't be seen to be going anywhere *together* —"

"Then meet me there," he persists. "At midnight."

"In secret?" My eyes widen at the illicitness of his proposal.

"We'll be like a couple of old movie spies!" he murmurs huskily. "What do you say?"

I give him a bold smile. "Oscar Kilo!"

"Excuse me?" This wasn't the response he was expecting.

"Okay." I give him the more traditional response. "Midnight tomorrow, I'll be there."

* * *

Any chance of an afternoon snooze is now out the window, for me at least. It's all I can do to stop squeaking with glee — I just can't believe it! I've only been away from London for a couple of days and I have a date lined up with this amazing man! Yes, I did experience a brief twang of disloyalty to Lee but then I reminded myself that this is exactly the kind of change I have been hoping for.

Giving up on trying to keep my springy eyelids closed, I start reading up on Café Tortoni — gazing at pictures of its yellowing marble, stained glass and venerable bronzes. I can't think of a more atmospheric setting for a tryst. I might just have to take up smoking and wear a beret.

That night Beth does everything right at the *milonga* — from following the *codigas* to playing novice to perfection, knowing that freedom will come soon enough.

"I think we're going to hang out for a while longer," she tells Lucy when the rest of them prepare to leave.

"God, I wish I could stay with you guys and just have some fun."

"Mmmm," Beth grimaces, afraid of saying anything that might encourage her and thus ruin our plan. "Maybe tomorrow night?"

Now it's me flinching — I don't want anything getting in the way of my sneaky pursuit.

"I can't believe what risk-takers we've turned into overnight," I marvel as I help Beth out of her padding

— no easy task in these tiny toilet cubicles. "Do you think it's going to keep escalating?"

"What?"

"Our lies and deceptions? I mean, by the end of this trip, do you think we'll be wanted for fraud in three different countries?"

Beth shrugs. "I don't know but it's always good to have ambitions!"

I take her discarded padding and stuff it into a zippy holdall, which I then wedge under my chair beside the dancefloor. Beth looks good — and reassuringly different — in the slinky black shift she'd packed for the end of the trip. Enjoying dance after dance, she comes back to give me a report on each partner:

"He may be as round as a beach ball but he has style!"

or

"He's from Japan, came here purely to Tango, dances eight hours a day. Wonderful!"

But then she watches back the mini-movie footage I've been filming on my camera and slumps a little.

"Well, obviously I'm no Dan —"

"It's not that," she sighs.

"What then?"

"I don't know if it's because I'm trying too hard but it still looks like I'm doing the dance as opposed to letting the dance do me." Then she tilts her head my way. "You know that first night with you and Rafael, there was something genuine about the way you two moved together."

"Well, it was an unusual circumstance —"

"You really should give it another go out on this dancefloor."

"After what happened last time?" I shake my head in a firm no.

"You can't let one lousy experience put you off the Tango forever," Beth protests.

"I know, but watching lessons is hardly the same as taking them."

"True," Beth concedes. "You know what? Tomorrow I'm going to ask if we can bring an extra partner into the classroom for you. In fact, why don't we pick someone from tonight? Who do you like the look of?"

"Oh hell no!" I turn to face the wall.

"Well, that's not very constructive."

"No!" I squeak. "It's Twinkletoes from last night. I can't believe it — he was trying to give me the *cabeceo*!"

"The Lee of the *milonga*?" Beth's eyes narrow. "Don't tell me, he's the one wearing the white suit?"

I nod. "He's only trying to come back for more with me because he knows how disadvantaged and apologetic I was."

"You could be right," Beth admits as she watches assorted eyes turn away from him. "I think every other woman in the room has got wise to him."

I am therefore all the more stunned to see Beth giving him an encouraging nod.

"What are you doing?" I gasp.

"I just want to say thank you to you for staying out late with me tonight."

“What?” I frown. “I think you might be taking the gratitude attitude a step too far!”

“Revenge,” she whispers in my ear before making full use of her dazzling stage school smile as she accepts his extended hand.

I’m not quite sure how she expects to punish him but I’m eager to find out. For three and a half songs she grins and bears it — all in the name of “etiquette”, rolling her eyes at my camera as she passes and digging her nails ever deeper into his back. Several times I capture the shock on his face as she resists him with the same force that he is attempting to manipulate her — she may be back to her slim self but she is pure, toned muscle.

I’m just wondering what on earth Adriano and Adriana would make of the pair of them when the song crescendos and Beth executes a series of deft moves — first a seductive cat rub with her ankle, then her trademark ocho, then a devilish hook — unbalancing him and sending him crashing into the table containing the most glasses of red wine.

Beth is clearly picturing Lee’s head on his body as she watches the dark pink stains seeping over his white suit.

I’m busy taking in the delight on the faces of the other women he has harangued — a few even applaud — when Beth hurries past me and hustles, “Let’s get out of here!”

I’m eager to follow her but the body suit bag has got wedged under the chair and I can’t free it. Oh crap. He’s coming straight for me.

"*Usted no debe demostrar esto*!" he says, jabbing at the camera dangling from my wrist.

As he continues babbling, I finally get it — he's afraid I'm going to post the footage on the internet.

"I give you *dinero*," he offers.

"Dinner?" I reel. Why would I possibly want to eat with him?

"*Dinero*! Money!" he says, taking a wodge of notes from his pocket.

Oh jeez! Now we can add blackmail to our crimes.

"No, no!" I begin but Beth has returned to find out what's holding me up.

"It's the bag!" I point to the seat.

She removes it with one yank and then contemplates the cash in his shaking hand. "Please tell me you didn't give him money for dry-cleaning?"

"No, he's trying to give it to *us* so we don't post footage on YouTube!"

"Ohhh!" Beth grins and then whips it out of his hand with a cheery, "*Gracias!*"

"What are you doing?" I fret as I chase her out of the door.

"It's not for us," she tuts as she hails a cab. "Remember those people we saw on the way home last night?"

And then I smile. Something tells me that the *Cartoneros* are going to get a nice bonus tonight!

CHAPTER THIRTEEN

Today's the day! I think as I wake.

Fifteen more hours and I'll be sipping Argentine wine with Dan, hopefully leaning closer with each sip until finally our lips meet in a blackberry-imbued kiss!

At the present moment, I'm even more eager than Beth to get to the dance studio because it will mean being beside him and feeling that sense of expectation grow between us.

But then Lucy announces she has a surprise in store for us today — we're getting out of Buenos Aires, going on a little road trip.

"But we're coming back here tonight, right?" are the first words from my mouth.

"Oh yes, we should be back this afternoon."

"Okay," I sigh, comforted that our plans can remain intact, if a little uneasy that we're heading so far away from Café Tortoni.

Don't you just wish life had a fast forward button for times like these?

As we hit the freeway, Beth and I try to reconcile the names on the signs we pass with a possible route, though it isn't easy to read a map with Dan driving. This man likes to change lanes a lot.

There are a good many beauty spots in Argentina — the Iguazu Falls, the glaciers of Patagonia, the peaceful lakes of Bariloche — but any of those would take a flight to get to. This country is massive — over two thousand miles from tip (where it meets Bolivia) to toe — a.k.a the southernmost point in the world.

"Ushuaia," I read the name of the town that marks the spot. "Shame we weren't there a week ago."

"How come?" Beth frowns.

"Well, then we could've claimed 'It's the end of the world!' and no one would have contradicted us."

Beth gives me a fond snicker. "You're feeling better, aren't you?"

"Well, I'm certainly feeling things other than utter despair which I take as a very good sign."

"Me too!" she grins. "Things are looking up!"

We remain peppy and engaged for another twenty minutes or so but then the scenery becomes so uniformly flat and samey we may as well be driving on a giant tarmac treadmill. Beth reverts to her iPod while I find myself hypnotised by the swish of the pale grasses and drift in and out of sleep. I have no idea how long I doze for or whether we are any further along because every time I open my eyes the same vision greets me. And then it dawns on me — this is Argentina's infamous Pampas.

In my hazy state, I see myself running through the feathery grasses, imagining that it would have the same prickly-tickle as the inside of a duvet, leaving me fluffy with down . . .

Part of me wants to make a break for it and experience the sensation for real but then Dan turns off the main road onto a hard-packed, sandy-coloured track. I expect the minibus to start juddering and become a real bone-shaker but, other than a stirring of golden dust whisked up by our wheels, there's barely a change.

"A few more kilometers of this and we're there," Lucy advises Dan.

I'm happily staring at the back of his head, imagining my fingers entwining with his hair as he rocks me in a slow, close-body Tango, when we come to a sudden stop.

"Okay, ladies." Lucy turns to face us, motioning to Beth to lose her headphones. "Time to saddle up!"

"Did she say *saddle*?" Beth blanches, gripping my arm. "Oh my God! I know what it is — we're going to play polo!"

"Of course!" I gasp as we hop from the van. Why didn't I think of this sooner?

"Don't look so excited!" Beth complains. "What if they try to get me — or rather *this*," she motions to her bulk, "into jodhpurs and those shirts — what are they called again? The ones with the short sleeves and little collars . . ."

"Polo shirts?" I venture.

"Oh!" Beth clunks her forehead. "This is not good. I couldn't bear —"

"Beth!" I hold up my hand to stop her.

"What?"

"It's not polo players."

"What then?"

I take her by her shoulders and rotate her so she can see the group of men approaching us.

There's no mistaking their distinctive outfits — wide trousers tucked into dusty boots, once-white shirts, red neckerchiefs and berets of rough wool. Their hair is wavy raven-black and their weather-worn skin leather-brown.

They are *Gauchos*.

"The name comes from the Quechua language," Lucy reads from her notes. "It means 'orphan' or 'vagabond'." She looks at them in awe. "I've always thought of them as a mix of cowboy, gypsy and nomad. Folk heroes of a kind."

In other words, the antithesis of the groomed, privileged, Rolex-wearing polo player.

"Do they dance?" Beth eyes them with suspicion.

"Actually we had something a little different in mind today," Lucy informs us. "Good for working those inner thigh muscles . . ."

It is then we remember the main thing *Gauchos* have in common with polo players:

"Horses!" Beth cries in dismay as an older *Gaucho* leads the steeds into view.

"Aren't they beautiful!" Lucy coos, admiring their velvety nostrils and sweat-sparkled coats.

"I don't have to get on one, do I?" Beth's voice is strained.

"Don't worry — we're not going to make you round up the cattle," Lucy laughs. "Rick just wants a shot of you clip-clopping into the sunset."

"Right, right," Beth gulps. "And I can see why you wouldn't think that would be a big deal but I'm really not . . . Eek!" Beth jumps back as one of the horses shakes its head upwards, whinnying to the sky in a complaining fashion. "See, they don't like me!" Beth reasons. "I really don't think I should vex them further. Animal cruelty and all that."

"Oh, Beth —" Lucy begins.

"How about Carmen going in my place?" She quickly volunteers me. "If it's just a distant shot, we look the same from behind . . ." She turns the pair of us away from Lucy to prove the point, only now asking me: "You wouldn't mind, would you?"

"No, not at all," I say, recalling the exhilaration I used to feel when I rode my cousin's horse as a child — how I would relish that transition from uncomfortable jiggidy trot to rhythmical canter. It would be good to feel that again — to experience the gearshift to freedom.

"I'm sorry, Rick says no." Lucy returns from a ten second consultation. "It has to be you, Beth. But, if it makes you feel any better, he says Carmen can ride out with you, provided she's out of shot . . ."

I see Beth wrestling with herself. I know part of her wants to burst into tears and lock herself in the minibus with a bag of *alfajores* but, as ever, her "show must go on" side prevails.

"Okay. So long as I get the smallest one," she bargains. "Not so far to fall."

She becomes all the more convinced of the inevitability of this when we discover the absence of a traditional leather saddle. All these particular *Gauchos* use is a number of woven blankets bound to the beast.

"That's it?" Beth can't hide her dismay.

I try to get her to look on the bright side. "At least now the two of you can identify with each other . . ." I give her padding a playful pat.

"Yeah, just what I need — even more wadding between my legs." She mops her brow with her cuff. "My God, it's hot out here — you're definitely going to let me shed a few inches tonight, right?"

"Absolutely," I say, wishing I could do the same for myself.

There's a real sultriness to the air today — the kind of burgeoning humidity that has you lumbering and lethargic. I'm relieved that we're not obliged to wear riding hats, however irresponsible that level of authenticity might be. With any luck we'll gain enough speed to create a hair-frisking breeze . . .

But first we must climb on board.

"*Listo?*" A *Gaucho* approaches each of us, cupping his hand under our left knee and giving us an upward thrust so we can throw our right leg over. We do so in unison and our horses shuffle, readjusting their footing.

"Oh my God, oh my God!" Beth bleats, tensing, her shoulders up by her ears.

"You can do this," I reassure her. "Try not to make any sudden movements, just relax."

As I watch her *Gaucho* make a few adjustments to her posture and grip, I notice the ornate silver dagger tucked into his belt at the small of his back. I'm just thinking how beautiful the craftsmanship is on the sheath, how it wouldn't look out of place in *Lord of the Rings*, when I sense a very modern presence beside me.

"You look good up there!" Dan teases from the safety of the ground.

"I hardly recognise you from this angle!" I grin back at him, finding it quite the novelty to be looking down on him. "Where's your horse?"

"Ah, it's a terrible shame but I can't hold the reins and the camera." He gives a "darnit!" grimace.

I shake my head and then look out into the infinite fields. "How will we know when to stop?"

"Don't worry about that, you go as far as you like — I've got a really long lens."

"Hey, enough with the bragging," Lucy scolds. "Ride on!"

Within a minute of setting off, the *Gauchos* lead us in two separate directions, not that there is anything to really distinguish either route. I wonder if they see patterns in the grasses the same way Native American Indians read footprints in the earth. Perhaps each whiskery tuft tells a story?

All I know for sure is that something about this basic connection between man, beast and soil is making me feel calm and grounded. I never would have thought to do something like this back home. All I wanted to do was hide away in a dark nook and look at me now, out in the open sunshine, no shelter for miles and yet somehow I feel protected. I even feel a smile play upon my lips as I realise that there is no way Lee could ever find me here — I don't even know where I am!

Suddenly I hear a disturbance of voices and a penetrating scream. *Beth!* I turn and see her horse veering away from the others, thundering at the earth as it makes a break for who knows what. She's grappling for something to cling to — the reins have whipped out of her hands, one foot is loose of the stirrup and already she is bumping and sliding off at an angle. I lurch as if to catch her, forgetting that I too am astride a horse. I try to get my steed to gee up and careen to her assistance, but it's too late — she slams down onto the earth so hard it takes my breath away.

Keep those hooves away from her face, her legs . . . I wince, barely able to look but mercifully her horse rages onward, leaving my best friend in a heap.

"Don't move!" I call out to her but my horse seems to think the instruction is for him.

"Can we go faster? *Accelerato*?" I implore my *Gaucho* while trying in vain to kick-start my transportation. "Oh never mind!" I decide I'll be quicker on foot, swinging my leg over his broad back and jumping down. "Urrrrh!" It's further and a harder drop than I imagined. My knees jar but I quickly right them and now I'm running, running towards her. Through the pampas. I'm not thinking about the insides of duvets now, I'm just praying that the reason she isn't moving is because she's in shock. Hoping against hope that her spine and her skull and those recently-healed ribs are all intact. Trusting that she'll still be able to dance.

"Hang in there!" I cry out.

The minibus has pulled up a few feet away and everyone is now anxiously crowding around her. I push through, dropping to my knees beside her.

"Beth, can you hear me?"

"Is she sleeping?" I hear one of the *Gauchos* ask.

"I just need to lie here for a moment . . ." Her eyes remain closed as she echoes the words I spoke from the bathroom floor on our first night at the Faena.

"Are you in pain? Does anything feel broken?" I don't know exactly what to ask, how to tell. "Can we call a doctor?" I plead to Lucy.

"Rick's already on it," she tells me. "But I think we should try and pull these spikes out of her . . ."

It would seem that Beth has landed atop a porcupine-spined shrub, turning her padding — but apparently not her body — into a pin cushion.

"Gently!" Lucy winces as I start whipping them out by the handful.

"I'm sure she's too shocked to feel anything," I mutter, wanting them gone before eagle-eyed Rick comes over.

"Is she going to be okay?" Simon has a tremble to his voice.

"She's going be fine," Beth assures him, forcing open her eyes to add conviction. "I'll get up in a minute. I'm just waiting for the nausea to pass . . . Look!" She demonstrates to him that she can move her hands and her legs.

He smiles, relieved, until Dan says, "Is that blood?"

"What? Where?" I gasp.

"There are a lot of sharp stones around here," he continues.

And that's when I see it — a red splotch spreading out across her shoulder.

"There's a doctor at the *estancia* nearby," Lucy passes on the update from Rick. "We'll take you there right now."

"That's not necessary." Beth tries to battle to her feet, clawing at me to get upright but she moves too fast and no sooner is she up than she passes out. Landing heavily in Simon's arms.

"We should loosen her clothing." Lucy begins unbuttoning her shirt.

"Best to leave this to the doctor." I try to politely divert her hands but she persists.

"My mum's a nurse, I think we should just see how deep the —"

Oh no.

"What's all this?"

Lucy has found the top of the body suit.

"Well, you know how nervous she was about falling off the horse," I babble. "I guess she wanted an extra layer of protection."

"She didn't know we were coming horse-riding today. You saw how surprised she was."

I gulp. I can't for the life of me think of another excuse for why their leading lady has the body of a stuffed toy. Perhaps if I made out she had some dreadful skin condition and it needed ointment and swaddling at all times . . .

"It's actually kind of embarrassing," I begin. But then in one move Rick reaches over and tears her shirt apart, exposing all my handiwork.

I hear the gasps of confusion.

An explanation is needed. Everyone is looking at me.

"What's going on?" Rick wants to know.

I open my mouth, nothing comes out.

Rick obviously thinks I need a jolt because he now roars in my face, "What the *hell* is going on?"

"Rick, chill." Dan steps between us.

"Chill? *Chill?*" He turns on him. "Our entire shoot is in jeopardy here! We've got an air date for tomorrow!" He's back in my face now. "You have to tell me what is going on!"

"She's a dancer."

"What?" Rick spins round to face Simon. For it is he, not me, who has spoken these words.

"She just wanted this chance to show the world what she is capable of."

"You knew about this?" Rick spits. "You knew she was a fake and you didn't tell me? Oh, you are so fired!"

"Wait!" I have to speak up but I can't help but shoot a bewildered glance at Simon. How could he know?

"Sometimes you forget that her microphone is still on."

"Lucy!" Rick barks, instructing her to try and get Legal on the phone.

"Wait!" I cry again. "Please just let me explain. I know this won't make the situation any better but you have to at least understand *why* she did it. She's not a bad person —" I turn to Lucy, our greatest ally, but even her eyes are downcast. "You have to know that we were especially sorry to have deceived you. As soon as Beth met you, she wanted to pull out — remember the whole drama in the bathroom?"

She concedes a nod.

"But then you said she was your last hope and so she went ahead. I think in that moment she felt she was doing it for you as much as anything."

Rick is getting impatient. "So let me get this straight — she's a dancer, a ringer, and she's padded herself up for what reason?"

"To be your perfect reality TV girl — the one who could be physically transformed and streamlined by the dancing."

"And all that guff about the abusive boyfriend —"

"Actually that's true. It just happens to be about me, not her."

Rick is so incensed he can't even speak.

"Um." Lucy has reached out to touch his sleeve. Despite the fact that he looks like he might punch her if she continues, she does just that. "I have an idea. A possible solution."

"There is no solution to this mess."

"An alternative then. What if . . ." She looks like she's about to lose her nerve.

"Yes?" I encourage because I know Rick won't.

"Actually it's something Beth said earlier about you being her body double . . ." She turns back to Rick. "What if we switch to Carmen — she's a genuine non-dancer. She has the looks and the size you said you wanted. She's viewer-friendly."

Oh no.

"But all the footage we've shot —" he begins his protestation.

"Really, they look so similar from behind," Lucy reminds him. "It's possible we could edit around her . . ."

"Actually, I do have some footage of Carmen dancing," Dan chips in.

Rick's eyes narrow at Dan.

"I mean, you know when I've been shooting B-roll, sometimes she's been in shot." He tries to sound casual. "It could be enough."

"And what do you propose we do with all the personal guidance with the experts?" he snaps. "Throw it all out?"

"We could re-shoot it with Carmen."

"*When?*" he spits. "Tomorrow is our last day in Buenos Aires."

Silence. It's not going to work. I hate to admit it but I'm relieved. I wouldn't have been comfortable revealing myself to the world as Beth has been doing. Then again, I could find that a tad more comfortable than prison. I'm a definite aider and abetter in all this.

"Of course, we could just carry on as we are . . ." Simon offers.

"What?" Rick scoffs. "Are you mad?"

"Only the six of us know the truth. No viewers have seen the padding. No one back in London knows . . ."

"You do realise that lying would implicate all of us?"

"Well, what about this?" Lucy is determined to find a solution. "What if we told the truth?"

Rick's brow rucks but he's still listening.

"That way we could keep all the footage up 'til now and then — *scandal!* We discover she's been lying, there's a big confessional and then the redemption . . ."

Rick purses his lips and then looks over to where Beth's body lay. Past tense. Only the padding remains.

For a moment we all look around in a panic but then we see her over by her *Gaucho*. He has blotted and bound her wound with a cloth, the buttonless shirt is now knotted at her trim waist, her skirt belted several notches tighter.

She has moved into his arms now and, in answer to the earlier question, he can indeed dance.

"What's she doing?" Rick is perplexed.

"Her last Tango," I whisper, transfixed.

This isn't a performance for the benefit of others. There are no tricks and flicks, no stage school schmaltz. It's slow and intimate and lost-to-the-moment — a culmination and expression of all the regrets of her life.

I wish those casting directors could see Beth now. There would be no questioning the rawness of the emotion here — it's so captivating and heartbreaking to see them move as one that we find ourselves stunned to silence.

All except Rick, who turns to Dan and orders, "Film it!"

CHAPTER FOURTEEN

And then the skies burst and the rains came down.

Of course Rick insisted on interviewing Beth at her most raw and sodden. It seemed cruel to have her standing there, cheeks streaked with mascara, rain drops strung like glass beads on her straggled hair, but he said the viewers needed to see her in a state of penance in order to forgive her.

I suppose we should be grateful he decided to let her ride in the minibus with the rest of us, instead of dragging her behind on a rope. Especially since the track is now basically a chocolate sludge of mud.

"Ooomf!" Beth's eyes flick open as we hit another rut.

I was going to urge her to try to sleep more but Lucy informs us that we're nearly there so instead I take Beth's hand, comforted that we're in this together, though I don't know exactly what we're "in" except a lot of trouble.

"Wow, check this place out!" Dan whistles from the driving seat.

I wipe the misted window to my right and see that we're now advancing down a tree-lined avenue reminiscent of a French country estate. Ever more

Beauty and The Beast is the building we're drawing towards — a fairytale confection of dusky-pink stone with piped icing trim and moss-fuzzed statues perched atop its pinnacle.

"It's so beautiful!" Beth coos as we take in the elongated leaded windows and guardian lions set before a sprawling lawn.

As far as I knew, *estancia* meant "ranch" and thus herds of cattle so I was hardly envisioning this level of elegance. I almost expect a man in velvet breeches and ruffled silk shirt to greet us but in actuality our primary point of contact is a fluffy Lassie dog with fur clomped into muddy dreadlocks on his underbelly and leaves woven between his toes as if he has stepped prematurely from a woodland pedicure.

There is a noticeable lack of over-excitable barking, panting or slathering, he simply approaches and surveys — his face noble with small, kind eyes — and then trots off. A few seconds later a petite woman appears from the shiny-leafed undergrowth and we discover a second building beside us, entirely shrouded in lush green foliage. "I am Claudia," she introduces herself. "Please follow me."

"After you." Simon continues to extend Beth every courtesy.

We move on to a grand but rustic atrium with bare brick walls, jangling chandeliers and a sunken seating area of faded coral velvet.

"You must be my patient." A genteel-looking doctor is awaiting us beside the open hearth.

Beth insists on visiting his office alone, while the rest of us are invited to enjoy afternoon tea.

Well, why not — when in crisis, brew up!

Apparently tea is usually served in the courtyard beside the fountain, but Claudia explains that the weather has caused the tables to be shuffled inside and lit with candles, on account of the power cut.

It really is surprisingly dark outside, I think as I go to pull up a chair beside Lucy but Rick halts me: "We need to talk business."

"Oh. Right. Sorry." I withdraw, taking a seat at the furthest table from them. There I fold my hands in my lap, trying not to feel like an outcast with people talking about me behind my back, even though they are.

I'm not alone for long. No sooner is the cake plate presented — little cubes of jam tart, a dry sponge and some brittle chocolate cookies — when in scuttle two chickens and a parade of ducks, waddling like old men with hip replacements. They flap up onto the seats of the table beside me as if expecting to be served themselves and then jump to the tabletop itself, jerking eagerly around. Once they realise they didn't quite pull off their masquerade as fellow guests, they resort to scavenging around my feet, getting increasingly vicious, one getting a good beakful of his rival's feathery neck. Excessive but a vision of harmony compared to what is going on at the crew table.

"Excuse me, *signora*." Claudia approaches, looking apologetic. "I'm afraid we just have two rooms available; would you approve that I place the three gentlemen together and the three women?"

"Oh!" I chuckle at the prospect of Rick sleeping dormitory style. "Actually we're not staying, my friend is just visiting the doctor . . ." I point off down the hall.

She shakes her head. "There is no return to the city tonight."

"No return?" I repeat.

"The roads are . . . how do you say? . . . impassable. Hopefully tomorrow the sun will dry them."

For a second I think of Café Tortoni but of course a scuppered date is the least of my worries right now. I look across at Rick. Face appropriately like thunder. I can't see this news cheering him up at all. Then again, maybe it buys everyone a little more time? This being an act of nature as opposed to anyone's actual fault.

As I direct the woman to their table, I urge her not to take offence if the man in black starts shouting. I estimate he's just coming up to his eighth expletive when Beth and the doctor reappear.

"What's the verdict?" Lucy is the first to ask.

"We have cleaned the wound, it is not so deep," he shrugs, rather too nonchalantly for my liking.

"So no permanent damage?" I double-check.

"She may turn a few pretty shades of purple and yellow but nothing breaks."

I barely have time to sigh with relief when Beth turns on Rick. "What about you?" she confronts him, ready to take whatever he has to say on the chin. "What's *your* verdict?"

I can tell he's a little put out by her directness, her lack of fear.

"Well, it turns out that we are trapped here until the morning so the jury is out until then."

"You're still deciding?" Beth crumples visibly.

Now Rick smiles. This is more like it. "I need to speak with London," he taunts. "I'll let you know tomorrow."

Spoken like a true reality TV suspense puppeteer. Oh, how they love to make the contestants wait until after the break to learn their fate.

Beth sighs as she looks out of the window at our captor, a.k.a. the raging rains. "So we're stuck here overnight?"

"Yes."

When she turns back to Rick, I see a new look on her face, one I can't quite place. "Will you be needing me any more today?"

"Nope!" Rick is triumphant in his dismissal.

I think everyone expects Beth to excuse herself and huddle under the nearest blanket but instead she cheers, "Good!", grabs a handful of cookies and heads for the door.

It takes me a moment to process what just occurred.

"Beth! Wait!" I hurry after her.

"Are you okay?" She turns back to me with a look of concern.

"*Me?*" I splutter. "Yes, yes, I'm fine."

"Fantastic, then I'll see you later." She gives me an excitable squeeze, leaving me with a whispered, "Don't wait up!"

I look after her in bafflement — who would choose to go walking in this weather? Surely the doctor would have advised her to rest?

But then, through the blur of the rain, I make out a figure sheltering beneath the far ombu tree. It's him — the dancing *Gaucho*.

"Where on earth is she going?" I hear Simon call over to me.

I give a noncommittal shrug. I don't want to get involved in any more deceit.

"Do you think someone should go after her?" he asks, all too ready to volunteer.

"No, no!" I insist, walking towards him in a mildly obstructive manner. "She'll be fine."

"Relax." Dan puts a matey hand upon Simon's shoulder. "She probably just needs to lick her wounds."

Or better yet have someone to lick them for her . . .

Or am I being presumptuous? Maybe she's just going to dance with him. After all, who could blame her for wanting to recreate the intensity of their earlier connection?

"Carmen?"

"Yes?"

It's Lucy addressing me now. "We're going to take one of the rooms to review the footage and strategise," she informs me. "You'll be all right by yourself?"

"Of course," I nod, though as soon as they are gone, I find myself feeling a little dejected — so recently spurned by the crew and now the hand I was holding so tightly has released me.

I realise now just how much I was depending on my rendezvous with Dan tonight, hoping we could lose ourselves in some dark nook in Buenos Aires and he could change the fact that Lee is still The Last Man I

Kissed. I don't want him to continue to hold that place of significance. I want my life to take a different turn and I thought Dan could be the man to make that happen. But there will be no chance of sneaking out from Rick's night watch and tomorrow Beth and I could be deported, sent back to London and, despite all the illuminating thoughts I've had along the way, I am still aware of a vulnerability towards Lee. I want love and he continues to be the only man making me a definite offer in that arena. I take out my phone and scan through the texts I have kept from him — the loving ones that I treasure and can't bring myself to delete, just in case he's the last man to ever say these words to me:

> I love being with you.
> I am so in need of your sweet affection.
> Always thinking of you and missing you.
> Love you sooooooooo (endless oooos)

Why couldn't he have always been this adorable? We could have been so happy.

Enough! I flip my phone shut and look for distraction on the bookshelves but the musty tomes are all in Spanish. I turn instead to my bag, looking for something to occupy me, even if it is just removing old chewing gum wrappers and Pret a Manger receipts. And then my fingers locate my sketchbook.

Beth suggested I bring it away with me in case costume inspiration struck. Now would be as good a time as any for that to happen . . . I fold back the first page. Since Beth resumed her natural figure it's easier for me to think of designs for her. I close my eyes and play back the image of her dancing with the *Gaucho*, re-imagining a sleeker outfit for her . . .

My pencil starts moving before the thought is even fully formed — I veer from a traditional split skirt to an all-in-one lace catsuit, all the better to curl around him. My coloured pencils favour a moody burgundy palette. I think of fabrics I could ruche up the front and drape to a flippy tail at the back. Then I experiment with going backless altogether, bar a few base-of-spine jewels.

It's then I remember the women who appeared to be sleepwalking at the *milonga* and I begin working on a gauzy black and gold negligée. For me, this is the outfit that works best with the *Gaucho* scenario — perhaps it would be taboo for this high society princess to dance with such a man by day, but by night when he visits her dreams . . .

Before I know it, a couple of hours have passed, my mood has shifted and dinner is announced.

Claudia is smiling *buenos noches* and beckoning me to a mid-size table with multiple settings.

"Actually . . ." How to phrase this? "I'm not allowed to sit with the others." I grimace. "Would it be possible for me to have a table by myself?"

She gives me a pitying glance and then seats me back at my earlier teatime spot. I make sure I am positioned with my back to the other table but a few minutes later

Lucy comes over to let me know that I am welcome to join them.

"Oh no, really it's fine," I smile. "I understand you have a lot to discuss."

"We're taking a break from that."

"All the same —"

"Is she resisting?" Dan appears by her side.

"Honestly," I blush. "I'm perfectly happy reading my book."

"Well!" Dan huffs. "We asked you nicely but now . . ." He places one hand on the chairback and one on the seat between my legs and the next thing I know he is carrying me — chair and all! — over to their table. I am so dumbfounded that even the jolt as I'm plonked in place doesn't re-set my gaping jaw.

"Bread roll?" He offers me the basket as if nothing out of the ordinary has occurred.

"Any word from Beth?" Simon tries to sound casual as he fills my glass with inky Malbec.

I shake my head. "The mobiles don't seem to work here."

"Should we be worried?" he asks. "I mean, she needs to eat."

I imagine her squatting beside a remote campfire with the *Gaucho*, barbecuing assorted meat cuts while flutterings of pale grey ash dance for them in the night air.

"I'm sure she's fine," I tell him. "I think she just needs a night off."

"How about we toast her wellbeing?" Dan holds up his wine glass. "To Beth!"

"To Beth!" three voices chorus.

It's only now that I realise Rick isn't at the table.

"He's dining in his room," Lucy informs me.

"And when she says 'his' room," Simon pulls a face, "she means it."

I scrunch my brow.

"He said that seeing as we're all so 'buddy-buddy' and 'keen to stick together' he's giving us our very own slumber party . . ."

"There were five in the bed and the little one said, 'Roll over! Roll over!' Dan trills, clearly untroubled by the arrangement.

Meanwhile my stomach is looping wildly. There's still a chance! All things are possible. Especially since Dan is already ordering another bottle of Malbec.

"Well, if he's going to treat us like naughty children, I think we should behave like them!"

"Drink a lot of wine as a child, did you?" I tease.

"Oh yes, I'm practically French!" he winks, then leans over and nuzzles my neck murmuring, "*Ma cherie! Champs Elysées! Chanel!*" in an exaggerated accent.

I know I should push him away but I can't curb my delighted giggling. It feels so good to laugh and feel frivolous.

Over the course of dinner we talk about life from our different perspectives in the "entertainment industry" and share stories of our worst job nightmares over the years. Simon talks about one boozy female presenter who would always show up so hungover her mouth would make all these sticky clicking sounds due to lack of saliva. "I wanted to squirt WD40 on her tongue!"

Dan runs through the bizarre array of things that have occurred in the background of his filming that he didn't even notice until reviewing the footage.

"The man who fell into an open wine cellar behind Kylie Minogue was particularly choice."

Lucy shudders, remembering the time she had to blast a celebrity with a fire extinguisher when her hair extensions caught light in a candlelit dinner scenario. As for me, I tell them how last year I'd devised a nun's habit held together with Velcro for a quick costume change (the actress was playing two roles in this serious wartime drama). As she was exiting one scene to do something selfless and pious, another actor accidentally trod on her hem and the whole thing whipped off, leaving a surprisingly curvaceous Sister Agnes exposed in a lacy balconette bra and thong.

"Speaking of getting undressed . . ." Dan deems it is time for bed.

I couldn't agree more.

Our room is essentially a honeymooner's dream — a vast four-poster bed with a shimmering peacock-blue canopy, glazed walls hand-painted with idyllic country scenes and a Juliet balcony jutting out into the pine-sprigged woods.

"So how about we draw straws to see who gets the bed with me?" a wine-emboldened Dan jokes, splaying out on the cover in his best come hither pose.

I can't even look at him in an amused fashion, for fear that my real want will shine through.

"Ignore him." Lucy places a protective arm around my shoulder. "You hounds are on the floor where you belong." She kicks Dan's dangling foot. "The bed is ladies only."

"And Beth?" Simon enquires.

I check the dimensions. "There's room for her too if she comes back."

"*If*?" he startles. "She wouldn't try to escape in this weather, would she?"

"Escape?" I hadn't thought of that possibility. "Noooo," I assure him. "Trust me, she wouldn't leave me alone to deal with the aftermath."

As soon as the words are out of my mouth, I have a moment of doubt. When I saw the *Gaucho* under the tree, my mind immediately went to a sexual liaison, but what if she did have escape on her mind? A horse could indeed get through the mud where a car couldn't. Then again, I can't see her wanting to ride again so soon after her fall. Besides, what would they do — clip-clop up the entrance of the Faena, squelch along to the room, change clothes, grab her passport and then have him canter along the *Avenida 9 de Julio* to the airport? No. We're in this together. She wouldn't leave me.

Unless she thought she was doing me some kind of favour . . . Separating herself to make sure we didn't get lumped with a joint punishment? Oh, I really don't know what to think any more! And I can't presume to know what she is going through. I remember all too well how low she was in London, how this opportunity offered temporary — if slightly delirious — distraction. Now look at what has happened! She's in even worse shape than she was then.

Apparently there is another level below rock bottom.

"Okay! I'm ready for my bedtime story!" Dan's mind is clearly in a more carefree place.

I look at him, already stripped to his boxers, and envy the way men have it so easy in these situations. (Especially ones with strong shoulders and tapered torsos.)

"A ghost story would be fitting in this weather," Lucy decides as the windows rattle ever more urgently.

"Or maybe, Lucy, you could tell us how *this* story ends?" Simon ventures as he slips under the covers of his makeshift bed, still sporting his T-shirt.

I like that. His modesty is so becoming. To me at least.

"Look, I promise you I don't know what Rick is thinking any more than you do," Lucy insists. "I've put forward a couple more suggestions but . . ." She gives a hapless shrug.

It must be weird for them, not knowing if they will have jobs in the morning. Yet still Simon's concern lies elsewhere.

"I just hope Beth is safe and well," he sighs as his head meets the pillow.

It's certainly strange not having her here, especially since she's been the focus of all our attention for the past week. I'd rest easier if she was lying safely beside me but then again I'm glad she's following through on her passion. She certainly doesn't do that enough with men. To be honest, I don't think I've ever seen her with such a glint in her eye. She always seemed to view sexual liaisons as an energy-sapping distraction. I suppose in this instance she has nothing left to lose.

As for me and Dan, I am intrigued to see how we will get together tonight. Will he wait for the others to fall asleep and then creep over and lure me into the bathroom? Will he give me a signal to meet him downstairs in the candlelit atrium? Or will he be so bold as to try and sneak in the bed beside me? The suspense is spine-tingling!

I give an exaggerated yawn to demonstrate that I'll be out for the count any minute and Lucy takes the cue to reach for the bedside lamp.

"Well, goodnight everyone!"

"Goodnight."

"Goodnight."

"Goodnight."

I smile to myself, my toes jiggling in excitement under the covers. Of course I'm probably not the only one whose eyes remain open. I know Simon won't be able to sleep for fretting about Beth, Lucy is no doubt wondering how her first big TV job could have gone so awry and Dan . . .

I hear a light snoring coming from his portion of the floor.

He's bluffing, right?

I wait patiently for the noise to subside but it only gains gravitas. My heart sinks. That is not the sound of a man poised for a moonlit assignation.

Instantly my eyes well with tears — not more disappointment! I can't bear it! This could be our last chance to be together and he's just fallen asleep!

But then maybe he has more faith than I do. Maybe he doesn't necessarily see this as our last chance. He lives in London, after all, not the Argentine Pampas.

As I take a calming breath, a well-worn but rather wise Spanish phrase comes to mind — *Que sera sera!*

Whatever will be will be.

CHAPTER FIFTEEN

The morning light encourages my eyes to open. I look towards the window and see the sloshing rain has subsided, leaving nothing more than a dripping-trickling on the uneven panes of glass. Inhaling a musky, tobacco-y smell, I trace it to a woodland bonfire — its smoke fogging between the tree branches like a mist in an enchanted forest.

It's almost eerily peaceful. Until the cockerel starts.

Clearly in training for some cock-a-doodle-do competition, he practises his call over and over as if a vocal coach is urging, "*Once more with feeling! Really let it out!*" Apparently he won't rest until he perfects a real eardrum twanger.

I'm amazed he hasn't awoken my slumber buddies until I sit up and find them all gone. Why does this keep happening to me? I never knew I was such a heavy sleeper. Or perhaps I dreamt the whole thing. Perhaps I'll go down to breakfast and find seven years have passed and I'm happily married to some Argentinian count. Meanwhile Beth has taken to herding cattle for a living.

And then I smile to myself — I can't wait to hear about her night . . .

* * *

By the time I descend the stone staircase, the sun has declared a beautiful day — the terrace is buzzing with guests and there is a completely different atmosphere to yesterday's gothic tale. Reality has returned. Though I've yet to see a familiar face.

I suppose I ought to worry but it's hard to summon angst in the face of such serenity. I lean upon one of the pillars as if it is my dance partner, soft cheek to its beige grit, and gaze out across the acres of lawn. If Tango began the healing, this place is pure cooling aloe.

Even the air temperature seems a precise match for my body, making me feel in perfect equilibrium with the world.

I shrug myself off the pillar and stroll out onto the grass, heading for the shade of a tree, when I catch sight of a man cantering towards me on a pure white horse. The image is so in keeping with the fantasy of this place it makes my heart leap. I turn to face him, imagining that as he passes he will reach down his arm and swoop me aboard in one seamless movement . . .

"Dan!" I gasp as he gets close enough to identify.

"My lady!" He taps his forelock as he stalls his steed beside me.

"I didn't know you could ride!"

"There are many things you don't know about me," he rumbles provocatively.

I find myself smiling, quite delighted at the prospect of finding out more.

"I was just heading over to the pool." He nods ahead. "Care to join me?"

"You mean —?"

"Plenty of room," he says, inviting me on-board.

Unsure of the strength in his bicep and my ability to get airborne, I use a nearby bench to climb up, this time onto the back of a real polished leather saddle, the slope of which causes my pelvis to slot extremely snugly around Dan's bottom. In turn, my torso has no choice but to align with his back.

"Hold on!" he says and my arms lock comfortably around his chest.

Ironically it is now, with all this idyllic scenery to behold, that I close my eyes. I seem to have found my preferred partner hold — my front to his broad back. No possibility of a kiss or an impregnation. This is how you hug someone you've loved for years. You come up behind them, pull yourself in close, rest your head on their shoulder. And suddenly everything is all right with the world.

"Carmen?" he checks on me.

"Mmmm," I sigh in submission. I know we've come to a halt but I don't see that as any real reason to let go.

"You guys look so cute up there, mind if we take a picture?" An older American couple have approached us from the poolside.

"Sure." Dan is happy to play along while I burrow my head into his back.

"You here on your honeymoon?" the wife asks.

"Oh no!" Dan chuckles. "If we were, she'd be asking for her money back — I fell asleep far too early last night."

So maybe he did have intentions!

"Oh, don't worry!" The wife winks. "Plenty of time to make it up to her!"

As they walk on Dan and I are silent for a moment. Time is one thing we don't have any guarantee of — depending on the verdict from the head honchos at Experience TV, this could be our last moment alone together.

"Of course we can always meet up back in London," Dan suggests.

"Yes, of course," I agree. "When do you get back from Cuba?"

"About a month from now."

"Right." My heart slumps in "never going to happen" defeat.

Then the horse shuffles to the side and Dan curses vigorously.

"What is it?"

He nods back over to the main building where Rick is standing hands-on-hips and ready to roar.

"I was supposed to knock him up half an hour ago."

I swing my leg over the saddle and drop down to the ground. "You'd better get back."

He looks down at me with something I like to interpret as frustrated longing. Or is it just me wishing that we were like the other guests — here on holiday and free to indulge every sun-kissed whim?

"Go, go!" I send him on his way, impressed as he takes off with starter-pistol speed.

Strange how quickly people can come in and out of your life. I feel a little foolish now, thinking I was on the verge of romance.

I may have no say in what happens next but as some mild form of defiance I decide to take the walk back with slow, deliberate steps, taking in every blade of grass, every frond of palm, every fallen fig that gives an almost cobbled effect to the lawn. I'm reaching down to pick up a plump one — stroking its dusty softness, admiring its dusky purple hue — when I hear all manner of squawking. Wow, Rick really has reached an all-time shrill! But then I look up and realise that the noise is coming from a tree filled with parrots so startlingly green they look like they've rolled in powdered paint. A great cluster of them appear to be having a family barney, quite literally ruffling each other's feathers.

It's not much different inside the building.

Everyone is fractious and squabbling.

"If you'd done a bit more research!"

"If you'd spoken up sooner!"

"If you'd taken a closer look at the footage . . ."

I don't get involved. I'm preoccupied with the fact that I'm about to discover my fate wearing slept-in clothes, it just feels so tawdry. Then again, I look like a candidate for *The Apprentice* compared to Beth.

"Holy scarecrow!" I gawp, taking in her dishevelled form as she ambles in the door — sex-tousled hair, traces of ash and dirt on her skin, the brazen display of the *Gaucho*'s red necktie.

I take a furtive look at Simon. He looks suitably crushed. Beth is oblivious. She gives me a heavy hug and slurs lustily in my ear, "No four-song *codigas* in the Pampas — we didn't stop all night!"

As she flumps down on the sofa looking so very sated, I feel a twang of envy. Of course there is always payback when you behave with such abandon but for a few glorious hours you are untouchable!

Even by Rick, who looks her up and down and sneers, "We'll get to that in a minute."

The time has come for his announcement.

"So we had some serious debates about the survival of the show and this is the conclusion we have come to." Cue the inevitable pause for effect. "*We're going to tell the truth*."

The ensemble slumps and murmurs in relief. Apologetic hands reach for hands. They are once again united. It's all going to be all right.

Or is it?

"We're going to tell the story of two women," Rick continues. "Two dreams."

"*Two?*" It's my turn to squawk now.

"Best friends who hatch a plot to dance their way to salvation!"

Hold on a minute!

"So now we have the contrast between the polish of the professional and the naïvety of the novice —"

"About the novice part . . ." I cut in.

"Yes?"

"I don't mean to be difficult but I'm really not cut out for reality TV. I think it's probably best if you focus —"

Rick holds up his hand. "Before you say anything more, let me spell out the alternative — I spoke to the legal team, and we would be obliged to sue you for the costs of the entire production."

Even though I am seated, I feel myself stumble backwards. I look at Beth in despair.

"It's not so bad in front of the camera," she assures me. "We're amongst friends."

"But the edit!" my voice curdles. Isn't that what every ruined reality star blames their downfall on?

"Even if that was iffy, what harm would a few duff moves do to your life, really?" she reasons. "It's not like you're trying to get a job as a dancer."

"No, but I would like to be employable in some context. What if I do something really awful and people spit at me in the street and leave hate mail at the stage door?"

"That's not going to happen," Lucy assures me.

"And even if it did," Dan chips in, "I bet you could come up with a great disguise for yourself." He gives me a broad grin. "Come on, I'm not here to make you look bad."

"And I'm not here to make you *sound* bad," Simon confirms.

"You probably won't even get that much screen-time," Rick colludes. "I mean, right now all the viewers are going to want to know is how the *Gaucho* was in the sack!"

"I'm not talking about that!" Beth huffs. "That happened on my time."

"No such thing, love. Or do I need to remind you of the contract?"

Beth gives me a look as if to say, *How did we get into this mess?*

"I know," I grimace, realising we're done for. "Springing you from the strip club was a breeze compared to this!"

"The strip club?!" Rick, Lucy, Dan and Simon chorus.

Oh no. I give Beth a rueful look. "I thought you said you'd told them *everything* after you fell off the horse?"

"Not quite."

I look back at Rick. "Forget what I just said and I'll do it."

"You're on."

Wow. I was not expecting him to agree so fast. This is crazy!

"Welcome to show business," Beth winks.

As the crew rally to capture Beth in full *après-Gaucho* glow, it starts to sink in just what I've agreed to. Not that there was any choice really — home alone with a gargantuan debt or TV humiliation with the possibility of kissing Dan in three different countries . . .

Nevertheless, I have a few unanswered questions . . . Presumably since we are leaving the country tomorrow I am fairly off-the-hook as far as Tango goes but does this really mean I'll be trying to master the Paso Doble in Spain? The Salsa in Cuba? Of course there are worse activities in worse locations but it's all the scrutiny. I'm one of those people who start making mistakes when I'm being watched. I drive fine by myself but the second someone is in the passenger seat I start missing turnings and eliciting honks . . . I insist boyfriends turn around when I take my shot at the pool table. I don't like birthday parties because that's too much attention on me — especially if (horrors!) I have to open a present in front of everyone and I'm so terrified that my face won't come up with the appropriate expression of gratitude and delight. It's all too much pressure!

And I know I'm not going to be able to take in any of the dance instructions because I'll be thinking, *What if I just can't get it?* and then the teacher will say, "Okay, let me see you do that!" and I'll realise that I hadn't heard a word she said so I'll stand there like an utter fool getting increasingly tense and frustrated with myself until I tear out of the studio humiliated. This does not bode well.

I want to voice my concerns but Beth's chat is underway and as I shuffle closer I find my anxiety giving way to curiosity — what exactly did happen between her and the *Gaucho*?

"So I guess that post-fall dance really started something?" Lucy prompts with a grin.

Beth nods, her face a picture of misty arousal. "I've never known such a connection. We didn't even have to speak, he knew all my pain and I knew all his."

Simon snuffles, ruining the take. Lucy glares at him.

"Sorry, my nose is kind of stuffy."

"Go on, Beth."

"He was just so all-embracing."

"I bet he was," Simon mutters.

"Simon!" Rick reprimands. "This does not require commentary."

"Sorry." He bristles with frustration. "It just makes me uncomfortable hearing about a man taking advantage of a woman in such a vulnerable state."

"He wasn't taking advantage." Beth turns to him. "He was comforting me."

"Well, maybe there are better ways to find comfort," Simon snips back.

"And by 'better' you mean less slutty?"

"I suppose I do." He juts his chin.

Oh dear. He's gonna get it.

"And who are you to judge?" Beth is fuming now. "As far as I can tell, you make a living from listening in on other people's conversations; since when did your opinion count for anything?"

Ouch.

"At least when I speak I tell the truth," he retaliates. "I don't go around misleading people about my identity, making them think —"

"*Jesus!*" Rick cuts in, throwing his hands in the air. "Can I get some professionals on this team? Let's take it from the top. This time without the morality assessment."

Though I know he'd like to walk away, Simon holds his position, only this time he removes his headphones. He doesn't need to hear the details in stereo.

Beth begins by describing the magnetic pull she felt when she saw the *Gaucho* waiting beneath the ombu tree for her. "In that moment, he represented a portal to another world, somewhere purely sensory." Not that they had sex straight away, she insists. First they huddled together around a fire and drank *yerba mate* out of a gourd, sipping the bitter tea through a silver straw. It was so strong it made her feel a little heady but she liked it. She wanted to feel different.

"I think I've always been waiting to get my career in place before I address the other areas of my life. I didn't want anything to get in my way. I've seen women give up their dreams for a man. That's what happened with my mum — she was an amazing dancer but then she met my father, fell in love, got pregnant, had me and that was it. By the time he left her, it was too late for her to start again. Her dream had passed." She expels a troubled sigh. "Men always want too much from me. I know that sounds ungrateful. I know I should feel lucky that I get the offers but it doesn't feel like an offer to me, it feels like a demand." Then her face changes. "Suddenly here was this man, solitary and nomadic by definition, and he wasn't asking for any more than one night."

I half expect Simon to make some dig about there being a plethora of men willing to offer a girl a one night stand, but this time he remains silent.

"He wasn't taking advantage of me. There was no manipulation. He was there. I went to him. We sat together. And then we danced. *For hours*. So close." She twiddles the tips of her necktie. "After a while I couldn't even distinguish where my body ended and his began. And then our movements became ever more subtle. Our feet barely moved. It was more of a sway than anything. I felt his breath on my ear, my lips met his neck, he held me tighter. And then we kissed."

Lucy looks utterly transfixed. All she can manage is a "go on" nod.

"It was such a release. I've worked my body in every other way, always straining for the perfect line but when we made love it was so raw and unexpected it took my breath away." She smiles. "I know I'm a mess." She flicks her birds' nest hair. "But I've never felt more alive!"

"Great!" I mutter to myself. How exactly am I supposed to follow that?

CHAPTER SIXTEEN

I don't know quite how to take this but Rick has decided that the ideal setting for my first on-camera interview is a cemetery.

Of course *La Recoleta* is no ordinary cemetery. Set in the heart of Buenos Aires, it's like a miniature marble city unto itself with mausoleums resembling scaled down cathedrals and wide, tree-lined walkways a-slink with stray cats. One of the more curious aspects is the juxtaposition of all this gothic grandeur with the boxy apartment blocks that surround the cemetery.

"Does it bother anyone else that the dead have fancier accommodation than the living?" Dan wants to know.

"It bothers me that Beth is missing this," I sigh as I gawp up at a life-size statue of an angel, wings outstretched as if to stabilise its precariously elevated position.

Rick insisted on dropping Beth back at the hotel before we set off, instructing her to spend the afternoon catching up on her sleep as we have a big night ahead of us.

"I'll get all the sleep I need when I'm dead!" Beth had protested — rather aptly, considering our current location — but Rick was adamant.

I suspect his intention was to deprive me of my support system but I'm ready for him — I spent the entire journey back from the *estancia* predicting questions and rehearsing responses in my head, so now I just want to get this introductory interview over with. Preferably somewhere in the shade . . .

"It's going to be too crowded to shoot here, chief," Dan grimaces as we approach the black granite encasement of the cemetery's most famous resident.

"Eva Perón: 1919–1952." I read the bronze plaque as I zoom in alongside the other camera-wielding tourists, many of whom are as surprised as me to learn that Evita was just thirty-three when she died. "To think of the command she had when she stood on that balcony —"

"How about here?" Lucy has already moved on to a positive penthouse of a mausoleum. But my eye lingers on a simple headstone etched with the name "Elena", putting me in mind of Granny Eileen and the promise I made on the plane to bring her along on this trip.

I wonder if she's frustrated by the way I've been holding the Tango experience at bay — I haven't even tried since my dud experience with Twinkletoes. And I certainly don't want him to be my lasting memory.

"Tonight I'll take you dancing!" I make a promise to a symbolic puff of cloud.

"Right, let's get to why we are here." Rick claps his hands together and nods to Dan to start rolling.

I clear my throat and prepare to deliver my neat little soundbites only to be thrown by Lucy's first question:

"When we were going through the tapes, we picked up on something Beth said about her supposed relationship with Lee — how at one point her/your life was in peril. To what was she referring?"

For a second I think about dismissing this as one of the lies we told for added drama but Lucy is too quick for me.

"I know it's real, Carmen. I can tell by your face."

I don't respond straight away. Instead I find myself looking around me — wondering how many of these neighbouring bodies went to their graves prematurely. I still get a chill thinking I could've been one of them.

"Carmen?"

I look up at her, still in two minds. But then I hear a screech of tyres from beyond the cemetery wall and the sound takes me right back to that night.

"We were on our way to a birthday party in the country," I begin.

"You and Lee?"

"Yes . . ." Most of the guests were arriving the night before but we couldn't leave until after my show. Lee was fine with that, said he'd rather travel on traffic-free roads. It wasn't until we hit the motorway that I started wondering how many beers he'd had that night —" I take a breath. "I asked him to slow down but the more tense I got the faster he went. I remember closing my eyes at one point, trying to imagine I was somewhere else. I kept thinking that as soon as we were on the country roads he'd ease up but instead he started acting like we were on a racetrack. Now I was really scared — the lanes were so narrow a car could come around the corner at any moment and there'd be a head-on collision. I was begging him to slow down, but he wouldn't listen.

"'You think I'm a bad driver?' he was taunting me.

"I tried to sound calm. 'I think there's a really good chance we'll have an accident if you carry on like this.'

"And then he said, 'Well then, why don't you just get out, *right now*'. And he reached over and released my seatbelt."

"What?" Lucy is aghast. "Surely he didn't mean while he was still driving?"

"That's exactly what he meant." For a moment I allow the full force of the memory to rush at me. The realisation that he actually meant me harm. The panic pounding in my heart as he started shoving me towards the door. The dizzying sensation that this could be the end.

"What happened next?"

"We rounded this corner and nearly hit another car. He swerved to avoid it. We hit the verge and the jolt made me fall into him. Then it was like he woke up and realised the madness of the situation."

"What did he say?"

I get an uneasy, twisty feeling as I remember. "'You're not going to leave me, are you?'"

The crew gives a collective shudder.

"I wanted to get out of the car while it was stationary, to get as far away as possible but it was pitch black out there, ram in the middle of nowhere." I feel a little teary now remembering how shaken up I was. "I thought if we could just get to the hotel, at least there would be people I knew. But of course they were all asleep by the time we got there. And then the next day it was supposed to be a celebration, I didn't want to be a downer. Besides, it was mostly his friends."

"So you didn't tell anyone?"

"Actually there was one girl but she just said, 'Aside from a few bruises you're okay, right?' And I said yes and then she changed the subject. I thought about calling Beth but she was so far away, I didn't want her worrying about my safety when there was nothing she could do."

"So, let me get this clear, even after he basically threatened your life, you continued going out with him?" Lucy is incredulous now.

"I know it sounds ridiculous but by the time we'd got back to London I almost felt like I'd missed my slot to break up with him — the moment had passed." I shake my head. "I think when something so terrifying happens, some part of your brain tries to play it down, making you question whether it was really as bad as it seemed. He swore nothing like that would ever happen again. I wanted to believe him," I sigh, "but the feeling never went away, I was constantly on edge. Even if he was yelling at the TV, it would leave me shaking. And then I did the one thing I knew would make me leave . . .

"I told Beth what had happened." I feel a lump rising in my throat. "Could I have some water?"

"Of course!" Lucy hands me a bottle and gives me time to take a few sips before we resume. "Ready?"

My energy is so low now I can barely nod.

"So how did she react when you told her?"

"She was stunned. She couldn't believe someone could risk another person's life like that. She told me it was only a matter of time before he'd do something like that again and if I stayed even another day it would be some kind of death-wish."

"Wow. That's intense."

"Mmmm," is all I can manage.

"And so you left."

I nod.

I know they won't understand the tortuousness of that act, or the fact that both Lee and I were crying and kissing right up until the last moment. I barely understand it myself.

It's then I notice a small woman dressed from head to toe in black, laying flowers at a graveside and I find myself standing a little straighter. "You know, I've been mourning this relationship long enough. Where better than here to make a pact to rejoin the living?"

I hear a murmur of approval from Rick. He nods to Lucy that he's got what he needed here.

Thank God for that. I have nothing left to give and already feel like I said too much. Especially in front of Dan. What must he be thinking right now?

But then, as we prepare to relocate, he discreetly brushes up against me and gives me an under-the-radar wink. My heart gives a little leap of encouragement. Maybe in some strange way I needed to say all that out loud? Maybe it was time for me to say boo to my demons?

This optimistic feeling lasts for a whole five minutes until I realise that in a couple of days' time Lee will be watching me on TV — seeing and hearing every word I just said.

CHAPTER SEVENTEEN

"Beth!" I call ahead as I open the hotel room door, keen to have her assure me that I haven't just poked an almighty hornets' nest, but the face that greets me is way too gleeful for me to consider bringing her down.

"Look what I got to Tango in tonight!" she trills, burrowing in a Gallerias Pacifico bag and pulling out a swathe of shimmering scarlet. On first glance, it appears to be backless, sideless and frontless but as she holds the collar in place I see sufficient drapery to cover her boobs. "See, it has these stick-on cups and built-in knickers because the side slits are to the waist!"

"Feels good to have your old body back, huh?" I laugh, already wondering how Simon is going to cope. "But can we talk about your hair?"

"Two hours it took to get back to blonde!" she wails. "Feel the texture!" She grabs my hand and musses her freshly-coiffed straw. "It's so matt I've had to buy a can of spray-on shine!"

I can't deny it does look a little like an Eastern European bleach job. I'm about to suggest we style her hair in the classic Tango chignon for tonight when she drops a second bag in my lap.

"I got a couple of little things for you too."

I feel inside and pull out a red silk rose ("For behind your ear," she tells me) and a jet necklace designed to lace my décolletage with twinkling beads.

"I know you're not keen on all these tight Tango clothes but that doesn't mean you can't look stunning!"

"Thank you!" I reach to hug her.

"It's just the beginning of a lifetime of repayments," she tells me earnestly. "I know I've got you involved in something you would never have chosen for yourself —"

"It's okay," I shush her, squeezing her tight. "It's worth it to see you happy."

"Honestly?"

"Yes," I assure her.

Well, there's no sense in us both feeling bad about this.

But then she adds, "I know you don't really want to speak about Lee —"

I try to turn away but she catches my arm. "Uh oh. What is it?"

"Is my face really that much of a giveaway?"

"Yes," she confirms. "What happened?"

I flump down onto the bed. "I told them about The Incident."

Her eyes widen. "Okay . . ."

I look earnestly up at her. "How do you think he's going to react when he sees it on TV?"

"Maybe he won't be watching," she soothes me. "This show isn't exactly his cup of tea."

"But someone somewhere will see and tell him . . ."

Beth nods and bites her lip a while before saying, "You told the truth, didn't you?"

"Yes."

"Well then," she shrugs. "Maybe it'll do him good to hear how it affected you. Maybe it's even therapeutic for you to talk about these things — as opposed to hanging out with friends who tell you that you're crazy and ban you from even mentioning his name!"

I smile. "Don't feel bad about that. It's natural you would feel that way — you just wanted him *gone!* Besides, I never told you what I was really feeling so how would you know to have a different conversation with me?"

Beth sits down beside me on the bed. "So tell me what you wouldn't want Lee to hear you say — what you couldn't say to Lucy on camera."

I blink at my friend. She's right to know there's a difference. "What I don't want him to know is that there is still a weakness for him, still a pull. Please don't look disappointed in me!"

"I'm not! Am I? I just . . ." Beth shakes her head. "I can't bear that he still has this hold over you."

"It's not as strong," I tell her, "and even if I do experience a wayward urge to contact him, our current geography certainly prevents me from doing anything rash."

And then I look her dead in the eye. "Can I be honest with you?"

"Absolutely!"

"Okay, here's how it is: I don't want to pretend that everything is hunky-dory and that I've moved on because then I have to have all my sentimental feelings about him in secret and when I do that it starts to feel . . ." I search for the right word, "*romantic*. In a really odd way. Like no one else understands our bond . . ." I pull a face.

"I can see how that would be dangerous," Beth concurs.

"So what I want to do now is admit to you that I still have yearnings for Lee even though I know it defies logic. I want to get credit for the twenty-three hours of the day that I hold it together, not feel weak for having a pang in hour twenty-four. I want to be able to tell you that I miss him even though I know that makes me seem certifiable."

Beth nods her acceptance. "I'm here for you." She reaches for my hands. "Whenever you want to feel out loud."

"Thank you!" I breathe a sigh of relief. "There's just one more thing."

"Yes?"

"Dan."

She looks expectantly at me.

"Do you think I really like him or am I just trying to Velcro myself to the first available male in a bid to stay away from Lee?"

Beth cocks her head. "Tell me how you feel around him."

"Hopeful," I decide. "I get a buzz of excitement when he looks my way, like anything is possible. He just seems so luminous after Lee."

"Luminous?" Beth coos. "That sounds pretty good to me!"

I look down at my feet. "I just hope I'm not wishing for something unattainable."

Beth gives my hair a tousle. "Why is it so hard for you to believe that you actually deserve a good man?"

I squint back at her. "I could ask you the same question."

And so we reach an impasse. Until there is a rap at the door.

"Well, hello blondie!" Lucy gasps as she beholds the new Beth.

"You said you wanted me to be my true self from now on."

"You certainly are full of surprises!" Lucy smiles as she requests a twirl. "Actually that's great. No mistaking the two of you now!"

"Especially when she's wearing this!" I hold up the fragmented dress.

"Oh poor Simon!" Lucy groans as she inspects the clingy fabric.

"I had the same response," I laugh.

"Poor Simon nothing," Beth huffs. "It's none of his business what I do or say or wear."

"Anyway." Lucy attempts to breeze onward. "I just wanted to let you know we need to leave in half an hour."

"WHAT?!" Beth and I screech, instantly a flurry of fishnets and false lashes.

And so begins our last night in Buenos Aires . . .

As it turns out, it's not just Beth debuting a new look tonight.

Obviously her entrance causes quite a stir considering she was last seen as a mud-spattered *Gaucho* groupie and here she is now, the bright blonde lady in red. But I get a few double-takes of my own.

None of my dresses said Tango extravaganza, even with the addition of the jet necklace, so I used the pinstripe waistcoat and fedora I had bought for Toby and teamed them with my one pair of flattering black trousers. For a moment this fashion twist gave me a flashback to my childhood ballroom experience — only this time, instead of a sheriff's badge on my lapel, I have the red silk rose tucked into my amped-up cleavage.

"Now that's hot!" Dan comments, to my delight.

Rick is less thrilled. "Don't blame me if you only get asked to dance by lesbians tonight."

"Ignore him!" Lucy tuts. "I like it."

Simon says nothing. His eyes are still extending from their sockets in Beth's direction.

We enjoy a celebratory steak at La Cabaña — a restaurant so passionate about its beef that they actually inform you of the pedigree of the cow before you chow down. It's all very deluxe and delicious but we know that this isn't what we dressed for.

"So what is the occasion?" Beth wants to know as she reapplies her lipstick.

Lucy looks rather pleased with herself as she announces, "Tonight is the annual Argentine Tangothon!"

"And what exactly does that mean?"

"Remember the *Avenida 9 de Julio*?"

We nod, recalling the vast multi-lane highway that stunned us upon our arrival.

"Tonight, instead of cars, it will be filled with Tango dancers!"

"Wow!" we chorus. This actually sounds fun to me. The bigger the crowd, the more lost I can get.

"Just remember that if we do get separated at any point you need to get back to the hotel by 2a.m. to give you an hour to pack before the flight."

"I can't believe that tomorrow we will be in Spain!" I marvel.

"And what does that mean to you?" Lucy enquires.

"*Amor*," I breathe, knowing that a date with Dan awaits.

"You sound very certain of that!"

Fortunately I can back up my claim: "Adriano told us that if there was a party attended by representatives from each of the countries we're visiting it would look like this: the Argentinian man would be standing alone in the shadows, the Cuban would be laughing and joking with a big gang of family and friends and the Spaniard, well, he would inevitably be entwined with a woman."

"What about you, Beth? Are you open to being entwined with a Spaniard?"

"Oh yes." She sounds excessively blasé. "Especially since they all smell like Antonio Banderas."

"Huh?"

"I hear his aftershave is very popular out there," she deadpans. "I'm also looking forward to visiting the city where the legend of Carmen was spawned!"

"Good point." Lucy reaches for a pen as we head out to the main event. "I must add that to the list since she is now one of our leading ladies!"

I don't know about that but I do know that I am in need of being led. Adriano was going to bring a friend to partner me but, thanks to the crush of black-clad bodies, it doesn't look like either of them are going to make it across from his apartment on the other side of the world's largest avenue in time for the first step.

More fool us for arranging to meet "by the Obelisk". We can't even get close to it. Currently we're wedged at the junction of *Avenida Corrientes* but I'm not complaining — this street is known as the Broadway of Buenos Aires and just standing in theatreland comforts me. I find myself imagining how I would dress the masses if this were a group scene on stage. I like the idea of the men and the women having sparkly red fronts and matt black backs so that as they twist and shift they would create glinting patterns.

Dan is also considering visuals, announcing that the blaze of bulbs promoting rival shows would make a suitably dazzling backdrop for our last interview.

"Tell me in what way you feel most changed from this trip?" Lucy requests.

Beth goes first, talking about how she has always danced in studios and on stage, "and then I come here and find my most memorable experiences to be *al fresco*: first in the Pampas with the *Gaucho* and now out here in the street!"

"Any other differences?"

"Dancing with people who are not critiquing me on a professional level. And realising what a truly universal experience dance is. I've always danced to convey a certain story on stage, I'd forgotten what an amazing way it is to communicate, full stop — I mean, I can't speak Spanish but I feel like I've had some very interesting conversations with the men I have danced with here!"

Not a peep from Simon.

"Carmen?"

I gesture to the couple beside us getting into the mood before the big surge — her hand snaking up to the back of his neck, his hand clasping her close, their furrowed brows united, the unspoken message of "I feel your pain."

"I think the major change is how I view heartache," I decide. "I no longer see it as something to be cured or jollied over, it's simply a part of life. I was always too eager to find a quick fix or a way to numb it but, from what I've seen here, if you find the courage to dance a while with those feelings of loneliness and disappointment, there's a chance they can become almost beautiful."

"Wow, Carmen," Beth whispers an aside. "Do you really believe that?"

"I really nearly do!" I blink with a dazed smile.

"Come on. We need to get these girls partnered up," Rick cuts in. "The countdown has begun!"

Naturally Beth is inundated with offers and busily tries to fix me up with one of her spare suitors.

"Oh Beth, that's just cruel!" I protest.

"Whatever do you mean?"

"This is a really big, once-a-year event, they don't want to be dancing with a novice."

"Don't be silly!"

"I'm not being silly, I'm being realistic. I'd feel the same way if I was really good, dragging along someone who can barely keep from tripping over their own feet. Besides, it's such a crush I don't know if I'd even feel comfortable being held that close by a stranger."

"Would you feel comfortable with me?"

"What?"

"I'll lead you!" she says, excusing herself from her partner of two minutes and taking me in hold.

"But —"

"Just go with it!"

"What's going on?" Rick steps in to the fray.

"This is who I want to dance with."

He looks at us — the vixen leading, dancing the man's steps and the woman in the man's clothes following — but before he can protest, the music starts.

I was expecting them to be blaring only the most traditional music from the speakers so I am quite surprised to hear a song I actually know — *Santa Maria* by The Gotan Project.

"I love this!" I rave. Hip yet oh-so-atmospheric.

Perhaps it helps that I can anticipate the twiddly bits of the song but I must say that Beth's direction is masterful, accentuating the strutty-strummy reverberations with stylised jolts and body slams. Instead of being preoccupied with apologising for my shortcomings, I actually feel emboldened to go with the flow, even adding a little slink and tension to my moves. As a male voice darkly murmurs, "*Argentina, Buenos Aires*", I feel my cheeks pinken with pleasure. I know it's probably sacrilegious to smile while tangoing but I can't help myself.

"Oh my God, Beth!" I gasp mid-swivel. "I've just had a revelation!"

"Tell me!"

"*I'm not a sad person!*"

"Did I ever say you were?"

"No, but I've just remembered what Adriano said about Tango attracting people of a melancholic nature — that explains why I've never felt at one with this dance — I was melancholy due to my circumstance, not my nature! I *am* going to be happy again!"

Beth dips me for effect and then raises me upright and proceeds onward with new vigour.

"Exactly how long is this avenue?" I ask, already craving a celebratory glass of Malbec.

"No idea," she shrugs unconcerned. "All I know is that I'm not stopping until we get to Spain!"

Spain

CHAPTER EIGHTEEN

We arrive in Seville in the midst of the Spring Fair, known as *La Feria de Abril*: a fantasy of Spain made real with Zorro-hatted men parading on horseback — cue castanet-clacking of hooves on cobblestones — and women sashaying down the streets in eye-popping polka-dotting.

I try not to stare but the sight of grown women in outfits I'd only previously seen on dolls is so captivating I can't help myself. There's just no ignoring the exuberance of the colour palette: fresh lime, gobstopper pink, electric blue — only the brightest, boldest hues need apply. Trim with ruffles, frills and flounces and you've got the absolute antithesis of sombre Tango sleekness.

Better yet, the women showcasing these dresses have *curves!*

"I've found my people!" I whoop, delighted at the way the taper and flare accentuates their womanly shape to almost cartoonish proportions.

"I think this is the happiest I've seen you look," Lucy beams at me.

I can't deny it. Just being in the presence of women exuding such enviable "this is me" defiance has me brimming with *bonhomie*. "I want to be them!" I hear myself blurt.

"Your wish is our command!" Lucy grins as she bids us enter the *Corte Ingles* department store on Plaza Duque, across from one of the six or so Zara stores we've encountered since we arrived in this sunny and vibrant capital of Andalucia.

"Holy cornucopia!" Beth reels at the psychedelic selection before us. "It's like fancy dress week but everyone has opted for the same costume — just in different colours."

"Actually, there's quite a variation in the size of the dots . . ."

"Only you!" Beth rolls her eyes as I size them up, from penny to jam jar lid. "I like this one!"

"You can't wear a paisley Flamenco dress!" I splutter, surprised that such a thing even exists.

But then we spy a New Look version of a Pucci print, an *Austin Powers Goes To Spain* number, even neon *broderie anglaise*!

Beth puts on her sunglasses to inspect one vibrant orange number then cheers, "When in Seville . . ." as she heads for the changing room.

"Carmen?" Lucy prompts me to brandish my choice.

"I have to go for the traditional red and white polka-dot." I go to lift the hanger to display it for Dan but buckle under the weight. The material has the same density as curtain material and the frills layering up from the hem may as well be fashioned from lead.

"Walking in this is going to be like wearing those workout weights strapped to your ankles!" I groan as I join Beth.

"I know. I can't believe how starchy the fabric is!" She frowns as she steps into the dress — which practically stands up of its own accord. "I can hardly imagine traversing the floor with all this bulk."

"You managed with that huge *King and I* ballgown for Toby's party last year."

"Yes, but that skirt was hooped and full of air," Beth reasons.

"Zip me up?" I turn my back to her.

"Wow!" Beth steps back to assess my form.

My hand flies to my rear, concerned that my wobbly bits are distorting the line, but I am amazed to discover instead a perfect demi-sphere. "The cut of this dress is incredible!" I marvel at my reflection.

"Come on!" Dan calls from outside. "Let's have a look!"

"Ready?" Beth dares me.

We throw back the curtain and strike a pose.

It's amazing what a new outfit can do for you. So many actors I've worked with speak of how the right costume helps them get into character and it really does seem the case with these Flamenco dresses — you wouldn't get anywhere with timid tiptoeing, you have to stride boldly just to set the fabric in motion. Even when you are standing still, there is no facility for stooping or Kate Moss arched-shoulder waifery, the dress demands you stand strong and your hands instinctively find your hips. As for the colours, how can you do self-pity in scarlet?

"Give us a twirl!" Lucy toots excitedly.

I may have been pleasantly surprised by my reflection but I'm even more delighted by the look in Dan's eye. We haven't had much contact since we left Buenos Aires — it was a night flight to Madrid and even when we were connecting to Seville Rick made sure our seats were as far apart as possible before arranging separate cabs to the hotel. I think his motivation was more about keeping Simon and Beth at a distance after their tiff at the *estancia* but the effect was the same. I'm toying with the idea of passing Dan a note but then, as we head to the accessory department, he sneaks up behind me whispering, "You and me tonight. Secret assignation. You game?"

Rick is, of course, watching so I grab a fan and crack it open, batting my eyes at him while shielding my lips so only Dan can see me mouth, "Absolutely!"

I then tilt the fan so Dan can't see the enormous *Viva España!* grin on my face.

"Does this go with my dress?" Beth is oblivious, holding up a peach lacquered design for my assessment.

"Looks a bit Japanesey to me." I frown at the hand-painted blossoms. "How about one of these lacy ones?"

There really is a wide range of options — from gold-tipped antique fragility to kitschy plastic and nylon, printed with '70s photos.

"Will you look at the sideburns on this fella?" I peer a little closer at one dated image. "I am so getting this for Toby."

"I hate to rush you ladies while you're shopping," Lucy apologises. "But we've just got five more minutes."

"You okay?" I ask. She looks unusually flustered.

"Remember how Rick pulled this trip forward, ahead of Cuba?" She gives me a conspiratorial look.

I nod.

"I lost most of my research time to re-scheduling the flights and hotels so I'm basically making up today as I go along."

"Well, you're doing great so far!" I commend her. "If there's anything —"

"Carmen, help me!" Beth issues a *crie de coeur* as she steps into the jewellery aisle.

"You finish up the outfits, I'll do my calls."

"Deal!" I grin as I join Beth.

Cheap and cheerful seems to be the motif here. The plastic bangles and clip-on earrings look like they've been sprung from the cardboard-backed children's sets you buy at supermarkets.

"Don't even try to match the orange, go for a complete contrast," I advise Beth, quickly locating a short strand of beads in shiny turquoise.

"This is so *Ugly Betty*!" Beth hoots as she plucks a yellow fabric flower from the crispy green oasis.

"I need a second head!" I decide as the assistant loads in an assortment of combs. I particularly like the mother of pearl ones — their spiky teeth making them look like multi-legged sea creatures, which I suppose is appropriate given their origin.

"Two minutes!" Lucy shrills.

I quickly reject the fake gold earrings so weighty they droop my lobes to my shoulders, settling instead for a white pair with a circular blob at ear and a big vinyl hoop the size of a curtain ring.

All we need now is a pair of drag queen size stilettos, some badly applied lippy and we'll look like kids playing in their mum's wardrobe!

"This is hilarious!" Beth cheers as we're hustled out the door. "I don't know why we waste so much time trying to look classy and designer in life, tacky is so much more fun!" But then the playtime glee vanishes from Beth's face. "You're not seriously expecting me to get in that?"

I turn and see Lucy negotiating with the driver of a horse-drawn carriage.

"Is this entirely necessary?" I challenge Rick on her behalf.

"It's just a leisurely ride, the traditional way to approach the Feria."

"But after the fright Beth had . . ."

He gives me a withering look. "We're not asking you girls to re-enact *Ben Hur*."

"But what if the horse bolts?" Beth whimpers.

"You'll just get there quicker."

Wow. His insensitivity is stunning.

"I will have my revenge on that man," Beth mutters as she boards. "I don't know when and I don't know how, but I will."

As we clip-clop down the street, every misstep by the horse causes Beth to flinch and grab for security. She's so on edge she doesn't even realise that her hand is repeatedly clamping onto Simon's knee.

As for me, I'm still beaming. For too long I've been living with a fear that I'd blown the fuse that makes true top-to-toe happiness possible, but here I am brimming with it! I wonder if my instant infatuation with this place has something to do with the fact that it looks like a giant stage set swarming with colourful extras.

Even more theatrical is the Feria site itself — the Los Remedios district over the river may be a tad insalubrious compared to the chic city centre but it has the space required to accommodate a temporary village of candy-striped cabanas — or rather, *casitas*.

I'm fascinated to discover that each one is uniquely decorated on the inside: here's a perfect recreation of a family dining room with lacy drapes, antique lamps and heirloom art on the fabric walls while its neighbour is large enough to house a dancefloor and DJ. Either way, every guest seems to be sipping chilled Manzanilla sherry, nibbling tapas and dancing Sevillanos — which Beth tells me is basically Flamenco-lite.

We join the masses parading along streets strung with white and green paper lanterns which, due to their spherical form and the intensity of the sun, are creating distinctive polka-dot shadows on the golden sand beneath our feet.

"I'm sooo glad we're wearing costumes," Beth notes. "The tourists are totally the odd ones out here!"

I still can't get over the variations in the dress designs and long to know more about the trends — is sleeveless in or out this year? How come they never use any shimmer or sparkle in the design — would that be considered a Feria *faux pas*? And where exactly do they keep their cash and lipstick since no one seems to be carrying a handbag? It's then I see a girl lift up her skirt to access a garter-style money-belt . . .

"Ahhh!" Lucy and I exchange a knowing look.

"Will you look at this mama and her mini me!" Beth nudges Dan to make sure he films a mother and daughter in matching fuchsia dresses.

They do indeed look adorable but I'm equally delighted by the groups of pre-teen girls who, rather than pouting and rolling their eyes, are taking just as much pride in their ensembles as their elders.

"I wish we had an annual event like this in England," I lament.

"I suppose the closest thing we have is Ascot," Beth decides, looking a little skittish as we pass a row of ten horses, though they are as calm and impeccably turned out as their riders.

"Now that's an outfit!" I stop to admire a young horsewoman sitting side-saddle in a long dogtooth skirt and immaculately tailored cream bolero jacket. A dove grey hat sits jauntily atop her glossy chestnut hair and simple pearl globes adorn her ears. Just as I am about to declare her most chic of them all, Beth points to a ten-year-old Natalie Portman lookalike holding the reins of a passing carriage.

"The deportment of these young girls is killing me!" she wails.

I roll back my shoulders and ponder, "Do you think we're too old to go to finishing school?"

"Okay, this is the spot!" Dan halts us at a crossroads, pleased that the backdrop now includes the adjacent fairground, as if the immediate scene weren't colourful enough.

"Right." Lucy checks her notes. "I just want a few words from Carmen on the Paso Doble — you said this is one of your favourite dances?"

I nod enthusiastically. "It's just so feisty and wilful and impassioned," I rave, before adding a reflective, "Everything I am not."

"Can you remember the first time you encountered it?"

"*Strictly Ballroom*, the movie," I grin, remembering how "Paso Doble" was like a password, taking Paul Mercurio from a luridly spangled world filled with day-glo eyeshadow and cockatoo hairdos, to a lantern-lit courtyard on the wrong side of the railroad tracks.

"Show us your Paso Doble!" the swarthy gypsies goaded him from beside the fire pit, and then laughed at his fancypants flicks and balletic arms, compelling the ringleader to retort with the unmistakable arched-back lunge of a matador and a fierce rat-a-tat-tat of nailed heels on wood.

"I think deep down that's what I want to happen to me here: a Spanish granny to rap out the beat on my chest and urge me to, '*Listen to the rhythm!*' "

Beth chuckles along with me and then prompts, "What was the other line you loved from that movie?"

"*A life lived in fear is a life half-lived . . .*"

I take a breath. So apt. So true. For a moment I feel my energy dip but then I spy two fifty-something females dancing, beaming as they rotate and circle one other, never losing eye contact, smiling so naturally, so delightedly, as if they were dancing to an ABBA song.

"They're my new role models!" I cheer.

"What about the men, Beth? Do you think you could find a good dance partner here?"

"Oh, you know me, I could find a partner anywhere — I'm the slutty one, remember?" She gives Simon a pointed look.

This really isn't like Beth. She's not usually one to take offence, not after all those years of audition critiques. Then again, it is awful to be misjudged. Especially when, for the first time in a long time, you felt liked for yourself.

"You know he never actually used the word 'slutty'," I remind her as we move on. "That came from you."

"Yes, but he went along with it!"

That I can't dispute. "I just don't want you to let it spoil your time here."

"How could I?" She forces a smile. "This is all too lovely."

"Isn't it?"

I turn to congratulate Lucy on what a great job she's done with her swift location research but find her in deep conversation with Rick. For a minute I think he might actually be praising her. Naturally he's doing the opposite.

"God, what now?" I accidentally blurt.

"What now?" Rick repeats before growling at Lucy, "Why don't you tell them what?" And then stomps off.

Lucy gives us girls a "don't hate me" look. "There seems to have been a small misunderstanding regarding the Paso Doble."

"And by 'small' you mean 'huge', right?" I try to make light of the situation.

"Go on," Beth encourages.

"Well, when I spoke to my Seville contact and explained that we wanted to experience *authentic* Paso Doble he got very excited and said he could get us prime seats for one of the most prestigious events of the Feria."

"Did he let you down?" Beth is ready to offer her sympathy.

"No. He got the seats. It just turns out that, as a dance, Paso Doble is not exactly the everyday/everywhere occurrence that Tango is in Argentina. It's not even on a par with Sevillanos. In fact," she gulps, "it's rarely ever danced outside the realm of competitive ballroom."

"Oh. Well. That's disappointing but it's not the end of the world," Beth decides. "At least we have the show to go to."

"And that's where the misunderstanding comes in." Lucy sighs. "To a Spaniard, Paso Doble is the marching music played at a bullfight."

Our eyebrows raise.

"Apparently there's this little brass band that announces the matador's entrance. You can buy compilation CDs of these tunes at every other shop in the city, you just can't get anyone to dance to them with you."

There is a short silence.

"I suppose it makes sense." Beth remains surprisingly calm. "The two things are inextricably linked — I mean you never see a Paso Doble danced without the man mimicking the moves of the matador."

"Do you mean we're actually going to attend a bullfight?" I am rather more alarmed.

"I understand if it's too gory or if you are morally opposed —" Lucy looks close to tears.

"What does Rick have to say about this?" Beth cuts in.

"That my ineptitude and sloppy research has ruined this whole segment."

"Seems a little harsh," I begin.

"He's got a point," Lucy grimaces. "Short of flying in Karen Hardy, there's no one here to teach you this dance."

I can see she's ready to admit defeat but I lay my hand on her arm and then nod towards Beth who has the same "obstacles-be-damned" expression I saw on her face the night of the ad application. "Just give her a moment."

Beth begins pacing before us, dragging her orange tail back and forth in the dusty earth. And then she stops. "So Paso Doble isn't performed on every street corner, big deal. What we're interested in is the origin and essence of the dance. Yes, the man represents the matador so it makes sense to learn from him but the woman is so much more than the cape or the bull — remember what I told you at the audition?"

"She's also the Flamenco dancer!" Lucy gasps.

"Exactly!" Beth confirms. "So logically, seeing as we are women, Flamenco is what we should be learning."

"And there's no shortage of that dance here," I chip in, referencing the dozens of show posters we passed en route.

"You're right!" Lucy cheers. "It couldn't be any more culturally iconic!" And then her face falls. "But Flamenco is not a partner dance. I know that much about it."

Beth muses for a moment, refusing to be deterred. "How about this — while we're at the bullfight, why don't you see if you can hook us up with one of the matadors? Even if we're not dancing set steps, I'm sure we could improvise a little." Beth positions me in classic *toreador* stance. "See, I can weave around him, respond to his arcs and flourishes . . ."

Beth is inspired, Lucy is encouraged but I'm still uneasy.

"Are we seriously going to watch a bullfight?"

CHAPTER NINETEEN

"Think of it as a dance between man and beast," Beth advises as we approach the bullring. "Ceremony over cruelty."

Initially this is easy enough to do — the surrounding streets are thronging with ticket holders resplendent in their Sunday best, socialising animatedly as they bustle along. Despite the heat, men are pristine in classic navy suits with pink shirts, silk ties and glinting cufflinks. Their hair and skin are expensively oiled — not exactly the bawdy "throw the Christians to the lions!" crowd I was expecting.

"It feels more like a day at the races," I note, surprised by the number of women I see excitedly fanning themselves, including a select group wearing elevated mantillas draped with fine antique lace.

"Like a bride, no?" enquires a man Lucy introduces as her contact, Felipe. "Those are the wives of the matadors. And this," he bids us step back to fully contemplate the vast circular building before us. "This is the *Plaza de Toros de la Maestranza*. One of the oldest and most beautiful bullrings in the world."

The exterior is stark white with garish mustard detailing and a series of hefty oxblood doors studded with iron nuggets. Felipe leads us along a crowded but cool stone corridor to the open-air arena, pointing out its border of elegant arches at the top and a band of bull-butting boards at ground level. The sand is a dazzling ochre-gold, raked to perfection and taking on an almost suede-like texture through sun-squinted eyes.

It impresses me greatly that there is a petite hand-painted tile denoting each seat number, especially when Felipe informs us that this place seats fourteen thousand!

Less quaint is the fact that, despite all the designer clad bottoms, we are required to sit on bare brick — hence the need to purchase a square of fabric-covered foam. And a bag of candied nuts while we're at it.

"All set?" Lucy checks on us before she goes on her matador mission. "The guys are seated in the next section" — she points across to Dan/Simon/Rick — "so they can film you and the action. I'll meet you all out front once you're done."

"You know, Lucy," Felipe chuckles as she goes to leave, "now you tell me about the dance concept, it is a shame you were not here a short time ago when Joaquin Cortes performed here."

"Joaquin Cortes?!" Beth's jaw drops. "As in the Flamenco legend? As in Naomi Campbell's ex, Armani's muse and one of the most feral, sexual dancers to ever flick his hair on stage?"

"Yes, yes," Felipe cheers. "He danced right here in the bullring. It was magnificent. Of course, if you are a purist you would prefer Farruquito —"

Before Felipe can expound further, the brass band strikes up, all parping trumpets and tinny cymbals.

"And that would be your Paso Doble!" Lucy groans as she scuttles on her way.

The "show" begins with a procession of all the "performers", like an early curtain call, possibly because not all of them will make it to the final act.

I can't help but get a thrill at the sight of my first *traje de luce* or "suit of lights". What other sport can claim such glitzy costumes? No concession has been made over the centuries to streamline the bulky, tassled epaulettes on the boleros or switch those stiff satin knickerbockers for a more flexible, horn-proof textile. And where else would you get to fight for your life in a starched collar and tie?

"I like the coral outfit best," Beth decides. "The one with all the black embroidery."

"He's the one to watch!" Felipe smiles at her good judgement. "Juan José Padilla. You will see."

"What about the guy in the white and gold?" I would have thought he was *numero uno* based on the glitz quota of his outfit but it turns out the opposite is true, he's merely a *banderillero*, assistant to the main matador.

"Well, he's obviously pretty confident — that's a bold colour to wear around so much spurting blood." (I notice most of the other aspiring matadors have chosen a more forgiving burgundy.)

"Do you think they're wearing Spanx?" Beth giggles, pointing to their impeccably pert rears.

"I think a couple of them have a pair stuffed down the front of their trousers!"

"Oh, dear Lord!" Beth reels as one fellow turns our way. "That's obscene!"

"Wouldn't you wear a little padding in their situation?" Felipe puts the bulbous bulge in context.

"So now what?" Beth wants to know why the "cast" are just milling around as opposed to doing some big opening number.

It's certainly a vast stage to fill. (The gate through which the bull will burst is bigger than my last theatre's safety curtain.) I look at the men adjusting their capes beside the barricade and wonder how many of them are thinking, *I don't want to go to work today*! Maybe they've even had bets with their friends on which body part will get skewered. Felipe tells us that seventy per cent of injuries occur between the belly and the knees. Feeling that he may be heading towards death statistics, I divert him onto the cost of the *traje de luce* which, I learn, start at two thousand euros a set. He's just explaining to Beth where she can buy a pair of their candy pink socks for about thirty euros, when it begins.

I can't believe they'll be able to show much of what follows on TV. Certainly not the horses that are blindfolded so they don't see the bull charging for them or the lances that their riders are jabbing into the neck of the bull. Felipe says it is the job of these *picadors* to test the bull's strength and weaken the muscles, thus lowering the head. Then come the *banderilleros* who stick the ruffled picks in the bull's shoulders, and leave them dangling there as the startling crimson blood streams down his black coat. Already Beth's face is in her hands.

While she can't bear to look, I can't tear my eyes away. Feeling a mixture of repulsion and indignation, I find my own nostrils flaring, actively willing the bull to punish these ridiculous prancing taunters in their overly bedazzled costumes.

Meanwhile, Felipe is trying to explain how the matador earns kudos, as well as identifying the distinct postures and "*faenas*". I register the name of the cape swish as a "*veronica*" but overall I am too crippled with empathy for the beast to take in what he is saying. At one point the bull tries to make a run back through the gate from whence he came and his confusion is palpable and heartbreaking. I almost get the sense that he's wondering what he did to deserve this treatment. And then I think of how Lee weakened me with his barbed words. How he would repeatedly jab at my wounds. No one believes it but I did try to fight back. I did try to retaliate. I just never won.

But then, as the matador makes his final deadly incision, I find myself reconsidering that claim. I'm alive, aren't I? Isn't that a victory in itself?

While the audience applaud, I feel nothing but disgust. I know there are two more matadors on the bill but I think we've seen enough. In Lucy's absence, I look to Rick to arrange our departure, just in time to see him collapse onto the row ahead of him. He's out cold. Apparently the sight of the bull being dragged out of the ring, turning the sand red in its wake, pushed him over the edge.

While Simon attempts to retrieve and revive him, I notice Dan tilt the camera his way — perfect blooper reel fodder.

"Beth, look!"

"I can't, I just can't!"

"Not the bull — it's Rick, he's passed out!"

"What?" She looks up in time to see Simon trying to slap him back to consciousness. "Oh, I wish that had been me!" she laments.

We're lamenting even more when we realise our gawking has cost us our chance to exit — there's no getting out now without creating a Mexican wave of spectators and seeing as the next bull is already in the ring, it's probably best not to make any distracting movements.

"Oh God, here we go again." Beth hunches into a forward foetal position while I try counting the rows of the stadium seating. I'm only up to fifteen when I hear the unmistakable sound of mooing and look back to see a farmer-type herding a dozen or so cows into the ring.

"What the —?"

Felipe explains that if the bull does not respond to the initial baiting and trots in the opposite direction instead of charging at the cape, they send in a herder to remove him as he is deemed unworthy of a fight.

"So he gets off scot-free?"

He nods.

Wow. If ever there was an argument for turning the other cheek, this is it. Now if there was just some way he could pass the message on to his fellow bulls . . .

But that's not all.

If the bull makes a magnificent defence, he can be pardoned and will return to his life in an Andalucian pasture where he will be put to stud and die of old age.

I'm really quite taken aback. "So they basically have to be really good or really bad to get to those Elysian fields?"

"Yes, but you should know that even the ones that die here today spent four or five years in those fields before they came here. No human contact."

"Really?" It's certainly a better existence than those factory-farmed animals. I get out my phone and do a little maths on the calculator setting, wondering about the pleasure/pain ratio. Say four years of unbothered bliss in the countryside versus the rather less idyllic twenty-five minutes in the ring. It's a horrible way to go but I console myself that it represents 0.002% of their life.

"Next you'll be saying that they die in a state of nirvana as their formerly idyllic life flashes before their eyes!" Beth takes no consolation from my statistics.

"I'm just saying —"

"I don't want to hear it."

I look back at the calculator and tinker with some new figures. Right now, Lee feels like the dominating factor in my life but in actuality, percentage-wise he has only been present for eight per cent of my time on earth.

So ninety-two per cent of my life has been Lee-free.

It's up to me now whether I let his percentage creep up or whether, with every day that passes without him in it, it gets smaller and smaller . . .

"Ladies." Felipe gets our attention. "Juan José Padilla has entered the ring."

And this is when everything changes.

For a start, he's fighting a Miura bull, known as the "bulls of death" because they are notorious for killing so many of Spain's matadors, including the legendary Manolete, whom Felipe gets a little teary-eyed at the mere mention of.

Secondly, the man has a death wish.

"What's he doing?" I gasp as Padilla kneels just metres before the gate from which the bull will erupt, and then drapes the cape over his body. I look around in amazement — isn't anyone going to stop him?!

"Felipe!" I tug on our guide's sleeve but he's too caught up to respond.

I have to look away as the gate opens.

Miraculously, Padilla doesn't get trampled. Seemingly miffed by this fact, he then elects to do the *banderilleros*' job himself, in a series of heart-stopping fly-by piercings.

"Do you think he knows that he's fighting one of the fiercest bulls in existence?" I wince as he lingers a little too long in his opponent's path, even turning his back on him. "Oh jeez!" I squirm as they rotate around each other, so close that he actually now has his hand upon the bull's rump. Another time he places himself against the backboard like the target for a knife-thrower, only in this case the knives are the bull's horns.

"The man is clearly insane," I say, scandalised by his kamikaze approach.

The other matadors were poised, cautious and precise. Padilla's outrageous, noisy, reckless ways are making the whole situation seem all too real, to the degree that I can actually imagine myself in his slip-on pumps. And I don't want to be in them.

Especially not when he is gored, tossed in the air like a rag doll and seeping scarlet through his satin sheathing.

Hearing the audience gasp in horror, Beth opens her eyes just in time to see his team-mates carrying out his limp body. I am quaking with shock.

What have we just witnessed?

But then, just before the exit, he regains consciousness, fights back and — though he is now wearing just one shoe — returns to triumph over the bull to thunderous applause. The arena is a-flutter with white handkerchiefs showing audience approval. Even the bull itself is given a posthumous lap of honour.

I am stunned. I look to Beth, back in her "brace-brace" aeroplane crash pose.

"Is the matador dead?" she asks out of the corner of her mouth.

"No," I mumble. "Unbelievably he's not."

I have to link arms with Felipe just to stay upright during our exit — unable to mentally process what I have just experienced, my body is nonetheless juddering with adrenaline. I feel like a blender switched to high. I don't remember ever feeling quite like this before. A thousand unanswered questions bombard my brain. There's a new "*Why?*" in town. Why do they do this? What attracts them, what *compels* them to do such a thing?

"Wasn't that wild?" Dan is equally strung out by the experience. "I can't believe that last guy, what was his name again?"

"Juan José Padilla."

We turn to find Lucy holding up a piece of paper. "That's the name of the matador I got for us. What's he like?"

She awaits our reply but we're all too dumbstruck to respond.

"It was his lambchop sideburns that sold me!" she chuckles. "Can you believe it, he's even invited us to his house?"

My eyes widen. "Are we insured?"

"What?" Lucy frowns.

"I mean, if anything happens to us, I presume the TV company has comprehensive insurance?"

"There aren't any bulls there!" Lucy tuts.

"It's not the bulls I'm worried about."

En route, Rick talks non-stop on his mobile phone, probably so no one can tease him about fainting during the bullfight. Meanwhile, Dan fills Lucy in on our matador's antics and Simon tries to shush him, no doubt concerned his enthusiasm is offending Beth.

"I'm sorry." Felipe looks repentant. "I didn't realise you were a vegetarian."

"I'm not," she replies.

"Oh," he says, neatly folding his hands in his lap. Point made.

When Beth refuses to be interviewed, the camera is turned on me. After pondering the notion: "Life and death packaged as entertainment or ancestral art form?" Lucy asks if I found myself relating in any way to the relationship between the *toro* and *toreador*.

"Absolutely," I nod.

Just like the bull who knows the matador is nothing but trouble, yet returns again and again until its ultimate demise, I would repeatedly respond to Lee's baiting and taunting. I thought I was going back to defend myself but I can see now that I was just getting in deeper. I can imagine the bull reasoning with himself — *I'm bigger than him, way more ferocious, I should be able to vanquish my aggressor. I'm not going to let the fact that he has a sword bother me*. In the same way, I thought I could love and reason Lee into a state of submission. Good would triumph over evil. He'd be nasty to me, I'd be nice back. That would show him! Hah!

"And in reality?" Lucy prompts.

"In reality, I would end up sobbing and pleading with him to be a little kinder to me," I sigh. "I can only imagine how powerful that made him feel. What a trip, being able to reduce another person to tears on a whim."

"So what have you learned today?"

I think for a few moments and then come to this conclusion: "Don't go towards the pain. Walk in the opposite direction. Get out of the ring."

"A beautiful pasture awaits," Felipe adds, rather charmingly.

* * *

"Okay, pull over here." Lucy has us stop by a nondescript roundabout.

"What's going on?" Rick wants to know.

"Apparently Padilla's house is tricky to find so he said to meet us here. He should be along in another ten minutes or so."

I get out of the taxi and stand beside Lucy, who is eagerly watching for the first glimpse. I can't deny that I have a few butterflies myself.

"Do you think it is politically incorrect to sleep with a matador?" she asks me.

"Well, I don't think that PETA are going to ask you to be their next spokesperson if you do."

"Actually I was thinking of you, technically it is your turn."

"What?" I hoot. "Is there some clause in this contract I don't know about?"

"Aren't you even a little bit tempted? They're like rock stars or footballers here. Plus there's the whole Ava Gardner thing . . ."

"I was thinking about her at the bullring. Did you ever hear about a musical called *Matador*?"

She shakes her head.

"Short West End run in the Nineties. Part of the story was actually inspired by her affair with a Spanish bullfighter."

"Really?"

I nod. "Only one song really broke out — you know *A Boy From Nowhere*?"

Her brows knit together. "Isn't that Tom Jones?"

"Yes!" I cheer. "If you listen to the lyrics you'll hear him singing from the perspective of a poor but proud matador, fighting to survive."

"I always thought he was talking about coming from a little town in Wales!"

I can't help but giggle. "A lot of people do."

We chat a little about the nature of pride, and how Spain could be just the place to regain mine and then Lucy asks, for the tenth time at least, "Is that him?"

"No," I say to the assorted Peugeots and Audis she points to. "He wouldn't drive that type of car."

"What then?" she demands.

"I don't know, it would be something more —"

Before I can complete my sentence, a souped-up monster ATV last seen in *Mad Max* bounces over the verge and, I swear, lands in slow motion with a boom and fanfare of dust.

"That's him," I assert.

CHAPTER TWENTY

We follow Juan José Padilla to what he would call his *casa* but what we would describe as a shrine to his profession.

The exterior of the house is normal enough, in a modern mansion kind of way, but once you pass the front door there is no *Through the Keyhole* mystery about who lives here. A dozen bull heads are mounted in the lobby area alone — like gold discs commemorating his greatest hits — alongside a life-size oil painting of the man of the house looking stately in full raspberry-pink bullfighting regalia.

The most surprising thing is that, in manner, JJ is actually more akin to this painting than his kamikaze alter ego — apparently the adrenaline junkie is part of his showmanship, behind closed doors he is decidedly debonair.

Well, as debonair as you can be when your gouged calf is bulging with bandages.

"Are you in pain?" I ask, via Felipe.

"This is minor!" Felipe translates as JJ flips his shirt to show the scarring from when his back got ripped from neck to waist in Pamplona last year.

Despite the appealing toned brown sheen of the rest of his torso, we turn away, wincing, only to be confronted with a multitude of photographs of him leaking blood in assorted stages of bull confrontation.

"Don't you think it's a bit weird to have all these near-death moments framed on the walls?" Beth whispers to me as we begin our tour. "Like me putting up a big poster of Baby landing on me or you being drunk-driven by Lee . . ."

It does seem a macabre celebration and yet JJ assures us this is absolutely typical of a matador's house — even when we discover that the lounge and dining room are also brimming with memorabilia, including dozens of trophies and awards.

"Just how many bullfights has he done?" I gawp.

Until now, I had presumed that these death-defying acts would take place a couple of times a year — I mean, how much drama can one person stand? But Felipe explains that during the summer season a top-ranking matador like JJ could be fighting three or four times a *week*!

I am stunned. Surely his heart barely gets the chance to settle back to its normal pace? I don't know if I could live with that many reminders of my mortality.

"And yet think how much aggravation you endured from Lee on a weekly basis," Lucy notes. "We all make choices other people cannot comprehend."

She makes a good point. Though I certainly didn't earn tens of thousands of euros for each of our fights.

"You also weren't so well-dressed," Beth observes, nodding to an Aladdin's Cave of costumes — *traje de luce* of every hue displayed in custom-built glass cases.

"May I?" I take out my camera, absolutely entranced.

JJ nods and then holds out a particularly exquisite pearl-white gleamer for my inspection. I insist on washing my hands before I trace the pink-to-crimson floral embroidery and yellow-gold embellishments.

"The craftsmanship is exquisite," I gasp in reverence.

I have a million design questions but Rick curtails my feverish interrogation with a casual sneer: "Just a reminder to everyone that this is a *dance* show!"

Ah, yes. That.

With Beth refusing to cavort with JJ on moral grounds, it falls to me to partner him. How I wish I could trade this experience for a couple of hours with his tailor. But at least Dan is psyched.

"Awesome," he cheers as JJ leads us outside to his practice ring — a scaled-down circle of sand, shimmering gold in the setting sun. "This will look great!"

After all the interior and night shoots in Buenos Aires, he's happy to have at least one dance scene in natural light. Of course I use the term "dance" in the loosest sense of the word. The best I'm going to be able to offer is a series of postures directed by Beth and translated, where necessary, by Felipe.

"I've been meaning to ask you," I turn to our guide while Simon prepares the music, 'Bullfighter' sounds so ugly and aggressive while 'matador' has a far more romantic, passionate air about it. What does the word actually mean?"

"Matador?" he repeats, making it sound even sexier with his accent.

"Yes?"

"*Killer*," he growls.

"Oh," I gulp as I turn to face my new dance partner.

There is an intensity to this man that I cannot match. He seemed so convivial touring us around the house but now he's back in work mode I get a true sense of his power. I don't know if I'm ready for this.

"Let's start with the cape," Rick directs.

I'm relieved to step back and let him do his iconic swishing, even if I am rather disillusioned to learn that the raging red is redundant as bulls are in fact colour-blind.

"It's all about the movement," JJ explains.

Like now I can tell that he wants me to come towards him . . .

"Hold on." Dan halts me just as I step into frame. "Can we use that larger cape?"

"Just what exactly are you implying?" I turn to him, hands on hips.

"Nothing personal," he grins back at me. "It's just that the pink and yellow combination would contrast better with your dress."

JJ looks a little unsure but obliges nonetheless, again holding it low at first and then twitching it to entice me. I can't help but go for the gag and as he swoops the fabric towards me I charge, pointy fingers at my brow, only to fall back into the sand with a clunk.

"Jeez! What the hell is that cape made from?" I rub my head in a daze.

"Carmen! Are you alright?" Beth rushes to my side, helping me get back onto my feet.

"I'm fine but that was not what I was expecting."

"*Es muy pesado.*" JJ holds out the offending article by way of explanation — I can barely lift it off the ground it's so heavy and tarpaulin-tough.

"My bad," Dan grimaces and then pulls my head to his mouth and kisses my crown.

I gawk back at him. Did he just kiss me in public?

"Don't worry," he winks. "Rick's off making a call."

"Do you feel well enough to continue?" Lucy joins the huddle.

I nod, now rather enjoying the mild concussion.

"Since the Paso Doble is the only Latin dance where the man is the centrepiece, we will start with Senor Padilla." Beth sounds convincingly professional as she begins to read from the print-out Lucy has provided. "His arrogant stance displays bravery and defiance in the face of the enemy."

"I think he's got that down," I opine.

"Actually I think he's already nailed most of the things on this list." Beth scans the page. "Ruthlessly in control, impregnable air, proud chest . . ." But then she lowers her gaze. "Apparently there needs be an 'uplift' through the abdomen and his buttocks should be locked."

I take a surreptitious peek at his shiny bottom. "Everything seems to be in order there."

Beth bites back a smile. "Let's get you in position — the hold is high: raised approximately fifteen centimetres above eye level."

He takes me in his arms, most definitely offering a strong frame. I feel like a child reaching up to dance with her dad.

"Now, Carmen, you need to assume the role of a Spanish dancer."

"Well, at least I'm dressed for the part!" I chirp.

"Your chin is slightly lifted on a long neck."

I extend like a swan. Or possibly a meerkat.

"Do my buttocks need to be locked too?" I enquire, feeling a touch of hysteria brewing.

Beth ignores my nonsense. "The woman is not timid or coy, she is *sensual* — all woman and proud of it. Ready to move?"

I nod, desperately trying to keep in character and not get too distracted by the proximity to his lambchop sideburns.

"Okay, Felipe, could you ask JJ to improvise in time to the music, keeping the moves staccato and precise. Feet always worked strongly against the floor."

I can't help but yelp as he sets us in motion — he's going at quite a pace and, with every jolty, syncopated move, I come unbalanced. My nerves aren't helped by his all-too-authentic calls of "*Hah!*" making me jump out of my skin every time.

"Try and stick with him," Beth urges.

I'm clinging on for dear life but then he begins twirling me like a top. I thought this dance would be empowering but more than anything I feel dizzy. Suddenly he grabs me, holding me steady and daring me to stare him down. So much for a *Strictly Ballroom*-style granny tapping out the beat on my chest. We're but a hair's breadth apart, breathing hard, when Beth asks JJ to perform "a bragging gesture of bravado". I've seen a few of these in the ring but at a far greater distance. When he unleashes his machismo this deep into my personal space, it makes me flinch and stumble backwards.

"Oh, for pity's sake, Carmen! Stand up to him!" Rick has returned with his delicate tuition style.

I'm trying desperately to summon enough latent fierceness to fight back when a Spanish goddess steps into my line of vision — you know how men make that curvy out-in-out shape with their hands? This is the figure they are describing. Her hair is a raven cascade while her facial features have a dainty, doll-like perfection.

For a moment I wonder if she is one of Rick's model/waitresses, making an impromptu cameo, but then JJ reaches for her, kissing her on the lips and announcing, "This is my wife."

Of course! I roll my eyes. Of course he would be married to some stunner. I bet matadors attract all manner of groupies. Seconds later I am obliged to *unroll* my eyes when he reveals that this gorgeous woman is in fact his childhood sweetheart. They first met when he was working behind the counter of a family bakery. How harmless an existence that must seem now, bringing home bear claws instead of bull heads.

"Maybe she just thinks of the blood as jam?" Beth offers her particular take on the situation.

Before I can respond, two little tots come running out, calling, "Papa! Papa!"

JJ seems utterly delighted by the little boy and girl, leaving me all the more astounded that he puts himself in such regular peril. Speaking of which . . . Rick is now bearing down on Lucy.

"*His wife?*" he roars, all too audibly.

"Yes, isn't she pretty?" I hear her whimper.

Rick growls his displeasure. "You didn't think to ask if he was single?"

"Well, they told me he was the most remarkable performer —"

"I don't care about that!" he spits. "How are we going to recreate the *Gaucho* chemistry with this guy's wife looking on? Get me an unmarried one."

"But —" She looks at her watch.

"We'll re-shoot tomorrow," he asserts. "And for heaven's sake get these girls some Flamenco lessons."

I sigh heavily as we are ushered out the door with only the briefest *adios*.

"You don't think that was a little rude?" I can't help but speak up once the taxi door slides shut.

"I get paid for providing show content, not manners," Rick snaps back.

"It's not possible to do both?"

Rick twists around so he can give me the full benefit of his incredulity. "*Now you want to get confrontational?*"

We drive the rest of the way back in silence. Not least because almost everyone has dropped off to sleep. It's been a long first day.

But apparently not long enough.

* * *

Instead of returning to our hotel, Rick has the driver pull up beside the fairground, telling Dan to prepare his hand-held crowd-friendly camera while Lucy is instructed to infuse us with sangria. I'm not entirely opposed to the idea, until I realise it's a ploy to get us to board a ride called *Maxima Sensacion*.

"I would sooner impale myself on the matador's sword." Beth digs her heels in as we survey the multi-armed metal monstrosity before us.

"I thought you dancers were supposed to be all about physical sensation?" Rick attempts to goad her.

"It's precisely because I am so in touch with my body that I know when to avoid things that might harm it and thus end my career." She gives him a supercilious look. "Besides, what exactly do rollercoaster rides have to do with dancing?"

"Oh, excuse me for wanting to inject a little variety."

In a bid to end the squabbling, Lucy moves us over to the children's carousel — rather disturbingly featuring real miniature ponies plodding *ad infinitum* nose-to-tail — and explains that Rick is concerned that we're going to be doing nothing but frowning and snarling for the Paso Doble, so he wants to capture some lighter expressions.

"What, like fear and nausea?" Beth retaliates. "Why does he insist on pushing us in this merciless way?"

Lucy shrugs. "All I know is that he's not going to let us go home until it looks like you're having fun."

I'm just wondering how to muster that on demand when I see the very thing guaranteed to put a big smile on both our faces — a sign saying "Churros & Chocolate", taking me back to the one good memory I have of my dad taking me to the Costa del Sol as a child.

"What exactly are they?" Beth inspects the crispy coils in the glass display.

"Basically a light, battered donut in stick form." I point to the man breaking the coils into pieces and wrapping them in paper like fish and chips. "You dip them in the hot chocolate, which is so much thicker and silkier than normal, more like chocolate custard in a way."

The most surprising thing is how unsickly the combination is.

"Oh Carmen, this is beyond delicious!" Beth raves, munching happily. "They taste so fresh."

"Well, they're only just out of the deep-fat fryer," I say, pointing to where the cook is adding new batter, cigarette lolling from his mouth.

"That's one for the health inspector!" Beth tips Dan the wink. And then orders a second portion.

Suddenly all is well with the world.

We find some rides with gentler undulations and a boxing booth with a drop-down speedball that Beth has a good go at, no doubt imagining that it's Rick's head.

The deeper into the fairground we go, past bumper cars and mechanical bulls and stalls selling every type of nut brittle, the busier it gets.

"We're going to get separated if we're not careful," I observe, to no one in particular.

But then I hear a voice say, "Would that really be so bad?"

I turn back and meet Dan's eye. Before I know it, he's grabbed my hand and is pulling me to the side of a gang of boisterous teenagers, leaving them to engulf the rest of our group. Now he's weaving me through the crowds, picking up pace, jostling a path for me and only stopping when we reach the big wheel. Or in this case the *massive* wheel.

"Come on!" He goes to tug me towards the ticket booth.

"Are you crazy?" I falter, gawping up and up.

"No one will be able to see us at the top!"

This is not something I would normally even consider. Not for a second. Yet something about his daring is contagious and a minute later I'm sitting beside him, grabbing at the bar for security and wending upward, feet dangling precariously.

"Oh wow!" I gasp as the people shrink below us.

I can't understand why I'm not hysterical, then again it's been quite a day — the Feria, the bullfight, the *frisson* with the matador and now this spontaneous, illicit move! I can no longer distinguish between adrenaline rush and sangria blur. All I know is that when Dan leans in to kiss me, right at the pinnacle, I don't hesitate in kissing him back. Voraciously.

His mouth is unfamiliar — his taste, his technique. He's not Lee. I've crossed the line and it feels *good*.

"Look! There they are!" Dan chuckles as he looks beyond my mouth to the masses below.

I can see a mini Lucy and Beth on their mobile phones, Simon turning in circles and Rick throwing up his hands in despair.

"This is so risky," I squeak. "And you're not even drinking!"

"No, but I did just see the way you ate that *churro*," he growls. "That was motivation enough!"

"Dan!" I slap him, instantly regretting my sudden move as I set the carriage a-jigging. "Yikes!"

"Seriously," he says, tilting my chin towards him, "I've never envied a donut as much as I did just then."

"Will you please stop!" I protest, hands masking my blushing face.

Though, I have to say, some part of me is getting a kick out of being thought of as sexually provocative. I even find that, as he leans in for round two, I kiss him with a little more confidence, imagining myself to be the temptress of the hour.

"You taste yummy," he says, licking his lips. "Take my room key, go on ahead when we get back to the hotel . . ."

"Really?" I can't believe how bold he's being.

"I have to be with you tonight."

"O-okay," I agree, pocketing the key as we make our descent. Wow. It's really going to happen this time.

"You know this has to be our secret?" he reminds me as we dismount.

"I know," I confirm. "I won't tell a soul."

"Not even Beth."

"I promise."

And the reason I can make such an assertion is that I know I won't have to say a word.

"You little devil!" Her eyes widen the second we reconvene. "You kissed him, didn't you?"

"Who?"

She rolls her eyes at me. "The candyfloss man!"

"What makes you say that?" I play innocent.

She just giggles as she takes out her lipgloss and applies a fresh coat to me. "You definitely have to sleep with the new matador now, just to throw Rick off the scent."

"Oh, alright." I pretend to play along. "I'll take one for the team!"

I really do feel giddy now. As if a whole new world, or rather, forgotten world, has opened up to me. A world of possibility, flirtation and surprising arousal.

"We've got time for one more ride," Lucy tells us. "What do you want to go for?"

For the new, bolder me there can only be one choice: "*MAXIMA SENSACION*!"

CHAPTER TWENTY-ONE

There can be no better location for an illicit affair than the ochre-yellow labyrinth that is *Las Casas de la Juderia*. Never mind the fern-tickled courtyards, blue-tiled fountains or corridors a-tumble with crumbling pillars. The key is the multitude of asymmetric levels offering alternate entrances, hidden stairwells and secret nooks — so many places to divert to when you step out from your lover's room of a morning and look across the balcony to see Rick heading straight for you.

"Yikes!" My heart is going like the clappers as I dart up a narrow stone staircase. I don't know where it leads but decide it's best to just keep going up, up and away. Before I know it, I'm careering along a narrow passageway, only to find myself at a dead end. Forced to backtrack, I take a tiny two-person lift to its highest point, figuring Rick is most likely heading *down* to breakfast . . .

When the lift door opens, I am surprised to find myself amid the turrets and potted geraniums of the roof terrace. Crossing the emerald green faux turf, I find myself contemplating a large swimming pool. Or do I? In my current dehydrated state, I wonder if I am experiencing a mirage. But then a breeze chases a ripple across the surface of the turquoise water and I smile in the knowledge that this panoramic oasis is real.

With no one else around, I can't resist slipping onto one of the sun loungers, keen to hold off the "morning after" by reliving every detail of the night before. The only snag is that the excess of sangria and surprisingly potent sherry has blurred my memory.

I know that we had little concern of being spotted at the local bar because the rest of our group was so clapped out they went straight to bed. I know that the venue was lively and we had to shout to be heard, talking excitably about all the fun things we'll do when we get back to London. He told me that he'd ultimately love to be a movie cameraman and that we'd make a great team because I could be the costume designer on set and thus we'd get to travel to ever more exotic locations together! I smile to myself, reexperiencing that "anything is possible" thrill.

Closing my eyes, I tilt my face to the sun, remembering how he pulled me onto his lap and kissed me and how easy it all felt. At one point, Lee came up in conversation and he sounded so empathetic as he whispered, "Love hurts". It felt like he'd kissed my wounded knee and made it all better. Then he said, "Let's go home," as if the hotel were our own personal palace.

I went ahead of him, straight up to his room with his key. Even though I had a couple of minutes to collect my thoughts before he arrived, I already knew I was going to sleep with him. I couldn't think of one darn reason not to.

Apparently he felt the same way. Quite enthusiastically so.

I move on to the wooden decking at the pool's edge so I can swish my toes in the cool water. Despite the hangover and sleep-deprivation, I am feeling rather pleased with myself.

"*Buonas Dias*!" The pool attendant greets me from behind a huge stack of fresh towels. As he sets them down, his smile widens, reminding me that I'm still in last night's outfit.

Time to go back and prepare myself for the day ahead. Now if I could just figure out which building I need to get back to . . .

Much furtive scurrying later, I locate the room, only to be greeted by the unmistakable sound of vomiting coming from the bathroom.

"Beth?" I hurry to the door.

"Don't come in!"

"What's going on?"

"I ate some bull's testicles."

"*You did what?*"

"Not on purpose," she wails. "Rick was the only person down at breakfast and I didn't want to sit with him so I went out looking for some food and this restaurant across the street smelt so good I just pointed to what everyone else was eating and then when I got back I looked up the translation online and —"

She retches again on cue.

"Can I get you some water? Actually, Sprite is supposed to help with upset stomachs . . ." I rummage in the minibar for a bottle and then return to the bathroom door, tapping my request to enter.

She gingerly turns the lock.

"Oh Beth, you look awful!" Her hair is damp and her face pallid. "Do you think we should call a doctor?"

"Lucy's already done it," she pants. "They should be here soon."

"I can't believe I wasn't here in your hour of need!" I say as I slump down onto the floor beside her.

"There's nothing you could have done."

"Well, for starters I would have suggested *churros* instead of mystery chunks of meat."

"*Oh God!*"

She's off again. I scuttle out to give her some privacy and hear a knocking at the door. It's Lucy and the doctor.

"I'm going to call ahead to Havana and see if I can find any Salsa dancers who also happen to have had medical training!" Lucy jokes as we await the verdict. "The good news is that Rick says it's okay for her to skip the initial lesson, seeing as she's a pro and should be able to pick up the steps quicker."

"You don't mean —"

"Yup! You're going solo."

Oh no! *No, no, no!* "I can't possibly leave her like this!" I protest.

"It's best she has some peace, the doctor says it's most likely psychosomatic so she just needs to rest and rehydrate."

"But —"

"Don't worry, I've told her I can be back in a flash if it gets any worse."

And to think I was worried about looking bad dancing next to Beth. That's nothing compared to doing this *without* her.

"In a way, it's kind of appropriate," Lucy decides. "Seeing as this dance is all about standing on your own two feet. Rick thinks it'll give the piece a nice twist."

"Of course he does," I mumble. "Anything to amp up the levels of discomfort."

And then Lucy frowns as she looks me up and down. "Don't you think your dress is a bit too evening wear for a dance class?"

"Um —"

"CARMEN!" Beth saves the day, calling me back into the bathroom.

"All better now?" I ask, ever the optimist.

She shakes her head and weakly announces, "I want to give you something."

"This is all too deathbed scene!" I complain. "I can't leave you."

"Don't be silly, I just got a little present for you while I was out." She bids me retrieve a box from the bed. Inside is a pair of red and white polka-dot Flamenco shoes. So very Minnie Mouse.

"They're adorable!" I chuckle as I try them on, surprised at how light they are — possibly made from some kind of laminated cardboard.

"Just a cheap bit of fun to amuse you," Beth smiles. "Enjoy!"

I lean down to give her a delicate squeeze, whispering, "Where's this restaurant again?"

"Oh no you don't!" Lucy is in the doorway holding up a change of outfit.

Curses! There really is no getting out of this.

I daren't even look in Dan's direction as we join the crew outside, fearing I'll blush or swoon or become suspiciously flustered. Fortunately Simon offers a distraction, obviously concerned at Beth's absence.

"She's not coming with us?" He looks devastated.

"Maybe later on."

"Well, just in case she doesn't make it, can you give her this?" He discreetly hands me a small envelope. "It's just an apology for my behaviour at the *estancia*. I wanted to put it in writing."

If Rick wasn't so close I'd give the poor man a hug.

"I know I've blown it with her but I want her to know how sorry I am. I had no business saying the things I did."

I emit a sympathetic sigh. "We all do crazy things in the heat of the moment."

"Hallelujah to that!" Dan chips in and I have to fake-drop my bag just so I can conceal the look on my face.

"Christ, Lucy, this place is a bit low-rent, isn't it?" Rick is clearly not enamoured with the scuffed backstreet location of the dance studio.

"We'll just shoot the interior," she advises, only to lose yet another brownie point when we discover that she's inadvertently booked a group class as opposed to a one-to-one. With no other space, or teacher, available Rick agrees to go along with it.

Frankly, I'm delighted. Far better to be part of the chorus than facing the spotlight alone. I just hope the other ten or so women don't think I'm taking the Mickey (or rather Minnie) with my shoes. The pros clearly favour sober blacks and burgundies but Lucy assures me that the contrast is a good thing because it will help the viewer identify me in the mass. I just wish Dan hadn't added that I look like "Dorothy in her ruby slippers at an Amish hoe-down".

As I follow the slo-mo clapping and tapping of the warm-up, I feel my nerves begin to ease. As intense and ferocious as Flamenco can be, it doesn't seem horribly difficult in terms of technique — no acrobatics, no teetering around on point, no jumps or lifts. Everyone can do an impression of a Flamenco dancer — just raise your arms, twiddle your fingers and stomp your feet.

I soon discover that is like saying Tango is just a matter of taking long strides with a carnation between your teeth.

It doesn't help that the synthetic quality of my shoes has got my feet sweating obscenely, causing me to skid every which way as the pace quickens. Within minutes we switch to farce as the ensemble suddenly breaks into a synchronised routine, all side-steps and body shrugs like Michael Jackson's *Thriller*, but with swishy skirts instead of dangling bandages.

I look at Lucy with "what the hell?" open hands.

It turns out that, though this is indeed a beginner level class, these particular beginners have been working on this routine for the past three months.

We can't get out of the place quick enough.

Once outside, I expect Rick to go ballistic at Lucy but instead I find him grinning at me. "That was hilarious," he crows. "You should have seen the look on your face when you realised you were the odd one out!"

"Don't worry," Lucy quickly soothes me. "I've already organised an upgrade to the esteemed *Museo Del Baile Flamenco*."

"And you're sure it's one-on-one this time?" Rick resumes his sneer.

"It should be — the teacher is charging eighty euros an hour."

My eyes widen and then I look down at my feet. "I'm going to need some better shoes."

This time I'm going for the real deal: robust black suede with a chunky heel inset with nails for maximum clackability.

Conveniently, all the traditional shoe shops are clustered together down a bustling alleyway running between two picturesque plazas. The only snag is that it's simply too much of a crush to manoeuvre a five-piece, so the boys cool off in an ice-cream parlour while Lucy and I venture into the narrowest of stores.

Instantly, I feel swept into a kind of stock exchange insanity as the masses clamour towards the counter, holding up the display shoe they need an alternative size for. When my turn comes, I bleat a hopeful,

"*Trenta ocho?*" only to have the hubbub halt as everyone turns to look at me as if I just spoke Japanese. Okay, so my accent may not be perfect but I'm in a shoe shop asking for the most common size, could they give me a break?

Resorting to mime — holding up three and then eight fingers — they finally twig and call up to a woman who leans over the staircase and drops a box down from above, rather like Wile E. Coyote might drop an anvil on Roadrunner.

Though I enjoy the show of the men below catching and juggling the boxes, one even balancing a heel on his chin, the shoes don't fit well so we move on to a store with rather less flamboyant customer service — basically, if they have your size they bring the shoes to you, if they don't, you're dead to them. You wait and wait, see them deal with other customers that came in after you and think maybe someone else is looking, checking the store room. You don't want to harass them but finally you crack and ask the equivalent of, "Soooo, any luck with that lovely claret number?" And they look at you like you're crazy, as if to say, "Obviously not or we would have brought them to you." Ah. I see. Well, thanks for letting me know.

It's only when we step into leafy and relatively deserted *Plaza de la Alfalfa* that I feel myself decompress. One store, set apart from the rest, has its blinds drawn so low you'd think they were closed but Lucy susses that they are merely preventing the sun from bleaching their wares, so we duck under the awning and into a shoe oasis. There's only one other customer, two attendants and seating for ten. Suddenly I feel like I'm in one of those old movies where the heroine has models parade outfits before her so she doesn't have to go through the inconvenience of actually trying anything on.

Though when I do, I make this joyful proclamation: "These are by far the least uncomfortable of all!"

"Sold!" Lucy cheers on my behalf.

As we hurry back to rejoin the menfolk, I ask how Lucy's stress levels are faring.

She rolls her eyes. "I honestly don't think I slept more than two hours last night."

"You and me both," I accidentally say out loud before quickly adding, "Jet lag."

"Thank heavens for the internet though," she continues, oblivious. "I think I've pretty much sorted the schedule for the rest of our time here. I managed to convince Rick that we'd be better off using a dancer dressed as a matador and wait 'til you see the hottie I have lined up, you're going to love him."

"Oh. Well," I squirm, unable to feign arousal, my attention being so skewed Dan's way. "I'm afraid I'm a bit of a lost cause in that direction."

"I know it's difficult for you to get close to any man after Lee."

"Mmm," I mumble noncommittally, feeling awful that we always seem to be lying to poor Lucy about something.

"I'm just saying, don't rule out the possibility of a holiday romance. It could be just what you need!"

"It could indeed," I say as Dan comes into view.

For a moment I have a fantasy of Dan grabbing my hand like he did at the fairground, only this time the two of us would steal through historic *barrio Santa Cruz*, exchanging ice-cream kisses under Moorish archways.

It's so bitter-sweet that we find ourselves in these insanely romantic places with multiple chaperones, having to curb every natural instinct. I wonder if the viewers will notice that I am starting to look at the camera in a very particular way? Or if Rick will get suspicious at the amount of times we "accidentally" collide with each other, desperate for some physical contact.

I expel a long sigh. What I wouldn't give to be taking a traditional siesta right now.

CHAPTER TWENTY-TWO

"*Museo Del Baile Flamenco*," Lucy announces our arrival at the Flamenco museum.

Not exactly the classic hangover destination but, as museums go, this is actually very hip. We walk through a sun-streamed courtyard, take the zippy modern lift up a couple of floors and then enter an exhibit with mood-lighting to rival the corridors of the Faena + Universe hotel in Buenos Aires.

Only the projected images and the informative panels are lit, everything else is in darkness. Too dark to film. Too dark to see Dan's hand brushing mine or to realise just how close he is standing beside me.

The main room taking us through the history of the dance has a series of divider screens and, provided we time our hang-back from the group just right, we can steal a kiss. I gasp inwardly as his lips meet mine, so bold and ardent. So more-ish . . .

"Carmen?" I hear Lucy's voice, backtracking in our direction.

"Yes." I quickly disentangle myself and scoot around the corner to face her.

"Can you make sure you digest this bit on the history of the Flamenco? I'll ask you about it when we're back in the light."

"Yes, yes, of course." I try to focus through my giddiness.

Late fifteenth century: Catholic persecution of Jews and Moors. Must convert to Christianity or face expulsion from Spain. Gypsies face attempt to exterminate them from the race altogether. Wow. That's harsh.

As Dan comes around the corner, I can't help but comment on what I'm reading. "Can you believe they actually passed laws forbidding gypsies anything to do with their identity — no more speaking Romany or wearing their particular style of dress. They even had to 'end their wanderings and seek steady employment'." I shake my head. "When I was a little girl, I thought being a gypsy was the most romantic and exciting thing in the world — I desperately wanted to be barefoot with wild black hair, big gold earrings, travelling in one of those hand-painted wagons."

"I'd like to —" Dan suddenly stops. ". . . know what happened next!"

I turn and see Rick watching us. "Well, let's see . . . along with the Jews and the Moors, they ended up taking refuge in the treacherous mountain areas, too desolate for the authorities to pursue them." I read on. "For many years these three radically different cultures lived in relative harmony and the fusion of their music and dances are what we know today as Flamenco."

"Any personal thoughts?" Lucy asks when I parrot the information back to her.

"Actually, the history did remind me of the way the immigrants who came to Argentina ended up blending their music and dance as a form of solace." I pause. "The main difference seems to be that, whereas Tango evolved into a dance for sophisticates, Flamenco is considered to be at its best when pared back to its most raw and untamed state."

I must confess there is something very appealing to me about the earthiness of this dance. I'm actually starting to think it might be fun to connect to my inner gypsy.

Until, that is, I discover that the studio where I will be taking my class is essentially a glass cube. With no curtains. In a prime position off the main courtyard.

All I need now is to be mistaken for a live exhibit and draw a crowd — isn't it bad enough that Dan has to bear witness to my ineptitude?

"Your instructor is on her way," Lucy informs me.

"Okay," I nod, trying to quell my nerves as I unwrap my new shoes. So much for comfort! I swear I can actually feel my bones splintering and re-aligning as I crunch out my first steps.

Sadly Ugg boots are not an option so I take a steadying breath and switch my focus to conjuring the regal yet provocative stance this dance requires. I want to do Beth proud but my shoulders slump the instant I catch sight of my teacher.

Maria Del Mar is skinny as a *churro*, which is actually a ridiculous comparison as they're so calorific but, really, I can't believe we've been assigned the one un-voluptuous Flamenco dancer in Seville. "Shouldn't you be teaching Tango?" I want to query as she approaches. Black hair yanked into a severe bun, she is basically Olive Oyl in polka-dots.

But then she smiles and the empathy and playfulness in her large, dark eyes coaxes me back from the verge of a sulk.

"*Bailemos el flamenco*!" she cheers. And who am I to argue?

From the exhibit, I know there are dozens of different styles of this dance from *Farruca* to *Fandango* and *Soleares* to *Seguiriyas*, there's even a style known as *Tangos*! But the one I'm hoping for is the cheery *Alegrias*, meaning "happiness". But Maria has other ideas.

"Today we dance *Tangos*."

I give a wry smile, I guess there's just no escaping it.

After the chaos of the earlier class, I am delighted to find that Maria plans on breaking the routine into manageable segments, starting with clapping.

Standing opposite me, she guides me through the one-two-three pause, one-two-three pause. Palms are at ninety degrees and at the end of each sequence her fingers fold into a clasp, like a full stop.

"*Siempre uno dos tres*." Always one, two, three.

Got that.

The opening move seems so simple it almost throws me — I have to put my hands on my hips and step forward on my right foot, bending the knee as I do so, and then bring the foot back. Same on the left — step forward, flexing the knee, bring the foot back. We do a sequence of four and then she adds a pantomime prince thigh-slap. I'm just thinking this is going to be a breeze when she turns to the signature hand flourishes . . .

I watch the exquisite control and elegance of her fingers — so dainty and fluid — while mine look like a bunch of twigs. What's going on? I thought with all the hand-stitching and precision sequin application I do at work I'd have supremely dexterous digits but, as I attempt to follow her lead and conclude with thumb and middle finger creating an O, I look like I have arthritis.

She shows me again, in slow motion. Visually I get what she is trying to convey but my brain impulses just don't seem to be reaching my fingertips. The harder I try to mimic her, the worse I get. In desperation, I resort to the cliché of imagining myself unscrewing a lightbulb to get the twisting motion but the second she incorporates a raising or lowering of the arm, I start doing an itsy bitsy spider routine.

Was that Dan laughing? Oh, this is so not what you want to be doing when you are trying to impress a man — standing next to someone skinnier and sexier doing something you're bad at.

Mercifully, Maria has decided to leave the hands for now and move onto the Bavarian beer festival move — lean forward, one clap, then give a smack to each thigh. I may now feel primed for a round of pat-a-cake but anything that doesn't require elegance, I'm down with.

And so to the real meat of the dance — the heel stamp.

Her foot hits the floor with a definitive whip-crack. She nods to me to try. Even though I have the greater weight on my side, my stomp barely makes a sound. Oh. She urges me to try harder. I do, attempting to combine all childhood tantrums with every time I wished I'd said no to a man. Still barely a sound, and from Maria a quizzical look of "where's your oomph?"

"Again!" she encourages me, this time cheering, "You are *mujere*!" *You are a woman!* As if being a woman is the strongest thing in the world.

I turn to my reflection to psych myself up, lowering my jaw, narrowing my eyes and trying to look fierce. I go for the angriest, most defiant clash between metal studs and wooden floorboards but find myself blinking baffled at what shows up in the mirror — is this what men see when they look at me? I think I'm being sassy and challenging when in fact the overriding impression is *meek*.

This has to change!

As we pause for a water break, I try to figure out why I'm finding this so challenging. More than anything, I identify a fear of looking like I'm trying too hard. Which is ironic since this is something I'm constantly accused of with regard to my relationships with men. I am The Accommodator: How can I make it better? I'll change so you don't have to. Watch me morph to fit your schedule, tell me your plans for the week so I can make mine. Which is fine, I suppose, if the guy in question is doing the same for you. But I haven't dated a man yet who did that. Why would he need to?

"Again!" Maria invites me back onto the floor, continuing with great patience and kind words — "*bien*" and "*muy bien*" — even looking a little impressed as I get the new addition of a four-pronged swivel spot-on. (Teeny swell of pride.)

Then we go back to the beginning and go over and over the routine from the top. This is the tedious, back-breaking aspect to dance. The only way to get it right is to do it again and again and again. I'm sweating now and my hair has kinked.

Truth be told, this whole experience is way more exacting than I was expecting — in a one-to-one situation, there is simply nowhere to hide. How those celebrities on *Strictly* endure day-long sessions, week after week, I don't know. Those giggling fits they have? Hysteria, I am now convinced.

When Maria pauses and turns to me with an expectant look, for one joyful moment I think our hour is up but then I hear these dread words, "With music?"

I'd almost forgotten about that aspect, I've been concentrating so hard on the moves. I ask her to give me a run-through, to show me how it should look, and get chills as I watch her interpret the song. She knows just when to flick from softness to shazam! This is not a frantic routine by any means but certain sequences are now much faster and I have trouble switching gear. All the while I am dancing, I never take my eyes off her reflection; the one time I try to assess myself in motion,

I immediately go wrong. So when she suggests I try it solo, I practically shriek, "*Are you crazy?*"

Despite the language barrier, there is no confusion about my reluctance. On the upside, I think she's encouraged to finally see some real emotion so she lets me off the hook and says we'll do it tomorrow, giving me a bit more time to practise my Flamenco stance — to demonstrate, she draws herself up, throws back her shoulders and juts out her chin. I do the same and she nods approval, as if to say, always carry yourself like this now.

It feels good, if a little haughty, to stand this way but I know I won't be able to maintain it.

"It's just not me," I explain to Lucy after class. "I'm not a fierce kind of *mujere*."

"Would you like to be?"

"Are you kidding?" I hoot. "I'd love it!"

"Really?"

I nod vigorously. "To be one of those women who can slay a man with one look? To command respect and send a clear message that I am not to be trifled with?" I stare mistily into the distance. "That's my dream!"

CHAPTER TWENTY-THREE

"How'd it go? How are you feeling?"

Back at our hotel room, Beth and I are equally eager for news of the other.

My friend smiles and tells me that she's had a good sleep followed by three scoops of peach *helados* (ice-cream) and now feels sick in an entirely more pleasant way.

I tell her about the farce of the first class and the intensity of the second and then attempt to show her the routine we'll be polishing tomorrow. (She's already way more adept than me at the hand twirls, having been practising them all day from her sickbed.) But before I can even get to the thigh slapping, the phone rings and Lucy informs us that we have just ten minutes before we leave to meet the new — and available — matador at the park.

"Cripes! I need a shower, I'll show you the rest later." And then I spin on my heel. "I almost forgot, Simon gave me this note for you."

As I close the bathroom door, I see Beth slump onto the edge of the bed. When I emerge, she's lying flat on her back, staring up at the ceiling.

"What did he say?" I ask, noticing a little trickle of a tear escaping her eye.

She sits upright and blots her face.

"Why did he have to do this?"

"Do what? What's he done?" I can't believe he'd do anything bad.

"Why did he have to be so sweet?" she huffs. "Now I'm the one who looks like a complete ass!"

I give her a fond smile as she hands the page to me.

Dear Beth,

It's hard to write an apology knowing it will draw all the more attention to my foolishness.

But I don't know any other way to begin to make amends.

I had no business reacting as I did at the *estancia*. I think it came from a place of misguided protectiveness but I can see now it was just plain rude, and didn't in any way reflect the high esteem in which I hold you.

The worst thing about my blunder is that we don't get to talk any more. Our conversations were the best part of my day. I miss them.

As I write this, I am playing Timbaland's "Too Late To Apologise". I hope that isn't the case for us. I really am very sorry.

Your dumb but repentant soundguy,

Simon

"Nice," I nod. "Not too mushy-gushy —"

Before I can complete my assessment, the phone goes again — time to leave.

"Wait!" Beth pulls me back from the lobby. "What am I supposed to say to him now?"

"You could start with a simple thank you and then ask him to forget the rather cruel things you said to him."

"That was in retaliation!" she protests.

"You don't have to justify yourself to me," I remind her. "I'm just thinking it would be nice to clear the air. It's not like he's angling for any romantic result. He just wants things to be as they were between you."

She gives an old codger grizzle, as if he's deliberately making things difficult for her. I almost think she was more comfortable being mad at him. Well, she may not be ready to be loved by him, but at least now they can get back on speaking terms.

Or not.

When it comes to the crunch, Beth opts to completely avoid and ignore Simon, looking everywhere but his direction, busying herself with the contents of her handbag and fanning through the leaflets advertising local attractions. I decide it's best that I do the same, that way he won't get the chance to ask me whether I gave the note to Beth, so he can at least presume that I've forgotten and that she hasn't read it yet. Jeez! The contradictory things we do to protect the feelings of others! (Especially others who you are still secretly hoping will one day hook up with your best friend . . .)

Now I can't claim to be a world authority on parks but I have to presume the Parque de Maria Luisa is one of the world's most elegant. One would be enchanted enough with its hundred acres of gentrified jungle —

the wide boulevards, secret gardens and dazzling bursts of flora — but then behold the Plaza de España: a sweeping arc of a building with ornately tiled recesses depicting every province in Spain from Cataluna to our current position in Andalucia.

Today this most regal of settings has an unusual crown jewel — our mock matador, Lorenzo, standing mid-point on a stepped bridge, in full regalia. The tourists can't believe their luck and snap excitedly. I don't blame them. He really is every bit as stunning as Lucy promised: floppy blue-black hair, long-lashed dark eyes and a bold, leading *hombre* jawline.

There's just one problem — he is alone.

"Where's Felipe?" Rick demands. "Wasn't he supposed to be here with him?"

Through a series of exaggerated mimes, we learn that our oh-so-vital translator brought him to the spot, deposited him and left. Some kind of family emergency.

Rick looks like he wants to stick his head in the nearby moat until bubbles cease to rise. Meanwhile Lucy, ever resourceful, starts darting frantically between tour groups, trying to poach a bilingual guide for an hour.

But I have a better idea.

"Couldn't you do it, Simon?"

"What?" He looks perplexedly at me, wondering how I could betray him like this, not realising that I am trying to do him a favour.

"If you don't speak up, we're going to lose him." I motion to Lorenzo, talking agitatedly into his mobile phone. Even without subtitles it's obvious he thinks the set-up is a shambles and is considering bowing out.

Simon gives Rick a rueful glance, takes a deep breath and then launches into an artfully pronounced appeasement, "*Con permiso, senor. Perdone nuestro desorden*."

Beth blinks in amazement. "I didn't know he could speak Spanish."

I just shrug and turn to Rick. "So how about I take over the sound equipment for a bit?"

He gives one of his trademark snorts. "This isn't a game of musical chairs!"

"Don't worry," I patronise him. "No one's going to ask you to dance." Before he can retaliate, I add, "Go on — I've been watching Simon working for a week, I know the basics and he can check the levels between set-ups."

"Look at you with the lingo!" he sneers. But he doesn't say no. "I suppose we do have an excess of footage of you from this morning . . ."

"You little bugger," Beth mutters under her breath, knowing I've just extricated myself from the matador fix-up.

And then comes the best bit. As Dan returns from shooting B-roll of the surrounding area, Rick slaps him on the back and says, "Looks like you've got yourself a new partner."

As Lorenzo leads us back to the park proper, I feel a swell of satisfaction. I've never liked the word partner before, certainly not in a relationship context, it seemed so unemotional, so *strategic*. But now I hear it in a newly positive sense — two people working together towards a shared goal. Maybe instead of seeing Dan as a potential boyfriend I should consider him more as a partner with whom I can dance through life . . . Perhaps tonight we'll even try some *vertical* manoeuvres?

I go to give him a discreet twinkle, easier now that we are obliged to walk together, but find he is already giving me a knowing look.

"Not too heavy, is it?" He gives the strap holding the equipment a jiggle. "I mean, what with that solid gold bow and arrow you're carrying around."

"What?" I chortle.

"I know what you're up to, Miss Cupid." He nods to where Simon and Beth are now framed by a pergola erupting with deep pink bougainvillea. "Just don't let Rick catch on. The bigwigs back home are baying for another rendezvous."

As am I, I think to myself. But there's no chance to reply, we've reached our shooting spot.

"Ahhh, Bécquer!" Lorenzo introduces us to a tree-encircling monument honouring his favourite nineteenth century poet — Gustavo Adolfo Bécquer.

Beth looks a little bemused as the dancer takes her hand and presses it, not against the statue, but the fraying bark of the cypress.

"This tree was planted in 1870, the year he died, aged thirty-four," Simon translates.

"Ohhh," she nods solemnly.

"These bronze figures at his feet represent two of the most common themes in his work — wounded love and love that wounds."

Even though he has only to repeat the matador's words, Simon seems painfully self-conscious having to address the woman who so recently cold-shouldered him. I'm sure the romantic subject matter doesn't help. It's certainly giving me pause — what phrasing: *Wounded love and love that wounds*. I can't imagine a more apt caption for a photograph of me and Lee. I suppose in that way at least, we were the perfect match. Both are *versions* of love, after all. Just not healthy ones.

As Rick adjusts the positioning of his subjects and tells Simon to stop acting so tense, I spy a laughing couple on a nearby bench and wonder why we can't all love each other the right way? When it's good, it's so good. But when you're "wounded", and I include Beth in that category, the whole romantic arena just feels like a minefield, best avoided. No matter how endearing the suitor . . .

"Well," Simon clears his throat as we resume. "He's quoting poetry now so here goes:

" '*I saw you for a brief instant, floating before my eyes . . . the sight of you took hold in me like that dark stain rimmed with fire that blinds when looking at the sun.*' "

I feel for him. On the day that he writes, if not a love note, a love apology, he finds his words compared to one of Spain's most celebrated poets. All the while facing his genetic opposite.

And it's all my fault for volunteering him.

I'm just wondering whether I'll have to write my own apology letter when Lorenzo recalls another verse:

"Tears were welling in her eyes
Words of forgiveness were coming to my lips
Pride spoke and she dried her tears
And those words went unspoken.
I go one way, she goes another
But when I think of our mutual love,
I still say: Why didn't I speak that day?
And she: Why didn't I cry?"

I feel like I am watching the scene before me in slow motion — something intriguing is occurring in terms of eye contact. Lorenzo may be addressing Beth but as she looks to Simon for the translation, he looks beyond her to Lucy. Who in turn has to reach to stabilise herself on a nearby railing. After a few exchanges, I notice that Beth is barely turning back to her proposed dance partner at all. Her gaze is lingering on Simon . . .

"*Venido conmigo*." Lorenzo leads us around to the other side of the tree trunk, to a white marble sculpture of three women looking as if they are sitting on the sidelines of a grand ball — all corseted waists, full skirts and centre-parted ringlets.

"These show three stages of love," Simon explains.

Lorenzo points to the first — eyes watchful, hands raised to her cheek.

"Hopeful love."

Then to the second — eyes closed, hands clasped to her heart.

"Fulfilled love."

And finally to the third — face downcast, hands crossed in her lap.

"Lost love."

We heave a collective sigh. Who can't relate to that?

And then Lorenzo bows low and invites Beth to dance.

The guy's got great timing, I'll give him that.

As we prepare to move on to the dance setting, I hang back and take a quick snap of the three women as a visual reminder of my own transition from lost love to hopeful love. Before I came away, I wouldn't have thought such a thing was possible. Who knows, maybe there's even a chance that I can reach the elusive fulfilment stage this time?

I look for Dan, to see if any such ponderings are showing on his face, but he's busy managing a group of American students, curious to find out what we are filming. He gives them an animated description, pointing first to Beth and then to me. I give the group a little wave, thinking back to when I was young and how wide-eyed such a sight would have made me. The fact that I am now an element of the filming is really quite surreal to me.

I'm just glad that I don't now have to dance in front of them, as Beth and Lorenzo must do.

Of course, she's always thrived on having an audience and he turns out to be the consummate showman — as an opening gambit, he plucks a scarlet bloom and tucks it behind her ear. It's the perfect match for her slip-off-the-shoulder top. She lowers her lids and hitches up the layers of her white skirt, giving him a tantalising glimpse of toned thigh.

And so they begin.

This is a very different presentation to my twitchy encounter with Juan José Padilla. Beth does not flinch. No matter how hard Lorenzo stomps or how loud he heckles her as if baiting a bull. Though she has the power to face him down and match his ferocity, she chooses instead to counter his extreme masculinity with femininity of an almost balletic nature, especially in her high, skirt-fanning arcs and the extension of her arms. I remember the dance notes decreeing the woman must always go to the man but when Beth executes her seductive finger twirls, he comes towards her in a hypnotic trance. Only to be punished for her allure — he makes a fatal lunge and they conclude, as it seems all Paso Dobles must, with the kill.

The applause sends the sound needle way to the right.

Even Rick looks impressed.

And then a surprising thing happens — even though the American students are predominantly female, they begin clamouring for a solo performance from Beth.

Lorenzo is the first to endorse this. Rick gives his approval. But Beth falters.

"What shall I do for them? I can't Paso Doble by myself and I'm just faking the Flamenco."

"Do whatever you like."

This is a true gift — carte blanche — and yet still Beth seems uncharacteristically uncertain. "I have no music —"

"You can pick a song from my iPhone . . ." one of the teenage boys offers, clearly smitten. "There's over three thousand songs on there."

Beth starts flipping through the options, clearly feeling ever more pressured. But then she looks up at Simon. "Could you choose something for me?"

His face brightens. "I'd be honoured."

So dutiful is he in the process of his selection he doesn't even look up as she peels off her red top to reveal a white camisole and then sheds her ankle-length skirt in favour of my baby-pink pashmina. There's no mistaking the ballerina in her now. She wants to show them her training, her expertise, her grace.

I turn to Simon to give him the heads up but he's way ahead of me — already hooking up the iPhone to the sound equipment and opting for Beyoncé's ethereal *Halo*.

As the piano tinkles the opening bars, Beth begins with dainty steps and impeccable posture. The singer's voice lowers and so she performs a toe-sweeping arabesque. I expect her to keep it purely classical but it seems as though the words of the song are infiltrating her body — ideas of awakening, rules breaking, risks being taken . . . Her movements are becoming more fluid and responsive. Lyrical was never her style but now she is truly letting the sentiments motivate her to discover new shapes and expressions, blending contemporary dance with ballet and even incorporating a little Flamenco flair in her fingertips.

As the chorus chimes "halo-halo-halo," so she turns-turns-turns, executing three flawless pirouettes. She repeats this to dizzying effect, leading us down the pathway — the dappled light rippling over her body, making her seem all the more fleeting and mystical.

Just as Beyoncé speaks of being addicted to a person's light, she emerges back into full sunshine.

I think of how tragic and burdened Beth looked dancing Tango in the Pampas and how optimistic and winged of foot she looks now.

Especially as we reach a clearing with hundreds of white doves pecking at scattered seeds and bathing in shallow pools. She moves deftly among them *en pointe*. Then, as the song crescendos, so Beth leaps high and long, sending the doves flurrying skyward.

In the headphones, I hear the sound of their wings beating the warm air and the admiring gasp of the onlookers.

"*Que Linda*!" Lorenzo is mesmerised by the fluttering vision before him. "So beautiful!"

The music slows and she turns towards him, her face glowing.

Suddenly he's shaking off his heavily jewelled jacket and engaging Lucy's help in freeing him of his shirt and tie. Her hands are shaking as she reveals his gleaming, sculpted torso. His tight satin leggings have the appearance of ballet hose now his chest is bare. Despite the fact that I know Lucy would rather pull him into the nearest bush, she releases him to Beth.

Approaching with his arms outstretched, the music surges again and she knows instinctively to run towards him and he raises her up to the heavens, his arms bolt-straight and strong. He's spinning on the spot now, lowering her gradually so that she becomes part cape, part angelic apparition, floating above the earth.

When the song concludes, she is cradled in his arms, his brown hand hovering above her shimmering blonde hair. No kill, this time. Just a protective caress.

Once the performers have taken their deserving bows and posed for a series of photographs with the students, Simon hands Beth a single white feather. "A memento."

"Thank you." She curtsies before him.

"You looked like a barefoot angel out there."

"Is that what he said?" Beth looks towards the matador.

"Actually no." Simon pulls himself together. "He said you looked *hot*."

"*Muy caliente*!" Lorenzo jiggles his eyebrows provocatively.

As she grins back at her dance partner, I see Simon's shoulders slump in defeat. But I know Beth. I know what really matters to her most. Lorenzo may have the heaving chest and arms to carry her aloft, but that's nothing compared to a man who knows just the right song to play for her.

And if Simon looked up, instead of inspecting the dust on his shoes, he would see that Beth is now smiling at him.

CHAPTER TWENTY-FOUR

For a moment the world seems as picture-perfect and fragrant as the surrounding orange trees: Beth is back chatting with Simon, I am looking forward to my next secret assignation with Dan, Lorenzo is flirting ferociously with Lucy . . . And Rick is alone.

Ah yes, everything is as it should be.

For our last interview of the day, Rick decides we should make use of the Neo-Renaissance splendour of the Archaeological Museum, also within the park grounds. Hang on, did he say last interview of the day?

"Yes!" Rick confirms. "I don't want to see you girls until noon tomorrow."

"And we don't want to see you!" Beth cheers before pulling me off to the side.

"Listen, Simon has asked me to go with him on a riverside stroll. What do you think?"

"Sounds amiable enough."

"I agree," she says, curiously confident. "But what about you?"

My face brightens with mischief.

"Dan?" She raises a brow.

"Mmm-hmm!"

"Well, enjoy it! You deserve some fun!"

Fun, yes, but maybe a little less sangria. This time I want to be able to look him in the eyes between kisses and really register the emotion between us. I want to savour every sensation.

My tail is practically wagging as I sidle up to him to garner our rendezvous point.

"Sorry, babe," he grimaces. "Rick wants to review the footage and we could be looking at an all-nighter."

My tail sags. "Really?"

"It's a bastard, I know. Tomorrow?"

I nod bravely and then feel a lump forming in my throat. That's what you get for being too cocky. I feel myself on choppy seas again but then reassure myself this isn't one of my usual fob-offs — I really will see him tomorrow.

Maybe it's for the best anyway. I would have pushed through my exhaustion to be with him but this way I can get a good night's sleep and be extra fresh and alluring for our next encounter . . .

On the way back to the hotel, I admire the energetic conversations taking place at assorted tapas bars on *Calle Mateos Gago* and then dare myself to sit amongst the throng, pulling up a little wooden stool at *La Sacristia*. For once, I don't mind eating by myself because I know it's just temporary. "Don't pity me!" I want to say. "My man is just working late."

While awaiting my fried fish and *espinacas con garbanzos* (spinach and chickpeas — what was I thinking?), I get the chance to peruse the leaflets I picked up at the hotel this morning, including one for the Aire de Sevilla Arabian Bathhouse. How perfect is that — a tourist attraction and muscle soak in one! Twenty euros will buy me the ideal presleep activity and better yet it's just a pebble skim away . . .

The second I enter the sixteenth century palace with its trickly fountain and tranquil courtyard, I feel my inner zen unfurl.

Donning the equivalent of shower caps for my feet, I venture up the creaking staircase and along the balcony to the changing room to slip into my cossie and robe. I exhale even deeper as I enter a marble ante-room with its ancient lanterns casting geometric patterns on the mellow yellow walls.

Only whispers are permitted and after all the clattering of the day my ears enjoy the soothing hush.

A guide bids me pad forth down mysterious corridors to an assortment of water therapies, including a circular tub with jets as powerful as fire hoses and a darkly claustrophobic steam room that sends me skidding for relief into the gasp-inducing cool pool.

Ultimately I settle into a multi-chambered expanse of thermal water — so very welcoming and enveloping. I swish my hands back and forth, then let my feet slip from under me and float on my back, feeling the warm water lap at the contours of my face. I think of the kisses Dan placed on my cheeks and neck, and sigh. I wish kisses didn't evaporate. I wish there was some way of preserving them and re-experiencing them. All I can really do is look forward to the next.

Of course, anticipation is a wonderful thing but I have to say it's even better to look forward to something while you are actually enjoying the present moment. Just as I am thinking I couldn't feel any more fortunate, the water swells beneath me as some new guests enter the pool.

I open my eyes and spy an older couple edging in, hand-in-hand. Suddenly I see how far I have to go. Suddenly it's not enough to just have one night with Dan under my belt and another on the horizon; I long to be them — to have been married for twenty or forty years and have the closest thing to certainty that you will be together forever.

What must it be like to live without that precarious, on-edge uneasiness, fearing it could all be taken away from you in a moment? Does it ever really go away, I wonder? Of course it's ironic that the one person I felt wasn't going anywhere — i.e. Lee — was the one I most needed to separate from.

Tipping myself upright, I decide to swim over to a new nook in the hope of regaining my former contentment but a younger and decidedly frisky couple are obscuring my path. It seems almost seedy being in the same water as them as they canoodle — her legs clamped around his waist, his hands in her wet hair, pulling her closer, nuzzling deeper. Then again, maybe it's because I felt those sensations myself so recently that it seems particularly indecent to me. Either way, I'm mentally propelling them into the icy plunge pool when the girl arches backwards and the man stands to his full height.

I feel myself reeling backwards — it is unmistakably Dan.

CHAPTER TWENTY-FIVE

It's a good thing the water is supporting me because my legs have completely buckled. I see now that the girl with him is one of the American students who stopped to watch the filming earlier. The rushing in my head suggests I might faint but the shock proves too stinging to allow me to opt out. How is this possible — that man was supposed to be my salvation!

And then I realise that, though they have yet to see me, I am not an invisible onlooker — *I have to get out of here!*

Consumed by shame, I turn back to the steps and attempt to slide out on my belly, keeping the lowest possible profile as I slither towards the doorway. But then I catch sight of my low, low form in the sheen of the marble and ask myself, "Is this what a Flamenco dancer would do?"

That's when I stop. This is not my shame. It's his.

I feel a sense of outrage welling within me. Everything he said last night — all the excitable "*When we get back to London . . .*" promises. How could he lead me on so blatantly, knowing full well my situation? How *dare* he mess with me like this!

I have no skirt to swish, no nailed heels to stomp — my feet are bare, my body dripping. But still I rise up, roll back my shoulders, raise my jaw and place my hands on my hips, for once unapologetic about my body.

"I am *mujere*!" I tell myself as I turn back to face them down.

"Oh shit!" Dan releases the girl in a panic as he sees me.

Watching him flounder in the water, I feel a strange sense of satisfaction — I did it! Somehow I summoned a look that could make grown men weep! Maria would be so proud!

"Carmen, wait!" Dan tries to scramble up the steps after me but in his haste slips and goes down hard on the marble. Now he's the one flat on his belly.

He looks up to me for sympathy — the girl who's always there for her guy no matter what. But this time I make a different choice and exit, shrugging, "Love hurts!"

In the changing room, adrenaline gives way to disillusionment. The fantasy that I'd found a new kind of partner is over. I may have only had that fantasy for a few days but the euphoria was so heady and hopeful I can't believe it wasn't real. Didn't we seem like such a good match? Didn't it make sense? I feel so duped — he came to *me* with all that crap. I was minding my own business and he charmed me, made me believe. What was he thinking? Was he just telling me what he thought I wanted to hear? All the talk of the fun we were going to have together, was that simply a ploy to get me thinking we had a future and thus make me more receptive to his physical advances? Could he really be that conniving?

I am dumbfounded. What is the point, really, in deceiving women like that? There was enough stuff to enjoy in the moment, I didn't need the pretty lies and he didn't need to tell them.

"Wounded love and love that wounds," I repeat to myself, thinking just how apt a caption that is for us right now.

So what next? On the most practical of levels, I want to know how the hell I'm going to get through the rest of the shoot with this guy literally in my face all day long?

I sit down on the wooden bench, curious as to why I'm not crying when I sense a presence behind me.

It's the girl from the pool.

"So, just to be clear," she begins, "that guy had a thing going with you too?"

I nod.

"Damn!" she curses. "I could have sworn my taste was getting better!"

I give a hapless snuffle. "Me too!"

For a few minutes we share a companionable silence.

"You know, they do really good mint tea here?" she offers.

"Do they?" is all I can manage.

"I think we should have some. I'm Kelly, by the way."

⋆ ⋆ ⋆

Still in our robes, she leads me out onto the white-washed terrace overlooking the cathedral, now glowing gold with its night lights. Our tea is poured from an elongated silver spout into petite engraved glasses. We chink and take a sip of the sweetened mint. I always wondered what it would be like to join forces with a fellow Woman Scorned but instead of plotting further revenge — Kelly reckons Dan may have already done himself some lasting damage in the fall — she gives her take on why men do these things.

"Well, first and foremost, it's because they can. They'll say anything in the moment to get their needs met. Whatever it takes."

"But don't they feel guilty about doing that?"

She shakes her head. "Hedonists don't have well-developed consciences. They are too busy seeking the next stimulus to get around to any navel-gazing."

"How old are you?" I ask, wondering how someone so fresh-faced got to be so knowing.

"Twenty-three," she tells me, with this caveat: "I'm a psychology major."

"Ohhhhh!" I nod. And then I tilt my head. "So you knew what you were getting into with Dan?"

"It's my last night in Seville," she shrugs. "I just wanted to have some fun."

"That's how they get you . . ." I mumble.

She smiles kindly. "Am I sensing a hint of romantic disillusionment?"

I look into her clear eyes and wonder if there's a chance she can offer any psychological insight into the questions that continue to plague me regarding Lee:

How did a girl like me end up in a relationship like that? Why do I still feel so attached? What can I do to stop myself a) going back or b) repeating the pattern with someone new?

"Well, I do have a few theories about the attachment aspect, if you're interested?"

"Go on," I encourage.

"Here's the key factor — almost no abuser is mean or frightening all the time. I'm sure you found your guy was at least occasionally gentle and loving with you, maybe even humorous?"

"Absolutely!" I nod.

"Well, intermittent kindness is critical to forming traumatic bonding," she continues. "When you experience harsh treatment over an extended period you naturally feel a flood of love and gratitude towards anyone who brings relief. But here's the kicker: in abusive situations, *the rescuer and the tormentor are the very same person.*"

I shudder in recognition. "That actually makes a lot of sense. A bit like Stockholm Syndrome?"

"Exactly like that," she confirms.

I shake my head. "All this time I thought it was just low self-esteem."

"You'd be surprised at the number of super-confident if not mouthy women this happens to. Sometimes I almost think the guy gets a bigger thrill out of dominating a woman with a bit of spirit to her."

"I never thought of it that way." Maybe I'm not as weak as I thought. "Have you had this too?"

She nods. "For me, the worst thing was the daily confusion — my every waking moment was spent puzzling over his behaviour. And that's what he wanted: all my energy directed towards him, leaving nothing for me." She sits up a little straighter. "But you know the one good thing about having had that experience? You start to notice the tell-tale signs a lot earlier on . . ."

For the next hour we compare horror stories and — shocker — even start to laugh at some of the absurdities of our former situations.

"I can't believe talking about something so horrible has put me in such a good mood," I marvel. "I'm feeling this huge sense of relief."

"The truth will set you free," she grins.

I smile back at her. "You know, this evening could have gone a very different way." I think of how I felt when I first saw her with Dan. "I wish there was some way I could thank you, other than paying for this tea," I say as I summon the bill.

"Well, there is one thing . . ."

"Anything. Seriously."

"Teach me how to do that look you gave Dan," she begs. "The one that brought him to his knees — that was fierce!"

"My pleasure!" I cheer.

Deciding it loses a little something in flip-flops, I strap on my Flamenco shoes to give Kelly the full effect.

"That's it!" she claps, mimicking my strut and stance. "From now on, I'm going to be unapologetically *Spanish!*"

As we hug goodbye, she grimaces, "I'm just sorry you've got to suffer the rest of the shoot with that fool."

"Oh, don't worry about that," I snort. "I'm barely even angry at him any more — if not for him, we'd never have had this conversation!"

I linger a while after she's gone, thinking that I'll change back into my other shoes but then I decide against it. I need to register how it feels to walk through life with impact, to turn heads and own the sound of my clacking heels. I'm used to tiptoeing so softly, no wonder I felt like no one was there to back me up. Now there's me and my attitude to contend with. Me and my feminine strength. Me and my determination not to be walked all over.

As my heels click on the cobbled streets under a starlit sky, I am filled with a strange calm. Suddenly I know exactly how I'm going to get through the rest of the shoot — *with dignity!*

CHAPTER TWENTY-SIX

I'm lying on my back, looking at the wood-beamed ceiling, still mildly in awe of the major shift that took place last night.

When I reach for my water on the bedside table, Beth whispers, "You awake?"

"Yes." I turn to her, pleased to have her company.

"You look different." She tilts her head in assessment.

"So do you," I reply, noting that her face seems softer somehow, less guarded. Until, that is, she asks this question: "Did you see Dan?"

"I did," I reply with a sigh. "But not quite in the way I was expecting."

"Was he with another girl?"

"How did you know?" I blink back at her.

"Oh, Carmen!" She scoots up in bed. "Simon told me all sorts of stories about him last night — how his nickname is Dan Juan because he's all about the conquest — I was so worried about you!"

"Well," I take a breath, "it actually worked out perfectly."

As I give her a summary of all that occurred, her face switches from horror to defiance to commiseration to fascination and ultimately to triumph.

"So it really was meant to be!" she marvels. "I was feeling so bad, thinking that if I hadn't been giving Simon the silent treatment I might have found out the truth about Dan earlier and then I could have warned you . . ."

I shake my head. "It's fine."

"Really?"

"Honestly," I insist. "It's like some kind of exorcism has taken place — Lee is no longer inhabiting my body!"

"That's it!" Beth snaps her fingers. "That's what's different — you look like yourself again!" She reaches over and gives me a big congratulatory hug. "It's just a pain that we have to carry on seeing Dan."

"I know," I concur. "You know the thing that's bothering me the most is having to perform the Flamenco routine solo in front of him . . ." I shudder. "I don't want him to see me at a disadvantage. I want to stay feeling strong."

"What time is the class again?"

"Noon."

"And what time is it now?"

I turn and look at the bedside clock. "8a.m."

With that, Beth throws back the covers. "Come on, let's get rehearsing!"

I can't help but snort. "I don't think the rooms below would thank us —"

"We're not doing it here," she cuts me off. "We're going to the river."

"The river?"

"There's something there I want to show you . . ."

* * *

The milky green Guadalaquivir looks so beguiling with its borders of bougainvillea and assorted palms I'm surprised that Christopher Columbus felt so compelled to sail for the new world from here! Personally I'd be perfectly content with the distance travelled by one of the shiny white riverboat cruisers, currently snoozing at their moorings.

"There's something calming about being beside water, don't you think?" Beth muses as we roll along parallel. "The flow reminding us to keep moving forward."

She then contradicts herself by telling the driver to stop. Right beside the bullring.

"*Really?*" I frown.

"Look across the street," Beth instructs me.

"Another statue?" I can't hide my dismay. That's all I need.

She takes my hand and scuttles me over to it. "Read the plaque."

"Carmen. *Carmen!*" I gasp. "It's me!"

Beth laughs. "I think in all Lucy's rushing around she forgot about this major connection."

I step back to inspect the woman who inspired Bizet's hot-blooded opera. Instead of a Salma Hayek type busting from a bodice, I find a relatively plain figure in a drab skirt and heavily fringed shawl. "She doesn't exactly look a wild gypsy temptress."

"Well, maybe her appeal was more apparent when she was in motion — the most ordinary woman can become provocative with the right walk."

Beth demonstrates this theory, looking like an early-rising streetwalker as she leads us down to the riverside.

"Your turn!" she dares me.

I'm trying to look bold and enticing but fear I more closely resemble Jack Sparrow out for a stagger.

"I know what you need!" Beth sets out her iPod and speakers. "Simon added this for me last night — it's *Habanera*, kind of like Carmen's theme."

"I know this!" I chuckle at the minxish opening.

"Come on then! Put some seduction in that sashay!" Beth urges me to be ever more brash to the point that it actually starts being fun.

"Now I know why people love appearing in panto!" I laugh.

I don't even mind when we get whistled at from a passing boat.

"Gotcha!" Beth gets serious as the song comes to an abrupt end. "Now I want you to put that attitude into your routine."

I take a rousing breath. I can do this.

"Go!" Beth cues me.

I begin clapping. And then slapping. And then stomping.

"Come on!" Beth rallies. "There's no one here to wake but the fish!"

"I really don't think all this is good for your knees."

"*Harder!*" She overrides my concern.

Gradually I start to notice a transition. As the steps become second nature I am able to shift my focus to improving my posture, then the positioning of my arms, then the rotation of my wrists . . .

Still Beth bays for more. “More passion! More flair! More Carrrrmen!” She rolls her “r”s before calling, “Again! From the top!”

By the time we’re done, I’ve worked up such a sheen it’s all I can do to stop myself from teetering over the edge and sploshing into the water.

“You worked hard this morning,” Beth acknowledges as she hands me a bottle of water from her bag. “Well done.”

I’m too busy glugging to respond.

“You know, I’ve just remembered something very apt that Simon told me last night.” Beth bids me sit beside her. “We were talking about the gypsy culture and he said that because their community is so close, when couples split they will inevitably have to see each other again on an almost daily basis — it’s not like London where they disappear into the masses — so they have to find a way to be civil around their ex.”

“Just as I will have to with Dan.”

“Not that he deserves it,” she clarifies. “But for the sake of the community.”

“Right.” I take on board what she has said and then look back at her. “You do realise you haven’t told me anything about what you two got up to last night!”

“Oh, there’s not much to tell.” She looks away but not quick enough to hide her creeping smile.

“Beth! Spill!” I give her a playful jolt.

She looks back at me with compassion. “I’m sure you don’t want to hear about it now.”

I sigh. "Or maybe now is the best time! Maybe it's absolutely vital that I hear about something good happening between a man and a woman."

She holds my gaze for a minute and then shrugs shyly. "Well, I mean, it's not like we kissed or anything."

"At least tell me how it felt to be alone with him!"

She thinks for a moment and then frowns. "Strangely comfortable! You know, I wouldn't have expected that to be possible after what happened but he really didn't seem to have an agenda, other than walking and talking and enjoying the sunset."

With a little more prompting, she reveals that they stopped off at a riverside bar with little wooden rowboats dragged upon the shore as seating. As she describes how they lay back on the cushions, gazing up at the stars, speaking of places they would like to drift off to, I can't deny my pang of jealousy. Or is it just longing? Longing to be attracted to a good person. Longing to attract someone who would row me towards my dreams not throw me overboard in favour of the first mermaid we encounter . . .

"You know one of the greatest pleasures of being with him?" Beth continues. "The fact that he wasn't *scrutinising* me the whole time."

I tap her with the empty water bottle. "I've never thought about this before but it's funny how you are happy to have an entire auditorium watching your every move but when one man really looks at you —"

"It makes me squirm!" Her body crumples inward. "I know."

I cock my head to one side. "Maybe it's because you are 'performing' to the crowd but when it's one-on-one, it's just you."

"There is that," she concedes. "But more than anything it's the *way* men look at me: I either feel like they're only humouring me until we have sex or, on the rare occasion I actually like them, it just feels like another form of auditioning!" She strokes the petals of a fallen blossom. "It didn't feel like that with Simon."

I smile knowingly. "That's because with him you've already got the job!"

Back at the hotel, I let Beth have the bathroom first, keen to just lie flat out for a minute or two. As I kick off my shoes, I have one of my once-in-a-blue-moon inclinations to contact my father. Texting is the only surefire way to get a response — the brevity and impersonal nature suiting him well. I take out my phone and type: "Today I saw a statue of my namesake in her city of birth!"

He taps back straightaway. "What are you doing in Brooklyn?"

What? I frown at the screen.

"I'm in Seville, Spain," I reply.

"You're not named after that Carmen. Your mother was a big fan of Rita Hayworth."

I'm fearing senility has snagged him when he follows up with: "Formerly Margarita Carmen Cansino."

I can't help but smile. I never knew that!

"Have to go now. Race is about to start."

My heart sinks. That's it?

I bat away disappointment by quickly typing, "May your greyhound's nose be first past the finishing line!" and then reach for my laptop and Google Rita Hayworth.

I get so little chance to feel close to my mother but now I devour the online information as if the words are coming from her own secret diary. What was it about this particular movie star of the Forties that resonated with my own flesh and blood? Why her over say, Lana Turner or Jane Russell?

As my eyes dart around the screen, I see that my dad is right about her real name and that, highly coincidentally, she once made a Seville-set film called *The Loves of Carmen*, taking the title role. Better yet, her father was a renowned Flamenco dancer from Seville!

"Whaddayaknow?" I smile to myself as I scan through the list of her other movies from *Gilda* to *Pal Joey*. And then I read the description of *You Were Never Lovelier* with Fred Astaire. "Lavish musical set in Buenos Aires!"

How about that. All I need now is a movie set in Cuba and I've got the complete set. Scouting around I actually find that in *You'll Never Get Rich* — her other Astaire musical — the two of them dance in front of a painted backdrop featuring the famous Malecón seawall in Havana! What's that phrase, close but no cigar? I'd say this is close enough with a big aromatic Cuban one!

I'm bursting to tell Beth of these quirky coincidences, feeling as though this trip is somehow fulfilling a destiny of which I was hitherto oblivious, but her shower is still raging. So I move on to reading about Rita's personal life. And this is where things get way more intense. She was married five times: her first husband was a domineering older man who became her manager but left her penniless. She divorced Prince Aly Khan on grounds of extreme mental cruelty. Her fourth husband, Argentine singer Dick Haymes, reportedly struck her face in public at the Cocoanut Grove nightclub in LA. Her fifth and final marriage was to a film producer named James Hill. Once again, mental cruelty was at play, confirmed by Charlton Heston in his autobiography. Heston and his wife joined the couple for dinner in a restaurant in Spain while he was filming *El Cid*. He describes how Hill subjected the woman known in Hollywood as the "Love Goddess" to "obscene abuse" until she was "reduced to a helpless flood of tears, her face buried in her hands." Heston went so far as to call it a "marital massacre" and said he was "strongly tempted to slug him" but instead took his own extremely upset wife home. He concluded by saying, "I'm ashamed of walking away from Miss Hayworth's humiliation. I never saw her again."

I can feel my heart pounding. Strange that I feel so protective of a woman I have never met. I want to steam in where Charlton Heston didn't and —

"Carmen, are you all right?" Beth looks wary as she steps back into the bedroom.

"It has to stop," I tell her. "This ridiculous battle between men and women."

Before I can expand further, the phone rings.

It's Lucy, letting us know that we need to show up for the day's filming in full Flamenco regalia.

Though Beth feels that the look has been done, I welcome the chance to get back into my polka-dot armour, all the better to connect with my warrior alter ego.

To aid the transformation, I give myself a precision middle parting, a voluminous yet sleek bun and groove a hair comb into place. Leaning closer to the mirror, I apply black kohl, false lashes and red lipstick. No sepia face for me today. I then trade accessories with Beth — her blue with my white — so that she feels her look is fresh.

"Ready?" Beth enquires as we prepare to greet the team.

I nod, only to turn and slam straight into Dan.

"My God!" I gasp as I behold the grotesque purple bruising around his jaw. "You look like you've been slugged by Charlton Heston!"

Not exactly the comment he was expecting to hear.

Even Beth gives me a quizzical look, deciding it's best to hustle me onwards, in the direction of another altered face . . .

With so much having happened since we last saw Lucy in the park, I'd forgotten we'd left her flirting with Lorenzo. There is, however, no need to ask whether the pair of them got it on — her eyes are glazed and her fingers twirling a small gold tassle.

"You little devil — is that a love bite?" Beth blurts as we get closer.

"What?" Lucy's hand flies to her neck. "I thought I'd covered it up."

"That is not a job for concealer alone," I pronounce as I take off my fringed shawl and style it accordingly.

"Now if we could just do something about that sex-drenched look in your eyes!" Beth teases.

Lucy quickly slots on her sunglasses and tries to look businesslike as Rick joins us. "Right!" She clears her throat. "Slight change of plan for today — Maria has arranged something special for us."

"What kind of special?" I can't help but feel a little uneasy.

Special means different. Special means something other than a class at the Flamenco museum. Something other than what I am prepared for.

"She wants you to experience a *tablao* performance."

"A what now?" Beth frowns.

"It's basically a Flamenco show with live music. Better yet, we get to eat while we're watching."

Watching! Ah, heaven! Back where I belong!

"Isn't life funny?" I ponder as Beth links arms with me. "It seems that whenever you are genuinely prepared to face your worst fears, suddenly you don't have to."

El Arenal has one of those "knock three times and whisper a password" doorways. I've seen a few of the other Flamenco venues in passing — one quiet, ivy-draped courtyard and the rowdy former coal bunker that is La Carboneria, but this place is a vision of old world sophistication with its immaculately laid tables and Andalucian artwork, including several bronze figurines. There are no coach groups here, just well-dressed families and couples. I only hope we're not going to lower the tone with our TV presence. I have a horrible feeling that the front and centre table marked RESERVADO is for us.

I'm looking for Lucy to check on the plan when I see a familiar face, one I barely recognise without his tassels . . .

"Lorenzo!" Lucy gasps as she too spots him.

"*Hola, mi amor*!" he growls with unmistakable lust.

"What are you doing here?"

"I wanted to see you." Simon translates.

His directness silences her for a moment. "Oh-oh, well, the thing is, I'm working —"

"*Debo estar cercano a usted*."

"I have to be near you."

Her mouth opens and closes. She looks anxiously towards Rick who surprises us all by striding over and welcoming Lorenzo with open arms.

"Nice work, Lucy," he winks at her.

"Excuse me?" She flushes. Does he know?

"This guy is getting us the most You Tube hits so far! And that's just from the preview clip that went out last night! I was going to ask you if we could get another session with him but I see you're already on it."

"On it! Under it! At it!" Beth giggles in my ear.

As Rick adds, "Try and get his shirt off again if you can!" we have to turn away to disguise our mirth.

"It's a good thing we're leaving tonight," Lucy puffs as he strides on his way. "I couldn't stand much more of this!"

"*We're leaving?*" Beth and I chorus in shock.

"So soon?" I add with a definite pang.

"The show is doing so much better than ETV expected so they want us to finish up early in Spain so we can stop off in London for a press conference."

"As in being interviewed by professional journalists?" I blanche.

"It's such a great opportunity to boost our viewing figures for the Salsa section," Lucy explains. "It'll just be the newspapers and radio and maybe a couple of the weekly magazines that go to press the next day."

While Beth is no doubt thinking of popping flashbulbs and front-page splashes, I'm imagining terrifying interrogations. I mean, if I was going to present myself to the nation I'd like to come across as one of those breezy, got-it-together people not the work-in-progress I am right now.

Beth clicks her fingers in front of my eyes. "Oh no you don't!"

"What?"

"Don't go to that place! Don't ruin your last few hours here worrying about what is coming next."

She's right. If anything, I need to be even more present — tomorrow I could be tested on my Flamenco knowledge and I want to do justice to this dance that has already given so much to me.

I take a heartening breath — if all I have is now, then I'd better make it count.

CHAPTER TWENTY-SEVEN

They say that to have the full Flamenco experience you need to be close enough to become anointed with sweat from the dancer's brow and to feel the juddering of the floorboards beneath their feet.

Seeing as our tabletop is actually aligned with the stage, I'm predicting our dish of pimiento olives will be dancing like Mexican jumping beans in no time.

"How exciting is this?" Beth attempts to supercharge me with her pep.

"So very!" I give an exaggerated grin, aware that Dan's camera is trained on me.

It's bad enough when you're at the same party as an ex, trying to look like you're having a ball every time he glances over, but here there's just no let up!

Fortunately the musicians have me at the first strum of that magically melodic Spanish guitar. Then come the singers with their triple-speed clapping — a stop-starty beat so fiendish and ever-changing I find myself tutting, "You just can't clap along like you can at a Neil Diamond concert."

The truth is, I love the enigmatic quality of this music, particularly the deep-smoked vocals — so raw and charged and gut-wrenching they resemble an invocation.

"I wonder which came first?" Beth whispers across to me. "Do you sing Flamenco because you have a natural hoarseness to your voice or do the songs themselves cause the laryngitis effect?"

I don't know but there's certainly a lot of straining involved — one man looks like he is trying to contain a fit — his body twitching and spasming as he expels every last bit of anguish from his soul.

"You can really hear the Arabian influence in the wailing, can't you?"

I beckon Simon over and ask him to translate a random line for me so I can get an insight into the agony I just witnessed. I'm rather surprised when he says, "When she walks, cinnamon and roses fall to the ground."

But maybe he's just talking about Beth again.

As the dancers file onto the stage, so platters start arriving at our table — principally a series of mystery bite-size appetisers. After Beth's unfortunate encounter with the bull's testicles, I'm nervous about popping a whole nibble in my mouth so I go to cut a taster piece, only for my knife to slip, sending the toasted base ricocheting onto the stage.

"Nooo!" I blanche at my culinary clumsiness.

"Don't worry." Beth dismisses my concern. "They'll crunch that underfoot, just be grateful it wasn't one of these smooshy white asparagus spears or we'd have a dancer down."

As the footwork gets more frantic, I can't help but think what a wonderful job they'd do at tenderising meat.

That said, I'm really not sure eating is compatible with Flamenco — it's pretty nerve-racking being so close to the machine gun fire of heels, I can feel my stomach agitating, in no mood for digestion. Worse yet, when the dancer with the long acrylic nails moves forward and strikes a dramatic pose at the edge of the stage, I see her nostrils flare wildly, inhaling my just-delivered fish dish. I almost expect her to look down and enquire, "Seabass?"

It's a relief when the meal is done and we can concentrate on the dancing.

Or more specifically, the facial expressions that accompany it: one woman seems to be doing Lamaze-style childbirth breathing with her mouth in an O shape. Another prefers to clench her jaw down, the bite-release synchronising with her footwork.

"I've never heard of keeping time with your teeth before." I blink.

"They are definitely a very rhythmical people."

Also very supportive. I remember Maria telling me that Flamenco has four key elements: *cante* (voice), *toque* (guitar), *baile* (dance) and *jaleo*, which roughly translates as "hell raising" but basically comprises "handclapping, foot-stomping and *shouts of encouragement*."

When fellow performers call out "*allez*!" it's almost as if they're saying, "Oh, I *know*! I know just how you feel!" It puts me in mind of the cocktail chats Beth and

I have — the way that when we dare to reveal something we think makes us peculiar or emotionally-stunted and then the other squeals "Me too!" we actually get giddy with excitement.

"Wow, look at this guy go!" Beth gasps as a sinewy fellow in a cravat rivals the women's *tour de force* performances, whipping himself into such a frenzy that his sweat does indeed fly from his brow and spatter those of us in the front row. You'd think he'd shed his jacket but instead he lifts up its tails, rather in the way the women hoik up their skirts to direct attention to their feet. Not that his jacket tails are obscuring his footwork but I suppose it's symbolic — focus not on my now-liquid hair or the ferocity in my eyes, instead lower your gaze to where my legs are going like the clappers.

My ears are seriously shocked by the clattering his heels produce — the aural equivalent of having your knuckles rapped with a wooden ruler. I look back to see whether Simon is wincing beneath his headphones and notice that Dan is now using Lucy's shoulder as a prop for his camera, obviously having trouble holding it up himself. Interesting. I wonder what other bruises are veiled by his clothes?

"Not often karma kicks in that quickly," Beth notes with a wink and then draws my attention back to the stage with the words: "And for the grand finale, a grand dame!"

Until now, all the female dancers have had raven hair, primary-coloured outfits and perfect pear-drop bottoms. This *señora* is considerably older with dark gold hair and a dress of lustrous lavender, atypically fluid in silk. Even her make-up has forgone the signature black liquid liner for an iridescent shimmer and she is the only one with painted nails — all the better to bewitch us with her fingertips . . .

I don't know what style of Flamenco she is channelling but it has a different feel and I find myself mesmerised as she flips and swishes her frilly Godzilla tail and then breaks out the castanets to such wondrous clickity-clickity effect she almost seems to be making them purr. The tall, white-bearded singer looks equally entranced, all but bowing his respect.

I suppose I would normally have commented on her magnetic stage presence but Beth tells me that in the Flamenco world a transcendental performance is attributed to "*duende*" — hard to define but loosely translated as "spirit". Rather than inducing the *Bravo!* reaction you might find at the ballet, it's more akin to the audience member getting a "someone just walked over my grave" shiver. We've seen the male performers juddering their bodies like pneumatic drills in pursuit of this phenomenon, but I prefer this woman's worldly sensuality. She doesn't seem so wracked and ruined by life as the others — it's as if she's matured beyond railing against the world and reached a wiser, more knowing level. But then again, maybe she couldn't have got to that stage without years of this emotional exorcism?

It really does seem that Flamenco has a "better out than in" mentality. And apparently Beth and I are about to find out just how therapeutic this can be.

"Please tell me Maria did not just beckon us to join her on stage!" I gurgle, horrified.

"Oh wow, we're going to perform with live musicians — what an honour!" Beth is already leading the way.

I knew I was naive to think we were going to get away with just watching and eating this afternoon. As I take my first step on stage, I wonder if this poor audience know what they are about to let themselves in for? Despite all my feverish practising this morning, something tells me I'd be better off if they handed me a guitar.

And then there's the thought of Dan watching. I'd like to smear the last of my orange mousse on his camera lens but the waiter has just cleared our table.

"Can Beth do it with me?" I plead, confident she'll have the routine locked down from this morning's observation alone.

"All three of us dance!" Maria declares.

"Oh, thank God!"

"After you have performed solo."

Oh no, no, no. I'm desperately fighting waves of panic, wondering how on earth I'm going to carry off "feisty" when my whole body is shaking.

"Just close your eyes," Beth recommends. "Forget about Dan and everyone else in the room and imagine yourself back at the riverside."

I am about to take her advice when I catch the eye of the lavender *señora*. Something about the penetratingly confident look she gives me prompts a radical decision to go the other way . . .

Instead of blocking out Dan, I multiply him, picturing a line up of every man I've ever humiliated myself over/begged to love me/pursued after they rejected me/carried on dating even though I knew it was wrong-wrong-wrong.

The last time they saw me, I was crying or pleading or trying to finagle "one more chance". Now I want them to see me strong and self-assured. I want to change the feeling I have when I think of them. I want to let go of the shame and trust that I won't behave like that again.

To that group, I add a couple of Rita Hayworth's husbands.

And then, finally, my father.

Hearing the live hand-clapping and knowing it is for me gets my heart thumping in an altogether more positive way. When the singer starts rasping, it is as if his voice is emanating from within me. And so my feet dare to begin.

"*Hassar!*" Beth cheers at my first sassy hip swivel.

My heels clack, my shoulders switch and my hands have finally found some flexibility. Before I know it, I've gone beyond the routine — my feet tantrumming as they summon all my leftover self-pity and purge it from my body. I don't even know what steps I'm doing but I'm no longer afraid.

As the song ends and the audience surprise me with their rousing applause, I experience a sensation I barely recognise — a big, chest-swelling, chin-raising, eye-flashing burst of pride!

CHAPTER TWENTY-EIGHT

When I awake to grey skies, English accents and the smell of bacon, I think for a minute that the whole thing has been an elaborate dream.

But then I see the castanets hanging from the bedpost and remember how, following our flight from Seville to London last night, Beth and I were shuttled directly to a West End hotel so there could be no chance of us being late for the press day ETV have planned.

Apparently, the morning will be spent doing photo-shoots and interviews, then at 3p.m. there will be a press conference in the ballroom.

"Bucks Fizz?" Beth holds out a champagne flute to me.

"Is this wise?" I ask, still in a daze though we are now up and dressed and contemplating the breakfast buffet.

"Well, it's sitting right here and if anyone needs a little Dutch courage, it's us."

"What are you nervous about?" I frown at Beth. "I thought you'd be raring to go!"

"I was until it occurred to me that I could be in for a lynching — I am the liar, remember? The deceiver! The thin girl in the fat suit!"

"Ooh, that's not good," I grant.

"I know ETV are trying to spin it as 'the forgotten dancer's last chance' but really this could go either way. At least you're the innocent one."

"Hardly!" I snort, jabbing a sausage onto my plate. "I made that fat suit, modelled it on my own body, if you recall! Not that I was even fretting about that until now . . ."

My concern grows when I see just how we are being portrayed in the photo-shoots — Beth in all her shimmering glory, raised up on a podium, with me kneeling at her feet, stitching her hem. This is of course a familiar pose for me but I wonder if the stylist had to go quite so frumpy with my outfit.

"Do you have anything a little less drab?"

I feel like I spoke too soon come the next scenario — this time they have me in full-tilt ballroom — canary-yellow feathers and billowing lemon chiffon sleeves with gobstopper pink lips. Meanwhile, Beth is essentially a spray-tanned babe in a bedazzled bikini.

"I look like Dame Edna standing next to you!" I despair.

"Last one before the interviews," Lucy urges me to hang in there.

As Beth is shoe-horned into skin-tight satin to play a female matador, I have a flare of hope.

"You know I actually have my own Flamenco dress?" I offer.

But they have a better idea: I get to play the bull, complete with nose ring.

"I'm starting to get a very particular idea about how I am being perceived," I mumble to Beth as we take a donut break.

"Well, bear in mind that the people who came up with these concepts have yet to see your Flamenco extravaganza from last night."

"That's true."

"If they'd witnessed that then they'd have you dressed in red PVC with flames coming off your feet."

I chuckle at the image.

"Besides, you wouldn't want to play the dollybird, would you?"

I shake my head. "I'd just like to be a better version of me."

As Beth peels off her false eyelashes, she sighs, "Can you imagine what it would be like to be happy with yourself, just as you are?"

I tilt my head as I assess her mood change.

"I always thought that if I were ever the girl being photographed for a magazine I would feel differently than I do right now."

"How did you think you'd feel?"

"As perfect as I appear to look!" she smiles. "I thought my inner critics would be silenced forever."

"But they're still yapping?"

"As a matter of fact, they're gloating. They're saying that I've been wasting all these years chasing an illusion when the joy of dance was always there for the taking, I was just too hung up on seeing my name in lights to know it."

"Is that your phone?" I inadvertently ruin her profound moment.

She reaches for her bag. "It's Simon," she beams at the display. "Just wanting to know how we're getting on."

"That's sweet."

She nods. "It's nice knowing someone out there is thinking of you."

"Yes, it is. It's one of the best bits. The little reminders throughout the day that you are not alone."

"See, you know that. I don't."

"Well, I know it in theory —"

"No. You've experienced this!" She holds her phone up to me. "You put yourself out there. You got involved." She hangs her head and then reaches for my hand. "I'm sorry for being so down on you about putting up with Lee so long. I had no idea how much you were having to let go of."

"Oh, Beth!" I give her a teary-eyed hug, grateful for her understanding.

"Okay, ladies. Time to meet the press."

The interviews go pretty much according to plan. We've had so much practice describing our feelings that trotting out soundbites has become the norm. As for my issue with "telling the truth", it dawns on me that I was never supposed to be perfect in the first place. Besides, I find the women journalists in particular to be more sympathetic than scathing and instead of dwelling on my bad choices with men they seem keen to use them as a springboard for a little education.

"So what potentially abusive warning signs would you tell girls to look out for when they start dating a new guy?"

I actually feel prepared to answer this following my Arabian mint tea chat with Kelly.

"It all seems to begin with disrespect," I tell her. "If he puts you down, sneers at your opinions or is rude to you in front of other people — these are major red flags. Also, if he has a negative attitude to women in general: does he talk about his ex-girlfriends in a degrading or condescending way? If everything was always this other woman's fault, pretty soon you will be the one to blame in this new relationship." I take a sip of water and continue, on a bit of a roll now. "You also want to watch for signs of controlling behaviour. This can start with subtle comments about how you dress, your weight, your friends, etc. Often he will give too much advice on how to manage your life and then get impatient when you resist his recommendations."

"Possessiveness?" one woman suggests.

"Yes, definitely. Though Lee wasn't particularly that way. He did however fit with the trait of rushing into planning a future together. Obviously, in a world full of commitment-phobes, this can seem really flattering but if he won't respect your wish to slow down a little, there is usually trouble ahead."

"You sound quite the guru now!" a younger woman teases.

"Well, I've done some pretty intense training on this topic!" I chuckle, amazed that I can now joke about such things.

"Is there one thing to beware of above all else?"

"I would say intimidation — if he towers over you or shouts you down. If he gets too close to you when he's angry, pushes you or blocks your way or restrains you. If he punches walls or kicks doors or throws things, even if they don't hit you. Basically anything he does that makes you flinch or feel afraid."

"Like undoing your seatbelt while reckless driving?"

"That's a definite no-no," I confirm.

"Or a GO! GO!" one of the guys quips.

"Exactly," I confirm. "Of course, it's easier said than done when emotions are concerned but knowledge is power. The more you know about the characteristics of abuse, the looser its grip."

This clearly isn't enough for one older woman. "You still need closure," she decrees. "I've already spoken to Rick about you facing Lee in person while you're in town."

"Oh no, no, no!" I protest. "That is not a good idea."

"See!" she toots. "You are still afraid of seeing him."

"With good reason!" I snort. "The man has some kind of weird power over me. Or at least he used to. Either way, I don't want to risk being in his presence again. I don't know what might happen. And please don't write that. I don't want anyone getting the wrong idea."

"So how do you feel about meeting someone new?" A male journalist mercifully moves things along.

"Honestly? I feel massive trepidation. The thought of something going wrong again . . ." My voice quavers. "But at the same time," I pause, thinking of Simon and Beth to get me back on track, "I still have faith that true love exists and that when the right two people come together, they can really bring out the best in each other. That is what I am striving for now — love that raises you up!"

* * *

"How was it for you?" I ask Beth when we are reunited.

She rolls her eyes. "All the women wanted to know was why I didn't get it on with the dancing matador and how they could get in touch with him."

"Really?"

Beth nods. "I think the chick from *Cosmo* wants to get him for their Naked Men issue."

"What about the men?"

"One guy asked if I was planning on having any tropical romances in Cuba and, if so, could they actually capture it on film this time."

"Oh gross."

"And then this other guy told me that he sees me as a blonde Catherine Zeta-Jones and insisted I could totally take Hollywood by storm."

"Well, that's very complimentary."

"Then he asked if it was true that I used to be a stripper."

"Oh dear."

"It's okay — any publicity is good publicity, right?"

"Right!" Rick confirms, looming in the doorway of the dressing room. "We just need you to make one last outfit change before the press conference."

"Here we go!" I brace myself, knowing that if anyone is going to end up with a turban of tropical fruit on their head, it's going to be me.

But then Rick hands Beth a scoop-neck leotard, black fishnets and a gold belt, and I get a pair of pastel pink shorts and a matching top.

Beth and I look at each other and then back at the clothes.

"Are you thinking what I'm thinking?"

When Beth's hair is styled in voluminous waves and mine is side-parted and curled, our suspicions are confirmed.

"So if you're Penny . . ." I begin.

"And you're Baby . . ."

"Where's Johnny?" we chorus.

"Son of a gun!" Rick hurls his mobile at the wall.

Uh oh.

"The lookalike has stood us up! I can't freaking believe this — the press call is in *nine minutes*."

"Cool your jets!" Beth attempts to soothe him. "If you just need a hot-bodied dancer guy, I've got numbers by the dozen."

"And can they magically appear here in . . ." he checks his watch. "*Eight minutes*?"

"Well, if you give me an hour —"

"These people won't wait!" He motions to the other room. "They're unveiling the new Cheryl Cole at Madame Tussauds at 4p.m. We can't compete with that."

"You know," the hairdresser starts circling Rick, "I have a great Swayze wig; I think it would really suit you —"

"What about you?" Rick turns on the hairdresser. "Would you do it?"

He looks at Rick as if he's lost his mind. "I'm Chinese!"

"Rick," I intervene before he starts propositioning the heavy-set doorman. "It's just for a photo opportunity, right?"

"Yes."

"No one would have to know that you are the show's producer."

"But if I do this, who would make the announcement?" he splutters.

"Lucy, of course."

"I don't know if she's up to public speaking."

"She'll be fine," Beth assures him. "That girl is way more capable than you give her credit for."

He looks at his watch again, puffs in anxious frustration and then rips off his shirt.

"Woah! Ricky!" Beth gasps as he reveals an armour-plated torso and highly-defined biceps. "Work out much?"

"I was a swimmer before I got into TV."

"Ah, but can you dance?" she teases.

The second Rick's new hair is secured, Beth has him doing the basic back and forth.

"That's it! Back two, three, forward two, three . . . Keep your hold strong. No spaghetti arms!" She winks at me.

"Ready?" Lucy sticks her head around the door and then does a double-take. "Rick?! Is that you?"

"You don't know me!" he barks, thrusting a sheet of paper at her. "Just read this out when the curtain opens."

For a moment I see Lucy at a crossroads — one way leads to panic, the other calm competency.

But then she points to the stage and instructs, "I need you guys in position now!"

Rick leads the way, taking me in rather too firm a hold — "Ouch! Ease up a little!" I squirm — while Beth slots in behind me, one hand on my back, the other on my hip.

I can feel her hands guiding me but Rick doesn't have the benefit of her touch and all too soon he loses his footing. And his nerve.

"I can't do this!" he bleats, genuine fear in his eyes as he glances towards the curtain.

We can hear the sound of the crowd on the other side now — the murmurs of anticipation and test-clickings of assorted cameras and tape recorders.

"I'm going to ruin the whole thing!"

"No, you're not." Beth places her cool hands on top of his clammy claws. "I want you to look at me the whole time, just keep doing those steps back and forth, back and forth. That's right," she encourages as he re-connects with the rhythm. "Don't let anything distract you. Nothing exists except for the three of us. This is your entire world. Got that?"

He nods, submissive for once.

Lucy clears her throat and then speaks confidently into the microphone: "Ladies and gentlemen, I give you Beth and Carmen," adding a muttered, "*And special guest . . .*"

The curtain flies back to reveal the three of us mid-motion, creating a whoop of delight and amusement from the women in the audience. I'm guessing the male journalists are probably a bit bemused, not being so familiar with the movie scene we are recreating, but with Beth's body doing its slinky-hipped thing, no one is complaining.

"Who's the hottie?" one woman calls out and Beth and I can't help but crack a smile.

Even Rick looks mildly flattered, muttering, "It's been a while since I've been called that."

As the song draws to a close, I feel like a new kind of bonding has taken place. We've been through a few dicey situations since we first came together as a unit but here we are again, finding a way to make it work.

All we need now is for Lucy to pull off the mystery announcement.

"Okay, so you'll see from the press releases we are handing out that *Dirty Dancing* is actually the musical where these two girls first met. And if you have watched our TV show, you will recall that Beth lost out on the chance for her breakthrough role as Penny when a fellow dancer slipped and landed on her."

The audience winces accordingly.

"We at Experience TV believe that Beth has true talent and we want to see her reach her optimum potential, which is why we have arranged for a uniquely talented choreographer to be with us in Cuba."

Cue dim lights and movie projection: a montage of exquisite dance sequences, all choreographed by the legendary Miriam Gilbert.

Beth looks both shocked and confused. "What's going on?"

"Is she here?" The journalist from *Dancer* magazine looks excitedly around the room. "I've been trying to get an interview with her forever!"

"Actually, I believe she is currently in mid-air." Lucy looks at her schedule. "She wanted to go ahead and hand-pick some Cuban dance partners for the girls."

"You mean —" Beth gasps.

"Yes. Miriam Gilbert is to be your personal dance coach!"

For a second I think Beth might faint — this woman is one of her all-time idols and it's taking all my strength to keep her upright. As I jolt her back to a standing position, I inadvertently jig a tear from her eye.

"Is this real?" She looks to me for assurance.

Before I can reply, the journalists demand Beth puts her reaction into words.

She shakes her head in wonderment. "I can't say it's a dream come true because how could I have ever dreamed such a thing were possible?" She looks back at the screen. "I've admired her work for so long and now I'm actually going to meet her? This is more, so much more, than I could have ever hoped for."

"What about you, Carmen?"

"I don't know what to say," I laugh, still reeling. "TV is the new Fairy Godmother!"

There is a responsive chuckle from the masses but then a lone voice asks: "What about your wish?"

"What's that?" I squint into the group.

"Well, Beth is getting her career ambitions fulfilled. What about your dreams?"

For a moment I am at a loss. My major goal of late has been to stay away from Lee. Not exactly terribly aspirational.

“I think I’m still in a state of transition,” I address the TV reporter who has now stepped to the fore. “I haven’t thought much beyond getting back to normal and feeling like myself again.”

“That’s it?”

I think for a moment. If I were to dare to hope for more, what would it be?

When the answer comes to me, I look directly at my interrogator. “Honestly? If I could have anything, I would have that one perfect dance — the one where you merge with your partner and move so seamlessly that they become your other breath.”

She smiles back at me. “Me too.”

“Me three.”

“Me four.”

As assorted women throw in their vote, I feel the anxiety of the day subside. I am not an interloper. I am an explorer! On a mission on behalf of my fellow women to see if new levels of bliss can be attained with a trip to Old Havana.

Cuba

CHAPTER TWENTY-NINE

Havana is everything you want it to be.

As soon as we exit the airport we're greeted with blue skies, palm trees and classic cars — some gleaming with pearlised paint jobs, others matt from the relentless sun, all happily cruising alongside banana trucks and makeshift horse and cart combos.

But the greatest number of people seem to be getting around on their own two feet.

"My, these Cubans are a good-looking people!" I wind down the taxi window to get a better look.

There's definitely a lot more skin on display here — an abundance of bare biceps and midriffs and toned brown legs in cut-off denims.

"I love the way they sashay," Beth observes. "Shoulders back, chest out —"

"And that's just the men!" I note.

"We could certainly learn a thing or two from the women." Beth directs my attention to a pair of curvy girls in hot pants and hoop earrings. "Don't they seem in harmony with their bodies?"

"They do!" I confirm, coveting their brazen confidence.

"So if you had to describe your first impression of Cuba in one word?" Lucy enquires, just as we draw level with a stunning man with mini dreadlocks peeking out from under his white mesh trilby.

He turns and smiles at us — his eyes may be ebony dark but the light behind them is dazzlingly bright.

"SEXY!" Beth and I gurgle in unison.

Even the old, peely-paint buildings look good.

"Can you imagine this place in its heyday?" I sigh.

"Oooh! I can see the sea!" Beth leans forward eagerly.

"This is the famous Malecón." Lucy points to the concrete seawall that protects the city and doubles as a hang-out spot for the locals — we see men fishing, couples kissing, groups of teenagers bantering and one lone trumpet player wending a tune into the early evening air. "Cubans treat it like it's another room of their house."

"One that just happens to get frisked with sea spray," Beth observes as a wave rears up, sending a fanfare of froth into the air.

I'm just insisting that I want to walk the length of it — even when I learn it is seven kilometres long — when the car containing Rick and the rest of the crew draws level with us. Beth gives her nemesis a cheeky wave. He doesn't know it yet but she's re-christened him Ricky Ricardo after the Cuban husband from *I Love Lucy*.

"Hey!" Beth grabs my arm. "I've just realised we've got our own Lucy too!"

This tickles her greatly but the most pleasing thing to me is the new face behind the camera — apparently Dan needed to "tend to his injuries" so he won't be joining us for the last leg of the trip. Whatever the excuse, I'm thrilled that he's out of the picture. Especially since the last image he has of me is cracking that Flamenco stage with my cheater-stomping heels. Feels good to go out with a bang instead of a whimper!

"I'm Guy." The replacement introduces himself as we step out of our cars, a couple of cigar puffs from the hotel.

"Well, that's nice and easy to remember — Camera Guy!" Beth teases.

"Or Camera Gay, as I'm often known."

"Ah!" Beth gives me a "bang goes that foursome" look.

Maybe they knew more about the Dan situation than I thought.

"So this is our home for the next week." Lucy turns to face the Hotel Santa Isabel. "Isn't she lovely?"

She is indeed.

Fronted with a shady twelve-pillared colonnade, the elegantly-tiered building may be only three storeys high but its breadth dominates one side of a large, leafy square. The pale gold stone is offset with cobalt blue awnings and even from this angle I can see that the entire roof is a terrace. I can't wait to get up there and survey our new kingdom.

Beth, meanwhile, is distracted by the numerous bookstalls across the way — predominantly featuring

Che Guevara imagery — not to mention the cafés and restaurants with pavement-seating and tableside musicians. It turns out this is the *Plaza de Armas*, one of the liveliest squares in Havana. If we weren't burdened with suitcases, I have a feeling we'd already be sampling pineapple-flavoured rum, but Lucy keeps us on track, chaperoning us through to reception.

While I take in the lobby and its modest chandeliers, velvet couches and granny's best lace doilies, Beth is wandering amid the potted palms of the inner courtyard, studying a photo of Jack Nicholson, looking as delighted with himself as ever.

It really is a wonderful, romantic hotel, borderline boutique, with just twenty-seven unique rooms. The only thing that gives us pause is knowing that right up until a year or so ago, Cubans weren't allowed in their own hotels unless they were staff. Only on their honeymoon were they permitted to stay overnight, for two whole nights, at a government-appointed property. Which really takes signing in as Mr & Mrs Smith (or in this case Mr & Mrs Perez) to a whole new level.

Lucy tells us that one of the ways we can give a little back is to save our hotel soaps and shampoos as Cubans are scrupulous about cleanliness and love to be fragrant, but such products are hard to come by.

"I'm going to give them that perfume I bought on the plane," I decide.

"The one you chose for the pretty bottle but makes you smell like a public lavatory?" Beth scrunches up her nose.

"I'm sure on someone else's skin it will be divine," I pout.

As we locate our room and insert the key, we see Simon doing the same across the hall.

"Convenient," I observe.

"Oh don't!" Beth squirms, scrabbling with the lock.

Just when I thought everything was on track for a beautiful romance, Beth has discovered a new resistance, one she broached with me on the plane: "What is it like having sex with a nice man?" she asked oh-so-casually as we were handed our movie choc-ices.

I scanned through my repertoire of partners and then gave my definitive answer: "I have absolutely no idea."

"I mean, how does it even happen when they are so courteous and patient?" At this point, she looked almost disapprovingly at the back of Simon's head.

"I thought you liked the fact that he wasn't putting any pressure on you."

"I do, I do. But then, in a way, that puts the onus on me to decide when the moment is right."

"And that's a problem because . . . ?"

"I'm worried that I'm never going to feel that *Gaucho* passion for him. I mean, I definitely missed him on our day apart in London and I have to confess my heart did do a little leap when I first saw him today . . ."

"That's a great sign!" I encouraged. "And don't forget you basically turned down the world's hottest fake matador for him. That has to count for something."

"I suppose," she conceded. "But the warm feeling I have for him is here," she laid her hand on her chest, "rather than here," she pointed to her lap.

"I believe the thing that can connect the two is a kiss."

"But what if I never have the inclination to kiss him?"

"Fortunately there is a time-honoured helper available — booze."

"Well, that's all very well on the evening of, but what about the morning after? I don't want to lead him on if I can't deliver on a more long-term basis."

I removed the ice-cream wrapper from her fiddling fingers. "That's very conscientious of you, Beth, but you may be thinking too far ahead, to things neither of you can predict. Besides, there's no real rush, is there?"

"I don't know, I feel like I'm trying to play catch up."

I sighed. "So his feelings may be a little more advanced than yours. He seems more than happy to slow down so you can catch up. And really, isn't that the ultimate sign of respect — allowing you to have your own feelings in their own time?"

"Yes, yes, it's very nice," she mumbled before putting on her headphones and pretending to be interested in a sci-fi movie.

"Carmen!" Beth snaps me back to our present situation, still struggling with the lock of our hotel room. "Would you please put me out of my misery and open the damn door!"

Fortunately her mood lightens as soon as she steps inside.

"Oh, it's such a peachy delight!" Beth twirls amid the antique furnishings, running her hand along the writing desk, setting the rocking chair in motion and then polishing the brass of the *Bedknobs and Broomsticks* bed.

Better yet, our balcony could host a small cocktail party and, just as we step out, a horse and carriage rattles by beneath us, for added atmosphere.

"Is that our phone?" Beth darts back inside and then calls out to me that Lucy needs us up on the roof terrace pronto.

We've become savvy enough to re-do our make-up before we step off the plane but both of us are keen to change outfits. I opt for a blue and white striped shirtdress and pin a star brooch on Beth's red T-shirt to reflect the colours and patterns on the Cuban flag.

"It's not for nothing you do the job you do!" Beth grins as we head on up.

"Oooh! You can see the sea from here!" I gasp.

"And the old harbour with the lighthouse that we saw from the taxi!"

"And all our neighbours' laundry." I point to the apartment building directly across from us. "Look at that old birdcage hung in that window."

Last time I saw a parrot we were at the *Estancia Santa Rita*. That was the day I got enlisted to become part of the TV show. Look at me now — oh so *au fait* with the interview process: I know that we won't be able to wear sunglasses because the viewers need to see the expression in our eyes and that we mustn't sip on the mojitos that Lucy has prepared as props otherwise the levels of liquid in the glass could jump up and down in the edits.

"Got your lines down?" she checks with us as we are put in position.

"Yup," we reply.

On the plane she gave us brief notes on the history of the Salsa and now she wants us to tell it back to her in our own words. Starting with Beth.

"In the beginning 'Salsa' was a general term used for a whole group of different musical styles — Merengue, Cha Cha Cha, Mambo, Son, Rhumba —"

"Which is different, by the way, to the Rumba you see on *Strictly*," I chip in. "The Cuban Rhumba is more earthy and tribal with African roots. Plus they pronounce it more like 'roomba', you know like those robot carpet cleaners?" I hand back to Beth.

"So. While you can still hear all these forms of music in their own right, the mixture is Salsa."

"Which, by the way, means 'sauce' in Spanish," I add. "Befitting its mixture of ingredients."

"Including a fair amount of spice," Beth winks. "Because, let's face it, Salsa is hot!"

That was our sign-off line but Lucy wants more.

"So, Beth, what comes to mind when you think of Salsa?"

"Men in satin shirts with fast-moving hips and women with glossy legs and spangly costumes!"

Lucy gives a "that'll do" nod and then turns to me. "Carmen, how would you say this dance compares to the Tango and Flamenco?"

"Well, it definitely seems the happiest dance of the three." I muse for a moment and then pontificate: "If you think that Tango began as a kind of homesick lament and Flamenco was a dance of defiance against oppression, it seems that Salsa is saying, 'Look, we get it, life is hard but for tonight let's forget our troubles and have some *fun*!' "

"I'll drink to that!" Beth raises her mojito glass and we chink and slurp in perfect unison. All the way down to the bottom of the glass.

"Okay!" Lucy signals to the guys to stop recording. "You *chicas* can take a few moments to enjoy the view but don't forget that we need you in the lobby for 9p.m."

"9p.m.," Beth repeats as she gives Simon a discreet "see you later" smile, and then reaches to refill our glasses.

"Any chance of telling us what tonight has in store?" I chance my arm as they turn to leave.

"Oh yes." Lucy sounds misleadingly breezy as she replies, "You're going to dinner with Miriam!"

We wait until everyone is out of sight and then Beth rushes at me with such bounding dog force that we both topple backwards against the iron balustrade, sending the freshly-filled mojitos sloshing down onto the poor soul enjoying his balcony below.

"Oh God, it's Rick!" Beth hisses, ducking me down with her as we watch him wipe his face and then take a taste of the liquid on his fingertips. "It's raining rum, hallelujah!" Beth starts singing before I muffle her mouth.

"We have to apologise!"

"Are you crazy?"

I get to my feet, ready to face his wrath, but when I look down, he's gone inside. No doubt to clean himself up.

"We'll explain later," she shrugs.

"I really don't think we should leave this — you know how cranky he gets after a plane ride, do you really want to put tonight in jeopardy?"

Beth shakes her head.

"Besides, if anyone should know how shocking it is to have a drink thrown in their face . . ."

"You have a point," Beth concedes. "But we really haven't got time to get blasted by him right now. What if we had a mojito sent to his room with an apology note?"

"Deal!"

We trot down to reception only to realise we don't know Rick's surname. As our Spanish fails us once again, we try to describe him through mime and for one awful moment I think the receptionist thinks we are trying to order a man on room service. But then Beth manages to convey that we are with the TV group and he finally hands us a list of our names and respective room numbers.

"Here we are — Richard Martin, Room twenty-two."

"You're kidding?" Beth smirks.

"What?"

Beth waits for the penny to drop.

"Oh my God!" I hoot, grabbing her hands. "We're *Living La Vida Loca* with Ricky Martin!"

CHAPTER THIRTY

"This is the best restaurant in town?" Beth looks mildly concerned as we assess the ramshackle street that houses La Guarida.

"It's certainly atmospheric," I note as Lucy ushers us through a giant black door into a cavernous entrance hall dominated by a crumbling curve of staircase. The surrounding walls are flaking with what looks like caked-on sugar, fraying around a hand-painted inscription to Fidel. I wish Simon was here to translate but it turns out the restaurant is too discreet to allow filming so the rest of the crew have been obliged to stay home. Besides which, Lucy seems eager to hustle us on our way. "Up, up, up!"

I feel a certain trepidation as we begin our marble-stepped ascent, as if to lay a hand upon the wrong portion of wrought iron balustrade might cause the whole thing to collapse and engulf us in dust.

"Did we miss the bit where they hand us hard hats?" Beth wants to know.

"Up!" Lucy instructs.

At the next level we inadvertently find ourselves peering into people's apartments, spying washing strung on indoor lines, steam rising from cooking pots and old men in vests watching the tourists instead of TV.

"One more." Lucy motions to the next staircase, and then guides us across the landing to a heavy wooden door. "See you in a couple of hours . . ."

We ring the bell. There is a short delay and then it creaks open, welcoming us into another world.

What was once just another apartment is now a multi-roomed dining hide-out, all creaky-cosy tables with mismatched china and gem-coloured glasses refracting the soft candlelight. Now the meaning of La Guarida — The Den — comes into its own.

"Something smells good." Beth's nose twitches as a preview of creamy mushroom sauce and sheeny mango glaze is brought to us on a waft of night air.

"Do you feel that lovely breeze?" I look towards the balcony and then startle — there sits Miriam Gilbert.

Beth notes my inhalation and matches it. "She's really here!"

The legend rises open-armed and envelops us in a warm hug, making us feel like her long-lost nieces. Her hair is a lustrous white wave, her sixty-something skin supple and gleaming, her trademark damson lips a perfect match for her tunic and trouser ensemble. I remember reading once that, when she's not dancing, she favours outfits that closest resemble pyjamas. I also remember Beth telling me how intuitive she is when it comes to mentoring dancers and I certainly get the feeling I am meeting someone who can see your very essence, even when you can't.

"Isn't this a charming place?" She bids us sit. "When they first opened, the owner would sit here, playing dominoes, waiting for people to come, and now look at it — every table filled!"

"And palpable appreciation in the air," I note.

"When you eat, you will understand why," she winks, nodding for our cocktails to be served.

I am almost hesitant to drink any more as Beth and I rather made up for the mojitos we spilled while we were getting ready.

"Sleepy, tipsy and jet-lagged!" she accurately observes. "Just how I want you!"

We laugh delightedly and then listen up as she begins our intensive session.

"From the footage I have seen of you two, it seems as if you want to master the steps first and then add the style and personality later. But that is like an actor learning his lines without having any notion about the character he is to portray," she reasons. "I wanted to see you before class because, ladies, the dance begins *the moment you enter the room*."

I feel an internal surge of excitement.

"Tomorrow the Cubans will teach you their authentic version of Salsa — and it's going to be a fun ride: flirtatious, bold, exuberant — but tonight I want to get to the essence of all partner dancing, which is this: attention on the male. And the male's attention on you."

Now I have tingles!

"For your part, I want you to notice the smallest detail — the smell of his cologne, the feel of his cotton shirt beneath your fingertips, the form of his shoulder beneath that cotton. I want you to hang onto him *like a breath*," she husks. "Now, if you can finish the dance and report back to me every nuance of his being, you danced well. If you can't, you're a soloist." At which point she gives Beth a knowing look. "And this is going to be harder for you because of your training. I've worked with so many professional dancers who can't even *look* at their partners let alone allow them to lead."

"If only half of them knew how!" Beth counters.

"You have a point there," Miriam concedes. "Fortunately here in Cuba you will be experiencing a nation of dancers, they have been training since they were children."

"Oh jeez!" I reel. "I'm going to be so out of my depth!"

"On the contrary, you will never be in better hands."

"Really?"

She nods. "A good partner will bring out a whole new colour in you as a woman — he will take you in his arms and if there's any of that monkey chatter in your head — any of that '*I won't be able to keep up!*' or '*I can't do this, I'm English!*' — he will slide his middle finger up your back like a zipper and hold you there until you close your eyes half way and allow yourself not to think, not to know yourself, but simply to suspend yourself in his action and let him float you through instincts."

I am in a stupor now. I love the way she speaks — equal parts with her voice and her body, so expressive and engaging!

"Oh, Miriam!" I sigh, giddily. "Do you really think it's possible for someone like me to experience something like that?"

"Absolutely. You just have to let the layers fall away so you can access your feminine self."

Oh dear. I hear a screech of brakes. Female I can do, but feminine is a whole different ball game.

"Is that absolutely essential?"

"Yes," she confirms. "Your femininity will allow him to puff up and feel good about being the leader. It empowers him."

" 'The man is the boss on the dancefloor if nowhere else!' " Beth quotes one of Penny's lines from *Dirty Dancing*.

"Exactly. It's a concept that has become so distorted in our culture. I'm not talking about the woman being a wimp — you'll still give him a run for his money in terms of resistance and compliance so that he's intrigued and wants to be the pursuer. Trust me, I always come back spicy!"

We laugh, not doubting that for a second.

"Of course, to really let a woman feel safe enough to soften and let go, he has to understand her pain and her frustrations. He has to read her like a horse whisperer."

"It was like that with the *Gaucho*!" Beth sighs, explaining to Miriam just what occurred amid the pampas grass.

She nods empathetically and tells us about the pock-faced gangster she used to Tango with. "We had this understanding whereby we could bring all our demons to the dancefloor and we would take each other on."

I reach for my drink, still trying to fathom the power and potential of these encounters.

"Carmen, you don't seem convinced?"

"Oh no! I love the sound of it, it's just the one partner dance I had with a man in Buenos Aires was quite the opposite — he spent the whole time chiding me and correcting me —"

She holds up her hands in horror. "Any man who asks you to dance and then gets petty with technique has missed the point entirely!" she rankles. "I know those people all too well — computer programmer by day, dance pretender by night! You know what I say when a man tries to bully me with corrections?"

My eyes are as big as saucers now. "What?"

She leans close. "If you can't get that you've got a woman in your arms who smells a certain way, moves a certain way and is begging to be taken on this fantasy journey with you, then I don't care how many dance steps you know or how many corrections you might *think* you want to give — you need to go back to a class with a better teacher and find out what is *really* going on!"

I can feel my face shining brightly back at hers — Beth may worship this woman's choreography but it's her attitude that is wowing me.

The courses come and go, all delicious, though I couldn't tell you what I ate, just that I feel like all my senses are being satisfied at once.

We're onto the liqueurs now and, inevitably, talk has turned to the man-woman dynamic *off* the dancefloor . . . Specifically myself and Lee.

"Speaking as someone who can relate, I would like to offer you this," Miriam begins . . . "Enough with the deep, psychological introspection!"

"Oh!" I wasn't expecting that!

"You're not a fool. These people are very good at what they do. You were feeling lonely and it's hard to give up the little perks you were getting. It happened, big deal. It doesn't mean you are a magnet for these people. He was simply the only guy in your field of vision at the time. Move on!"

I feel another avalanche of relief. First with Kelly, now with Miriam. Hoorah for wise women!

"The only thing I would say," Beth grimaces, looking a little cautious about raining on any parades, "is that she does seem to gravitate towards the damaged ones . . ."

I can't deny it.

Miriam turns to me. "You know what I would say to you when you meet the next one?"

She sounds so nurturing, so loving. "What?" I breathe.

"RUN!" she yells.

Beth hoots and claps her hands. "Exactly! Why should she get the duff one?"

"Look, it's like the old AA analogy." Miriam leans back in her chair. "I walk down the street, I fall down a hole. It takes me forever to figure out how to climb out. I walk down the street, fall down a hole, this time I know how to get out. I walk down the street, I walk *around* the hole. Next time," she pauses for impact, "I walk down a different street!"

As we chink glasses, I feel a sudden surge of optimism — I'm looking beyond Miriam to the balcony and beyond that to a very different kind of street. Maybe I'm doing better than I even realise!

"I'm going to find me a nice man!" I chirrup.

"Oh no, no!" Miriam looks horrified.

"What? I thought you said —"

"A nice man is as much of a label as a bad man. You have to look for your own principles first, find your own light, and explore your own darkness. Ultimately you want to meet someone who aligns with your life, someone who does no harm. You want to look for commonality of goals and probably a best friend, and then hopefully the hormones match that."

I cast a glance at Beth, who is indeed at the hopeful hormone stage.

She in turn gives Miriam a quick summary of her situation with Simon, along with her attendant concerns.

"I have to say, he sounds worth the risk," Miriam encourages. "Especially since your *Gaucho* experience was carnal and cathartic — the perfect Sorbet Guy!"

"Sorbet Guy?" Beth repeats with an intrigued titter.

"It's something a friend of mine calls the man who cleanses your palate for true love."

She explains that the ideal is someone with whom there are no real prospects — therefore zero complications — but who gives your self-esteem a wonderful boost and restores your dating optimism.

"I can't deny it, the *Gaucho* did all that but there's so much more at stake with Simon. And to be absolutely honest, I've never really been one for romance. Am I really missing out on that much?"

Miriam smiles knowingly and then leans in, close to the candle flame. "Last time I was in Cuba, I met a man who swept me off my feet — literally — and carried me through the streets of Santiago quoting poetry to me as he walked! When he finally set me down he told me he wanted to kiss my face a thousand times, and he did: '*Uno, dos, tres . . . cien . . . mil*' And when he was done naming every kiss in Spanish, he leapt to his feet and shouted up at the stars, 'This is the night of a thousand kisses!' "

Beth and I are agape with wonder.

"If you are on your deathbed and you've never had even one night like that . . ." she shakes her head. "More's the pity."

Beth grabs her glass and urges us to join her in a toast: "Here's to every night in Havana being one of those nights!"

CHAPTER THIRTY-ONE

I awake to Beth blaring the Seventies disco song *Cuba!* by the Gibson Brothers.

Before I know it, she has me up pogo-ing along side her, chanting the chorus and pumping the air like a revolutionary. I dance myself dizzy and then fall back onto the bed exhausted.

"Do you think that's how all Cubans start their day?"

"Absolutely!" she grins. "Mojito?"

"You're kidding?" I jerk upright, afraid she may be taking the hedonism plan a little too far.

"Of course!" she giggles. "Come on, get in that bathroom. We need to be fresh and fragrant for our new dance partners!"

I experience a surge of delight — today I am going to feel a man's arms around me and have another chance to *exhale* . . . And this time I don't have to worry about the implications or my screwy judgment, it's just a dance. All the comfort, none of the crisis. Right?

Our classes take place a short drive away at the legendary Hotel Nacional de Cuba — a Havana landmark which opened its imposing doors in the

1930s and has since welcomed the likes of Nat King Cole, Marlene Dietrich and Frank Sinatra.

Lucy also informs us that it hosted the infamous Forties mob summit run by gangsters Meyer Lansky and Lucky Luciano, as depicted in *The Godfather II*. Indeed, as we turn into the majestic, palm-lined driveway I can easily picture squat men in spats and sashaying, scarlet-lipped women. But I am rather perplexed by a road sign showing a trumpet, with a red line through it.

"No trumpets?" I hoot. "Of all the things to ban!"

"It's not a trumpet, silly," Beth corrects me. "It's a horn."

"Even so."

She rolls her eyes. "As in a car horn?"

"Ohhhhh!" The penny finally drops. After all the noise of the revolution, they are obviously keen on keeping the peace.

Guy films us skipping up the steps of the front entrance, gawping our way through the grand lobby and expansive colonial courtyard, and then revelling in the cool of the airy ballroom.

There we are greeted by our new dance partners, a.k.a. the three amigos — Alexis, Martinez and Russo. All are Cuban and yet each man has a decidedly different look:

Alexis, the eldest and official leader of the pack, has ebony skin, black bush-baby eyes and peroxide curls of duckling yellow. He's wearing Rupert Bear check trousers and a mischievous grin and, when he welcomes us, the deep raspy-croak of his voice reinforces the impression of him as a one-person-party.

Beside him stands Martinez, tall and lean with sheeny mocha skin and — as we witness when Lucy requests he changes his shirt on account of the brand logo — the owner of a highly-defined six pack. Beth and I shuffle a little closer together so no one can see as we dig lusty nails into each other's arms. He wears a bandana headband over his cornrows and his long legs end in a pair of giant trainers. He appears to be the quietest of the three, and the most soulful.

Russo, by contrast, is stocky and shaven-headed with green eyes and a bionic groin. I'm not kidding, that part of his body seems to have a life of its own, like a wind-up toy propelling him around the room. Any pause in the proceedings and it's off again. His big, shiny belt-buckle only serving to accentuate that area.

"That man could single-handedly create a demand for male lap-dancing," Beth decides.

He certainly has the flirtatious personality to go with it. I'm sure if he hadn't gone the dance tutor route he would have done a rip-roaring trade as a *jintero*, which is essentially the Cuban version of a street hustler with extras.

That said, for all his could-have-your-eye-out-with-that sexuality, he's not sleazy, mostly because he's cracking up the whole time.

Alexis gets us started with the fundamental footwork — *uno-dos-tres*, pause, *cinco-seis-siete*, pause — and then leads us in a series of drills. "To help with muscle memory," Beth explains.

Just as I master one sequence, we move onto the next, each getting increasingly complex until it feels like tongue-twisters for my feet.

As I've already established, I'm a pretty slow learner and now even reverting to the basic step is a challenge. I can do it copycat style in the line-up but ask me to add arms or turn and I'm instantly lost.

"Left-two-three, pause, right-two-three, pause" — I have to repeat the phrase over and over in my head or I end up on the wrong foot, thus throwing off my game entirely. Apparently, I'm taking too big steps (common mistake) and bouncing when I should be grinding into the ground.

As for Beth, her old nemesis — perfection — is back.

Alexis explains to her that Cuban Salsa is very different to ballroom Salsa or LA style, which is very precise, all straight lines, fancy arms and dizzying spins that Cubans think are farcical. Their style is much less manicured, more laid-back and, once again, far *sexier*.

As a result, Alexis insists that we need to work on liberating our hips. Which is where the real embarrassment begins.

Imagine standing in front of a man you really fancy (say, for the sake of argument, Martinez . . .) and you are required to stand with your legs apart, stick out your bottom like a duck and then begin rotating your hips in a full circle. The Cubans are fluid, uninhibited and effortlessly rhythmical. I am mortified. To me, the motion feels jerky and unladylike. Crude even. Beth is giggling at my flushed face but I want to cry, "I'm English! We don't do this!"

Still they make us continue. Now anti-clockwise. I look even more like a broken doll now. Am I really so hideously out-of-touch with my own sexuality?

"YES!" I exclaim when we take a break. "I just feel such an idiot!" I explain to Lucy. "I mean, to them it comes so naturally — it's so smooth and sensual — but if I were to gyrate and bounce like that in a club in London —"

"It would give entirely the wrong impression!" Beth politely concludes for me.

"But we're not in London," Miriam chips in, greeting each of us with a generous hug before she hoiks herself up onto the edge of the stage. "You know, I have this theory that there are the Equator People and the Snow People. Those who live near the Equator are very touchy, very pelvic and basically relaxed. It's just too damn hot to bother with formality!" she reasons. "And then we have you Celtic types . . . I mean, look at dances like the Irish jig — hands glued to your sides, hopping about because you're so bloody cold!"

Beth and I burst out laughing at her vision.

"Let's forget all about moving your hips for now." She hops down and stands before me. "I want you to hold your ribcage up like a Flamenco dancer, imagine your spine hanging down like a rope and the pelvis is just the pendulum hanging on the bottom on the rope. Then give me a soft flexible knee like a skier. Good," she encourages. "Now I want you to close your eyes and picture this scene . . ." Her voice becomes hypnotically low and seductive: "You are barefoot in the bathwater-warm ocean, fish are nibbling at your toes, there is a soft ocean breeze and the waves are knocking you a little bit from side to side. You've already had six mojitos and the band just showed up on the beach."

The music strikes up on cue.

"As you sway you become a little unsteady on the uneven sand but it's okay because there is someone there to catch you."

At this point I feel a pair of warm male hands rest upon my hip bones and realise that my hips are indeed moving of their own accord. I don't know which man is holding me but something about the sensuality of the moment makes me want to turn around and lose myself in a rum-flavoured kiss . . .

"Time for some partner work!" Miriam announces, not a moment too soon. "You remember what I told you last night?"

"I *dreamt* about what you said last night!" I confess.

"Okay, I want you to stand before your partner . . ."

Yes! I squeal internally as Martinez steps in front of me.

"Take a moment to become aware of the energy between you and then I want you to hold up your palm to your partner." She comes over and stands beside us. "Good, now I'm going to let him find you."

I watch as Martinez focuses his attention on my palm. For what seems like an eternity he remains intently in the same position.

"Try to initiate a little and see if it frightens her in any way," Miriam guides him.

He takes the most minuscule step, not timid but respectful. I don't know what to think. I don't know what to do to make him feel more "welcome". I may not know him but I trust him, why is he not moving closer?

"He's waiting," Miriam reports. "You're holding him off at a distance."

My eyes flick to her with concern. Do I do this in real life? Is this what keeps love at bay?

"It's okay to receive," she tells me, causing my eyes to prickle. "It's okay to receive."

I swallow hard, feeling unstable, unsure of what I "should" be doing.

"It's not in the head, it's in the body," Miriam advises.

And with that, I find my gaze dropping from his face to his chest. I stare a few inches below his collarbone and imagine a connection to the same place in my own body. I am aware of a wanting and I don't know if it's coincidence or mirroring but I feel a shift and here he is taking a step forward. And then another.

As our fingertips connect, I feel a ripple within so satisfying that when he clasps my hands I feel like we'll be bonded for life.

"There we are!" Miriam smiles. "Now I want you to practise doing a 'press-catch' motion to work on your tension." She demonstrates how it should feel to me, pushing our weight forward, towards each other and then releasing and catching one another's hands just about at the point that we would topple back.

"Keep practising that while I check on Beth — who is desperately trying to lead Russo."

"I'm not!" she protests.

"It's not your fault, it's your training, you don't even realise you are doing it."

It doesn't help that he's too transfixed by her boobs to put up a fight.

Miriam motions to Russo to step aside and takes Beth in her arms herself. As she tells Martinez to start doing the basic step with me, she holds Beth steadfast. "I want you to go completely neutral."

I see Beth getting increasingly restless but Miriam refuses her inclination to step — "*Ah-ah-ah! Don't you even think about it! Ah-ah-ah! Where are you going, young lady?*" as if she were breaking a frisky colt. Only when Beth is still and submissive does Miriam make her move.

"There we are," she soothes, before handing her back, now to Alexis.

She wants us to keep rotating partners. If the intention is to keep us on our toes, it works — just as the three men differ in looks, so their respective dance styles are equally diverse. Though I feel most attracted to Martinez, I feel most competent with Alexis, his lead is so firm and directive I don't think I could go wrong even if I tried. With Russo, I am hit and miss — he seems to have a bad case of ADD: one minute he's all grinding of hip and winking of eye and the next he's staring off around the room, missing his cue. Making me all the more glad to return to Martinez . . .

As Miriam reminds us to pay "molecular attention" to our partners I realise just how poetically beautiful his liquid brown eyes are and revel in the encouraging sweetness of his smile and the soft scent of his cologne.

I never thought of Salsa as a gentle or even particularly graceful dance but here he is manoeuvring me like I'm a delicate flower and sending showers of fairy dust into the sky with every turn.

"Now let's try this with some music."

"*Oye Como Va!*" Carlos Santana calls to us from the stereo.

I expect my attraction to Martinez to heighten the off-balance klutz in me but a voice tells me, quite clearly, that an opportunity to dance with such a wondrous specimen comes along once in a lifetime. And so somehow I find myself elevated to a higher plane, one where I am atypically calm and composed, and can savour every sensation from the silkiness of his shoulder to the coolness of his long fingers, all the while knowing that my body is moving in direct response to his.

"Look at you!" Miriam observes me from the side. "So delicately feminine!"

I practically choke on the spot. "I have never been told that before!" I splutter.

"Well, that's why you should keep going with your dancing, us working women can be tough cookies." She studies me some more. "You're quite lovely when you follow him, when you relax. And do you know why?"

I shake my head. I really have no clue.

"Because in this moment you're not trying to be interesting, you're just very interested in him! And he's delighted that you're giving him so much!"

If I was floating before, I am up above the clouds now.

When Lucy calls for another interview break, I am unable to censor my rapture.

"I know I've only been doing this for an hour or so but I can honestly say this is one of the best things I've ever done in my life!"

"And would that have anything to do with your dance partners?" Lucy smirks.

"Absolutely!" I cheer. "All three are fantastic but Martinez is divine!"

Lucy looks to Beth for similar droolings but all she offers is: "You can certainly tell he's a former Salsa champion."

I wonder if she is trying to protect Simon's feelings? I'm certainly glad that I no longer have to concern myself with what Dan might be thinking. Already he feels like a distant blip. That's one of the great benefits of learning a new dance — your brain is so consumed with trying to co-ordinate your body and remember the steps there's simply no room for lamenting. I only wish I'd known this sooner — that there is actually something practical you can do to give yourself a mental break from heartache.

Throughout the rest of the day, we learn moves with cute names like *sombrero* and *caramello* — there's even one called *Coca Cola*! Weirdly, the faster we do the move, the easier I find to grasp it. I remember in that "pie and mash" class in London everything was broken down into tic-tac steps and precision angles, I felt like I was doing vertical Twister, but here Miriam explains that as long as you are loose and receptive and "energetically connected to his power source", you can do just about any move he throws at you.

And she's right.

It's only when you cling on too tight that the problems start. You have to allow both partners the freedom to move.

"So spaghetti arms can actually be a plus!" I laugh at one point.

And then my attention goes to my hands and I notice that I have stopped letting go of my partner during the demonstrations. Earlier, when we would pause to take a new instruction, I would instinctively separate — disengage and step back — the hold was for dancing after all. But gradually I notice I am becoming comfortable with remaining in contact, even when we are just standing there observing. Like right now, I appear to be listening intently to Miriam translating Alexis' mambo adjunct to the *sombrero* but really I am bouncing off the walls with glee that I am standing here holding Martinez's hand! As if such a thing would happen in real life!

I do wonder if it is improper that I am getting such intense secret kicks but then I decide it's just a perk of learning Salsa in Cuba.

The downside is the sweating and inner thigh chafing and the toe blisters and waking every morning stiff and aching.

For the next three mornings, I hobble from the bed to the bathroom looking as if I have living rigor mortis. Gradually the heat from the shower loosens me up sufficiently to allow another battery of dance drills.

"It's basically exercise in disguise!" I complain as I mop my kinked hair after another rigorous session.

"You sound like you've been conned!" Beth giggles.

"I feel it! They get you so caught up with the moves you don't realise that you are working out! Look!" I pull at my waistband. "I can't remember the last time this gaped!"

Or the last time I was this happy. I love the fact that our dancers always greet us with sparkling eyes and a double-cheek kiss. I relish the way Miriam fills my head — and body — with such colourful imagery. And now that I have learned to bind my battered feet in advance, I am even starting to enjoy the routine of the warm-up. There is something satisfying about moving in sync with a group. Up until now, I felt as if Rick was constantly trying to catch us out but now he seems to be allowing more structure, possibly keen on amping up the quality of our dance. Lucy tells me he wants to run a sequence cutting from class to class, showing our daily development doing the same moves. Whatever his motive, I like the growing sense of familiarity and ease — I know where Simon and Guy will be positioned in the room, I know that Lucy will be following along with the steps out of camera shot and that Rick, no doubt bored by the repetition, will be making business calls from the courtyard.

Alexis will inevitably yell, "What happened?" when I make a mistake and bark at me to smile and breathe when I repeatedly forget to do either. I know that Russo will produce a grin so wild and wide that I can admire his gold fillings and that Martinez will cause my heart to levitate, especially when he sings along to the Marc Anthony tracks.

I wish I could better communicate with him but he speaks the least English of them all. Then again, maybe it's better this way. It certainly keeps things focused on the dance — it actually feels nice to adore someone without engineering a way for it to go further. He looks so good upon that pedestal, it suits him so well, I like keeping him there.

By day, that is. By night, as I lie in bed, I imagine what it would be like to have him look at me with desire. My physical limitations would fall away as he reveals that all he's ever really wanted is a girl with my precise personality. Yes, he might look like the type who should have something petite and toned on his arm but he's tried that and it's always left him feeling strangely empty. He had all but given up hope, and then along came me! Oh yes! Dream, dream, dream!

"Carmen!" Beth nudges me. "We've arrived."

I squeeze my eyelids together and try to blink myself awake.

I remember getting on the minibus. I remember the darkness and balminess of the night, I just don't remember our destination.

As I peer out of the window, looking for clues, I see Martinez walking towards us, dressed head to toe in white, like an angel.

"Are we in heaven?" I ask blearily.

"No, sweetie-pie." Beth helps me to my feet. "This is the *Casa de la Musica* . . ."

CHAPTER THIRTY-TWO

We step out into the leafy suburb of Miramar and follow Martinez over to what appears to be a crumbly old stone mansion. While I can't wait to get past the portico and onto the dancefloor, Beth is hesitant.

"Bit haunted house, isn't it?" She hangs back, sharing her fears of cobwebby curtains and fossilised harpists.

Martinez laughs as Simon translates her concerns and then promptly blitzes them as he pushes open the door to reveal a highly-animated Salsa band. We're told this group is an off-shoot of the legendary Los Van Van, hence the excitement amongst the glammed-up locals.

"They may not have much but they sure know how to work what they've got," I note.

"Do you think there's a single Cuban who can't dance?" Beth ponders as we watch them move with such natural ease. "I think the competition is tough in London — can you imagine auditioning here?"

I shake my head. "It's like this vast undiscovered pool of talent. Some of whom are about to get their fifteen minutes of fame . . ."

While Rick sets Simon and Guy to work, the rest of us form a Rum Club — apparently it's quite the norm to buy a bottle of Havana Club and a few cans of coke to make your own Cuba Libres. At least it's the norm for *tourists*. It is quite plain from the deserted bar area that the locals can't afford the drinks here, hence the tradition to treat them.

Alexis — who has been saving a prime table for us — holds up his glass to chink ours and introduces us to his babe of a wife, Daylin. She too has cropped peroxide curls and huge, bright eyes, just like him, but her knock-out figure is all Beth.

"Let me get a picture of the three blondes!" I grapple with my camera.

As they line up, they look like a transitional image — dark-skinned, blond male becomes medium-skinned, crop-haired female becomes light-skinned woman with long hair. The image tickles Alexis so much he insists Guy films the three of them dancing — manoeuvring the two women in perfect synchronicity, one at the end of each hand.

"Oh, this is great!" Lucy enthuses as he goes from basic steps to arm origami — the women passing under and over and at one point ending up side by side as if they are about to start Cossack dancing. Seconds later he separates them, twirls them, crouches down and spins them back from whence they came by placing a strategic hand below their knees, like he's setting spinning tops in motion!

"That's so cool!" I gawp at his control and their perfect mirroring.

Ordinarily, two women and one man might bring out a sense of competition but here there is no out-doing, just a wonderful sense of "All for one and one for all!"

And there's more group work to come — without missing a beat, Alexis passes Beth to Russo and then motions for Martinez to bring me to the floor. Three other couples join us and before I know it I find myself experiencing my first *Rueda* — Spanish for "wheel" — on account of the fact that we are all moving in a circle.

Here the beauty of being a woman really comes into its own — the men do virtually all the work! Yes, all of us listen to Alexis to hear him call out the next move — *un fly* is a single clap for example, *setenta complicado* is as tricky as it sounds — but it's the men who set it all in motion and they are the ones who have to move on to the next partner when Alexis calls, "*Dame*!" pronounced "Dam-ay", short for "*Dame uno*!" and simply translated as "Give me another!" Sometimes he calls, "*Dame dos*!" and the men speed past, grabbing the second girl along. But you are never alone for long — all this happens at such breakneck speed that I find myself shrieking as I'm spun and twisted and pretzeled every which way . . . Chaotic but utterly thrilling, this is the closest sensation I've had to hanging off a merry-go-round since I was a child.

"I think I'm going into cardiac arrest," I wheeze as the song comes to a frenzied end. "Seriously, feel how my heart is pounding!"

"That is fast." Beth's eyebrows raise in mild alarm. "But what a way to go!"

I burst out laughing. "You know, when I'm eighty-nine and I've had enough of life, I'm going to come back here and have some young Cubano take me out on the dancefloor and finish me off!"

"That moment may come sooner than you think." Beth nods for me to turn around.

Already there is a hand extended in my direction.

If it was anyone other than Martinez, I would sit this one out but how can I resist his open palm?

It's only when my hand meets his that I realise the music has changed from Salsa to something he introduces as Reggaeton — an infectiously staccato mix of reggae and hip hop.

Miriam arrives just in the nick of time to take responsibility for Russo's bionic pelvis and then directs the rest of us into two rows — men facing women, except we're now a man short.

"Simon! Come! Come!" Daylin beckons wildly.

"Oh no, no," he protests with a nervous look at Rick.

"Now, Ricky." She sidles up to him. "It's just one dance — you can hold his equipment for a few minutes, can't you?"

Instead of the snort of derision I expect, Rick nods dumbly. Or maybe it's wisely — something tells me that resistance is futile with Daylin, her vivaciousness could overpower any man.

"Okay, women follow me, men follow Alexis . . ."

Daylin then starts to do the kind of moves that would make a rap video vixen blush, punctuating every beat with a precision twitch of her plump but pert behind. We all gawp in awe. Not least because she carries off the most provocative moves with a joyous grin on her face.

Alexis then leads the men in a peacockish response, their entire bodies vibrating to the music and belt-buckles jiggling wildly. The brazenly flirtatious moves look great on them but on Simon — bless his M&S socks — it just looks agonisingly awkward. (I know the feeling.) And not just because he's English. Despite his obvious affinity with music, it would seem that his ears hear one thing and his body another.

I look to Beth, concerned this is going to do little to encourage her physical attraction, but she looks enchanted. The more he shakes his out-of-time thing, the more she cheers and encourages him. The song culminates with the men shunting toward us women, groin first. Shunt, shunt, shunt goes Simon until he is almost mounting Beth.

She couldn't look any more ecstatic.

I suppose in her line of work she actually doesn't get to see too many men dancing badly — maybe it's the sheer novelty making her giddy?

"Wasn't Simon fantastic?" she squeaks as we head back to our seats.

"Er . . ."

"Seriously! Can you imagine being that unco-ordinated and yet going for it with such gusto!"

I need to pick my words carefully. "He certainly was enthusiastic."

"I'll say!" she hoots. "God, how I'd love to get my hands on those hips!"

I blink back at her. "You mean in a dance teacher kind of way?"

She gives me a playful look. "Not necessarily . . ."

I can't quite believe it. Then again, she always liked the scene with the rhythmically-challenged guy in *Footloose* . . .

"Oh-oh-oh!" I suddenly leap back to my feet at a familiar trumpet toot. "I love this song!"

"What is it?" Beth frowns.

"All I know is that it's called *La Vida Es Un Carnaval* which I'm guessing is *Life Is A Carnival*!" I beckon Simon to see if he can translate for me but the only thing he can catch is the call of *Ahora!* meaning "Now!" and *Azucar!* meaning "Sugar!"

"I'd need to either see the words written down or spoken more slowly."

"Martinez?" I turn instead to my favourite native Spanish-speaker, though of course he has the opposite problem: struggling to find the English phrasing to convey the singer's message.

"She want you to understand that you are not alone," he begins. "You may feel it but it is not so. There is always another."

I blink back at him. I was expecting something more along the lines of *Get The Party Started* so this profound sentiment has taken me by surprise.

"When you have a time of much sadness, you must not think it will last," he continues. "It will move away. And you will be happy once again."

My heart glows a little in response — he may just be giving his interpretation of some lyrics but I feel as if he has just blessed me.

"*Gracias*!" I husk, still a little dazed.

"*De nada*," he replies. And then he invites me back onto the floor.

I look back at Beth in quiet despair. "I'm telling you, if you could harness Cuban energy, you could power the world."

More Reggaeton. But I'm not complaining. For me, dancing to a Salsa song is about as relaxing as taking a driving test — I have to concentrate so hard to remember all the pedals (footwork), check my wing mirrors (so I don't step back onto another dancer) and keep myself steady in reverse, etc. But seeing as I actually don't know any Reggaeton steps, I can enjoy the freedom of freestyle for a few minutes at least.

Which isn't to say that I don't feel a little foolish bobbing around trying to look "gangsta" but Martinez doesn't seem to mind. He's actually moved us over to the base of the stage now so we can have a bit of privacy, away from the camera lens.

But not for long.

Daylin is up to her minxing again, having everyone form one grinding line, pressing into Martinez who in turn is forced to press closer to me. I have nowhere to go with the stage behind me and as the pressure grows so I can feel his hips, his stomach, his thighs, his —

"Sorry!" I gasp, trying to co-ordinate my movements so I don't do him any damage.

What exactly am I supposed to do with my hands?

As the music amps up, so the others lunge harder. Still, Martinez manages to hold them off from crushing me entirely, expertly straddling the line between sexual and genteel.

I wish I had the nerve to respond in a seductive manner but I just haven't got the confidence. I can't look at him either. He's just too gorgeous. The last thing I want to do is pass out and miss all this. All I can do is surrender to his undulating proximity . . .

"I think you just found your Sorbet Guy!" Beth giggles when the press gang finally stop pressing.

"More like my Hot Tamale!" I inadvertently growl, pushing my damp, kinked hair from my brow.

"Now that sounds like a good combination!" Beth approves. "Best of both worlds!"

"Oh, if only!" I stare longingly at the man in question, body still popping even when he's pausing for a water break.

"I think he's perfect," Beth decides. "Barely speaks English, lives in a country with such strict exit policies you'd practically have to marry him before he could ever visit you in London, you couldn't work here —"

I hold up my hand. "Forget all the convenient obstacles, I think you hit the nail on the head when you said he was perfect. What would a man like that want with me?"

"You don't think you two have chemistry?"

"I think that was more *gravity* than anything — a dozen bodies pressing him into me."

"Well, I don't think it was coincidence that he chose to dance one-on-one with you for the sexiest song of the night."

"And that is why you will be my best friend for life."

I go to sit down but Beth pulls me back to her eye level. "Don't you want to go back to London a changed woman?" she persists. "That guy is your 'perfect dance' personified."

I can't argue with that.

"Just bear in mind we only have two more nights here," Beth reminds me. "I don't want you to end up missing out through dilly-dallying."

"Okay," I pout. "Tomorrow I'll make my move."

And then I strike a John Travolta/*Saturday Night Fever* pose to lighten the mood. Only to regret it the instant I see Martinez looking my way . . .

CHAPTER THIRTY-THREE

"Morning, ladies!"

"Morning, Lucy!"

"Slight change of plan today —"

If there is any phrase guaranteed to put me off my breakfast, it is that.

I set down my fork and prepare myself for the worst. "Don't tell me — we're the new star attraction at the Tropicana and we have just a matter of hours to come up with an act *and* design costumes made entirely of tobacco leaves."

"Actually, it's Alexis' birthday today so we thought we'd shake things up and head to the beach."

While Beth yippees, I feel a tinge of anxiety not even the prospect of a half-naked Martinez can appease.

"I think I need to have a little chat with Guy," I tell Beth as we board the bus, now accessorised in outsize sun hats and jewelled flip-flops.

"I'd wait 'til just before we arrive," Beth advises. "You know how these drives always lull him into a stupor."

"Good thinking," I reply. All the more time to daydream about last night's steamy dance with Martinez. I can still feel his body on me . . .

* * *

The minibus takes us out of the city and into untamed countryside. We pass so many hitchhiking locals that Rick finally cracks and allows a handful to occupy our spare seats. He even attempts to converse with them via Simon, making me wonder what he's up to. But then the glistening sea comes into view and I decide it's time to make my move with Guy.

"Soooo . . . Shooting at the beach today," I begin as I casually drop into the seat beside him.

"Yup," he replies without taking his heavy-lidded eyes off the speeding scenery.

"Not worried about getting sand in your camera?"

"Not as worried as you are about getting into your swimsuit."

Damn! He so has my number.

"About that —"

He holds up his hand. "Orders is orders."

I sigh in exasperation. "Look, I can imagine what Rick has in mind but I don't want it to be like one of those magazine articles featuring best and worst swimsuit bodies," I grimace. "Can't you just focus on Beth?"

"Maybe it's heartening for the viewers to see a woman with a real body, flaws and all."

"You don't understand how that works," I tut. "People want to see cellulite and buddha bellies on the so-called beautiful people — the actresses and models and dancers who are supposed to be perfect but with real people, it's different. We're the ones who get the makeovers and all the great tips on how to disguise our imperfections."

"Even so —"

"Come on!" I cut him off. "As a visual, wouldn't this scene be so much nicer; me in a brightly-coloured kaftan, Jackie O sunglasses, hair still looking good, massaging sun tan lotion into the shoulders of a stunning blonde *Baywatch* babe . . ."

Now he perks up. "That would satisfy a certain demographic . . ."

"So we have a deal?"

"Maybe if you could get her to run along the beach?"

I give him a withering look but I can tell he's serious. "Wait there."

Two minutes later I'm back.

"Well, she won't run but she will give you a full Bond girl emersion from the sea — pushing her hair back, shaking off the water . . ."

"She'll shake?"

"Guy!"

We look up to see Rick pointing out of the window to where the ever-curvaceous Daylin is bouncing excitedly at our arrival. She couldn't look any more ingénue-sexy with her white vest barely skimming her bottom, her legs golden, her feet bare.

"I'm on it!" he says, hoiking his camera into position.

Really, what was I worried about? With all these camera-ready Cubans, I am so off the hook.

The beach is buzzing with activity — it seems the locals even sunbathe in a lively fashion — but nothing can distract from the natural beauty of the powder-soft sands and magical aquamarine waters.

I breathe in the smell of salty air and coconut sun cream.

"I think these Cubans may be having the last laugh," Beth muses as it finally really registers with us that we are, well and truly, in the Caribbean.

"*Hola*!" Miriam welcomes us, pointing over to the birthday boy, clad in bright orange shorts, raising a beer to greet us.

"*Feliz cumpleaños*!" Beth and I give Alexis a verbal toast, as coached by Simon.

In turn, he introduces us to his teenage son and Daylin's sister, Jazbel, who has the most fabulous disco Afro. Meanwhile Russo waves and hollers to us from the shoreline.

"Saints preserve us," Beth mutters. "He's wearing Speedos."

"Those are some powerful thighs," I can't help but observe.

"Why is it that men with shaved heads always have the furriest bodies?" Beth frowns as he heads our way. "I want to wax him right here, right now . . ."

"Where's Martinez?" I ask, realising he has yet to catch my eye.

"He's gone away," Daylin replies all too matter-of-factly. "To Varadero."

"It's a beach resort a couple of hours up the coast," Lucy anticipates my next question.

"Oh. So he'll be back later?"

Lucy looks to Daylin. "Depends," she grimaces. "He must help his father. Maybe he comes back in two days."

Two days? I feel unstable. In two days, we'll be gone . . .

"Swim?" Russo suggests, now beside us.

"I just want to lie down for a bit," I quickly excuse myself and then place my scarf over my face like lots of people do on the beach. My features need to be able to crumple without concern for how it might look.

After five minutes, Beth checks that I'm still breathing. "You alright?"

"No," I reply.

She peeps under the scarf. "He still might come back . . ."

I shake my head. "But there's a good chance he won't."

"What's up with your stomach?" She notices me gripping at it.

"I'm getting this horrible preview of how I'm going to feel when we leave." I turn towards her. "I mean, I miss him already and it's only been a matter of minutes!"

Beth settles beside me on the sand. "Remember the whole deal with the Sorbet Guy is that the encounter is short and sweet."

"I know," I sigh heavily. "My brain gets that concept but my heart is still yearning for something more. I never did have obedient emotions."

Beth issues a snuffle. "As if any of us really do."

"I just hate that this amazing time with him has been cut short."

"Now you know how those *Strictly* celebs feel when they get prematurely eliminated!"

I can't help but smile. "You're right!" And then I turn over and start flicking sand off the waxy surface of the sunlounger. "I really thought I had it made — having a crush on someone I knew there was no future with — but it gets you just the same!"

"Oh, honey." Beth gives my hand a squeeze. "The universe does seem to be intent on testing your ability to let go — first Lee, then Dan, now Martinez."

"Well, at least the men are improving," I acknowledge.

All I can do now is wait for this leaden lump of disappointment to pass. But — oh no! — here comes cousin dread, that horrible fear that if I ever like a man again, something crushing is just around the corner.

I look up and find Miriam scrutinising me. "You're digging a ditch deep enough to bury your heart, am I right?"

I wasn't even aware that I was clawing at the sand until now.

"Would that be such a bad idea?" I squint back at her.

"Yes," she replies succinctly.

"Oh, Miriam!" I wail, inadvertently unbalancing my sunlounger as I sit up too fast.

"Woah!" She reaches to steady me and I find myself gripping onto her hand begging for answers.

"What are you supposed to do with all these feelings you have for people that are unwise or unreciprocated or cut short? I feel like they just keep mounting up — all these messy, leftover, inappropriate emotions!" I puff out a breath. "I just want to meet that one person so that I can do it right! Not all these beginnings and endings within a week of each other."

She peers down at me through her sunglasses. "You've had a pretty intense run lately, haven't you?"

"I've never had so many different emotions in such a short space of time!"

"Well," she begins as she kneels beside me. "As far as Martinez goes, you can't get too hung up on the significance of him leaving. It had nothing to do with you. He's just living his life."

"But why do I keep getting attached to these people who —"

"Who what? Who don't behave as you want them to?"

Now that shuts me up.

"Are you familiar with the saying, 'Sadness is a tantrum against what is'?"

I give a little snort of recognition. "That's what it feels like! I feel like there's a two-year-old inside me kicking and screaming because I didn't get my ice-cream today."

"Don't you mean your sorbet?" Beth queries.

Miriam smiles at her and then takes my hand. "You're so close to getting it, Carmen. And trust me, the answer is not for some fantasy man to come cantering along the beach on a white horse."

"I know," I agree. "I slept with the man on the white horse and it only made matters worse."

"Look, when bad things happen to good people, they can feel pretty sorry for themselves. It doesn't make any sense — what did they do to deserve this? Suddenly everything in the world looks skewy and they start to doubt that the love they have been hoping for will ever come. For everyone else perhaps, but not for them."

My shoulders slump a little as I relate to what she's saying.

"Read any book on spirituality and you will see that we attract what we fear — the rejection, the romantic disappointments, they'll keep on coming, proving your worst fear right. Until you change your attitude."

"Can't I just meet someone as disillusioned as me?" I half-joke. "That way we could cancel out each other's pain?"

Miriam gives me a "nice try" look.

I sigh. "Honestly, I felt sure I was making progress —"

"*You are!*" Miriam insists, cutting short my protest. "But don't let this situation be an excuse to slip back into your old thinking. Self-pity will not serve you. You have to embrace where you are right now, with all your heart!"

"Any tips on how to do that?" I ask in a small voice.

"I have a two-part plan for you," she asserts. "First, look and learn." She motions to the locals on the beach. "These people are not leading perfect lives but you don't see them sitting around feeling hard done by. No saying, 'If only I had a bigger house . . .' because that option is not available to them — they can only ever swap properties of the same value, there is no moving up in the world. They can't postpone their happiness until they are rich because, until there are some radical changes in the government, that day will never come. Their happiness is not circumstantial, it's a choice. You've seen how much *energy* they put into having a good time! And they reap the appropriate reward."

"I suddenly feel very spoilt!"

"What's part two?" Beth wants to know.

"For that, we need to get in the water." Miriam holds out her hand: "Beth, the sunscreen please."

"Wait!" I halt her. "I can't go in the sea, I'm not wearing my swimsuit under this and there's nowhere to change."

"I discovered a solution to that the day before you arrived . . ." Mirian summons our Cuban posse and before I know it I am encircled by them, all facing outwards, creating a human beach hut.

There's no excuse now. Even Guy is off shooting B-roll so there's no danger of being filmed. I can do this!

Swimsuit up to my waist, arms out of the kaftan, hook the halterneck over my head, final deep breath, cast off the covers. "Ready!"

On "Go!" all three of us slosh into the water — warm, enveloping and instantly therapeutic — all the way up to our necks.

"Doesn't that feel better?"

"It does," I concede, as I lick a flick of saltwater from my mouth.

"And now I would like to introduce you to a very special lady by the name of Yemaya."

Beth and I look around, as if a fourth head is about to bob up and join us.

"Yemaya is the Cuban goddess of the sea," Miriam explains as her arms swish sensuously back and forth. "Mother of all. Strongly protective of all her children, she comforts them and cleanses them of their sorrows."

"That sounds good!" I say, mentally picturing all my woes washing away.

"To get the full benefit, I want you both to submerge yourselves."

Oh! "The thing is, we haven't done our beach interviews yet —"

"Do you want perfect hair or healing?" Miriam counters.

"The healing," I respond reluctantly.

"Come on, we'll go down together." Beth reaches for my hand, we pinch our noses and on the count of three drop down under the surface of the water.

As Beth floats off to my right, I tilt myself forward and force myself to go deeper, flipping my feet and blindly feeling around the soft seabed, even twisting and tumbling as if I am in a washing machine, just to make sure I get a thorough cleansing.

We emerge at the same moment, gasping for air, curiously refreshed.

"Now just relax and enjoy!"

For a while, the three of us float contentedly on our backs and then I find myself nudging at Beth.

"Do you know what I've just realised?"

"What's that?" She tilts her head up so her ears are no longer filled with water.

"Even though we never kissed, Martinez was the best, purest holiday romance I've ever had!"

Beth smiles at me. "Who says you're not a quick learner!"

Miriam too is delighted, pronouncing: "And now you are open again!"

"So what now?" I eagerly enquire.

"I think that's enough emotional evolution for one day," she chuckles. "Let me see you move those hips!"

"What?!"

"Come on, you said you wanted your movements to be more fluid, didn't you? You can't get more liquid than the Caribbean Sea!"

As Beth and I do our best to visualise hula-hooping with giant squid rings, I look shoreward for Russo, the pelvic muse.

I expect to find him hungrily checking out the bikini babes but instead he's talking to a mum, who then leaves him with her child. Apparently he has some stray caretaking gene I wouldn't have guessed at — I watch him go about amusing the toddler, holding his little hands and bouncing him in the water with his customary grin. He's surprisingly attentive, a natural even.

"You were so good with that little boy," I comment when I'm back on dry land and safely swathed in a towel.

"I have two of my own."

"Really?"

"Twins. My ex-wife lives in Guanabacoa. It's not too far, I see them every week."

He goes to his wallet and pulls out a picture. We chat for a while about his family and then conversation turns to his tattoo — of a wolf and a dream-catcher, referencing his American Indian heritage. He shows me the woven bracelet on his wrist and explains how it is of red and white thread to show the two blood colours that run in his veins, whereas Alexis, for example, would be represented by pure black. It's interesting how there is zero racism in Cuba. They really do live in harmony — presumably, they have enough adversity without turning on their fellow man.

"Carmen!" Lucy summons me. "We need to do a quick interview slot, over by the raffia sunshade . . ."

As Russo jumps up to help me to my feet, I realise that it's not just Martinez I'm going to miss, but every one of our new Cuban friends.

The rest of the afternoon is laidback, I even get the chance to do some sketching, working on a Salsa skirt with turquoise silk ruffles trimmed with white ribbon, simulating the ocean waves as it twirls. I also do a co-ordinating outfit for Martinez — white cotton trousers for his long legs and an aqua silk shirt to compliment the sheen and hue of his torso — my way of wishing him well.

Meanwhile, Simon and Beth are sending each other smile-inducing texts — ah, the modern courtship! — but Lucy looks vexed by the bleating of her phone.

"It's Lorenzo again!" she confides at one point. "He wants to visit me in England."

"You're not keen?"

"I honestly don't know what I'd do with a man that good looking!"

"Are you sure about that?" I pull a face.

She chuckles back at me. "I suppose there are worse problems to have in life! Speaking of which, I meant to tell you — that dance last night with Martinez was totally hot," Lucy gurgles. "Rick said it nearly made up for your lack of sexual activity this trip."

"Cheek!" I huff and then I sit bolt upright. "You mean you got all that on film?"

"Absolutely!" She grins. "Pretty nice memento for you!"

Excitement overrides potential embarrassment — even if I don't get to see Martinez again before I leave I will be able to re-live one of the sexiest moments of my life over and over *ad infinitum*, and how many people get to do that!

I look around for Rick, expecting him to have set up a mini-office over in the shaded café area, but instead locate him in the water. Of course I've already seen him topless in London but what causes me to do a double-take today is the look of contentment on his face. If I didn't know better, I'd think he was almost smiling. Maybe he's connecting to his former life as a swimmer. Maybe Yemaya has given him a big wet hug. Most likely, he's just come up with a new money-spinning show idea. Possibly using Alexis as the front man — he's certainly getting louder and more enthusiastic with every beer, instigating a sing-a-long and assorted beach games before culminating in a spontaneous "all back to mine" invitation.

Miriam insists that we seize this opportunity to experience an authentic Cuban house party. Beth is raring to go, already packing up her beach gear, but Lucy seems hesitant. "You're absolutely certain that he wants us there?"

"Of course!" Miriam insists. "We're the ones supplying the alcohol!"

CHAPTER THIRTY-FOUR

We follow them from paradise to what is essentially a Cuban council estate. The tatty tenements are trimmed with metal link fencing, patchy grass and crumbling breeze blocks. Someone has jollied up a shed wall with a tropical fish design but the streaky, greying main buildings could definitely do with a La Boca makeover.

As we disembark, Alexis beckons us over to the shade of a tree to introduce assorted relatives and neighbours, including a two-year-old princess whom Daylin is teaching Reggaeton. I kid you not! This little girl in her pink bunny motif top with hair in bobbled bunches has her hands raised above her head and is gyrating up a storm.

"She's like Beyoncé's Mini Me!" Beth hoots, eyes wide.

"I told you we start young!" Daylin grins.

Miriam explains that Alexis is quite the chef and points to two *alfresco* cooking units — the first is a vast black cauldron on a makeshift kerb-side fire containing a bubbling soup . . .

"Here!"

I am handed a flat wooden paddle and encouraged to give it a vigorous stir, like I need the extra steam heat in my life.

The second is an old oil drum, ingeniously converted into a barbecue grill. (Set horizontally with a hinged lid cut into the metal.) We sniff at the aroma of charcoal-roasted meat and then file through a sparse white living room with a tiled floor to the kitchen where we unload the booze — three different ages of Havana Club rum and several cases of beer.

"Where's the water?" Rick looks impatient.

"Sorry!" Camera Gay cringes. "I knew there was something I forgot!"

Rick paws at his throat in full desert-parch mode. I see him reach to turn on the kitchen tap but nothing comes out. Possibly just as well.

"Thirsty?" Alexis slaps him on the back and hands him a "Bucanero".

The can does have a certain kiddy soda look to it with its bold red pirate design so perhaps in Rick's desperation he decides to overlook the words "*cerveza*" meaning "beer" and "*fuerte*" meaning "strong".

No sooner has the cooling froth met his lips, the whole can is downed. Alexis cheers and hands him another. As Rick continues his earnest pursuit of refreshment, it dawns on me that this is the first drop of alcohol I've seen him sup since shooting began. The effects are swift and deadly — as he attempts to transfer his body from the kitchen sink to the lounge doorway, he staggers at a misjudged angle and ends up facing the wall. The look on his face is pure "how the hell did that just happen?"

"Rum?" Beth offers, oblivious.

"Don't mind if I do, ron-ron," I reply.

Out of the corner of my eye, I watch as Rick now feels his way to a seat so he can settle in to watch the dancing. I'm sensing from the way he's gripping the chair that the room itself is taking him on a fair spin.

For a while I am distracted as Russo puts on a hilarious display doing the girl's Salsa steps — complete with diva attitude and pout — with Daylin's brother as his straightman beau. For someone so robustly masculine, Russo does a curiously convincing job playing the woman, even to the dainty way he holds his hairy hands during his free turn.

"Natural born entertainer," Miriam confirms, whistling encouragement.

When I look back at Rick, his feet are tapping along to the music and he has a glass of neat rum in his hand.

"Come, Ricky!" Daylin encourages him to join the dancing as a new song begins.

"Oh no," he protests. "I don't dance."

"It's Havana, everyone dance!"

She has him on his feet now, her hands on his hips.

"Really, it's too hot!" He tries to resist but his repression is no match for her powerhouse nature. "Too hot?" she repeats before flinging open his shirt. When she registers the fine torso that lies within, she quickly summons her single girlfriends to take over.

Realising it's just a case of damage control now, Rick orders Simon and Guy to turn off their equipment.

"Off-off?" Simon double-checks.

Rick thinks for a moment and then pronounces, "There will be no more filming tonight." And then pulls the petite Janet Jackson lookalike closer.

Everyone looks a little surprised but then Lucy shrugs and giggles, "I think this has just become the wrap party!"

Once everyone has a celebratory beverage in hand, Miriam shows us a Cuban version of cheers, using Simon and Beth to demonstrate.

"First, you tap the top of the glass and call '*Arriba*'."

"*Arriba!*" they repeat with a hearty chink.

"Then you tap the base and call '*Abajo*'."

"*Abajo!*" they chorus.

"And then you call '*El Centro*' as you slide the middle of the glass up and down against each other to simulate the friction between two bodies."

"Oh!" The two of them flush, suddenly pulling away.

"And finally, '*Adentro*'," Miriam concludes. "As in 'down the hatch!'"

On cue, we all throw back our drinks, all except for Beth who is too busy looking over Simon's torso in a whole new light.

"You're such a stirrer," I tease Miriam as I top up her glass.

"These windows of opportunity don't last forever," she smiles back at me. "Tomorrow's your last night, right?"

"Right," I sigh.

"Time to eat!" She changes the subject as Daylin hands each of us a plastic cup of the pale stew-like soup, adding a squeeze of fresh lime before our first sip.

I'm hesitant at first but then . . . Oh my!

"Beth! You have to try this!"

We've had a few iffy meals since arriving in Cuba but this soup is so exceptionally tasty I gratefully accept seconds. Then comes the meat. The last pieces Beth and I endured in a restaurant had the whole table juddering from the sheer effort of trying to saw through the leather-toughness. This, by contrast, is sublime — juicy, melt-in-your-mouth shreddings. It amuses me that all the women and children are herded into a back room to make sure they get fed before the men start scavenging but it certainly does make a girl feel cared for.

"Wait a minute, are they playing George Michael?" Beth jumps to her feet, leading me back into the living area where Alexis has decided to instigate a game of name-that-tune with a motley selection of Eighties music.

Kool & The Gang. Culture Club. "Michael Bolton?!" Beth despairs.

Then comes an eerie chorus of "*Turn around . . .*"

Russo, Alexis and various neighbours repeat the phrase while looking expectantly our way.

"B-Bonnie Tyler?" I falter.

"YES!" they whoop, delighted.

Beth and I burst out laughing — of all the least likely places to hear this song!

Things get even more surreal when I spy Rick in a corner with Miriam. He of the minimal/instructional/critical speech pattern is now blabbing his heart out as she soothes his fevered brow.

"Have you seen this?" I nudge Beth.

Her eyebrows raise accordingly. "Well, if anyone can discover a soul in that man, she can."

Now that Daylin has lost her protégé, she turns her attention to me, deciding — in her usual blunt manner — that I have no business wearing the baggy clothes I do.

"What is all this?" She yanks at the excess yardage of my skirt. "You have good figure!" She makes curvy motions with her hands. "Why do you hide?"

"Oh, Daylin," I sigh. "It's because I wear skirts like this that you think I don't need to."

"Pah!" She swats away my excuses and then beckons Simon over to translate.

"She says she wants to see you express your sexy side."

"Great!" I cringe. "Can you explain to her that I don't have one?"

"She says every one has one. You just need confidence. It begins with a look."

Daylin takes my hands and gives me a heavy-lidded look of devastating seduction. "Is easy!" she chirrups. "Now you!"

And I thought the hip rotations were embarrassing. "I just can't!" I squirm.

"Look, look!" She gathers all her friends around and bids them show me their sexy look — in a finger click they turn from buzzy, chatty, smiley people to a brothel line-up, each of them working their signature look — the Janet Jackson-alike is coquettish, Daylin's brother is honourable yet ardent, Russo is pure lip-parted lust . . .

"I need another drink." I go to escape to the kitchen but three glasses are thrust at me, obstructing my route. Against my better judgement, I take their challenge and drink all three.

"Now!" Daylin demands.

I make a strongman pose and growl out loud. "That wasn't it, by the way!" I quickly add. "That was just me psyching myself up."

They all wait patiently for me to get on with it.

Still I have nothing to give. This is worse than trying to conjure fiery pride for the Flamenco.

"Look at me!" Russo volunteers himself as the object of my affection.

I try my darndest but all I can summon when I survey his laughter-induced crinkles and gold-flecked eyes is "fond". Then I get an idea — using Beth's technique of blocking out the rest of the world, I switch my gaze to the side and imagine Martinez standing there, daring me to show the full range of my desire for him. Suddenly I find my head slanting to the right as I give him my sultriest, naughtiest look.

"That's it!" They all clap and do a victory dance.

"Really?" I blink, unconvinced.

Russo growls his approval and moves towards me but Daylin steps between us, announcing it is time for dessert.

"I think we need some air!" Beth diverts me outside, into the now cooler night.

"Did I just make a complete fool of myself?" I need to know.

"Not at all!" Beth assures me. "I just wanted to mark the moment — you know when you have those out-of-body experiences and you can't quite believe you're really here?"

"Want me to pinch you?"

She nods and then emits a little yelp as I oblige.

"So it's true," she smiles and then leans back on the rough bark of the tree. "You know, before I came here, I thought the highlight of the trip would be the show at the Tropicana — all the OTT costumes and the glitz and the spectacle — but this . . ." she nods towards Alexis' humble yet buzzing apartment, "This is where it's at!"

"The real deal!" I nod in agreement. "We're so privileged."

"Ain't that the truth!" she sighs, her eyes a little sad now. "They have so little . . ."

". . . but they share it all."

"Exactly!" Beth nods. "They don't hoard anything, look at how they were about the food, welcoming everyone in, no skimping today to save for tomorrow. They really are living for the moment!"

I pick at a loose piece of bark. "It makes me a little ashamed of the way we live at home, always wanting more. When I think how much time I spend fussing over the décor of my flat, getting everything all matchy-matchy but never having anyone over . . . All those microwave meals for one. All that shopping for shopping's sake. I mean, we even tried to do that here!"

I know we're both now thinking of our trip to the "mall" in Miramar. No more than a dozen shops with a handful of outdated items rattling around on the rails. I imagine if we took Daylin to TopShop she'd probably faint from the sheer volume of merchandise.

"You know, I actually think shopping is my primary hobby," Beth confesses. "I dread to think how many hours I've spent trawling around Oxford Street and how little I have to show for it. Imagine all the other things I could have done with my time!"

"No wonder we end up feeling so empty — our priorities are so messed up." I perch myself on the little wooden bench and then ask, "So how do we stay changed from this experience? I mean, we feel this way now but you know how it is, within a few weeks of being back we'll be wandering like zombies around House of Fraser . . ."

Beth nods understanding and then surprises me by saying, "I think I'm going to look into teaching dance."

"Really?"

"I don't want to look at every other girl dancer as competition any more. You've seen how these guys all work together — it just feels so much better. I want to be part of this kind of community."

"You've just given me an idea!"

"For what?"

"A way to say thank you to them all. It's just a token gesture but it'll take the two of us to pull it off — we have a free day tomorrow, don't we?"

"We do — what did you have in mind?"

"Mango?"

Beth and I look up to find Simon offering us a plate of expertly-sliced fruit.

"I'm sorry, am I interrupting?"

"Not at all!" I get to my feet. "I was just going to check on Miriam."

"Well, as a matter of fact," he halts me, "Rick got a bit teary-eyed so she's taken him for a little walk."

Beth and I exchange a stunned look.

"You didn't happen to hear what the tears were about?" Curiosity gets the better of me.

"He doesn't want to go back to England."

Beth nods empathetically. "Back to reality?"

"Well, that's just it — he was saying that it's not reality any more because everyone is too posturing and media-savvy, whereas here —"

"Oh no, please don't say he's going to exploit the Cubans?" Beth cries.

"On the contrary," Simon halts her concern. "He wants to stay here for as long as the country remains free of celebrity culture."

"Wow," I coo, understanding the appeal. "You know you'd make a good spy, Simon?"

"I know!" he chuckles. "It's my amazing invisibility that does it!"

"You're not invisible to me," Beth stills the conversation.

Immediately I feel the need to exit. As I back away, muttering something about getting more mango, I hear him croak: "Would you care to dance?"

I find myself hovering by the gate to the apartment, unable to take my eyes off the two of them. It's just so wonderful to see them finally touch. As she places her hand on his shoulder, I see his eyes flicker closed with bliss. Oh-so-gently he places his palm on the small of her back and I see her body yield to his . . .

Their tentative tenderness is a curious match for Whitney Houston's exuberant I *Wanna Dance With Somebody* — hardly what Simon would have chosen for their first embrace — yet the sentiment is not so very wide of the mark.

He says something I can't hear, maybe something about the way her face is aglow in the moonlight. Their moves are becoming slower, dancing to their own rhythm now. I feel mildly voyeuristic but I can't turn away — I'm too busy willing her to will him to kiss her.

"Yes!" I hear myself squeak as their lips meet.

I'd say Beth has just secured a way to stay changed when she returns to England.

I take a happy breath in but feel a little wistful as I breathe out — I wonder where my true love is tonight? Not in a self-pitying way, you understand. I'm just curious . . .

Just as I sense my eyes welling up, I feel a presence behind me and a familiar furry arm slips around my waist.

"*Amor!*" Russo comments on the romantic couple before us.

"*Si!*" I sigh, comforted by his presence. But then he requests, "*Un momento!*" and releases me, I'm guessing to get another Bucanero beer.

Seconds later, my waist is warmed again. But as I go to lean back and enjoy his strength, I find a distinct absence of furry chest hair cushioning my shoulder blades. My hand goes to his forearm — that is smooth too. Just like . . .

I gasp as I turn around. "Martinez!"

CHAPTER THIRTY-FIVE

My mouth is still parted in amazement but I cannot speak. This is more than I could've hoped for.

"Carmen!" His eyes are lightly sparkling yet intense. "*Qué tal*?"

"*Bien*!" I reply. "*Muy, muy, muy bien*!" I laugh. "I didn't think I was going to see you again! Daylin said Varadero —"

He nods. "I have to return before the morning but tonight . . ."

"Yes?" I look hopeful.

"Tonight is with you."

My heart flips in pure delight.

Motoring back to Havana, windows wound down to fully embrace the breeze, I feel so lucky. So. So. Lucky. I don't mind now that all we have is this one night, I'm just so grateful to have this second chance to revel in the bliss that is Martinez!

He tells me that we are going to a different kind of nightclub tonight, one with a theme of *elegance*. Ah. Not so easily attained when you are still shaking sand from your clothes.

"Can we stop back at the hotel, just for ten minutes?"

"Of course," he obliges.

While I do my make-up, my new Cuban stylist rifles through the wardrobe.

"What about this one?" He is holding out one of Beth's dresses — an elegant yet flirty creation in hot pink.

I go to tell him I couldn't possibly fit in it but then I wonder — the upper body fabric has a certain flexibility, the skirt a forgiving flow of silk. I've certainly dropped a fair few pounds with all this dancing . . . I can almost hear Daylin egging me on — "Tighter is better!" And so I dare to try it. Gosh. I can't believe it, I turn to take in my reflection from every angle — it's actually pretty flattering!

"May I see?"

"One moment!" I call back. With no time to wash my hair, I decide to scroll it up, the residual sea salt acting as effective setting spray. One diamanté hair clip and a strand of Claire's Accessories' finest metallic beads and I am ready to present myself.

"*Ay dios mio*!" His hand immediately goes to his heart. "You look beautiful," he sighs before offering me his arm.

After a week of sweating in semi-ventilated dance studios and eardrum-trouncing clubs, the Fifties stylings of the Havana Café take my breath away.

The room is dominated by two full-size classic cars and — believe it or not — a small Cubana plane suspended from the ceiling! The surrounding walls are layered with movie posters and old black and white photographs and I chuckle as Martinez points out the life-size cardboard cut-out of Ernest Hemingway mid-drink pour at the bar, all the more droll since he is juxtaposed next to a brightly-lit fridge of Red Bull, bringing us back to the present day with a caffeine jolt.

But best of all is the eleven-piece band on stage: all the musicians are dressed in white dinner jackets with black bow ties, set behind turquoise podiums, serenading us with *On This Night Of A Thousand Stars*. The song makes me think of Miriam's story about her Cuban love and the thousand kisses and my smile broadens further — frankly, every time Martinez looks at me feels as good as a kiss. He's just so lovely!

"You are well?" He looks quizzically at my fidgeting hands tapping the tabletop as we await the arrival of our drinks.

"Yes, yes!" I explain that I often get like this. When I'm somewhere inspiring I always want to get out my sketchpad. "You know, draw?" I mime the action.

"Ah yes. I like too."

"Really?" I brighten.

When the waitress brings our cocktails, he borrows two pens and then invites me to flip over the paper place-setting decorated with car illustrations and start getting artistic myself.

As much as I enjoy sketching the show dancers in their cute floral frocks and white patent belts, my eye repeatedly returns to Martinez. I steal a glance at his page and when I do I see he has chosen to draw not the lively bongo player or the vintage gas pump over in the corner, but me.

He's actually rather good — his lines have an easy, light flow — and before I know it, I am returning the honour, beginning a portrait of my new favourite artist!

It's a surprisingly intimate act, the pair of us taking in every detail of each other's faces in the ever-changing coloured show lights — the angle of the cheekbone in pink, the flare of the nostril in blue, every individual eyelash tipped with gold . . . The first few times I catch his eye, I feel self-conscious and flush a little but gradually a calm focus takes over. I never knew this could be such a sensual experience. When I realise he is studying my mouth, I feel my senses heighten and my breathing becomes more pronounced.

What I wouldn't do to reach across and kiss him now — to melt my lips upon his.

"I'll be back in a minute!" I blurt suddenly, feeling the need to visit the Ladies and take a moment to lean against a cool wall.

As I get to my feet, so does he, helping me out from the table. He's so close now I can't resist leaning in and kissing him softly on the cheek.

"Thank you so much for bringing me here," I whisper. "I'm having a wonderful time!"

He goes to speak but as I step back my necklace catches on his button and sends all the glittering beads scattering across the floor.

"Oh no!" I cry but he's already bent down, picking up every last one.

"Please don't worry about it," I insist, especially since most of them have conveniently tucked themselves under the table. "It's no big deal, it wasn't expensive or anything."

"I will arrange," he says, bidding me continue on my way to the bathroom.

I am reluctant to leave him but he assures me he has the situation under control. I feel even more of a klutz washing my hands alongside a series of intimidatingly tiny skirts and perfectly toned brown legs but when I return my state of rapture is quickly restored — there, lying on my napkin, is my necklace, not just repaired but good as new.

"*Gracias*!" I gasp, suddenly feeling as though this cheap item has been imbued with great sentimental value.

"May I?" He offers to place it back around my neck and, as he does so, it feels as priceless as diamonds. I get a sudden image of myself wearing it back in London and no one understanding why it is so very precious to me.

And then he says the words I've been longing to hear.

"Dance with me?"

I nod acceptance, tucking the necklace into the low neckline of the dress, only to look up and find him looking desirously in its direction. Oh God! Why is everything he does so infernally arousing?

Mercifully, the song is slow and he holds me so tenderly I find my body relax and respond with hitherto unknown grace. As we turn together, we seem to be following the flow of the mirrorball's reflections, the little white squares dancing around us like ethereal confetti.

I can't quite believe how good this all feels. I know we only have a few hours here, I know he will have to leave before sunrise and there's a good chance I will never see him again but I find myself in a surprisingly serene state of acceptance. I could not have conjured a more perfect Sorbet/Hot Tamale combo if I tried!

"We continue?" he asks as the music changes to a seductive Bachata.

Though this dance is new to me, I say yes. And then yes again as our bodies closely align and we rock one, two, three and then give a switch of the hips.

Again. One, two, three, switch. And again.

"*Esso*!" he cheers as I find the rhythm.

It would seem Daylin's flirtation masterclass has paid off — or maybe it's just the rum? Either way, my body feels more loose and responsive than ever before. Of course it's hard to ignore the sexual connotations of the movement but there is a sense of being cherished I would not have anticipated.

I allow myself to meld closer and as we become sublimely in sync I realise that the wish I made back in London has come true — my dance partner has become my other breath . . .

CHAPTER THIRTY-SIX

Beth and I wake up at exactly the same moment, both apparently equally surprised to find the other there.

"Why aren't you with Simon?" I startle.

"Why aren't you with Martinez?" she counters.

"He had to go back to Varadero," I sigh. "What's your excuse?"

"He turned me down."

"What?" I'm aghast. Surely he can't have changed his mind?

"He said he wanted last night to be all about our first kiss. Said if we went any further he might spontaneously combust."

"Really?" I giggle. "That's so cute."

"I think it was actually his polite way of saying that I was too drunk. Probably worried I might pass out halfway through."

"He may have had a point," I concede. She does look a little worse for wear. "Besides, there's no rush, is there?"

"Not now that I know that I want to."

"You do?" My eyes widen.

She nods emphatically. "You were right. The kiss sealed the deal. I get a funny feeling just thinking about it . . ." As she turns on her side to face me, she stops suddenly. "*Are you wearing my dress?*"

I throw back the covers and confirm that I am indeed sporting her party frock. But instead of apologising for the liberty, I find myself saying, "Hold on a minute, whose clothes are you wearing?"

Beth looks down and discovers a pair of skintight hot pants and a midriff-exposing polyester top.

"Jeez! No wonder I was so hot in the night!" She hurriedly whips off the top. "I think I traded outfits with that Janet Jackson lookalike."

"Do you still have all the measurements?"

"Hold on." Beth rummages in her bra and then triumphantly thrusts a scrap of paper at me. "Ta-daaaa!"

"Good woman."

During our last dance *chez* Alexis, Beth and I performed a covert mission with the tape measure — getting all the respective inches for our dance gang's chest, waist, hips etc., all without letting them know what we were up to. (That's the wonderful thing about Reggaeton — you can take a man's inside leg measurement without arousing the slightest bit of suspicion.)

The plan for the day is to create a signature wardrobe for Alexis & Co so they can present themselves as a coherent dance school and create a bold impression on a night out.

Whereas I was previously cursing the fact that we had to lug all our Tango and Flamenco clothes with us to Cuba (seeing as Rick refused to let us even swing by our flats in London), now I'm glad for the extra fabric options.

"We'll have one pile for items we can't live without and one for customisation."

As we start sorting our clothes, I realise the pair of us are tottering and repeatedly bashing into one another.

"Sorry," Beth apologises on the third clash. "I think I'm still drunk!"

"I was wondering why I didn't have a hangover!" I tut. "I guess it's just not here yet."

"Why don't I go downstairs and get us some breakfast so we'll be prepared for when it hits?"

"Good idea. And see if you can get a lead on a sewing machine while you're at it."

"You mean one of those old hand-operated jobs, like this one?" Beth points to the machine set beside the door.

"Where the hell did that come from?" I gasp.

Beth gives an exaggerated shrug. "I have no idea."

Fifteen minutes later, I've unpicked three seams and Beth is back with an array of breakfast goodies, including a portion of cold Brussels sprouts.

"Well, I thought we should try them once before we leave," she reasons. And then she asks me to tell her all about my night with Martinez.

"With pleasure!" I reply, regaling her with every detail.

Apparently I tell the story rather well — Beth is now clasping a croissant to her chest, with both hands.

"Wow!" she breathes. "And was there a farewell kiss at the end of all this dancing and romancing?"

"The most idyllic one," I sigh. "He walked me back to the hotel and we stood there face-to-face, smiling, as if we were just enjoying looking at each other. And then his gaze lowered to my mouth . . .

"Yes!" Beth squeaks in anticipation.

"I felt my eyes close as he moved in and then he kissed my lips so gently, so respectfully, so . . . *lovingly* I couldn't open them again. I didn't want to spoil the moment by seeing him walk away. So I just stayed there, under the stars, savouring that sensation until I was ready to sleep."

"And how do you feel now?"

"Not at all like I thought — I presumed I'd wake up feeling a massive downer knowing that it was all over but actually I'm still filled up with it all!" I grin happily and then add, "So in answer to your question, I feel hopeful." I reach for a slice of papaya. "You know, before I came here, I was so convinced that love was in short supply — such a limited resource — I had to cling to whatever scrap came my way but now —" Mid-sentence, I scrabble to my feet.

"What are you doing?" Beth enquires.

"Something I've been putting off for months," I say, tracking down my phone.

Beth nods sagely. "Old love texts from Lee?"

"Yup!" I reply, and then without even re-reading for nostalgia's sake, I press delete and delete and delete. "All gone!" I cheer. "Clean slate."

"I think this calls for a —"

"Please don't say mojito!" I beg, hand to throbbing head.

"Don't be silly," Beth tuts. "I'm all about the daiquiri now!"

As it happens, the daiquiri is rather good, like a buzz-inducing Slush Puppy, but of course the real highlight of the day is seeing our *Project Runway*-esque creations on our models.

For Daylin and her sister, we used ruffles from my Flamenco dress to make twirly polka-dot miniskirts that flare out and accentuate every Salsa turn. We also made matching bustiers for when they want to turn them into dresses. (I was even considering making a pair of trousers for Alexis for fun but then Lucy — who came on board to help with the bedazzling — pointed out that he'd almost certainly wear them.) For a more diva-esque ensemble, we used Beth's shimmering scarlet Tango dress to make two eye-catching tops. And, not wanting the boys to be outdone, we made bandanas from the scraps and then stuck crystals on the Che Guevara T-shirts we bought at the market, turning the matt black image of the bearded man in the beret into a twinkly attention-grabber. I even created a new belt-buckle for Russo from half a castanet.

They hoot and holler as they pull off their own clothes and try on the new stylings, seeming particularly delighted to discover the stack of brow-mopping cloths with individual monograms. (No one notices but the one I ask them to pass on to Martinez is embroidered with a small red heart.)

Despite the fact that we are on the minibus bound for our last dance venue, much hugging ensues, with Daylin squeezing hardest of all — especially when she notices that I have tapered my own top and shortened my skirt.

"Yes! Yes!" she commends me. "Much better! Show yourself!"

Apparently I mishear her as saying, "Embarrass yourself!" for as Russo kindly helps me down from the minibus, I catch my foot and fall forward with such force I topple him and land forcibly on his — thankfully — indestructible groin.

"At last! Carmen falls for a guy!" Rick cheers.

"What?" I look up and find him directing Guy's camera at us.

"Oh no!" I bury my head in Russo's shoulder, squirming at how this will be misconstrued.

"It's okay!" Russo soothes me and then winks directly at the lens. "I'm her dance teacher!"

"Hey! Enough with the horizontal stylings!" Beth helps me to my feet, leaving Russo in a happy heap. "Just take a look at this place."

Club 1830 (as in the year, not the age limit) claims a prime open-air position at the end of the Malecón. With the sea swishing and a-glinting beside us and a sunset sweeping across the horizon with such striking beauty, I almost kiss Rick.

"Sorry it's taken me so long to give you what you want!" I tease him as we find ourselves side by side at the bar.

"Are you kidding me? You've been great."

"What?" I splutter.

"Do you have any idea how hard it is to find people who genuinely don't want to be on TV?"

I chuckle at him.

"You know, if you ever decide you want to do costume work for television, I'd put in a word for you," he offers. "It has to be better paid than the theatre . . ."

I eye him up and down. "What's with the sudden benevolence?"

He shrugs and leans back on his elbows. "I think it has something to do with the fact that I'm never going to make another TV show as long as I live."

I look around for Lucy, curious to find out if he always says this at the end of a shoot, but then Miriam comes up and introduces a petite, tawny-haired woman — as Sylvia to me and "your new landlady" to Rick.

"She has a *casa particular* for rent," Miriam explains as the two of them chat. "He can stay there as long as he likes."

"So he really is done with TV?" I gawp.

"He's handing everything over to Lucy."

"But what's he going to do here?"

"I think for a while he's going to just *be*," Miriam replies. "He's been resentful of his job for so long he's forgotten what it's like to have a day without a snarl and a gripe in it. He just needs to reconnect with his pre-cynical, pre-materialistic self."

I struggle to imagine what that might be like but, then again, there can be no better setting for such a miracle.

"What about you?" Miriam enquires. "Back to the theatre?"

"As a matter of fact, the show I was hoping to work on has been shelved for a while so I'm not quite sure what's next. Although Rick did just suggest TV work . . ."

"It's certainly a tough time for the West End," Miriam sympathises. "Of course, you know Hollywood box office has never been better?" And then she gets a particular twinkle in her eye. "If only you knew someone based in Los Angeles with movie connections . . ."

I blink back at her. Is she saying what I think she's saying?

"There's a project coming up that I think you'd be perfect for."

"Are you serious?" I'm stunned. Talk about coming up with new dreams . . .

I'm about to ask her more when Russo bowls over on an urgent mission — he needs a partner for the *rueda*. As in me.

As he takes my hand, so a supremely attractive man reaches for Miriam, looking suitably transfixed.

"You've still got it," I wink at her as we get into position.

And then we're off.

"*Dame*!" The caller demands a switch of partner and I am passed onto Simon. Apparently Lucy is giving him a break.

As we execute our wobbly version of a *Caramello*, he whispers, "Thank you!" in my ear.

"For what?"

He smiles warmly at me. "I know you've been rooting for me with Beth."

I grin back at him. "Well, I had an ulterior motive — I knew you could make her happy!"

"*Dame*!"

"Oops, I'm off!" I laugh as I move onto Miriam's hottie partner.

Oh, he's good! Subtle and gentle, when he releases my hand he looks to the heavens as if he just sent a ribbon rippling in the sky. It's all the more galling therefore that my next partner is an out-of-time yanker. I do my best to withstand him, knowing that Alexis is next, only to be passed from him onto someone so sweaty I can barely keep my grip. I slip away from him too soon and collide with a strangely familiar body. The room continues to spin around me as I feel my way up his chest and then behold his careworn denim eyes.

"Lee!" I gasp.

I want to bite back his name as soon as I've said it but it's too late. He's here. In Havana. In the flesh. In my dance space.

My eyes dart around him in search of Beth but she's nowhere to be seen.

"Carmen."

As he says my name, I feel the first hook insert itself. I want to freeze him so I can have time to think or maybe even just run away but already he's speaking again.

"Can we talk?"

I don't know what else to do but follow him as he leads me off the dancefloor and out to the wave-splashed Malecón. I'm almost annoyed that the sunset is now a ravishing copper-glow, as if it is somehow in cahoots with him.

"How did you find us?" I hear myself asking, as a delay tactic as much as anything — of course there aren't exactly dozens of TV crews filming a couple of English dancing girls but then he reveals he had a little help from a certain UK newspaper . . . The stirring buggers!

I'm tempted to stay in the safe zone of small-talk and steer the conversation onto classic cars but then again I don't want to act too casual or familiar, I know where that can lead . . . I need to keep my distance emotionally, I have to remember that I have a choice in what happens next, like at the *milonga*. I don't have to go along with what he wants just because he's crossed the dancefloor to meet me.

Or in this case the Atlantic.

"You know I was missing you anyway but seeing your face on TV . . . Hearing your voice . . ." He gulps, trying to compose himself, but in actuality he looks ever more vulnerable and broken.

My heart crumples and tugs towards him. *Oh no you don't!* I rein it back in, trying desperately to stay centred. To connect to my core. What's the other thing? Oh yes — breathing. Keep breathing . . .

"I can't do it, Carmen," his voice cracks. "I can't bear my life without you in it."

"Please don't —" I try to stop him going on.

"I know I've treated you badly," he continues regardless. "I know you deserve better." He takes a step closer. "Let me be better. Let me be the man you always wanted me to be."

I look at him. I see the man I loved so dearly and also the man who is the greatest threat to my happiness and wellbeing. And I remember Miriam's words about avoiding men who do harm . . .

"I-I can't," I stammer and then remember my Flamenco stance and raise my jaw. "I'm sorry. It's too late."

"Don't say that —"

I feel my jaw clenching as I try to maintain my position. It's so hard not to pull him into an embrace — how can you not feel compassion when someone lays their heart at your feet? All it would take to ease his pain is my arms around him and my whispered assurance that we can try again. But I've been there before and it doesn't work. I know better now — I remember Kelly explaining how this kind of wounded display is all part of the act, playing to my weak spot to regain control. I have all these extra tools now. I just have to use them.

"There's no going back this time," I assert.

"So that's it?" he snorts. "I come all this way and that's all you have to say?" The anger and disgust in his eyes confirm I have made the right decision.

How quick he is to switch. My pity morphs into defiance.

"I gave you everything I had, Lee. All the love I had. And you squandered it. I could never trust you with my heart again."

"If you're afraid —"

"I'm not afraid any more," I say, my hands instinctively going to my hips, as I conjure a mental picture of a swishing matador's cape.

This time he looks at me with mild confusion. "Well, if you change your mind —"

"I won't," I assert, my fingers now reaching for my beads as if to connect with some lingering trace of Martinez — a reminder of just how good things can be if I hold out now.

"This is it then."

The finality gives my inner organs one more violent tug. Still I stand strong. Right up until the point that he turns to walk away. And then I feel my eyes welling up as I watch this defeated man skulking away from me, suddenly seeing him as the injured bull. My lips part to call out to him. My chest is heaving now, panic growing. Am I really going to let him walk away, all alone in a strange city?

Against all my new-found wisdom and knowledge and joy, I feel myself stepping towards him.

And then I get the most almighty wake-up call — a huge wave crashes up and over the Malecón and drenches me, head to toe. I gasp out loud, shocked and sopping and blinking through the salty water to watch him walk away oblivious.

"Oh my God!" I whisper, aware how close I came to making a huge mistake. And then I half-laugh as I turn to magnificent mother ocean and squeal, "Thank you!"

I push my wet hair from my face. I've done it. I faced my absolute worst fear. My insides still feel a little unsettled but my outsides are zinging and refreshed.

"Carmen!" I turn and see Beth hurtling towards me. "What the hell happened?"

Still somewhat stunned, I shake my head. "I just had the most almighty ablution."

"A-what now?" she frowns. "Miriam said she saw you leaving with a guy, it sounded like Lee."

"It was."

"WHAT?!" she shrieks.

"It's okay," I soothe her. "He's gone. For good."

"You're sure?"

I nod.

She heaves a long sigh and then asks, "Why are you so wet?"

"This massive wave —"

"Carmen! *Que pase*?" Russo is hurrying over now. Deftly wiping the mascara away from under my eyes with his new back pocket cloth. "Why are you here?"

I can't help but smile — the question seems positively existential! I may not have a conclusive answer but I know one thing for sure — I didn't come to this earth to have spirit-squandering relationships with troubled men. Or if I did, I've done that now. Crossed it off my list.

"I think she needed to cool off after all that crazy *rueda*!" Beth suggests.

Russo tilts his head. "So you use the ocean to make a shower?" he nods as if it's the most logical thing in the world.

I smile back at him. "Me and Yemaya have an understanding."

He looks tickled that I know the name of a Cuban goddess, but nothing can put him off his stride for long. "May I join you in the shower?" he enquires with a lascivious twinkle in his eye.

"Of course," I welcome him. "Beth, you in?"

For a tiny second she considers her outfit and then says, "What the hell!"

We link hands and step back against the Malecón wall.

"It's a big one," Russo warns us as he sneaks a peek. "You ready?"

As Beth starts screaming in anticipation, I hear myself whooping, "Ready for anything!"

And I mean it! I'm ready for a new Lee-free, fear-free life! Ready to fall in love, maybe even ready for Hollywood!

I know I should probably close my mouth but I can't — I just can't stop grinning.

ACKNOWLEDGEMENTS

I have such a bumper lot of thank-yous I am going for brevity and name-listing!

But first I must thank one man in an excessively gushy way: Lundy Bancroft is the stunningly insightful author of *Why Does He Do That? Inside the Minds of Angry & Controlling Men*. This book changed my life and gave me a euphoric dose of understanding and hope. For his liberating wisdom and compassion, I shall be eternally grateful!

MY NEW PUBLISHER HODDER
Sara Kinsella, Isobel Akenhead, Carolyn Mays, Sarah Christie, Lucy Hale, Aslan Byrne, James Spackman, Catherine Worsley, Katie Davison, Laurence Festal and Francine Toon.

MY AGENT WILLIAM MORRIS ENDEAVOUR
Eugenie Furniss, Claudia Webb, Dorian Karchmov and Alicia Gordon.

USA
Miranda Garrison, Edward Arriens and all Living TVs Dirty Dancers, especially James Collins, Pamela Smith, Vincent Viaren, Emma De Vees and Donna Gilkes.

ARGENTINA
Elsa & Julian Scopinaro, Oscar Moret and Christine Denniston.

SPAIN
Gilles Marini, Shirley Ayme, Rocio Galan, Petra Massey and Lesley Margarita.

CUBA
Karel Duvergel, Amanda Maitland, Robert & Jean of Mambo City, Rob & Enrique of Salsa Explosion, Susan & Dr Jim of Salsa Caribe, Roger Hall, Victoria Urmossy, Ysel, Roynet, Merwyn Manson, James Breeds (and Cabbage in spirit).

And finally, in a category all of her own, my mother Pamela for her fierce dedication, support and legendary high kicks.